Ask Me if I'm Happy

Kimberly Menozzi

Ask Me *if* I'm Happy

Kimberly Menozzi

Published by: Good to Go Press

Ask Me if I'm Happy

Cover design and photography Kimberly Menozzi

Copyright © Kimberly Menozzi 2010

ISBN: 0615490751

ISBN-13: 978-0615490755

Per Alessandro
Ti voglio bene.
Sei tu lo scatolone che mi tiene verticale...

Connections

(February, 2008)

Kimberly Menozzi

1

Restlessly, Emily's feet slid over the pockmarked concrete of the Rovigo train station platform, chips of disintegrating cement gritting under the soles of her shoes. Two hollow blasts of a distant whistle shook her out of her daze and she sat up on the bench to focus on the pinprick of light emerging from the fog.

The more you want something, the slower it comes. I suppose this includes Italian trains. But why today of all days? Why can't my last day here be different from the past ten years?

The concrete bench was freezing but she stayed put, her suitcase beside her. Weighted down by the sleep she'd missed the night before, her eyelids began to droop in spite of the cold. Emily shook her head suddenly, causing herself some momentary dizziness and drawing a disinterested glance from one of the other travelers on the platform. While digging around in her shoulder bag, she looked up at the station clock and sighed; her train was forty minutes late. Locating her planner, she pulled out her plane ticket and examined it once more.

Milan Malpensa, 15:00, British Airways to New York, window seat…

She clutched the airline ticket like a talisman before tucking it into place once more, briefly marking the blue edge of the photograph next to the ticket before closing the planner and shoving it back into her bag. No point in taking the photo out; the image of Jacopo seated upon the Spanish Steps in Rome, looking smug, was etched deep into her memory.

Still blindly exploring in her bag, her fingers slid over the surface of a thick legal-size envelope tucked up against the side. The contents of this envelope had, a few days before, rendered much of her life null and void in one fell swoop.

That was an eternity ago.

Shivering, she looked around at the other pre-dawn travelers. A few hopeful faces turned to look down the length of track visible from the platform in the faint light. However, the approach of the rhythmic clacking and chuffing didn't slow. A freight train rattled past and disappeared into the mists, taking Emily's fleeting optimism with it.

Earlier, after exchanging most of her euros for American dollars, she'd used the rest to buy a train ticket from the machine inside the station, and then a magazine at the Valentine-infested newsstand outside. Now she was obliged to forgo any additional purchases. Though as time dragged on, the station's offerings became more tempting. A shift in the wind nudged the steam of her nearest neighbor's tiny cup of espresso her way, bringing with it the warm, rich scent.

Maybe just a hot chocolate? Or a caffè macchiato?

Another passenger's watch beeped but Emily kept her focus out on the tracks, refusing to read the station clock.

Stamping her feet, she carefully rubbed her numbed, raw hands to warm them. Fingers aching down deep, she pictured her sheepskin-lined gloves, cozy, warm and forgotten on the kitchen table back at the apartment.

Yet another scatterbrained moment and here I am, paying for it.

Finally she stood up and scuffed to and fro, never straying far from the bench and her suitcase.

"Sei disattenta," Jacopo's voice chided inside her head. *"You're careless to do something like that, but that's just exactly what you always do, isn't it?"*

With a small mental jerk she drew her thoughts back to the present.

Stop worrying about Jacopo. Right now.

The cold air seeped through her coat and she rubbed her arms uselessly. The coat itself seemed to have stiffened in the frosty air, the sleeves bunching and folding between her fingers.

Closing her eyes, she blew into her hands and reconsidered buying a hot drink from the vending machine nearby. All at once, her fellow travelers began shuffling toward the yellow line. Emily opened her eyes to find them leaning forward as one to peer toward the approaching lights.

Wincing at the metallic grinding of the train's brakes, she braced herself for the ritualistic rush to attempt to board against the exodus of smokers heading for the platform to squeeze in a quick nicotine fix.

She managed to drag her suitcase aboard a bedraggled second-class carriage. Clinging to her last shred of optimism, she pushed her way along to the next. This compartment was no better than the last. Here she found only the same stale air, dull lighting and rows of seats covered in dreary Trenitalia green, two by two on either side of the aisle from one end of the carriage to the other. Most of the seats were already occupied, the passengers giving any newcomer the typical Italian once-over from head to toe and refusing to like what they saw.

Determined to ignore the stares, she pressed on toward the middle of the carriage. In passing, she noted a man standing beside a seat, breathing the outside air through an open window. He smiled at her, tugged the collar of his black wool coat more snugly about his neck and returned to his view of the depot. The train made a false start, lurching forward to an abrupt halt, and Emily stumbled, her suitcase falling to the floor with a loud *thud*.

Hauling her suitcase upright, she caught a glimpse of the man's dark eyes watching her. He moved away from the window as though to offer help and she turned away from him, dragging her case to the first empty pair of seats she found. When she put her hand to the vent to check for heat, she felt only a faint rush of tepid air.

"That's not good," she muttered, rubbing her hands again until the circulation resumed, stinging her slowly pinking skin. Snuggling deeper into her overcoat, she turned toward her own dim reflection in the window. Movement behind her image caught her eye, and she saw the man across the aisle by the window smiling in her direction. Years of married habit swiftly stifled her impulse to smile in return.

When he turned back to his own window, she tilted her head to watch him directly.

For the first time, she noted the crack spanning the length of the glass along the sliding window frame. He pushed the broken portion up as high as it would go, then wedged a small, tightly-folded piece of paper between the Plexiglas and the lower frame in an attempt to keep it closed.

At last the conductor's whistle signaled their departure. The smiling man moved to a different seat, leaving the row with the broken window vacant. They began to glide silently forward in the eerie, graceful way of even the most decrepit trains, before the momentum caught and the rattling and clacking began.

Emily took the magazine out of her shoulder bag but the glossy pages remained shut. Instead, she toyed with the wedding band on her left hand, idly tracing the ornate carving with the pad of her index finger.

With every bump and sway of the train, Rovigo slipped further behind her.

Shouldn't this mean something? I thought I'd feel better, or worse; instead, there's nothing in the end, even after ten years.

She shook her head and searched for an article in her magazine to lose herself in the language, a language still foreign to her in so many ways.

"How like you to choose something as dry as a teaching journal in order to pass the time."

She pushed away Jacopo's voice and squinted at the page, her eyes and brain refusing to work together to focus on the words.

"Mitologia Antica e Fiction Moderna, di Davide Magnani.

"Il ruolo che l'antica mitologia gioca nella fiction moderna è sottovalutato, ma tuttavia innegabile. Tutti i temi moderni non sono altro che mere rielaborazioni di antiche storie e sono stati raccontati attorno al fuoco sin da tempo immemorie..."

Drawing a long, quiet breath, she closed her eyes and pressed her cool fingertips to her temples. In time, her mind slightly clearer, she tried once again to read, translating as she went.

"Ancient Mythology and Modern Fiction, by Davide Magnani.

"The role that ancient mythology has in modern fiction is little appreciated, but nonetheless undeniable. All modern themes are merely re-workings of ancient tales and have been told around the fire since time immemorial..."

Emily let her attention drift away from the article, settling on the artwork on the page opposite: a chalk drawing of Proserpina and Plutone on a city sidewalk, drawn by a street artist in Rome. Her heartbeat trebled for an instant in recognizing the figures.

4

Proserpina, she thought, and tried to swallow the dry lump in her throat. *Proserpina, who stayed in Hades because she was tricked into doing so.*

Biting her lip, she folded the page with the photo back and out of sight, then focused again on the article at hand, determined to get through it this time.

Fifteen minutes later, that man was smiling at her again. His eyes tickled at her periphery like so many nimble fingers until she allowed herself to sneak a few peeks at him on the sly, using the reflection in the window. In only a few minutes, she noted he was Jacopo's exact opposite in many ways.

He's the other side of the same coin, though, I'll bet.

Still, he was easy on the eyes, with a strong jaw, dark eyes and dark, boyish curls which fell along his brow. His clothes weren't fancy, but simple in design. A pale blue chambray shirt peeked out from beneath his red scarf. There were no fancy designer labels, no ostentatious, trendy affectations on view.

She liked that.

When he crossed his legs, she risked a direct look at him and smiled in spite of herself. His shoes were black running shoes, rather scuffed up at that. She knew too well the premium Italians placed on footwear; it was nice to see someone who wasn't completely fussy about his appearance for a change.

When he drew out an eyeglass case from the inside pocket of his coat, she turned to the reflection in the window once more. He perused a copy of *La Repubblica*—not *Libero*, not *La Padania*—so she was reasonably sure he wasn't from Veneto. Despite her fugue, this thought made her smile again. A glimpse of his dark eyes straying in her direction, followed by his own secretive smile, sent a pleasant shimmy down her spine.

Her heart leapt skittishly even as she pushed the expression off her face and felt the blush creep up from her collar to tint her cheeks.

The broken window fell open with a soft *thump* and the banging and rattling of the train's progress drowned out the soft hum of conversation around her. A steady, chilling wind blew inside the carriage. Several passengers grumbled their disapproval and tugged their scarves and coats more tightly around themselves, but none made an effort to close the window.

After a moment or two, the man stood and pushed his glasses up the bridge of his nose with an air of determination. Emily observed even more openly this time as he returned to the broken window, shoved it upward and stuffed the wedge of paper between the Plexiglas and the frame once more.

When he turned, he saw her watching and his smile lit up his face again. His eyes met hers fully and she looked away, her cheeks tingling as she turned to the window and the countryside emerging in the growing daylight beyond it.

In spite of herself, her eyes shifted to follow him yet again when he stepped away from the row with the broken window.

His hair had been tousled by the wind, and upon settling back in his seat he ran one hand cautiously over it, taming any wild, out-of-place waves. His dark eyes behind the oval frames of his glasses flicked in her direction before he turned toward his own window. She thought it was clear that he was trying not to be obvious about watching her.

"*Emily, you need to get over yourself*," Jacopo's voice scolded. "*Pale skin and a mousy pony-tail on a dumpy thirty-four-year-old woman won't catch the eye of someone like him.*"

Still, it was just a fun little daydream, right? Then she considered why she was on the train and she revived her interest in the magazine.

With effort, she managed to make him fade into the background. By her reckoning, it was for the best anyway.

2

Emily never heard the arrival announcement at *Bologna Centrale* but the stirring of the other passengers pulled her out of the article. She checked her things to reassure herself she would be able to get away quickly and make her connection. Thanks to the delay, she was too far behind schedule as it was.

The smiling stranger stood up and put on his coat, adjusted his scarf and stowed his eyeglasses. Before he caught her eye she looked away but a pleasant little flicker of awareness told her he was still watching from time to time. While the train crept toward the station, the man sat down and trained his gaze out the window toward the red-roofed neighborhoods along the railway and the elaborate graffiti on the walls there. Afraid she'd already encouraged him too much, she did the same.

Oh, boy, that's just what I'd need, too—some egomaniacal italiano *chasing me to my next train.*

A small smile quirked at the corners of her mouth before the train stuttered to a squalling halt and she joined the line to disembark.

Suitcase in tow, she hurried as best she could along the platform and wove her way through the crowd to make an awkward descent to the *sottopassaggio* for the station. She paused in front of a monitor to read the display of departures and arrivals and her stomach twisted.

That has to be wrong, doesn't it? So many cancellations all at once?

When she finally stood in the ticket hall and stared forlornly at the board, embarrassment flushed her cheeks. A brief check of the newsstand confirmed what she'd somehow managed to forget during her recent preoccupation:

"*Sciopero Generale*," said the headlines in bold print. "General Strike."

No trains would be running from nine a.m. to five p.m. that day, leaving countless travelers in the lurch. Already an hour behind her original schedule, her last chance of reaching *Milano Centrale* on time had departed more than fifteen minutes before.

"I guess I'm stranded, then," she muttered, her voice faltering and cracking, her fingers twisting her ring again. She noticed what she was doing and parted her hands, shaking them vigorously as though trying to restart sluggish circulation.

"Stupid, stupid, stupid… I hate this damned country."

A soft cough to her right drew her attention to the fact she'd spoken aloud. She turned to find the man who had smiled at her on the train. Looking away hurriedly, she read the newspaper headlines to avoid the mild smirk on his face.

How could I not remember the strike? How could this have possibly slipped my mind?

Ignoring the clock of the timetable, she looked at her wristwatch as if the time there would be different somehow. Instead, the hands stood steadfastly at the nine and the three; the second hand spun with malicious speed. She was belatedly aware that she'd made some sort of anxious sound, as her persistent would-be travel companion gave another soft cough beside her.

Her temper flared, her hands balling into fists, while he continued to grin at her.

"*Tutto okay?*" he inquired gently, adjusting the strap of his knapsack.

"No," she answered curtly, putting her back to him. Her mind reeling, she stood that way for a moment before she crossed to the doors which led out to the tracks. She continued to the *sala d'attesa*—the waiting room—where she perched on the edge of one of the chairs, her legs bobbing with anxious energy. The businessman in the next seat tutted disapprovingly and Emily offered him a weary, embarrassed smile, slowing but unable to stop her agitated motion.

Only then did her eyes stray to the stylized crack in the wall, which served as both a window onto the tracks and a memorial of the 1980 bombing. She read and re-read the names on the plaque next to it, seeing but not seeing, and slowly sat back in her chair. Soon the names and ages posted there grew clearer, sinking in and cutting through the white noise in her head.

Get some perspective. You see, things could be a lot worse. Besides, are you really in that big of a hurry to go back? Really?

Flashing forward, she imagined the look she'd find on her mother's face when she arrived in Ypsilanti. It wouldn't be a pretty scene, even though she'd had plenty of advance warning.

And then the questions will begin, even though I've given all the answers I've ever had by now. At least, all the answers I can give her.

Catching a glimpse of the man from the train passing by the window, she breathed a small, frustrated sigh.

Don't come in here, for Heaven's sake. Just leave me be... Oh, of course.

When he paused in the doorway and held the door open for an elderly woman laden with packages, Emily took a swift look around. There were no other exits open and her urge for flight was already fading.

By the time her eyes had returned to the doorway, he'd already spotted her. He smiled.

Emily smiled, too, then forced the expression off her face.

"*Don't be ridiculous,*" Jacopo scoffed. "*He's got to be up to something.*"

She again pulled out her magazine and pretended to read, but Jacopo's voice persisted.

"*Why won't he leave you alone? He must have some sort of ulterior motive, no doubt.*"

The man from the train sat at the far end of her row. In her peripheral vision she noted him glancing in her direction and her heart skipped expectantly.

And if he does have an ulterior motive? What of it? Maybe it wouldn't be so bad.

She continued to feign interest in the article, shaking her head at such flippancy.

"What does that even mean? Of course it would be bad—how could it be good? This is no fantasy, stupid, and it's no fairy tale, either."

Chastened, she recognized the dull pain insinuating itself into her head. If she didn't calm down soon, it would escalate into a full-blown migraine. Pressing her hand to her forehead, she resisted the urge to sigh again, or to swallow down the pang of homesickness at Jacopo's voice, ever-present. The cool draw of her fingers across her brow soothed her a little, but not quite enough.

It's time to think; what do I need to do?

"I'll never make that flight now—it's impossible," she muttered, blushing when the businessman nearby looked sideways at her. While she searched her coat pockets she thought again of her gloves on the kitchen counter, then dug deeper for her cell phone.

I need to call the airline and shift the reservation to the next flight out. That's first and foremost. I'll call Mom later to let her know I'm taking a different flight.

A cold dread seeped into her limbs, her heart chattering frostily in her chest.

Oh, God; oh, no.

She pulled her shoulder bag onto her lap and rummaged hastily through it. Her fingers sifted through all sorts of identifiable detritus: her planner, her sunglasses case, travel packs of tissues, her hairbrush with the ponytail elastics around the handle, even a few pens and a stub of a pencil.

Her fingers clasped a small case and she exhaled with relief. *Ah, there it is!* Her spirits soon sank with the realization that she'd only found her mirrored compact. She took it out and stared at it, puzzled.

Why is that in there? I haven't worn makeup in ages—and certainly not today.

The businessman stood abruptly and walked away, tucking his newspaper under his arm in a pointed gesture and smoothing his coat as he went. Emily watched him go, then dropped her compact in her bag and resumed her search with unsteady hands.

She checked the same places again and again. Shaking all over, she let her hands fall to her lap on either side of the bag, resolving not to dump the bag out on the floor in a desperate last search.

My gloves are on the kitchen counter where I left them, right next to my cell phone. A fat lot of good any of it'll do me from there.

Her throat locked around the idea of going to the newsstand and sorting out a phone card. Using the last of her change for a payphone seemed somehow like another slap in the face from this infernal country. Her eyes closed in anticipation of that pain.

I really wanted to make this trip without speaking a word of Italian; now I can't, and it's because of yet another stupid mistake.

She shook her head and unshed tears burned behind her closed eyelids.

"*Scatterbrain,*" Jacopo chided. "*Always the scatterbrain.*"

Biting her lower lip until she feared it might bruise if she continued, she willed the day to end, just end. Opening her eyes at last, she stared dully at the floor and tried to take a few deep, calming breaths. A faint buzzing filled her ears, drowning out her thoughts and the soft chatter of travelers around her.

"*Scatterbrain.*"

It was a mild taunt, sometimes spoken as an endearment, but its relentless presence was no consolation. It was almost as though Jacopo were there with her.

The thought made her flinch, her heart clenching in her chest, and her hand rose to cover it until it beat more smoothly again. An instant of hope sent her hand into the inner pocket of her overcoat, to no avail.

Perhaps distance will help? When I get far enough away, maybe autopilot will kick in and I won't have to think about what I'm doing anymore...

She thought of the man from the train and his persistent, if amiable, pursuit of her. It would be so much easier if he would just come right out with it. This relentless but gentle quest of his was somehow reminiscent of Jacopo in Venice, ten years ago.

And look how that turned out.

Better that he should declare his intentions so she could refuse them and get on with the rest of this interminable day.

In spite of herself, she found her thoughts drifting resolutely back to the piazza with the paper shop, where Jacopo had found her, and where it had all begun.

3

"*Emily Miller, it's nice to meet you. Would you do me the honor of joining me for dinner this evening, or must I chase you across this city again?*"

At once, she pulled her hand out of his and stepped away from him. "Excuse me?"

"*I saw you when you arrived last night and I decided to make your acquaintance. As it turns out, however, you are a very hard person to get close to.*"

"*Why?*"

"*Why what?*" *He tilted his head to one side in a disarming gesture.*

"*Why do you want to 'make my acquaintance'?*"

"*Do I need a reason?*"

The row of seats creaked and she felt the shift and tilt as someone sat nearby. With some effort, Emily shrugged away Venice and the past and turned her attention back to searching her coat pockets and shoulder bag.

Maybe I missed it, that's all. Maybe I'm just imagining it on the counter at the apartment. One thing I know: I can't take another surprise this morning. I'm at my wits' end.

The clatter and shuffle of objects in her purse seemed loud in the solemn silence of the waiting room, but she continued digging, until the black jeans and scuffed running shoes of her new seatmate distracted her. Her breath caught in her throat at this sudden, unexpected closeness. She scarcely managed to resist the impulse to jump up and walk swiftly out the door. Dragging her gaze up over the black overcoat and past the red scarf, she finally reached his face.

Ever calm and relaxed, the man from the train smiled at her in his—by now—familiar way.

Emily returned to the exposed contents of her purse. Even after acknowledging the lack of anything incriminating in view, her ability to concentrate was well and truly shaken.

I wonder how long he's been there? Never mind; just focus on the task at hand.

"I don't believe it… Today, of all days–" Stomach churning, she cut off her thread of monologue. The thought of being caught talking to herself again, with *him* so close, was mortifying. Twisting away, she continued searching her bag with dogged determination, unable to accept defeat just yet.

I could swear I brought it.

While she searched, he stayed seated beside her, glancing around at other travelers, from time to time sending an indulgent smile in her direction. She thought he had the amused air of someone waiting for his companion to finish an unexpected, fussy task.

What nerve he has—and where do Italians learn that smirk, anyway? Is it genetic or something? If I never see that look again, it'll be too soon.

In time, he faced her and cleared his throat before he spoke softly. "*Parli italiano?*"

"*Posso, ma non voglio.*" Facing him, she enunciated each word with exaggerated care, since he had so spectacularly failed to get the hint so far.

How dare he address me so informally? How rude is that, using 'tu' instead of 'Lei'?

Untroubled, the man from the train nodded. "*Vuoi parlare inglese?*"

This second, softer inquiry, still lacking in formality even though they were strangers, felt somehow provocative. She deliberately turned away from him, biting back a clever retort. Her eyes still pricked with tears of frustration she refused to permit.

Forcing herself to take slow, even breaths, she scrabbled in her head for a calming thought. Her hands ceased their useless search but continued trembling in the depths of her purse. She hoped that he couldn't see them shaking.

I'm not hanging on by a thread here... I've got to ignore him, keep it together and figure something out. I'm going home today, no matter what.

Her resolve was slipping, though, and she stood and stepped away, still struggling not to become frantic. Part of her wanted to curl up in a corner somewhere and give in to the panic looming over her. Instead, she focused on directing her wobbly legs toward the door, a vague plan forming in the back of her mind: collect the change in her purse, buy a phone card and find a public phone that wouldn't eat the whole card before she'd made her arrangements with the airline.

It certainly seemed simple enough--on the surface.

"*Scusa?*" The man followed at a respectful distance now, his voice still low and gentle. "I'm sorry to disturb, but might I offer you some help?"

Oh, just go away.

"I'm fine, please, really."

He touched her arm from behind and she turned to face him, ready to hurl in his direction the dozens of Italian insults piling up in her mind. When her eyes met his, every last slur drifted away like pollen in the wind. Her throat ached and she swallowed hard, trying to ignore the stinging in her eyes.

"*Davvero?*" he asked, his tone gentle. "It is obvious that you are having some difficulties." His fingertips were still light upon her arm, steering her back toward the chairs inside the *sala d'attesa*, away from the door and the cold outside air.

In amazement, she allowed him to lead her.

Dammit, but he seems so sincere. Why does he have to act so nice?

"I, um... I can't find my cell phone. I thought I'd thrown it in here, but now I can't find it and..." She drifted off.

Why am I telling him this?

He nodded his understanding, intently reading her eyes, and she couldn't look away. Though his eyes were warm and comforting, most of all she found them friendly. She hadn't seen such open friendliness in a long time.

"Okay. But you are now quite certain you don't have your mobile?"

"*Sì*, yes, that's right." With a small effort, she looked away. To her surprise, save for a few like herself who had been surprised by the strike, the waiting room was empty.

"Some things are not so difficult, then, to fix, *sai?*" He reached into his coat pocket and took out his cell phone. "Please, use mine."

"But you don't know who I need to call."

"Your husband, perhaps? Does it matter?"

"*Oh, he's good.*"

"Actually," she began, abashed, "I was thinking more of the airline. I have to change my flight now."

"Oh. That is a good idea, as well." He continued to hold the phone out to her. "*Ti prego*; please, I wish to help."

"Uh… *Grazie…*"

Emily took the phone with her left hand so he would see her wedding band. "*Grazie mille.*" She turned away from him, dialed and then spoke to the ticket agent. The first flight she could book would leave the following morning.

"Thank you again," she said, returning his phone, her stomach fluttering anxiously all the while. "*Sei molto, molto gentile.*"

"*Di niente*—it is nothing. Do you need to make another call?"

"I don't think so."

"So… you're flying out from Marconi here in Bologna?"

A sudden, almost dizzying awareness swept over her. "No, Milan. From Malpensa."

"You'll need a room, then, for the night."

"That's right…" Frustration roiled in her stomach. She took a deep breath, willing the nausea away.

I should have thought of that.

"This is getting more complicated by the minute," she said.

"*Non è vero.*" He smiled, shaking his head. "If you stay at a hotel, you can leave with no problem in the morning."

"If I can get a room, that is. I'll be lucky to find a vacancy around there, this late."

"*Non ti preoccupare*—if you permit me," he said, already dialing, "I will try on your behalf. I fly out of Malpensa frequently, also—I like to stay there before a flight..."

"Well, I'm not sure I could ask –"

"*Ciao*, Giorgio!" He held up one finger to silence her and spoke rapidly into the phone. After what seemed like an interminable amount of chit-chat he turned to her again.

"Your name, *signora*?"

"Um, I'm Emily; Emily Spadon." She began to spell it for him but he cut her off.

"Spadon?" he echoed in the same Spanish-sounding, Venetian accent she'd spoken with, before relaying the information to the person on the line.

Belatedly noticing her compulsive ring-twisting, she steeled herself into stopping.

He ended the call with a cheerful, "*Ci vediamo, ciao!*" and scribbled something on a notepad he'd retrieved from his bag. "*Ecco fatto*," he said, handing her the page with a flourish and a smile. "He says he'll hold the room for you, no problem." The tattered edge of the paper shed a strip of semi-detached confetti onto the floor and he bent to pick it up.

"Wow, I guess chivalry isn't dead after all." Emily read the note and carefully placed it in her shoulder bag. "So...might I know the name of my knight errant?"

"*Certo*," he said, then made a small, self-mocking bow before offering his hand. "I am Davide Magnani."

"*Piacere*, Davide; it's nice to make your acquaintance. Thank you so much for your help today." A faint sense of recognition flickered, but disappeared. "I...um... How can...How *could* I repay you for this? I mean, I couldn't just accept your generosity without..."

"*Un caffè, forse?*"

"A coffee? That's it?" She laughed. "Are you serious?"

"You asked. I told you." He shrugged, still grinning.

"Well, if you're sure… You're one cheap date, *amico*." She looked around for the bar and felt his hand touch her shoulder.

"No, no… Not here in the *stazione*," he said, chuckling, "please."

"Okay," she said slowly, the skin on the back of her neck tingling. "Where would you suggest?"

"Don't worry; it's not far from here. It's a very good place," he added, when she hesitated. "It's warm, and they have such delicious brioche—you won't believe it."

She looked at him, still unsure. She was no longer concerned with being rude, but her gut instinct was speaking louder than ever, telling her to trust him. This, in spite of every warning she'd ever heard about strangers in her life.

I've only just met you, so why on Earth should I trust anything you say to me?

Seeking his eyes, she read deeply; she knew at once that she could trust him to be a gentleman. Of that, she had no doubt.

His own gaze never wavered in the least.

"If you're not comfortable with the idea, I understand," he said. "Still, it would be a pity if you missed out on the best brioche you've ever had." He paused, now seeming uncertain. "Will ever have," he corrected himself. "You haven't had it yet."

With his next warm smile, the last of her resistance melted away.

She realized she was smiling, too. It felt good to smile again, after so long.

"Thank you," she said.

Davide raised an eyebrow. "For what?"

"For the offer. I'd like to take you up on that."

"You would? *Sinceramente?*"

"*Sì*, I would."

As the relief showed on his face, Emily felt less doubtful. It felt good to be sure of something, too.

"Well, why not, then? Heaven knows I have all day now. Shall we?" She gestured for him to lead but he paused, seeming to consider her suitcase.

"Can I make a suggestion? Perhaps you'd like to check this in the left luggage lockers. It might be a bit cumbersome to you, here in the city."

"Good point." Looking down at the suitcase, she grasped the handle. "Where is that office, then?"

He led her back to the ticketing hall and then outside to the walkway in front of the station. "It is just through there," he said, pointing toward the other entrance on the right-hand-side of the building, "next to the *farmacia*."

"Okay. I'll be right back."

Of course, by the time I get this done, he'll have suddenly remembered a pressing appointment and be gone. He's bound to, right? It'd fit right in with the rest of the day, anyway.

However, when she returned, he was still there, waiting by the ticketing hall entrance.

The way this day has gone so far, he should have disappeared already.

"I cannot believe that you've never been in Bologna before," he said as they strolled along the walkway to the street in front of the station, under a cloudless azure sky.

"I can't believe I confessed it so quickly," she laughed.

They paused at the crosswalk to wait for the light. Davide grasped her hand to lead her against the flow of pedestrians in a gesture so familiar she nearly let him. When she pulled her hand out of his, a shy smile was his only response.

Denied her hand, he instead led her gently along by the crook of her arm, guiding her through the oncoming pedestrians who would otherwise have passed between the two of them. Once they'd crossed the road, he released her and they walked side by side under the porticos. She soon wished she hadn't pulled away so fast—how rude that must have seemed—and she missed the warmth of his palm against her own, his fingers closed protectively around hers.

"You've never been *here* before," he said as they strolled, "but you've lived in *Italia* for…how long?"

"Years, but how do you know I live here? I could be a tourist, or a student. A very 'mature' student, true, but still."

"No," he said with a confident shake of his head.

"My mistake with the strike alone should mark me as a new kid in town, don't you think?" she persisted, not altogether sure what point she was proving. They paused at the end of the portico where the winter sun shone down on Piazza 20 Settembre.

"No," he said, still more confidently, gazing out toward the stone archway of Porta Galliera.

"Why not?"

"Anyone could forget a strike. Normally it is something which is, at best, a minor inconvenience." He turned to face her. "Besides, despite your distress, you're too comfortable here. You show no signs of being a tourist and what's more…" He paused, his eyes crinkling as they met hers. "When you speak Italian, you have a slightly Venetian accent. Even a well-educated tourist would sound like a newsreader, at best."

"I'd never thought about that. I suppose you're right."

"I am." He clapped his hands together to produce a brief echo along the portico. "Okay. As you will find that Bologna is my town, would you like the tour?"

"Let's start with the brioche and see where the day goes, okay?"

He offered her his arm and she tentatively threaded her hand into the crook of his elbow.

"*Va bene*. Right this way." He folded his hand over hers and led her along the sidewalk under the warming sunshine.

4

"Wow. You weren't kidding, were you?" Emily took a small sip of cappuccino and sighed.

"It is as I told you, eh?"

"*Proprio così.*" As Emily looked around the bar, she felt a small smile blossoming. "This place is positively charming, too. How did you find it?"

"I told you before," he said in a bad imitation of an American accent, "'Bologna is my town.' I know where everything is here."

"Really?"

"*Sì.*" He nodded, raising his eyebrows a notch too high. "*Veramente.*"

"So you're a professional tour guide, then?"

"No. I spend a lot of time in the University *Quartiere.*"

"You're a teacher's assistant?"

"No…" He stirred his *caffè macchiato* idly, shaking his head.

"Well, a student, then. You don't seem old enough to be *un professore.*"

"Don't I?" He leaned forward and the small table jostled between them, the cups clinking in their saucers. "Look closer."

It felt like a dare, a childish challenge, so she leaned nearer too. Her courage faltered after a moment, but only after she'd noted the laugh lines around his eyes and the few gray strands in his hair.

"Don't fall for it," Jacopo's voice scolded at once, almost making her flinch. *"Kill time with him if you must, but for Heaven's sake, don't let this go any further."*

She pulled off another piece of her brioche and popped it in her mouth to keep from thinking about the hint of woodsmoke and earth in Davide's cologne.

"There's something I'd like to ask you," she said before she could lose her nerve.

"Che cos'è?" He was running a finger over a lacquered-over message someone had scratched into the surface of the table.

"On the train this morning—you *were* watching me, weren't you?" She laughed nervously and shook her head, blushed and looked away. "I'm sorry. You know, right when I said it, I realized how..."

"Sì," he interrupted softly. "I was watching you on the train, but there is a simple explanation."

"And what might that be?"

"Well, I confess: at first, I saw you across from me on the train, and I thought, 'What a lovely woman she is'."

Facing him once again, she chuckled in spite of her embarrassment. "Oh, please; I saw so many stylish, elegant women on that train. I'm not like that."

"I saw the magazine you were reading," he said, as if that would explain everything.

"Yes...?" she encouraged with her hands, drawing him forward.

"Well, then I thought, 'She's intelligent as well. That's wonderful.' So I couldn't take my eyes off you."

Emily laughed more freely, waving her hand, shooing his words away. "Oh, please..."

"No, *è vero, è vero,*" he laughed too. "But there's more, of course."

"Oh, really? Okay, what is it?"

Smiling, he nervously busied himself with brushing up the crumbs of his brioche. "I saw you with your magazine and then... I saw the article you were reading with so much interest."

"You could see which article I was reading?"

"*Sì.*"

"You'd read it, too?"

"*Sì, sì.* Many times, in fact."

"Imagine that... I would never have guessed something like *that* would catch your attention." A wave of relief washed over her, now that the mystery of his "attraction" was solved. "You know, I thought the article was very interesting, but I'm not sure I completely understood it. My Italian isn't perfect and there were some rather abstract concepts and complex language in it..." She trailed off, a realization dawning. "Oh, lord... 'Davide Magnani'." She put her hand to her forehead, embarrassed. "*You* wrote it, didn't you? That's why your name rang a little bell in the deep, dark recesses of my mind."

"*Sì*, I did. It's just that other thing I do when I'm not teaching or speaking to educational conferences in *Padova*..."

"Amazing... I mean, what are the odds of reading an article and having the author sitting right across from you on the train like some average Joe? Or, in this case, like some average *Giuseppe*?"

He chuckled. "I would think that the odds are probably quite small."

"So you were in *Padova* for a conference, then?"

"*Sì*, I was there for a sort of...*come si dice*—'workshop', for professors and enthusiasts of modern literature. I spoke about the article, explained my theory, that sort of thing."

"How interesting. I wish I could have heard it, too."

He laughed loudly before covering his mouth with his hand, abashed.

"What?" she asked, puzzled. "What was so funny about what I said?"

"I'm sorry. You must understand, though, that I'm not used to such politeness. Most people are not interested in what I talk about, except for my fellows and the students who are obligated to take my course to gain their degrees at university."

"Okay, but I *was* reading it, wasn't I? Wouldn't that indicate a sincere interest?"

He shrugged modestly, a faint pinkness shading his cheeks. "We all read the magazines in the doctor's office, whether we have an interest in fashion and gossip or not." He looked around the bar, his smile still pulling at his mouth when he faced her again. "Emily, tell me the truth: would you really be interested in the speech I gave?"

"I would, yes. I really would."

"Then I have something else you might enjoy equally. Come with me. We're nearly there, anyway." He stood and hoisted his knapsack over his shoulder while she got her coat and shoulder bag.

"Nearly where?"

"You'll see. Come." He held the door for her and once again they braved the February cold.

The porticos were even colder, channeling the wind and hiding the sun as they wound along the streets. Emily noticed that the people around them seemed to be getting younger and younger, the shops more outré and trendy. At the same time, the stationery and art supply stores multiplied, along with notices offering copy, fax and telephone services to anywhere in the world.

"Are we going to the university?"

"*Sì*—to my office, actually. If you enjoy the trappings of academia, I thought you might like a look into the heart and soul, the real *guts* of it." He gestured fervently as he spoke, as though the topic at hand were something more visceral, and she smiled at his self-deprecating attempt to enliven what he obviously thought she'd find dull. Instead, the idea gave her a little thrill.

Arm in arm they moved through a maze of turns and twists in the busy streets until they turned a corner, opened a heavy oak door and climbed up two flights of massive marble stairs. There was a reassuring weight to everything around them; the very solidity of the dark-paneled walls and the marble floors demanded an attitude of reverence, as though they were in a cathedral.

It feels like you could learn by osmosis, just by standing here.

They passed through an archway into a corridor filled with winter sunlight. Davide stopped, shook out a key ring, opened a glass-paneled door and moved aside.

"*Prego, dopo di te.*" He gestured politely for her to precede him and dropped the keys back into his coat pocket.

She stepped inside and needed to bite her lip to keep from laughing. Surrounding her in the tiny room were stacks of boxes and papers, bookshelves stuffed to capacity. There was scarcely space to turn around in a full circle to see it all.

"I guess now I see what you meant by 'the real guts of it'. I've seen larger cubicles in my day."

He closed the door and squeezed past her to step over boxes stacked haphazardly on the floor. He hung up his coat and scarf, then extended his hand to take hers, a wry smile on his face.

"I think you'll find it gets very warm, very fast, in here."

She scanned the bookshelves nearest her while he cleared a jumble of papers off a chair so she could sit down. He wrestled with the chair for a moment or two, jockeying it into a position amongst the chaos to face his desk and the narrow window behind it, which opened onto a view of the building directly across the narrow alley.

When he took his seat at the desk, a bluish aura surrounded him, a reflection of the soft gray light filtering through the window to bounce off his shirt. She watched him position himself in a rickety office chair, well-worn, no doubt used and abused over decades in this same tiny office. Once he seemed assured that it wouldn't dump him out onto the stacks of papers and oddities behind him on the floor, Davide relaxed and faced her directly for the first time since they'd entered the room.

He said nothing, his gaze meeting hers over the papers and books jumbled on top of his desk. Thinking back to their conversation in the bar, she noted again the crinkles in the corners of his eyes, the threads of silver in his dark hair. Before Jacopo, this was precisely the sort of man who'd caught her eye. A nervous rush of anticipation made her shiver inside.

But can he tell? Is it so obvious?

Davide's half-smile was enough to make her quiver now, and she felt the flush creep up into her cheeks at the thought.

Yes, he can tell, but he's showing restraint.

"So," he began with a sardonic grin, "it is everything you ever dreamed, *sì?*"

"To be honest, it really, truly is."

He sat up straight suddenly, nearly toppling his chair.

"*No...veramente?*"

"*Sì,*" she insisted, appreciating the puzzlement on his face. "I always used to imagine my professors in rooms like this, poring over ancient, dusty tomes under the light of a single lamp, searching for some elusive piece of knowledge to share with us. Imagine my disappointment when I went to speak with them and found them in some teensy cubicle with schedules tacked to the walls, or the department head in a nicely-appointed office with all the modern trappings, reading a Jackie Collins novel or playing solitaire on the computer."

"I have a fax machine," Davide said, with boyish eagerness. "Somewhere."

Emily laughed and looked around the room, trying to take it all in.

"Obviously, I'm not a department head. I've only been teaching here a few years," he said and shrugged, glancing around. "Most of what you see in here isn't mine. These treasures belonged to my predecessor."

"Oh, what happened to him?"

"He died."

Oops.

"I'm sorry," she said, chastened.

He waved a dismissive hand. "Eh, I never really knew him. So tell me, what did you study at university?"

"I'm afraid I wasn't particularly ambitious. I was an English major, basically—journalism, creative writing and classic literature." Shaking her head, she sobered while she resisted the pull of her hands, one to the other. "I never finished, though. Unfortunately, 'Life', such as it was, managed to interfere with my plans."

Davide regarded her quietly, waiting for her to continue, then cleared his throat. "I'm sorry. I didn't wish to make you uncomfortable."

"It's not your fault, Davide. You've been so kind, and this has been a nice morning in spite of everything—and it's all thanks to you. I just have something on my mind." She saw that he was watching her hands and realized she was indeed twisting her ring around her finger. Again she forced herself to stop. "I promise, I'm all right."

"Are you sure?" He glanced at her hands again and she understood he'd noticed her little habit.

"*Sì, certo.*" She smiled, putting as much sincerity into the effort as she could.

He smiled too, hesitantly at first, then with hopeful confidence. "*Va bene...*" After unlocking the drawer of his desk, he took out a diary and quickly consulted it. Then he closed and locked up the drawer and stood to open his knapsack. "Since you will not have an opportunity to hear my talk, why don't you take this? I would like you to have it." The plastic presentation folder he offered her was filled with pages covered in spidery scrawls between the lines and along the margins.

"Won't you need this? It's got all these notes scribbled on it and stuff. Don't you need to copy them down?"

"No, I've already done that. Please, keep it."

Emily paged through the speech and paused over one particularly re-worked section, as fondness for the tiny handwriting came over her. "*Grazie*, Davide. I look forward to reading this."

"I suppose you'll have time to begin it on your flight tomorrow."

"Yes, plenty of time." Her mood darkened once more as she thought of the journey ahead.

Davide knelt awkwardly beside her chair, one hand resting atop hers while he studied her expression. "Emilia, *dimmi... Cosa c'è che non va?*"

"I have to go back to the States, and..." She met his eyes at last. "I can't talk about it right now. You do understand, don't you?"

He nodded reassuringly. "*Penso di sì*. Come with me, then. We will get your mind on something else to pass the time for a while. There is much yet to see."

5

ownstairs, he pulled the door open with a bit of effort and
held it so Emily could precede him. They stepped out into
a rush of wind along the street and Emily shivered a bit as
she buttoned up her coat. Davide offered his arm once more and
they strolled in a companionable silence.

At length he drew a deep breath, then exhaled slowly. "So,
Emilia. Tell me a little about you."

"Like what?"

"Like, perhaps, why you are interested in mythology's influences
in modern literature? Or you might tell me why you were in Rovigo
this morning."

She could feel the tension in his arm as he spoke and she
squeezed it reassuringly.

"I live...uh, there," she said, second-guessing whether she
should have used the past tense instead.

"Are you sure?" he laughed.

"Maybe not so much. I mean, 'if you can call it living', as the old
joke goes," she said and laughed too.

"What do you do there? Or are you a lady of leisure?"

"No, I work. Actually, I'm a teacher, like you. Sort of, anyway."

"This explains your educational interests. But what does this
'sort of' mean?"

"It means that I, well… I teach English at a language school in *Padova*. It's nothing special, not a very big school. Just me and a few other English teachers, a Chinese teacher, a German teacher, a couple of Spanish and Portuguese teachers… I'm rambling, aren't I?"

"*Sì*," he grinned, "but it's quite charming. What was it like living in Rovigo?"

"Why do you ask?"

Davide shrugged, offering a half-grin. "I've never been there. In fact, I've only passed through there on mornings like this one."

"Yet you were surprised by the fact I'd never been to Bologna?"

The sound of the quiet, disapproving *tsk* of his tongue against his teeth seemed to rasp along her spine. "It's hardly the same thing," he said, his tone irritating in its inferred patience.

Emily squared her shoulders and kept walking, pushing away the memory of Jacopo's frequent use of the same critical sound.

"*How* is it different, then?" she asked, hearing the challenge in her own voice.

"*Cosa?*"

"How is it different? Or more to the point, how would *you* know, since you've never been?"

Davide stopped short, his grin fading. Standing tall, Emily cocked one eyebrow, folding her arms across her chest. Seeing the puzzlement in his face, however, she slouched and lowered her eyes to study the pavement at their feet.

"*Mi dispiace*, Emilia. I did not mean any offense by what I said. I only meant that Rovigo is a smaller town and Bologna is such a busy place. Everyone comes here eventually, it seems."

"You're right. I'm sorry. I don't know why I reacted like that." She shrugged and started walking again. "I don't know what to say, really. It's not much different than living anywhere else, I suppose. I worked, I took care of my house, I cooked and slept…just like at home. Venice, now? *That* was another story."

"You lived in *Venezia*?"

"*Sì*, I did. For the first year I was here. I moved to Rovigo after that."

Davide's smile returned and Emily's spirit lifted at the sight of it.

"How was *Venezia* for you? Did you enjoy it there?"

Emily realized she was twisting the ring around her finger again and she thrust her hands into her pockets to stop. "I liked it very much. I didn't speak any Italian, though, so I depended on his help quite a lot."

Davide nodded, his face almost expressionless save for a slight pursing of his lips at the mention of her husband. A stirring next to her heart made her breathless. Her hand went instinctively to rest there for a moment.

"But, in the end, you learned the language," he said, encouraging her to continue with a small movement of his hand.

"Of course. I had no choice, especially when I decided to get a job. But that didn't happen until we went to Rovigo."

"Why Rovigo? I mean, you were in *Venezia*, so why leave?"

"His mother was ill. She needed to be somewhere she could get to the hospital faster and he wanted to go with her, to take care of her."

Emily paused, remembering.

"His family owned a palazzo in Rovigo, so that's where his mother went. She had a private flat there, which was quite lovely, really. We had a house of our own, outside of town. It's the first piece of real estate I've ever owned."

"You own it?"

The sincere surprise in Davide's voice was too obvious to miss. "It was something he insisted on: half in my name, half in his. It gave me a reason to work, too, beyond earning my own spending money. I paid the taxes and he paid the house payments. It seemed fair enough."

He nodded, seeming to concede her point. They paused on the corner of Via dell'Indipendenza and he looked around, his eyes narrowing briefly.

"I have something I think you might enjoy." His smile suggested a new treasure. Emily thought of the copy of the speech he'd given her in his office a short while before.

"You do?"

"*Sì*. Being from *Venezia*, you might appreciate this on a different level, of course. Would you like to see?"

"Sure, why not?"

With no compunction, he took her hand to lead her across the street. This time, however, she didn't pull her hand away. Instead, she savored the heat of his palm against hers, the reassuring strength in his fingers as they walked along the nondescript city street.

They reached the first corner and Davide paused to point out the weathered, ancient archway under which the street itself passed.

"This was a reinforcement of the original city walls," he began, and as his arm moved in a semi-circle that seemed to outline the arch, she wondered if he used this tone of voice in his lectures. "It was built in the late twelfth century, when the city was experiencing a particularly robust period of growth. However, it didn't take long before the city outgrew the walls and assimilated them in the manner you see here."

He paused to let her observe the three windows in the center of the former tower, each window smaller than the first, closed and shuttered against the winter cold. He then turned and led her along the portico just past the archway. The peach tones of the building to their left changed abruptly to a deep russet red along a solid wall.

"*La Finestrella*, or the Little Window," Davide continued, "has one of the most unique views in all Bologna. It's one of our better-kept secrets, even though we all know about it."

She laughed at this statement, so contradictory and so sensible at the same time.

What is he talking about?

He stopped on the walkway close to a small window in the wall, which bore a palimpsest of graffiti. Bold permanent-marker-scripted messages in a host of different languages competed with spray-painted designs for attention. Other materials had been used, too:

Emily recognized correction fluid and the slightly darker color of scratches in the paint, perhaps made by the edge of a dead pen or the blade of a pocket knife.

"*Ecco: La Finestrella*," he said, indicating that she should look through the window.

Her brow furrowed as she stepped forward. Her eyes widened as she found herself looking down on a canal, reminiscent of one of the smaller canals of Venice.

She turned to him, finding his expectant and somewhat hopeful smile waiting before she turned back again. "Wow," she breathed. There was nothing else to say.

After a few silent moments passed, Davide stepped forward to look through the window as well. They stood shoulder to shoulder, silently regarding the water that flowed toward them. It didn't take much imagination to cast the earth-toned palazzos along the water as something grander.

"This canal is called *Canale delle Moline*, or Canal of the Mills." His voice was soft, his breath making small mists in the cold. "It is called this because there used to be many mills along the length of it. There are only two areas where it is visible. The rest runs under the city."

Emily's initial impression of a Venetian canal quickly faded, the reality before her somewhat less glamorous than the real thing. Just as the reality of Venice itself had overpowered its more mythical beauty for her.

At least *this* illusion had been conquered straightaway.

She shut her eyes and put her hands up to the edge of the window when a quick wave of vertigo crested and fell to make the sidewalk undulate beneath her feet. Davide's touch on her shoulder seemed distant and unreal, as though a dozen layers of clothing separated her from him instead of her sweater and woolen overcoat.

Icy cold filled her stomach while her skin flushed hot, the perspiration along her neck chilling in the winter air. She wanted to undo her ponytail and flail her hair around to cool and warm herself at the same time, but her hands remained still.

He held her arms in a light but firm grasp as he lowered his head to meet her eyes with his own.

"Emilia, *stai bene?*" he asked, a hint of startled urgency in his voice. "Are you okay?"

A nod was all she could manage at first, her head still reeling. "*Sì, sì...* I'm okay." She raised one shaking hand to her forehead to wipe away the sheen of perspiration there. "I suppose it's just been a very long day already." Meeting his eyes, she added, "I didn't sleep well last night. I never do before a big trip."

Davide raised one hand to press his fingers to her cheek, as though checking her temperature. Her heart clenched at such a tender gesture from a virtual stranger, but she didn't move away.

"But do you need to rest? Something more to eat, perhaps, or to drink?"

The cold air prickled at her cheeks, a good sign that her blush at his gentle attention was warming her skin from within.

Oh God, but his touch feels so nice.

A dry swallow at the thought somehow grounded her once more. "I think I'm fine. Really."

His eyes searched hers for a moment more before he straightened and moved a half-step away, his hand still on her shoulder. "*Sei sicura?*"

"*Sì, sono sicura.*"

"All right, then. Let's go this way," he said, taking her hand once more and leading her back the way they'd come. "I have even more to show you."

As they continued walking, Davide continued to explain in detail the significance of countless monuments and landmarks, one after another, only hesitating in his monologue to answer the questions she posed.

"It's simply astounding to me how Europeans retain all this information." She shook her head in wonder.

"It surprises you? Why do you say that?"

"It's just that, if you were to ask the average American the history of their town or their country—and I include myself in this, by the way—aside from the high points, we'd likely draw a blank. Ask a European the same questions, they're capable of giving you an informative but enjoyable tour. How is that possible?"

Davide thrust his hands into his pockets and hunched over a little, shielding her from the wind.

"I have a theory about this," he began, arching his eyebrows and pausing until she indicated he should continue. "I think this is, in part, because the United States is so young. Much of the history there is history only because it happened in the past—and you keep it there with a firm hand by destroying everything as you go along. Nothing lasts. But here –" He spread his arms out and turned in a circle in the middle of the piazza.

"Here, in *Italia*, at least, we live with our history—it is with us every day. We cannot forget completely because we see it every day of our lives. For example," he continued, gesturing in the direction they'd just come from, "I work at the university, so I show you the university. It is an important part of my life, *hai visto, no?* As it happens, the University of Bologna is the oldest university in all *Europa*. It started here, it continues here—it might always be here. Without this school, there would have been no Oxford, no Cambridge, no Yale, no Harvard, no University of… of… Indiana.

"Since we live our history in this quite intimate fashion—cheek to cheek, as it were—it is easier to recall. Throughout *Europa*, our history is the history of civilization, of humanity. Our history is the history of the world entire. It's not possible to set that aside so easily."

His constantly-gesturing hands fell at last to rest at his sides, his impromptu lecture at an end. Emily stood quietly, looking up into his face, expressionless.

"I see," she deadpanned, as brief as he'd just been verbose.

Davide rolled his eyes and took her hand with a resigned air to tuck it in the crook of his arm. His chuckle a moment later reassured her that he'd gotten her joke, and Emily giggled as they set off. They wound their way out of the University Quarter and past the Two Towers of Bologna—leaning at their distinctive angles—then along random twists and turns until Davide paused in a residential neighborhood.

"It's lucky that we met this way, you know," he said in a matter-of-fact tone.

"Why do you say that?" She grinned. "Is it because you've been able to show me around town?"

"In part," Davide nodded encouragement.

"So you could buy me the best brioche I've ever had?"

"That, too. But it is actually lucky because I could bring you here." He gestured toward a doorway and the small brass plaque beside it.

"*Il Cuore della Grassa*," she read aloud. "There's no menu posted. Are they open now?"

"There is no menu, because whatever they make, you eat—and I can promise you, you will enjoy all of it. This is perhaps the best place in all Bologna for true local cuisine and, as you may understand, that is no small boast in this city."

"Goodness. I hope I'm up to the task."

"Oh, you will be."

6

The shapely server swayed between the tables toward them. Angling to face Davide when she put down the platter of *antipasti*, the languid way in which she placed a second, empty plate in front of him was full of artless intent. Then she turned her hip to him while she put Emily's plate down with considerably less grace and attention.

Emily noticed how Davide's eyes trailed after the server sashaying her way back across the dining room. *Men.* Chuckling softly, she flipped her napkin over her lap and straightened it.

"*Cosa?*" he protested with an abashed grin, then selected a slice of bread from the flat wicker basket on the table. "I'm sorry, Emilia, you are right. That was very rude of me."

"Oh, please…as if you could help it," she said, smiling as he selected a few paper-thin slices of *mortadella* and *prosciutto crudo* from the communal plate.

Taking a sip of her mineral water, Emily looked around the restaurant. The dark oak of the walls and furnishings seemed to absorb the late winter sun peering through the sheer curtains over the windows, leaving the room in a half-light which encouraged low, even whispered conversation. The few customers there spoke only Italian, or what she surmised was a Bolognese dialect. When her attention came back to Davide, she found him focused rather intently upon the plate before him. Unfortunately, his expression was more of embarrassment than of hunger.

"Davide," she began, leaning forward to catch his eye, "I was looking at her, too. That's why she *exists*—she's here to look at and appreciate. Besides," she added, reaching out with a fork to choose her own slivers of meat from the plate, "it's not as though we're a couple or something. We're just two friends having a nice lunch together."

"I am beginning to take offense."

"To what?" Still using her fork, Emily delicately folded some *mortadella* onto a piece of bread.

"I did not bring you here for a 'nice lunch'. I brought you to this place so you could have one of the finest meals you will ever have. And so, we should begin." Grasping the carafe of wine by the neck, he moved to pour some into her glass, but she swiftly reached up and halted him.

"I, uh, I don't really drink wine."

"No... *Non è vero...*" He shook his head dismissively, tried again, and once again she stopped him.

"It's just not something I got into the habit of doing, not even here."

"You have not been here long, then."

The whole scene had become all-too-reminiscent of her first dinner with Jacopo. The dimly-lit surroundings, the lack of tourists, the mystery menu and the refusal of her companion to accept her dislike for wine; all of it echoed that night much too closely for her comfort.

"Ten *years*," she said, more defensively than she'd intended. In the silence that fell between them, Davide slowly put the carafe down and Emily felt the movement in her chest again, a chilly presence just below her heart.

"I'm sorry." Her voice was barely above a whisper.

He gathered her hand into his own with a delicate movement. The elaborate carvings of her wedding band sparkled faintly as he rested his thumb next to it. His gesture caused that sense of panic yet again. Deep inside, she had a light sensation of breakage: something at once white-hot and icy-cold, splintering but remaining intact out of habit.

She knew she was staring at his hand, but she couldn't draw her eyes away; nor did he release her. She focused on his thumb, on the small scratch across the knuckle, the clean, trimmed nail, the warmth of his touch as he gently, soothingly stroked her little finger. Tears yearning to be shed prickled behind her eyes, but she blinked them back, fighting to keep her breathing steady and calm.

"Emilia –"

"No, you're right. This *is* a special occasion, isn't it? I'm about to enjoy a fine meal with a charming gentleman who has been kind enough to show me around this beautiful city, so I should be able to be open to his suggestion. And you know, there is the wisdom of that ancient adage to consider."

"Which is…?"

"Correct me if I get it wrong," she said, pouring some of the wine with her free hand and raising the glass low over the table. He followed suit. She took a deep breath. "*L'acqua fa la ruggine*—'Water makes rust' — *giusto?*"

"*Giusto.*" His smile lit his eyes and he touched her glass gently with his own to make a tiny, melodic chime. "*Salute.*"

"*Salute,*" she echoed and he released her hand.

Her smile slipped for a moment at the loss of his touch, the cool air of the restaurant making its absence even more obvious. To mask her reaction, she brought her glass to her lips and breathed in the aroma of the wine.

Sipping hesitantly, Emily found the wine wasn't quite as dry as she'd feared. When Davide had ordered the *Lambrusco di Sorbara*, she hadn't known what to expect.

His eyes followed the glass, rising to her lips, one eyebrow raised. "Is it all right?" he asked, his voice low in deference to the quiet atmosphere.

"It's quite nice, actually." She smiled at him, recalling that Jacopo hadn't been so concerned whether she'd enjoyed it.

"*Bene.*" Davide smiled around a mouthful of bread and *prosciutto.*

Seeing his boyish grin, Emily felt the tightness around her spine ease and she sat back, relaxed at last. The muscles in her legs and lower back felt watery and disconnected, but the sensation was far from unpleasant.

I've been so unfair to him. He's been nothing but a gentleman so far and yet I insist on comparing him to Jacopo? I should wait instead and see if he earns the comparison.

"Emilia, *dimmi…* What have you thought of the city?"

Emily swallowed her own bite of *mortadella* before speaking. "Bologna is a beautiful place, Davide. Thank you for showing me around."

His face flushed slightly and he stared at his plate while the server's swaying gait brought her back to the table. As the woman collected the used plates, he glanced almost timidly in her direction.

Did I reduce him to this? The twist of guilt in her stomach was deeply discomfiting.

"The tour has been my pleasure, Emilia, I assure you. But I am afraid that I might have bored you a little?"

"*Bored* me? How?"

"Well, sometimes I forget that I'm not in a classroom." Color rushed into his cheeks again and she felt the empathic rush in her face, too.

He's nervous as hell, isn't he?

"I've enjoyed every minute of it," she said, and he looked up at her with something like hope in his eyes.

The familiar sting of tears burgeoned and she blinked it away, only managing to resist the urge to reach for him. The desire to feel his hand in hers was strong enough that she almost did, anyway.

After he took another small sip of his wine, she marked the way he licked the rosy sheen away from his lips. The stirring below her belly gave her pause and she shifted in her chair to shake it.

Still, the sensation came with a sudden unexpected thought:

I could stay here, couldn't I?

Pragmatism forced away the thought, yet it returned when his eyes met hers straight-on. The draw of his eyes was almost tactile. She straightened her shoulders until she felt the back of the chair, hard and unyielding against her spine.

No, don't…this isn't the time.

With no small measure of disappointment, she realized it was *her* silent voice, not Jacopo's, which had spoken.

The server returned, platter in hand, and set two bowls of soup before them. Emily was grateful for the distraction and was pleased to find it was another familiar dish, *tortellini in brodo.* The plump meat-and-cheese-filled rounds of pasta floated in a savory beef broth. The rich aroma reminded her that, aside from the pastry and cappuccino that morning, and then the bread and slices of meat just now, she'd had precious little to eat that day.

Davide slid a smaller bowl, covered with a hinged lid with a notch for a small serving spoon, toward her.

"*Prego*, Emilia—serve yourself first."

Smiling, she opened the lid and used the spoon to sprinkle some of the *Parmigiano Reggiano* over her pasta. She then slid it back to Davide, who eyed her bowl with suspicion.

"That's *it*? That is all you're going to have?"

"What do you mean?"

He took his turn with the cheese, scooping a few heaping spoonfuls over his soup. A chirping laugh escaped her at the sight, bubbling up and bursting over the table to draw a few bemused stares in their direction.

His laughter followed and the heaviness that had settled around her heart lifted again. Neither of them spoke until the soup was finished and the plates were collected.

His eyebrows arching in a curious expression, he led her wordlessly along.

"It was very good, Davide," she said at last, unable to keep him waiting another moment. "Honestly, you act as though you cooked this yourself."

"*Grazie a Dio…*" he said with a sigh, gesturing toward the ceiling. There was a hint of amused frustration in his tone. "I thought you'd *never* give me your opinion."

"But why are you so concerned? What difference would it make?"

His brow furrowed in what she took for genuine puzzlement. "I want to know that you are happy, Emilia. I already know this food is good. I need to know if *you* are enjoying it. What kind of host would I be otherwise?"

"You're worrying needlessly. I know I've never been in better hands."

It wasn't until he cleared his throat and took a long sip of his wine that she realized the potential double-entendre. To be honest, she was surprised that he'd picked up on it.

The next course arrived, tendrils of steam still rising as the server set out the plates. Emily looked to Davide, not recognizing the dish.

"*Cotoletta alla Bolognese,*" he explained. "Breaded, fried pork cutlet with *Parmigiano Reggiano* and.a slice of *prosciutto crudo* on top." He tilted his head toward the third dish, centered on the table. "And oven-roasted potatoes, of course."

Breathing in, Emily relished the scent of rosemary, sage and oil from the potatoes. Once again, Davide waited for her to serve herself first, before placing a generous portion of the remainder on his own plate.

His eyes darted to her face time and again, gauging her reaction to the meal until she struggled to hold back a fit of giggles at his attention. Pouring another glass of mineral water, she sipped it and tried not to think about what she found so humorous. Thinking about it only made her want to laugh; it was hard to resist.

With this course nearly done, she found herself spearing more potatoes from the serving dish, one by one. Davide did the same. When they reached the final piece, he put his fork down and sat back, conceding it to her. For just a moment, she wondered if perhaps she'd eaten an unseemly amount of food already.

No. That's Jacopo's thinking. Why would Davide care how much you've eaten? He's not judging you.

"Please," she said, feeling that absurd urge to giggle lying just beneath the surface. "Please, Davide, take it."

"Why don't you? I've had already the, *come si dice*... 'lion's share,' no?"

"No, I shouldn't."

"Why not?"

She shrugged, at a loss for words. He nodded, spearing the piece on one side with his fork. With his knife, he cut it carefully down the center with considered precision, putting half on her plate.

"*Eccolo... va bene?*"

The suppressed giggles welled up and out of her, and Emily covered her mouth with her napkin as though she could push the sounds back in. He began laughing, too, a kind, hearty sound that was perfectly at home between them.

There was something in his laughter that made her warm all over, a pleasant rush of familiarity she hadn't expected.

Oh, God... I don't want to leave. I don't want to go at all.

She busied herself with putting her napkin back in her lap before they both raised their potato pieces on the tines of their forks, touched them together as though in a toast and finished the course.

A different server came to clear the dishes this time and soon returned to deliver the next course. A few slivers of flatbread sat next to chunks of *Parmigiano Reggiano* and a portion of a soft—almost wet—white cheese, contained in a low, flat dish of its own.

"Oh, no... I don't know if I can..."

Davide smiled, pouring a little more wine into her glass. "It's up to you, but if you don't at least *try* a little, I will be rather disappointed."

"Blackmail? I thought we were friends."

He shrugged and spread some of the wet cheese on a piece of the bread. After eating with an exaggerated expression of enjoyment, he scooped more onto another slice of bread.

"What is that, then? Ricotta?"

"*Squacquerone*. It is similar to *stracchino* but is more liquid, as you can see. *Provalo*," he said, offering it again.

Taking it, Emily timidly tried some. Having expected a slight yogurty sourness, she was pleased to find a milkier sweetness instead.

"Another Bolognese specialty?" she asked. Davide nodded, watching with interest as she finished the portion he'd given her. "What?" She squirmed a little under his interest, shifting in her seat.

"I just like watching you eat," he said. "It's been a while since I've met a woman willing to enjoy a meal this way."

The rush of heat into her cheeks had to be obvious, though she didn't understand why it had happened. What was there to be embarrassed about, anyway?

Then again, maybe it isn't quite embarrassment.

At last the desserts arrived, along with a fresh bottle of sweet white wine.

"I don't know if I can…" she murmured, knowing full well Davide heard, and that she *would*. His smile over the top of the empty bottles and the plates of *torta di riso* as he poured the Malvasia into the fresh, small glasses warmed her yet again.

She averted her eyes, the flush deepening in her cheeks and throat.

The wine. I'll blame the wine.

When she faced him again, his eyes met hers steadily, just as they had in the train station that morning.

That morning, when she'd known without a doubt she could trust him.

7

"Well, I'm certainly fit to burst." As they stepped out of the restaurant, Emily had expected more daylight. "How long were we in there?"

"A little more than two hours." Also scanning the sky, Davide fussed with his scarf. "It's getting colder."

"It smells like snow."

"You noticed that, too?" Closing his eyes, he breathed deeply through his nose, held his breath and then exhaled. "Did you notice the other smells?"

"What other smells?" she asked, sniffing the cold air and feeling it chill the back of her throat. It should have been invigorating but the large meal was already making her groggy.

"Shut your eyes and try."

"Why?"

"Just try it."

Closing her eyes, Emily took in the air. The brittle, icy scent of snow was still there but other scents were, too: charcoal from a pizza oven, bread baking, the dusty aroma of concrete and stone and a savory smell she couldn't pinpoint, something more elusive than the rest.

Suddenly, the sound of something rasping near her cheek made her jump, even as she identified the scent. Opening her eyes, she found Davide rubbing a twig of rosemary between his fingers, grinning mischievously.

He tapped her cheek lightly with the twig before she snatched it out of his hand, laughing. She held it up and sniffed it, shaking her head.

"Where on earth did you get this?"

"There's a plant near the *cassa*. I took a little."

"Davide!"

His smile widened. "They don't mind, Emilia, don't worry." With no hesitation at all, he took her hand and led her along the narrow street.

"But why did you take it, anyway?"

"I like the way it smells, plus I find it refreshing after a meal. Don't you?"

Already raising the twig to sniff it again, Emily nodded in agreement. "I've always liked the smell of rosemary," she said, smiling. "My mom never did, though. She never used it in cooking or anything."

"No? She doesn't like it?"

"She hates it. I remember once I won a little plant in a contest at school. I brought it home, so proud because I never won anything, and my dad made a big fuss over it. He put it on the windowsill in the kitchen and everything." Her smile wavered in spite of her best efforts. "When Mom came in and found it there, she took it and chucked it out into the backyard. She didn't ask about it, just tossed it."

"What did your father say?"

"He knew there was no point in saying anything. I did, too."

Davide squeezed her hand in his, remaining silent. Squeezing his hand in return, she didn't look at him, certain she'd find sympathy in his eyes.

"Will you see her, at home?" he asked after a time. It took Emily a moment to understand what he meant.

"My mom? Yeah, sure. I'll stay with her, at least for a while."

"And your father will be glad to see you, too."

At this, she bit her lip, debating what to say and how to say it. "My father passed away a long time ago."

She felt him recoil in her grasp and knew he was embarrassed.

"I'm so sorry. I didn't know."

"Like I said," she tightened her hold on his hand yet again, "it was a long time ago. Before I came over here, in fact."

He nodded, frowning, and said nothing more. With a sigh, she stopped, took both his hands in hers and stood in front of him, making sure his eyes met her own.

"You didn't know, and I'm okay with it. Really."

"*Mi dispiace.* That's something else we have in common."

"Your father passed, too?"

Another nod. His eyes still held hers. "Several years ago. I think yours was a good man, though. I can see you love him very much."

That he used the present tense was not lost on her.

"I do, Davide. That's true."

She refrained from noting that it was apparent he couldn't say the same. Her heart ached intensely with the wish that her father could have known him.

But then, he would have had to know about Jacopo, too. That would have been terrible.

"Emilia? *Tutto bene?*"

Blinking, she realized she'd drifted away into her thoughts. Looking down, she found his hands gripped tightly in her own, leaving pale impressions in his skin around her fingertips.

"Oh, God!" She released him, gasping. "I'm so sorry."

He flexed his fingers and chuckled softly. "I know. You have quite a grip, though." He crooked his elbow toward her and she threaded her hand through it, the heat fading from her cheeks. He pretended to wince away from her touch and laughed. She laughed too.

Time and again as they walked, she had to resist the urge to pull him closer, to wrap both her arms around his arm. The desire to embrace him in this way came and went, which intrigued her. Was it really so easy to grow attached to someone? Over a matter of mere hours?

Sure, she'd stayed with Jacopo after she'd been in Venice less than a week, but that was different. He'd seduced and compelled her to stay, proposing marriage only a few weeks after they'd met. That whirlwind courtship had never been as chaste as this.

And oh God, similarities abounded, didn't they? But something was much, much different this time.

She choked back a startled laugh, disguising it as a cough. Davide's hand stole over hers where it rested in the crook of his elbow, stroking her cold fingers until they warmed under his touch. Something like nostalgia swept over her, casting the coming evening in a cozy, fuddled haze.

I'm already acting like this is going to go further. Am I crazy, or what? I'm going home tomorrow. Do not pass "Go," do not collect two hundred dollars.

I have to think about something else, before I get caught up again.

"Thank you for lunch, Davide—it really was wonderful. Still, it does bring to mind a certain question."

"What's that?"

"Well, that lunch wasn't unusual, I know. I've enjoyed many like that since I've been here, so I had an idea what to expect." She rested one hand on her belly, rubbing it ruefully through her coat. "All the same, I still don't know how you do it." Emily shook her head as they strolled along, winding from back lane to portico and back again.

"How I do what?"

"Oh, not *you* personally. I mean Italians or even Europeans in general. How can you possibly eat a huge meal like we just did and still look like, well...*that*?" She gestured toward a particularly wiry example ahead of them, slinking along in stiletto heels on the cobbled streets, adorned in a mish-mash of the latest examples of winter high fashion. "How is *that* even possible? Is it all the walking, or an obscure side-effect of the wine, or what?"

Stopping, Davide watched the woman in question disappear among the crowd along the street. "Emilia, I will let you in on a secret, okay? Something that very few non-Europeans will understand."

"Okay."

"Pay attention," he said, raising one finger in front of her face. "Because this is very, very important."

Emily nodded, resisting her urge to giggle at being addressed with such a schoolteacher's gesture, knowing he didn't mean to condescend. Besides, coming from him, it was rather charming.

"People like that woman up there?" Davide gestured in the direction the woman had gone, then turned to look that way. "They do not exist. She is a figment of the collective imagination—I swear it."

"Obviously people like her *do* exist, Davide. There she goes."

"Oh, you are just accepting the myth."

"All right, then," she said, sighing in mock frustration. "Don't answer the question."

"Fine, fine.... I will tell you." His voice turned cold and remote, and he bit out each word with crisp precision. "She does it the same way all the rest of them do it. She starves herself, works out to exhaustion and denies herself all the real pleasures that life has to offer. She keeps company with a good man who cares for her but she only stays until someone with more money comes along."

Voice rising, his eyes narrowed and he turned his cutting gaze to Emily, holding her fast in place. "Then, she takes a married lover who treats her like the *puttana* that she aspires to be and she calls that 'being happy.' As long as she has those useless labels plastered all over her body like some sort of high-fashion *Formula Uno* pilot, I suppose that she probably *is* happy."

Emily stepped away, taken aback. "I'm sorry, I didn't mean...I just wondered how..."

The lines around Davide's eyes softened and the tension in his jaw faded. He swallowed hard, looking away from her toward the passersby. His hands rose to adjust his scarf and collar needlessly, almost obscuring his face for a few moments. "*Mi dispiace*, Emilia. I did not want to..."

"I don't understand, though. You liked the woman in the *ristorante*, didn't you?"

"*Sì*, but there is a world of difference, *capisci*? She has curves, and warmth, and sensuality," he insisted, his hands shaping the air in subtle ways. "She has satisfaction with life and it shows. You can tell some things by observing a person and that is what I have observed in her."

"And *La Signorina* Dolce e Gabbana, back there?"

"Not a trace of life to be found. So many words are, are...*emblazoned* across her body, anywhere you look—but she doesn't have anything to *say*. She is thin, brittle... just lifeless." He fell silent, his brow furrowed, his lips pursing while he stood deep in thought. "No. There is just no life behind the façade. So many girls—women, I mean—are like this today. No depth, no life...no *hope*. Just empty shells."

Shoulders slumping, Davide stared unfocused at the stream of pedestrians that passed. There was such sorrow in his face, he no longer seemed the kind and confident man who had escorted her throughout the day. Aching to reach out to him, to erase whatever memory had ensnared him, the hurt and anger in his eyes stayed her hand. He seemed so far within himself she doubted she could reach him anyway.

Who was she? You're one of the good guys, aren't you? At the very least, you seem to be. So why would any woman ever want to leave you?

Her stomach twisted with the realization that she was about to leave, too.

The sky was darker, azure fading into late-afternoon violet, the wind colder than ever. She felt adrift without her friendly guide from the day's adventures.

I have no idea where we are, but I know it's getting late.

"Maybe we should be on our way, then," she said with quiet uncertainty. It wasn't at all what she'd wished to say.

Davide came back to himself, slowly focusing first on her and then on their surroundings while a faint flush of color rose into his cheeks. "Oh, *scusami*, Emilia. What a terrible host I am." He smiled uneasily and looked around. "I just realized where we are now. Come with me, we're nearly to Piazza Maggiore."

Already turning to go, he reached for her. Emily hesitated before taking his hand and the fresh flicker of hurt in his expression gave her heart a twist.

"Come with me," he repeated, feigning indifference, and led her along toward a busy thoroughfare, his grasp of her hand looser than it was before.

8

D avide resumed his role as tour guide as they moved through streets which were rapidly filling with people. They stepped out into a grand piazza and he led Emily around the periphery, launching into a description of the history of the palazzos and the church, animatedly demonstrating how the power play between the pope and the citizens had brought construction to a halt. His spirited re-creation of the dominance of the pope and the frustration of the Bolognese should have amused her but she just didn't feel it.

The coffee bars and the pubs were open; the heady, dark scents of coffee and hot chocolate wafted out of doors on waves of warmth from inside. Windows fogged at the edges, as lights switched on over displays of elaborate pastries and sandwiches, attempting to lure inside prankish students and retirees alike.

Emily saw it all as if through a haze. Davide spoke louder and faster but she was only half-listening.

It's too hard to believe that there are men who reject women like that. I mean, isn't that the standard here? It's certainly what Jacopo wanted — repeatedly, from the look of things.

How was it possible that the mere thought of Jacopo could stir her emotions so easily? She was trembling now, most certainly not from the cold. Her face warmed with her own anger and she wondered how Davide hadn't noticed. Was he really so oblivious?

Disappointed, she found herself resigned to boarding the train for Milan and resuming her trip. A sour hint of dread remained while she feigned interest in Davide's monologue.

I just want to get on the train and go home. I want this damned country behind me, for good.

"Emilia?" Davide said softly, leaning in close so she could hear him above the playful shouting of teenagers in Piazza del Nettuno, some of whom were threatening to splash their friends with water from the fountain of Neptune. Someone played a vaguely Celtic tune on a guitar outside a bar and a group of people sang along. "What is it? What's wrong?"

Emily barely heard him. Staring into the middle distance, she pushed her shaking hands into her coat pockets while he moved to stand in front of her, his eyes seeking hers.

"*Oddio...* Emilia, I'm terribly sorry... I never meant to upset you like this." He folded his hands in front of him and moved them in an unconscious gesture of supplication. "I know I overreacted. You must know that it had absolutely nothing to do with you."

"I know, I know…. I didn't think that."

Davide reached forward to draw her hands out of her pockets and clasp them in his own, but she continued shaking all the same.

"Emilia, please. You are very upset and I would like to know how to help you. You must tell me what is wrong."

"Honestly, Davide, I don't know what I can tell you."

"Just tell me the truth—that is all."

The truth. Emily looked around the piazza, taking it all in, chewing her lip. "I guess it's finally getting through to me."

"What is?"

"This place, these people—all of it."

"Emilia, I'm sorry… *non ho capito.*"

Pulling away from him, she began walking toward the Neptune fountain. Davide followed. When she stopped, he stopped, maintaining a respectful distance. "Everywhere I look, there they are:

beautiful people holding hands, sitting on the steps kissing, being beautiful together…couples in love, showing their love for each other and not caring who sees."

She gestured around the piazza so he could see for himself and his eyes followed, then returned to her face. His incomprehension was both frustrating and heartbreaking.

"It is true," he said, nodding, "and you are right. But why should this trouble you so? It has always been this way, has it not?"

"Yes, but my personal circumstances have changed." She swallowed hard, afraid to take the final plunge.

Once I've told him, there's no going back.

"Ah… I see." He nodded again, understanding. "You are going home without your husband and since it is almost San Valentino, you are already missing him—but he will call you, at least, *no?*"

"No." She climbed the steps to the edge of the fountain, studying it in the fading afternoon light. A dull ache emerged behind her eyes, stinging slightly. "No, but it's not that."

Davide stepped up beside her and placed his hand on her shoulder, tenderly.

"*Emilia, ti prego—dimmi.*"

"He won't be calling me."

"Of course he will. I am sure he is thinking about you right now. I would be, if I were him."

Turning sharply to face him, she spied his guilty expression a moment before it faded away. Hope and fear warred within her, neither one gaining the upper hand for now.

If anyone else had said it, I would swear it was a line.

"Maybe *you* would, Davide, but not if you were *him.*" Her shoulders slouched in defeat; her heart felt too big, beating in slow, heavy thumps that sickened her and shook her whole body. "He's not. I know it." Emily turned to him, her weary smile gone at last. "He hasn't thought about me in years."

Her right hand wrenched her ring ruthlessly around her finger, the friction warming her hands even in the cold air until she forced them apart. Tears welled in her eyes and Davide drew her close, forcing her hands still, holding her while her tears spilled over. At last, she forced the words out—the words she hadn't actually spoken to anyone in all this time. "He left me almost four years ago. The divorce was finalized last week."

Davide tightened his arms around her. He swallowed, hard, and she knew he was trying to think of how to respond. Cursing herself for putting him in this position, she tried to stop her tears.

"I'm so sorry," he began, at last. "I did not realize that *this* was your loss."

She pulled away and looked up at him, the cold air tightening the trails of her tears on her cheeks so that they felt like cuts in her skin. "I feel awful now for that, too," she said. "I should have told you the truth in the first place."

"The truth? Emilia, *non ho capito*," he said, shaking his head.

"I've let you entertain me all day long but I didn't even try to explain what was going on. It's no excuse, but I've been carrying this around with me for so long that it's just... a habit." She looked up into his eyes, imploring him. "You should know: I didn't want to lie to you, not at all."

"And you have not," he said, gently drawing her back to himself. His hands warmed her face when he wiped away the traces of tears, his eyes meeting hers, not shying away.

"It's just that...I've been so stupid. I could have gone home at any time. Instead, I stayed there, in Rovigo. I stayed, and kept hoping...I kept wearing this –" she raised her left hand to show him her wedding ring, "because I convinced myself if I stayed faithful, he might change his mind and come back to me."

Resting her hand against Davide's coat, she watched the ornately-cut band glitter in the lights of the piazza. "A few months ago, I found out that he'd *never* been faithful to me. Well, to be fair," she said, unable to keep the bitterness out of her voice, "he was, for the *first* year. I was so stupid... I refused to see what was right in front of me, even when he wasn't really hiding it anymore."

Davide's face twisted into a scowl, haunted by more unexpected emotions: shame in the furrows of his brow, deep sadness darkening his eyes.

Helpless to resist now that she'd begun, she continued her confession.

"I kept trying to be the perfect wife, to give him everything that he could want. I just didn't know what it was that he wanted. He never told me directly and once I'd figured it out, it was done. He'd found what he'd wanted most but it wasn't me.

"It never was.

"He went to Rome four years ago," she said. Davide tensed, his eyes widening before he shifted his gaze to the statue behind her. "All the same, I kept hoping, and dreaming, and deluding myself until... until the absolute end." Shaking her head in frustration, she pressed her forehead to his chest, relishing his closeness in the cold while she pushed the memories away with all her strength. "I always do that. I dig in my heels in the worst situations and let someone else make my decisions for me. This is where it gets me every time: lost and alone. I'm sick to death of it."

"We all make these mistakes, Emilia. I know. The strength to change comes slowly, though. You can't rush this sort of thing."

"I know that, Davide. But how long is long enough? How do you know when you're ready to move on?"

"You just do." He shrugged, the effort full of helplessness. "You just do. Then, you make the jump."

She pulled away from him once again, her fingers doing their familiar dance as she closed her eyes and drew a deep breath.

I need to make a real change. I need him gone once and for all.

With a swift, violent movement, she pulled the ring off her finger and tossed it over her shoulder into the fountain at her back.

Startled, Davide reached to stop her. "Emilia! *Che cosa hai fatto?!*"

"I made a wish," she said shakily and opened her eyes. "Who knows if it'll ever come true?" She stepped down from the side of the fountain, leaving Davide to watch the lights dance on the water where the ring had disappeared. "I've been going through the motions, alone, for over four years. Now I'm going back to a place I've hardly been for the last ten. I have no plan, no ideas and very few options open to me."

He joined her and Emily turned her back to him, her arms out by her sides as if she might take flight at any moment.

"So," she continued, "can you tell me why I feel like the weight of the world has just lifted off my shoulders?"

"Emilia," Davide's voice shook with apprehension from behind her. "I cannot even tell you why *I* feel that same way."

9

In a moment, the strength drained from her arms, which fell with a dull *clap* to her sides. She spun around to face him and found him looking as surprised as she felt.

"I—uh—I'm sorry," he stammered. "I should not have said that. Perhaps we should...um... Or I could arrange a taxi for you, or —"

"Davide?" She stepped closer to him; he edged a half-step away. "What do you...?"

Silence fell between them. The distant sounds of the piazza gradually filled it.

"I noticed you this morning on the platform when the train arrived in Rovigo," he said, his voice low so only she could hear. "You were standing apart from everyone else and you looked so sad, so alone, that I somehow wanted to make you happy. Then, when I saw you here in the *stazione*, and you still seemed so lost, so emotional... I wanted very much to help you." He swallowed hard, loud enough for her to hear. "I saw something of myself in you. I know how much it hurts to be alone like that. I know that sometimes it's something we've done to ourselves, for protection. At first, I thought perhaps it was just me, that I was seeing things that weren't there. But when you boarded the train, I was sure of it." He turned his eyes to hers again. "Either way, to see you look so sad—to look so much like I did, once...it broke my heart."

"You really have helped me, though—in so many ways," she said.

"*Grazie.*"

"I mean it."

"I know. All day, I thought someone was waiting for you, that you would be okay, in time. I believed that your hurt would heal. But now?"

"Now, what?"

"I don't know. Emilia, I would like to know that you are okay. I need to know that you *will be* okay."

"I'm sure I will, Davide."

"I wish to *know* it, though."

She began to tremble, tears threatening. "I don't know what to say to that," she managed at last, her throat so tight she could hardly breathe. "I can't guarantee anything."

In the silence following, Davide took her hand in his. She could still feel the fading warmth where her wedding ring used to be. The light brushing of his lips over her skin replaced it, along with a pleasant trembling at his touch.

All day long, he's taken my hand in his and I've hardly felt a thing. Now he does it and this *happens?*

She laughed quietly and he smiled, slowly releasing her hand. Without a second thought, she slipped her arms around him and he returned the embrace without hesitation. Davide rested his cheek atop her head and squeezed her gently, swaying ever-so-slightly in the middle of the piazza. He stroked her hair with a gentle touch and tears rose to her eyes at this tender show of affection. When they stepped apart, his hand slipped down to caress her cheek, to encourage her to smile.

"Emilia, *dai—fammi un sorriso.*"

There was no reason to resist, yet she felt the tugging at the corners of her mouth as though it was happening to someone else, somewhere else. The piazza, so bustling and noisy moments ago, seemed to have gone silent, or might have been drowned out by the rhythm of her heartbeat as Davide moved closer to her again.

His caresses hardly seemed to touch her, yet her skin tingled wherever his fingertips brushed. He framed her face in his hands as if holding her smile in place and he kissed her, the touch of his lips feather-light at the edge of her mouth. Her smile broadened and, closing her eyes, she sank into his arms. His mouth traced over hers, hesitant, not pressing for more than she was willing to offer.

The gentle skimming of his lips over hers ceased and when she thought he would pull away, he instead pressed his mouth more firmly to hers. His gentle parting of her lips wasn't rushed or intrusive, stopping shy of anything overtly provocative. Kept to a warm give-and-take between them, they lingered a few moments longer until they reluctantly parted on some unspoken cue and the sounds of the piazza came rushing back.

Too soon. This is ending much too soon.

"It's late." His voice was scarcely audible in the crowd. "I'm afraid it is time to go."

"Okay."

He led her through the piazza, toward the wide porticos along Via dell'Indipendenza. Neither of them spoke. She grasped his hand tighter and he dropped his pace to match hers, slower and more reluctant by the minute.

"Almost there," he said as they stepped out into Piazza 20 Settembre. "Now we have come full circle."

"I guess we have," she agreed. They cut through the gallery of shops adjacent to the piazza, angling toward the station. They joined a large group of pedestrians too impatient to wait; cars, trucks and scooters blared their horns in protest as the people crossed against the red light. Emily felt perfectly safe with her hand held securely in his, knowing that nothing would come of the complaining klaxons, but she still felt a new heaviness growing in her chest.

He's going to let me leave, isn't he? After his little romantic display to me in the piazza, he's still going to let me go?

The ticketing hall was packed. Emily was certain that the left luggage office would be, too. A sudden realization sent her hand plunging into her shoulder bag, seeking her ticket. "Oh, no…" she groaned, reading it.

"What is it?"

"I don't have a ticket for a new train. I forgot to get one this morning for another train to Milan. I bet they'll be booked solid, too…"

"Give it to me and I will trade it in for another, while you go and get your suitcase."

"You'll do that?"

"*Sì, certo.* It's not difficult to trade one ticket for another."

"Oh, well…okay. Let's do that." She handed him her ticket and started off for the luggage office. "I'll be right back—I hope."

"I will watch for you under the schedule board, don't worry."

Forty-five minutes later, she forged her way clumsily toward the schedule board, dragging her suitcase along behind. She searched for Davide in the mass of people in the hall with an increasing sense of agitation. The old panic returned, dragging with it a feeling of abandonment in this unfamiliar place, until she spotted him pushing his way toward her.

A surge of happiness erupted close to her heart as she hurried to meet him halfway.

"I took the liberty of validating this for you already," he said, stuffing the ticket into her hand, "but the train is leaving very, very soon. Let's hurry, or you're bound to miss it." He grabbed her suitcase and took her hand in his, then began to shove unapologetically through the crowd to the first track, using her suitcase as a makeshift battering ram.

"Wait a minute," she said as he pulled her along, checking the carriage numbers of the train waiting at the first platform. "Wait—this is a Eurostar. I didn't have a Eurostar ticket before."

"You do now. After this long day, I thought you could use a more comfortable post."

She looked closer at her ticket. "This is first class as well! I —"

"There is no problem, Emilia. It was the least I could do." He continued to read the numbers on the carriages beside them and guided her to the correct door. "*Eccolo.*"

"I don't know what to say."

"'*Grazie*' will suffice."

"Well, then... *Grazie*, Davide."

"*Prego.*" He pulled her close and she returned the embrace with a sudden sense of elation. He kissed her temple, her cheek, then drew away, releasing her little by little.

"I mean it, Davide." She reached up impulsively, placed her hand over his heart and stepped closer, feeling his heartbeat beneath her palm. "Thank you for everything you've done. You've made this a very special day for me."

"*Anche per me.*" He pressed her hand against him, then took her hand in his own and brushed his lips over the backs of her fingers. "Have a safe trip."

"I'll do my best." She shivered, then smiled as he released her hand. "*Ciao*, Davide."

"*Ciao*, Emilia," he said, stepping farther away and raising his hand in farewell.

A conductor was waiting to take her suitcase and help her aboard. At the top of the stairs, she turned toward the platform to smile and wave goodbye but Davide was gone. She remained there for a moment while the conductor placed her bag on one of the racks in the corridor. He led her to her seat with a polite touch on her shoulder and a gesture in the correct direction. His soft-spoken instruction was all but lost in the noise of passengers moving from carriage to carriage.

Emily found her seat and settled in, looking out the windows on the platform side of the train, across the aisle from her. Mostly she saw her own reflection there, owing to the bright lighting on the train and the relative darkness outside. She realized that she had been staring only after the passenger seated there gave her a cross look and an irritated flick of the pages of his newspaper in her direction.

Outside, the conductors blew their whistles to signal that all the passengers had boarded. The sharp trills grew closer, then faded down the length of the train before the hydraulic hiss of the doors closing followed close behind. Emily sank a little lower into her seat and turned toward her window. She closed her eyes to her reflection and to the view of the other tracks beyond it.

She flexed the fingers of her left hand; the absence of the small weight which had rested there for ten years made her feel lighter all over. She smiled, thinking of Davide's soft kisses in the piazza and beside the train. A faint heat rose in her cheeks when she thought of touching him when they'd said farewell. She would carry the sensation of his heart beneath her hand all the way home.

The whole day is beginning to feel like a dream. Maybe that's all it was—a pleasant dream? It's over now, at any rate.

The train was already up to speed before Emily opened her eyes and sat up. She sifted through her shoulder bag, past the legal envelope that no longer seemed quite so dreadful, under the Davide-illuminated copy of the speech, seeking the scrap of paper he had given her that morning with her hotel information on it. Glad to find that she hadn't lost it after all, she read and re-read the information, fighting the sense of melancholy that rose at the sight of his handwriting.

I might as well put him out of my mind, then.

She put away the paper and looked out the window at the lights along the landscape, flashing past in the darkness. The train swayed and she dozed with her eyes open, lulled to half-sleep by the droning conversations of other passengers and the occasional announcements on the PA system, first in Italian, then in English.

"*Il suo biglietto, Signora?*" the conductor asked, extending his hand. She nodded, already rummaging in her shoulder bag for her ticket.

As the conductor took it, she noticed a blue scrawl on the back. His fingers obscured the writing while he read and punched the ticket. He returned it to her unsteady hand and went on to the next passenger.

Emily paused in returning the ticket to her bag and took a deep breath. Had Davide given her a farewell message? She flipped it over to read the back and found that someone had scribbled on it in blue ball-point ink: "12C".

Oh, is that all?

Her anticipation flickered against a wave of disappointment.

Why on earth would someone write that *on my ticket? I'm in 14A.*

Another train rushed past in the opposite direction on the next track and she startled at the sudden burst of sound.

Oh.

She slowly turned toward her window and the reflection of other passengers there.

There he was, smiling at her again.

This time, she let herself smile back.

It felt good.

Kimberly Menozzi

Un Romantico a Milano
A Romantic in Milan
(the same day)

10

Checking his watch, Davide realized that he'd already glanced at it three times in the last minute. The seconds hand had barely enough time to make a full circuit before he looked again.

Inside the train station, the incessant rumble of suitcases trundling across the floors and the constant, garbled announcements on the PA added to the chaos. Now that the strike was over, new delays had befallen arrivals from the north, thanks to a snowstorm near Treviso. This much Davide had gathered from the conversations among the distressed in the queues to the ticket windows, once he'd returned to thinking in Italian. After an entire day speaking English, he was on the verge of mental exhaustion.

Before he could read his watch yet again, he forced himself to focus on the intercity ticket in his hand, hoping he really could exchange it. He'd made an impulsive promise to Emily to keep her from worrying about her departure. Now that he was nearly at the ticket window, he wasn't so sure he'd be able to follow through.

Divorziata. For the duration of the day, up until that moment, he'd found himself frustrated and distracted by her presumed marital status. He'd kept his flirting to a minimum, held back from making advances—and how many times had he wanted to try to kiss her as well? To just "go for it," as the Americans say?

Granted, he'd seen she wasn't ready for *anyone's* advances, but he would have been much more relaxed in her company had he only known.

And I did kiss her. He smiled at the thought of her welcoming reception of his kiss in front of the fountain in Piazza del Nettuno. He could have pushed for more than the one, yes, but it wasn't the right time.

And when will that be? She's going back to the United States in the morning. You'll probably never see her again.

Perhaps I should ask her to stay here tonight.

Shaking his head, he took a step forward in line and settled in to wait while the clerk at the window helped the perplexed German teen who was struggling to sort out which train to take.

Suppressing a sigh, Davide looked over his shoulder to the left luggage office. Outside the station doors, people gathered in clusters to chat or to smoke, blocking the entries in both cases. Every time a door managed to open, a blue-gray cloud filtered in along with the cold air, the tobacco stink mixing with the odors of stress and delayed travel that filled the large hall.

There was still no sign of Emily.

If he asked her to stay in Bologna, then where would she sleep? Hotels were notoriously difficult to find on short notice in the city center. He had plenty of room at his flat, of course, but how might she react to *that* proposition? They'd only just met that morning.

Our kiss notwithstanding, he mused, feeling a smile tug at his mouth. *No, that would never happen. Besides, her flight leaves early—she needs to be in Milano.*

"*Signore? Signore?*" the clerk called, his weary, uninterested voice breaking into Davide's thoughts.

Davide stepped up to the window, ignoring the grumbling of the people queued behind him.

"*Sì, sì,*" he said, sliding the ticket through the cutout in the Plexiglas. "I need to exchange this ticket for another to Milano, on the next train possible, please."

The clerk nodded, reading the print through his half-moon glasses, then turned to his computer screen. "There's a *regionale* leaving in twenty minutes–" he paused, "–make that forty minutes. You'll need to pay an additional seven euros."

Davide nodded, already taking the money out of his wallet, and the clerk set about printing the ticket.

"We should take the Eurostar," someone in the next queue said to their companion. "It'll be the fastest train to Milano."

Davide paused in accepting the ticket from the clerk. *I hadn't thought about that…*

"Is there a problem, sir?"

"Not a problem, no." Davide slid the ticket into his pocket. "I'd also like a ticket on the Eurostar to Milano. First class."

Behind him, another customer muttered something unintelligible. The clerk blew out a frustrated breath and started tapping keys on his computer, then stopped. "Are you sure, *signore*?"

"*Sì, sono sicuro.*"

"*Va bene…* That will be forty euros, ninety." The printer spit out the ticket and the clerk waited for Davide to sort out his bankcard. His eyes narrowed when Davide paused again and yet more muttering followed in the queue.

"Actually, could I make that two tickets?"

"Another first class?"

"*Sì.*"

"I don't have any seats together."

"Do you have two in the same carriage?"

The clerk frowned, nodded and tapped in the order. "Eighty-one, eighty."

"*Grazie.*" Davide slid his bankcard forward and the clerk completed the transaction with a relieved sigh.

Tickets in hand, he pushed through the straggling groups spreading in every direction from the queues. He watched the crowd for any sign of Emily and found none. With a frown, he turned toward the doors for the tracks and made his way to the validation machines to stamp the tickets.

He stepped to one side and squinted at the small print for the seat numbers, then dug out his glasses to read better. One ticket was for 12C; the other was for 14A. He took out a pen from the inner pocket of his coat and scrawled the opposite seat number on the back of each ticket, then put his pen and one ticket away.

A few paces from the trackside exit, a sleek, silvery Eurostar train waited. On the side of the carriage, next to the doors, was the electronic display of pertinent information: train number, carriage number, class, time of departure. He compared the time on the display to his watch and groaned. They were cutting it close, no doubt.

Sounds of complaint drew his attention away from the train and back to the validation machine. There an elderly couple stood, sliding their ticket into the machine and withdrawing it with disappointed frowns. Behind them, other travelers made obvious signs of displeasure, fidgeting, checking watches or craning their necks in exaggerated displays of impatience.

"*Avete bisogno di aiuto?*" Davide asked. He received their blank, worried expressions in response. "Do you need help?" he offered again, in English this time, and the woman's eyes lit up with relief, a smile erasing the worry lines around her mouth.

"Yes, young man, we do." Her accent was so similar to Emily's that Davide nearly did a double-take. "We can't seem to get this machine to stamp our ticket."

"May I?" he asked, reaching for the ticket.

She looked at her husband warily and waited for his nod before handing the ticket to Davide.

"You just have to make sure that you push it all the way in," Davide said, demonstrating. The machine made a soft *click* that he felt more than heard in the crowd.

"Grassie," the man said in an approximation of Italian.

"*Prego, di niente,*" Davide said and smiled in return, handing back the ticket.

Merda! Emilia!

Hurrying out into the crowd gathered to read the schedule board, he looked around for Emily once again, convinced that he'd missed her. The moment he spotted her, his heart gave a painful twist in his chest. She was searching the crowd, her eyes wide and despairing, her shoulders slumped in a posture of defeat.

Just as she'd looked that morning when he'd noticed her on the platform in Rovigo.

He began pushing toward her, forcing his way through the crowd, his heart pounding uncomfortably hard, threatening to leap out of his throat. He hadn't meant to leave her alone like that, not even for a second.

Her eyes found his as he shoved through the tail end of one of the queues, heedless of the protests he left behind him. She hurried in his direction, a smile lighting her eyes, erasing the helplessness he'd seen there.

His heart swooped upward with elation at the sight of her smile. It was all he could do to keep himself from gathering her in his arms and kissing her with all the joy he felt.

Overhead, the PA system broadcast an incomprehensible announcement; he understood only enough to know it was about the boarding of their train.

"I took the liberty of validating this for you already," he said, stuffing the ticket into her hand, "but the train is leaving very, very soon. Let's hurry, or you're bound to miss it."

He folded her empty hand in his and made their way toward the doors and the first track, leading with the suitcase and shoving it ahead when people didn't move aside fast enough. The blast of cold air when the door opened was sobering, indeed, after the warmth inside the station. More tobacco-tainted air rasped at his lungs as he led her along the length of the train, seeking her carriage.

"Wait a minute," Emily said, dragging her feet while trying to read her ticket and follow his lead at the same time. "Wait—this is a Eurostar. I didn't have a Eurostar ticket before."

"You do now. After this long day, I thought you could use a more comfortable post."

"This is first class as well! I —"

"There is no problem, Emilia. It was the least I could do," he continued to lead her toward the head of the train, stopping by the doors of the appropriate carriage at last. "*Eccolo.*"

"I don't know what to say."

"'*Grazie*' will suffice."

"Well, then… *Grazie*, Davide."

"*Prego.*"

Davide drew her to himself and slipped his arms around her, hoping she couldn't feel him shaking. She seemed to bounce into his embrace with a cheerful eagerness instead. He held her tight for as long as he could without risking the train's departure, taking a moment to inhale deeply her soft, subtle fragrance. He kissed her temple, her cheek and then drew away, releasing her as slowly as he dared.

"I mean it, Davide," she said, her hand fluttering up to rest over his heart. She stepped closer, pressing her palm firmly against him, and he swallowed hard. "Thank you for everything you've done. You've made this a very special day for me."

"*Anche per me.*" He pressed his hand over hers, the better to feel it, then took her hand in his own and brushed his lips over the backs of her fingers. "Have a safe trip," he said, releasing her.

"I'll do my best." She smiled, shivering as a sharp wind blew along the platform. "*Ciao*, Davide."

"*Ciao*, Emilia," he said, stepping away and raising his hand in farewell. She gave him another smile and turned to climb the steps onto the train. He darted off into the crowd, making for the doors at the far end of the same carriage.

This is crazy, he thought, queuing to board. *Why on earth don't I just tell her that I'm coming to Milano with her? Why go to Milano in the first place?*

Out of habit, he reached to adjust the strap of his knapsack and realized he didn't have it with him. He shook his head and felt a grin tugging at his mouth.

I need to be sure she makes it okay.

That wasn't it at all. It was true but it wasn't the only reason. He shook his head again, grasped the handle by the stairs and hoisted himself up and inside.

I can convince her to stay. I just need more time.

11

As he settled into his seat, Davide could still feel Emily's hand over his heart, her fingers beneath his palm as he pressed her hand closer. His heart was beating for her touch alone, so she could feel his life there, hers for the asking.

If only she *would* ask.

He wanted to touch her face, to press his lips to hers again if just for a moment, to express how he felt with all the conviction he could muster.

But first she had to *see* him.

Seated facing backwards, only two rows ahead of her seat, he was surprised that she hadn't noticed him already. Then again, she had a tendency to get lost in her thoughts, just as he did.

They had something in common. He smiled at the thought and realized that he hadn't smiled so much in ages. Surely *that* was some sort of sign? If one believed in signs, anyway.

Sometimes, he thought he did.

Too nervous to get up and go to her, he continued watching her, hoping only that she would look his way, or see him in the reflection in the window. Since he could see a sliver of her face reflected there, it was reasonable to think she could see him, too, wasn't it?

The desperate sadness he'd seen in her face that morning was no longer there; in its place was an expression that he took for wistfulness or a gentle melancholy. A smile strayed across her lips from time to time, only to disappear when her brow furrowed in deeper contemplation. He'd seen this look often over the course of the day in Bologna. Her thoughts were broadcast to the world in spite of herself and her reticence to share.

She seemed to dream and drift in her own thoughts, only to be interrupted by the passing conductor who asked for her ticket. As Davide had hoped while buying her ticket almost an hour before, she spied his blue scrawl on the back of her ticket and read it with puzzlement.

When another train rushed past on the adjacent track, barreling toward Bologna and pushing a concussive burst of air ahead of itself, she startled a little.

Then Emily turned toward her window, her expression dazed and disbelieving. He didn't realize he was holding his breath until he saw her smile in her reflection in the window. Then he exhaled quietly, hoping that the surrounding passengers wouldn't notice.

They sat that way for several minutes, the train swaying gently, the muted clacking of the tracks passing beneath their feet while they smiled at one another's reflection in the window. He wondered if she had any idea what he was thinking, if it was even possible for her to understand what the simple truth was yet.

Perhaps, perhaps not. There was no time like the present to find out.

He stood and made his way down the aisle toward her. With each step he took, both their smiles grew wider.

"*Ciao.*" She laughed softly, a little hiccup of a sound which caressed his heart.

"*Ciao,*" he said, sliding into the seat next to hers.

They were both silent for a while.

"I must say, it is quite a surprise to see you here," she said at last. "A pleasant surprise, though."

"I'm glad you think so. I was –" He stopped abruptly, uncertain why. The whole afternoon he'd spent with her had been so easy compared to this.

"You were *what?*"

"I was…afraid. That you might think badly of me."

"Why would I do that?"

"Isn't it strange to you that I've followed you here like this?"

"Maybe a little. But I'm glad you did. I was sad to think that I couldn't thank you again. You left me no option, hurrying off like that."

"*Mi dispiace*, Emilia."

"No, I understood that maybe it couldn't be helped. I just didn't suspect the reason for it."

They leaned close to one another over the armrests of the seats and he took her hand in his.

"Emilia," he murmured, closing his fingers tenderly around hers.

"*Sì?*" She moved closer still, her smile wavering.

A harsh cough behind him caught Davide's attention and he turned to find a rather peevish, balding man in a rumpled suit, waving a ticket.

"*Mi scusi; questo è il mio posto.*" His Milanese accent carried a distinctly condescending tone which Davide elected to ignore.

"*No, no; scusami.*" Davide said, turning to face the man. "I hope you wouldn't mind trading seats with me?"

"Why should I trade? I have a ticket for this one."

Emily sat back with a frown and Davide tried again, his smile fixed upon his face.

"I see that, sir. But as I said, I hope you wouldn't mind."

"I paid for this seat, young man, and I want it."

"*Ho capito,*" Davide said, determined to maintain his temper even after the snide "young man" comment. "But you see, we weren't able to book seats together," he gestured toward Emily, who gave a flickering smile to the newcomer, "and I was given that assignment right over there." He indicated his previous seat with a tilt of his head but the rumpled man didn't as much as glance that way.

"*Non è un problema mio.* You should have booked earlier, or something. Besides, how do I know if that was your seat at all? Now do stand aside, or shall I call a conductor?"

What the hell?

Davide looked at Emily, fighting to keep his embarrassment from showing. The muscles in his cheeks creaked in protest of his frozen expression.

"Go ahead," she said, her voice full of quiet disappointment.

Davide's smile faded at last. He pulled his ticket out of his coat pocket as he stood and faced the man in the aisle.

"This is my ticket, sir. Why not trade seats, then? As you can see, it's already stamped and –"

"I don't like to ride facing backwards."

Davide glimpsed Emily rolling her eyes and his heart sank.

She'll be stuck next to this cretino *all the way to Milano, no doubt.*

"Davide, I'll trade tickets with you." Emily stood up, sighing. "Give it to me—here's mine."

Davide and the man stepped aside to allow her to enter the aisle. She took the ticket from Davide's hand, gave him her own, and waited.

"Emilia, I–" He looked at the rumpled man, then at the ticket in his hand.

She said nothing, only smiled. Davide smiled in return.

"As you wish, *amore.*" He settled into her vacated seat and the rumpled man settled into his own with a smug grin.

She went to Davide's former seat, sat for a few moments, then returned.

"I'm sorry to disturb you," Emily said, leaning over the rumpled man to speak to Davide, "but would you mind if I sat here?"

"If you sat *where*, exactly?" Davide asked, leaning toward her in front of his seatmate.

"Well, there aren't any seats left, except that one," she jerked her head to indicate Davide's old seat, "and I don't like riding backwards...so I thought I'd sit with you."

"Certainly." He nodded and smiled. "I'd like that."

Emily turned toward the other man and gave him a smile. "*Lei capisce, naturalmente?*" she said, slipping into Italian for the rumpled man's benefit. "I'd hate to sit apart from my fiancée."

With that, she climbed over the man's legs and settled onto Davide's lap, putting her arms around his neck and her back to the other man.

Davide's eyes widened with surprise and he struggled to keep his expression in check while he wrapped his arms around her.

I never thought she'd actually do *it.*

Her cheeks were a livid pink now and he pressed a little closer to give her a gentle kiss, which, blessedly, she permitted. She shivered in his arms and he closed his eyes, breathing slow and delighting in the scent and heat of her skin. He'd never expected to get so close to her so soon, or under such strange circumstances, but he'd take whatever he could get.

It wasn't long before the rumpled man huffed scornfully and snatched up his newspaper and bag before shuffling off to the seat Davide had vacated. Watching over her shoulder as the man left, Emily feigned surprise before turning back to Davide.

"Gee, I wonder what's wrong with *him?*"

Davide chuckled and shook his head, giving her a squeeze before she got to her feet and they traded seats one more time. The man had opened his newspaper to block them from his sightline.

Emily looked out the window at the occasional flashes of light, the only indications of life in the darkness beyond the glass. Davide smiled at her, watching attentively until she faced him and smiled as well.

He opened his mouth to speak but she spoke first.

"I can't believe I did that," she whispered, blushing deeply and lowering her head. "I've never done anything like that before in my *life.*" She hid a soft giggle behind one hand.

Davide shrugged. "It worked, though. *Brava*, Emilia."

"*Grazie.*"

"But what would you have done if he hadn't gotten up?"

Her face colored deeper still, crimson going nearly violet.

"I guess I'd have stayed where I was."

Che peccato…It's a pity he had to go, then.

He couldn't keep the smile on his face from broadening further at the thought.

"Emily?"

"Um, hm?"

"*Fiancée?*"

Emily burst into giggles again, her hand pressed tightly to her mouth to hide them. "Sorry," she said when her laughter had subsided. "It just came to me. I didn't think he could refuse an engaged couple, you know?"

"It was inspired thinking, though."

"Thanks."

He held her eyes for a moment, relishing the happiness that shone in them. On impulse, he leaned in and gave her a small kiss on the cheek, then lingered as long as he could with his lips brushing the soft skin in front of her ear. He wanted to whisper something to her, to prolong the camaraderie, but his mind had gone blank when he smelled the scent of her skin, so close.

"Why didn't you say you were coming to Milan?" she asked, her voice soft enough to be nearly lost in the murmur of voices around them.

"I didn't know that I was," he confessed, unable to lie, and drew slowly away from her at last.

"Really?" Her smile flickered, uncertain.

"I have a room booked," he lied, fearful that she might think his accompanying her had been presumptuous. "I just wanted to be sure you made it there without problems."

She started to speak, faltered, and then simply laughed. Her hands toyed with the strap of her purse and he thought of how throughout the day she had twisted her ring around her finger whenever she was nervous.

Her ring finger had a thin band of skin paler than the rest, though not by much. He put his hand over hers and took it gently into his own, his thumb rubbing the base of her naked ring finger. Emily's eyes fixed upon their hands, following the movement of his thumb, her smile coming and going in time with his caress.

"Emilia," he began, falling silent when she raised her eyes to meet his.

"*Sì*, Davide?"

He felt the blush rise from his collar to tint his cheeks. The words weren't ready to be spoken—not yet.

Nevertheless, they would be. He was sure of it.

12

Davide sat serenely amongst the chaos of passengers disembarking from the train, Emily's hand in his. Watching the crowd force their way to the doors, the usual spectacle of healthy young men and women pushing past the elderly or infirm without a second thought, he wondered at the lack of civility in his countrymen.

A gap in the flow of humanity presented itself and he stood and stepped casually into it. Here, he was in his element—it was familiar, even comfortable—but he knew *she* was not and his heart went out to her. He could see she was uneasy with the prospect of plunging into the crowd outside. It was in the timid way she stepped forward, how she held herself back, as though making herself smaller to avoid intruding into someone else's path.

She flashed a smile at him all the same and he felt a pull at his heart when she did so.

Until I'm certain she's happy, I won't be able to be happy myself.

He knew this was indulgent, even melodramatic, but he permitted himself the indulgence. Besides, it wasn't every day that he blew his whole travel budget and bought a first-class ticket from Bologna to Milano, just to be sure a woman he'd known less than a day made it to her hotel safely.

Incredibly, that was precisely what he was doing.

Once they had disembarked, he led her through the stream of passengers flooding out along the platform toward the main entrances, her hand secure in his own. The immense, elegant arcs of iron gridwork and Plexiglas which sheltered the tracks did little to keep warm the crowds gathered there. Signs over the concrete peninsulas alongside the trains directed them toward the archway between ghastly gigantic D&G ads plastered to the walls. Beyond these monstrosities were the restrooms, bars, bus queues and gates to the other trains.

Quickening his pace, her hand clutched in his own, he pushed her suitcase ahead of them through clusters of luggage-laden passengers, muttering hasty apologies. Once through the archway to the main hall, he took her down the stairs which led to the bus queues.

He looked at his watch and sighed, his breath misting in the frosty air. A glance was enough to tell that the hotel shuttle bus had already come and gone—just a few moments ago, in all likelihood—and they'd have to wait for the next one.

"It looks like we've missed it." He paused to consult the schedule that hung on the wall. "The next one won't be here for at least forty-five minutes."

"Oh, well. That's okay." Emily peered around him to read the board for herself. "Why don't we wait inside? It's awfully cold out here."

"Good idea. I think the bar is still open. Perhaps we could have a coffee while we wait?"

Her smile seemed more tired than before but nonetheless sincere. "All right. That sounds good."

Though the initial rush of travelers had thinned out, Davide still kept her hand in his as they walked back up the stairs to the main floor and the coffee shop there. He liked how her hand felt, warm and small, fitting neatly in his own.

"So, what would you like?" he asked as they stepped into the bar. He led her to a tall table at the end of the long counter and tucked the suitcase between her and the wall. "*Un caffè? Un tè?*"

To his surprise, her already rosy cheeks pinked further before she responded. "Hot chocolate?"

"Okay. *Cioccolata calda* it is. *Aspetta.*"

He placed the order at the counter, distantly aware that his hands were shaking all the while. Had they been shaking when he held her hand too? Had she noticed?

A fresh rush of anxiety flooded through him, leaving his knees watery for a few moments while he waited. At last, the *barista* handed the drinks over and Davide threaded his way through the crowd to cross the few steps to his and Emily's table.

"*Grazie,*" she said, her voice almost lost in the shuffle and conversation of the customers crowded into the small bar.

"*Prego.*" His smile felt shaky and unreal.

An awkward silence followed between the two of them. He watched Emily stir sugar into the bitter dark chocolate in her cup. His own *caffè* now seemed like a spectacularly bad idea but he sipped it anyway. As keyed-up as he felt, he wasn't likely to sleep that night, anyway.

"Why were you embarrassed to ask for a hot chocolate?" he asked, unable to bear their silence another moment. "It's a perfectly reasonable request."

"I guess it felt a little childish to ask for this," she said, shaking her head. "I don't know why, though." Her fidgeting fingers returned to her cup and spoon, stirring the thick chocolate into a perfect swirl on the surface. She licked her spoon, first on one side, then the other and dipped it back into the cup, oblivious to the fact that he was watching as though hypnotized.

Davide swallowed hard and drew a long, deep breath, mentally cursing his own foolishness.

Any moment now, I'll devolve into a drooling idiot.

"I can't imagine why, either," he said, hoping his voice didn't tremble too much.

Their eyes met for a long moment, then she looked down at the cup in front of her. Her fingers traced the pattern along the edge of the saucer, sliding over the embossment of roses and vines with an unconscious grace. Davide found himself thinking of a musician's hands dancing delicately over her instrument and more heat rushed up from his neck to burn his ears.

He raised one hand to his ear to be sure the flush wasn't visible.

"I get the feeling there's something on your mind, but I can't be sure what it is." He gave a light, quick laugh, his nervousness returning. "Should I ask you to share with me?"

"If it's too personal, of course, you don't have to tell me, but…" She hesitated, still toying with her cup. "I was wondering about something. I got to thinking about it on the train and…. In Bologna, when we were walking after the meal, we saw that woman and I asked about how women stay so skinny here…"

Anticipating what had drawn her curiosity, he nodded and licked his dry lips. "You are thinking, then, as to what made me so emotional."

"I'm sorry—maybe I shouldn't ask."

"No, it's okay. You shared your story with me, so…it's just fair that I should too, isn't it?"

"I don't want to press, though."

"No, no. It's all right." Davide fell quiet, considering what to say. Would she be overwhelmed with the truth? Or should he just come out with it?

"Well," he began, lowering his voice, "I should tell you first that my parents divorced when I was very young. It was a long, ugly process and I suppose it made quite an impression on me. I decided that I would never marry, as I couldn't see the point in doing something that would make me hate someone I loved. Of course, this is the perspective of a child, not an adult, but I maintained this until I had gotten much, much older. Until about seven years ago, in fact."

Emily's eyes widened, a subtle expression of surprise, and he checked around to be sure no one else was listening, though he couldn't say why he cared whether anyone overheard him.

"I changed my mind about marriage after I met *her*. I thought I felt that certain something that my parents had somehow lacked and had failed to pass along to me. It's stupid, I know—but you must realize that I had never had a girlfriend and I'd abandoned that hope a long time before she came along."

Emily nodded with an air of recognition and brought her eyes to his. "How old were you? When you met her, I mean."

"I was thirty, she was twenty-seven. There I was, faced with this beautiful creature who—for reasons I couldn't have explained—was showing what seemed to be a genuine interest in me. I was overwhelmed but happy, and intoxicated by the fact my affections were returned to me.

"I'd proved my parents wrong, you see. My father was convinced that I'd end up alone because I always had 'a book on my nose', as he said. Never mind that I was studying at university. Never mind that I was pursuing my only natural talent—studying, learning, expounding upon my theories.

"*You'll end up alone and surrounded by these useless books,* he'd say. *Will they keep you warm at night? No! Not unless you burn them!*"

"That's awful!"

"My mother was even worse. She was convinced I'd turn out just like my father. As I got older she'd look at me, make a disgusted face and say, *Oh, it's just awful that you have to look just like him. You'll never be happy with one woman since you'll have so many chasing you.*

"Yet that wasn't happening and when I looked in the mirror I didn't exactly see Mastroianni. I'm average, I always have been, and since I was terrified of women, I didn't compel them with my lack of charisma."

Emily gave him an indulgent, disbelieving look and he sighed before continuing.

"And so, to find her there after all those years felt like a comeuppance to them both."

"What was her name?" She slid her fingertip along the edge of the saucer again, not meeting his eyes.

"Letizia. She was finishing her degree in economics and I had just started teaching at the university."

"Letizia," Emily echoed, as though trying the name out.

Davide stared into the last of the foam of the coffee in his cup. "We'd only dated a few months before we got engaged. It seemed like such a sure thing... But once I'd started teaching full-time she started acting dissatisfied. She didn't like Bologna, she didn't like my flat—too old-fashioned, too dark—she didn't approve of my office, my colleagues... I did my best to make her happy, to show her she didn't need all those things she craved and then... Well, that's when it all started to fall apart, I guess.

"Finally, to appease her, we made plans to spend a week in Roma. She was obsessed with the place; she always said that it was better than Bologna, more important, more metropolitan."

A bitter smile quirked at the corners of Emily's mouth. "All roads lead to Rome, they say," she said.

Davide nodded, recalling that she'd said that Jacopo had gone there, too. He stood straight, his back aching from a tension he hadn't felt until then.

"A few days before we were to leave, I was asked to assume some classes for another professor who had fallen ill. I felt I had to say yes—I needed to get in with the university heads, to show that I wanted to advance, all of that. In the end, she went to Roma without me.

"When she came back, she showed me all these photos of herself. *Here's me at the Coliseum, here's me on the Spanish Steps, here I am in front of the Vatican...*

"The photos were quite good—not just snapshots random strangers would take. Eventually, while she was packing her things, she explained that they were all taken by the same person—and so was she.

"Then she showed me a few other photos. Ones she'd kept hidden before."

He suppressed a shudder at the images, still salt in a festering wound. Letizia, nude, stretched out over rumpled bedclothes with a weary, satiated smile and her makeup smeared across her face. He'd found several photos hidden in a drawer after she'd gone. One of them had even offered a glimpse of her new lover, his face partially obscured by the camera, reflected in a mirror behind her. It was the way she liked sex best: messy, obvious, a display for others to heighten her own pleasure.

She was only happy if she was on display.

"She showed me those just to twist the knife a bit more. All the fancy things she'd brought back to flaunt in my face weren't enough. Suddenly it made sense. He'd paid for her company with designer goods, all the stuff I couldn't afford on my modest salary."

He thought of the woman they'd seen in Bologna earlier that evening. One look at Emily's pensive expression said she was thinking of the same. Another image forced his stomach into a slow roll: Letizia, her blonde curls straightened and pulled back in a sleek chignon, dressed in a tight green dress and heels so high and pointed that he'd actually wondered—in the midst of her departure, yet—just how far she'd actually be able to walk.

"Naturally," he went on, "I'm quite bitter. It gets worse and worse each year. I see these young girls in my classes—funny how the older I get, the younger they seem—and they just appear to be growing more materialistic. On the one hand, I fear for them; on the other, I hate them for it. I know it's not fair or rational, but this is somewhere that my trust in rational thinking falls through.

"After all these years, I'm afraid the subject is still too close to my heart."

Emily nodded sadly, gazing down at the tablecloth. Another long silence fell between them, filled with the clinking of cups in saucers and other murmured conversations in the coffee shop.

"In some ways it's the same for me," she said, at last. "I've never been one of *those* women and I've always felt out of place in their company. When I came to Italy, I'd never felt so isolated and alone. I had no hope of blending in, of becoming one of them, because I hated what I thought they stood for.

"Jacopo never understood that. He couldn't see why I might feel threatened by them, or hurt when he'd pay attention to them. Now I know why that is—he was with them all the time.

"Before she died, his mother used to praise me—in a rather backhanded fashion—saying that she was glad her son had chosen me over all those pretty, flashy girls. I never knew whether she meant well by that."

Davide smiled in sympathy. "I'm sure she meant well. It's the sort of thing we lose in translation, no?"

Her sad smile changed little. "Now I know that he chose me because I was gullible. I couldn't speak Italian, so he could speak with girlfriends on the phone in front of me and I wouldn't know. When I started learning Italian, he switched to dialect. Then he never spoke to them from home. He rarely introduced me to colleagues; he only took me to dinner at certain friends' houses or in restaurants far from town with quiet clientele. He said he didn't want to go to nightclubs or pubs with me because I wouldn't enjoy the atmosphere. Fancy dining was 'boring' because he 'did it with clients all the time'.

"I never knew he meant that in more than one way. He left me for one of the D&G girls, eventually," she said, her tone rueful as she tilted her head toward yet another poster on the wall across from the coffee shop.

Davide shook his head and took her hand in his own. "I'm so sorry."

She shrugged, a failed effort at nonchalance. His sympathy became empathy in a heartbeat as he read the story in her face. There was more there, much more, than what she'd said. He knew it as well as he knew his own story wasn't quite finished.

Not yet.

"It still hurts, though," he said, confessing in spite of himself.

"Yeah, it sure does." She breathed the words more than she spoke them.

Frowning, he reached out to stroke the back of her hand with his thumb. "I've been truly insensitive, Emilia. Here I'm lamenting an old wound while yours is still fresh."

"Perhaps not so fresh now." She squared her shoulders but left her hand beneath his. "He's been gone for four years, remember? Any pain I still feel is my own fault—really nothing more than force of habit. Moving on takes time. I kept putting it off, so I fell behind schedule." Her smile strengthened and Davide felt as though she'd given him permission to do the same.

He couldn't help wanting to smile whenever she did.

Four years, he thought. *Four years*. His eyes strayed to the Campari clock on the wall and he felt his jaw drop. At once he felt strangely awake, as though he'd been sleeping all along.

"*Vacca boia*! Look at the time! We should go, or we're going to miss the next shuttle."

Emily snapped to and Davide realized she'd felt the same as he had. In spite of their topic of conversation, another heartfelt smile beamed on her face, which was exactly how he felt in that moment.

He paid for their drinks and snatched up the suitcase, taking her hand in his once more.

Dio bon, it felt right.

13

"Here we are." Davide glanced at Emily, her eyes already drooping with fatigue.

I wish I'd brought my bag with me, he thought, taking her by the hand to help her off the shuttle bus. He picked up her suitcase and led her to the front entrance of the hotel. *Too late for that now. But that change of clothes in my office is going to be a sweet dream by the morning.*

A window at the front of the hotel gave onto the office and Davide peered inside to find who was on duty for the night. He could see a familiar shock of blond hair, nearly obscured by the computer screen, and he knew that an impassioned round of *Tribal Wars* was bound to be raging.

He pushed through the outer door into the anteroom before the lobby and heard the faint electronic *ping* in the office, indicating a new guest. Glancing up at the closed-circuit camera, he waved. A moment later, the door buzzed unlocked and he took Emily through to the reception area.

The door to the office swung open an instant later as the desk clerk came bounding out, all smiles.

"*Ciao, Davide! Che sorpresa! Come va?*"

"*Ciao, Giorgio. Tutto bene…*" Davide smiled, hoping to stifle the puzzled expression on his friend's face before Emily could draw any conclusions. Fatigue and anxiety took turns at his system until his nerves fairly sang from the stress of it. He felt faintly feverish but he was certain his friend behind the hotel reception desk couldn't discern his condition. "Giorgio, this is Emily Spadon. She has a reservation for a room tonight."

"Ah, *sì, sì.*" Still clearly befuddled, Giorgio set about printing up paperwork for Emily's check-in, his eyes darting to Davide from time to time.

Emily, meanwhile, was looking around the lobby with admiration. "This is some place, Davide. It's very nice—not what I expected from an airport hotel."

"The rooms are very nice as well. I think you'll be pleased."

Her hand rose to her mouth to cover a small yawn. "As long as it's clean and tidy, I'll be happy. I'm exhausted."

"Your key, *signora.*" Giorgio passed the key card in its paper folder to her over the gleaming wooden countertop. He gave Davide a sly wink and a grin over her shoulder. "Room 415, top floor, turn right. It's at the far end of the hall. Very quiet."

Davide blanched, hoping that Emily hadn't noticed Giorgio's suggestiveness. His eyes widened as he gave a single, sharp shake of his head to discourage his friend.

"*Grazie,*" she said with a weary grin, taking her suitcase in hand. "How late is the restaurant open?"

Giorgio gave her a most solicitous smile. "Our restaurant is open until eleven this evening, *signora.* The bar is open until one a.m."

"I see. I shouldn't waste any time, then. Could I leave my bag here and retrieve it on my way up?"

"*Certo, signora.* I would be pleased to keep it here by the counter for you." He was already coming around the reception desk to collect it before she turned to Davide once more.

"Davide, would you want to have dinner with me?"

"Yes, I would like this very much."

Her smile was the warmest he'd seen it all day. "Wonderful." She turned to Giorgio, who had watched the exchange with a smug grin. "*Vorrei la sveglia per le sette, per favore.*"

Davide could see that Giorgio hadn't expected her to turn to him so quickly, or for the request to be in Italian. "Of course, *signora*," Giorgio said, regaining his composure. "A wake-up call at seven a.m. Would you like anything else?"

"*No, grazie*," she smiled, turning back to Davide. "Shall we?"

"*Dopo di te*," he said, gesturing for her to lead and waiting for her to precede him before shooting an angry look and hand gesture behind her back at Giorgio.

There were only a handful of other patrons in the hotel restaurant. The hostess led them to a table in a quiet corner of the main room. Aperitifs arrived with the menus and they sipped in silence at the small flutes of light, sparkling white wine while soft piano music played through hidden speakers. Davide fussed with his place setting and water glass, his hands in near-constant motion while he tried to think of something to say.

But Emily beat him to it. "I have to admit... I never suspected this was how the day would end." She finished the last of her aperitif and put the glass carefully within the circle it had made on the tablecloth. "It makes for a very nice surprise, though."

He was both elated and embarrassed. "I, uh... I wanted to be certain that you made it here all right."

After she regarded him for what felt like an eternity, she chuckled and shook her head. "You could have just *called*, Davide."

"*Sì*," he said with a sigh. "I know."

"But... Well, I'm happy you came along, too."

Davide smiled, sliding his glass over the tablecloth and smoothing out the ripples in the fabric with his hand. "*Grazie a Dio.*"

A question lurked between them. It fidgeted behind her eyes, waiting to be spoken aloud. He wasn't certain whether he dared invite it, no matter how much he hoped it was the same question he wanted to ask.

The waiter arrived to take their orders and Davide was grateful for the chance to focus on something else for a few moments. Still, his eyes were drawn back to hers. Each time he found it harder to breathe, harder to focus on the world around them. Each time, he realized all he wanted was to be able to look into those eyes uninterrupted for an hour, or perhaps for a lifetime.

This is insane. You've known her less than a day!

And yet…

Abruptly he cleared his throat and brought his empty glass to his lips, tilting it back to coax the last few drops from the bottom. Emily seemed amused, though he didn't understand why.

"*Ho sete…*" he mumbled, as the waiter approached with a bottle each of water and wine.

"Me, too," Emily said, grinning. With considerable attention, she watched him open the bottle of wine.

He paused with the bottle poised over her glass. "*Sì, o no?*"

She tilted her head to one side in a becoming gesture. "*Sì,*" she said, nodding her consent.

Steadying his hand, Davide poured a modest amount into both glasses and sat back, struggling against the impulse to gulp down the contents of his own for courage. Pressing the back of his hand to his mouth, he swallowed a yawn as best he could.

Emily held her glass by the stem and swirled the wine with great care, her expression distant while she watched the liquid cling to the inside of her glass.

She's thinking of him. Again. Davide was sure of it.

"Sorry," she said, her voice only just carrying over the soft music of the restaurant. "I got a little lost there." She rubbed her forehead and mussed the fringe over it, so it lay crooked over her eyebrow.

It took all his will to keep from reaching across the table to smooth the fringe into place. The desire to follow yet another impulse emerged and his heart raced while he contemplated pressing a kiss to her brow instead.

He licked his lips, remembering their kiss in the piazza that evening. Dear God, why hadn't he tried for more?

Because it wasn't right, that's why. Get hold of yourself, man!

Davide gulped down the rest of his glass of wine, then poured more.

Emily's eyes widened in mild surprise. "Are you okay?"

"I'm fine," he smiled, waving one hand low over the table. "Really. Just a bit... I don't know. Embarrassed."

"Why embarrassed?"

He felt momentarily feverish and took another drink. "I'm not sure. Perhaps it is because I have acted so impulsively tonight?"

When she took a small sip of her wine, he noted how her lips pursed when she paused before swallowing. Another hard thud of his heart followed, strong enough to daze him. Fortunately, she didn't seem to notice.

"Sometimes, I suppose, 'impulsive' is good." She smiled very briefly. "Other times, maybe not so much."

"*Dimmi*, Emilia," he began, hoping to help her evade her dark mood, "When, in your opinion, is being impulsive a good thing?"

"What?" Her mouth twitched upward, giving him hope.

"When is being impulsive a good thing? Give me examples to make me feel better."

The laugh that escaped her was quiet but genuine.

"How many?"

"Three," he said, nodding decisively. "That's a good number."

"Okay, um..." Holding her hand up, she made a fist and extended her thumb. "One: when you allow someone to give you help when you'd prefer that he just go away instead. That was one of the best impulsive decisions I've made in ages."

Davide's heart skipped giddily. "You wanted me to go away?"

"In that moment I wanted it more than anything, yes. I'm glad you didn't, though—very glad."

He took a deep breath, gesturing toward her before taking another sip of wine. "Give me another example."

"Okay..." She seemed deep in thought for a moment, her smile playing over her lips all the while. "Oh!" she said, then gave a heartfelt laugh while raising her hand again to count off her second answer. "When they offer the dessert tray in a nice restaurant—that's a great time to be impulsive."

He laughed too, his stomach pleasantly shivering for a reason he couldn't quite fathom.

"Another, *amore*, please." Too late, he realized he'd said the endearment. He froze, waiting for her response. Frustratingly, thankfully, she didn't react to it at all. Instead, her eyes skimmed over the restaurant, as though seeking an answer in the cream-colored curtains and the potted plants.

She laughed once more, a soft puff of breath pushed through her smile, and he waited.

"Accepting a kiss from a man by a fountain is a wonderful time to be impulsive."

Davide had so intensely imagined her saying it, he almost believed she really had.

When her gaze had moved all the way around the dining room and returned to their table, it met his and held it in a gentle, tenuous grasp. He didn't want to look away and she made no effort to do so either, as far as he could tell.

If I kiss her again, what will she do? Do I risk it, or no?

He folded his hands together and rested his chin on them, his elbows on the table. His mouth had gone desperately dry but he didn't dare reach for his glass of wine to quench his thirst. He wet his lips and thought of their kiss in Piazza del Nettuno.

In an unexpected echo, she did the same, a flash of palest pink against the fuller flesh of her lips; he flinched, a low, unconscious twitch of his hips and his head at the same time.

He was certain that she'd seen his reaction but if so, she had the good grace not to show it.

The waiter arrived and Davide sat back, relieved, as the waiter placed their orders before them. Stomach rumbling, Davide considered the modest heap of pasta on the plate.

"Oh, geez…" Emily mumbled, her hand over her stomach an instant later. "Excuse me—I hadn't realized how hungry I was until I had something in front of me."

"Nor had I," Davide said, knowing that he meant it in many ways at once. "Nor had I."

Several forkfuls later, he caught her eye again.

"You owe me one more example," he prodded gently. "Remember?"

"You're right." Her brow furrowed as she considered her answer.

"Surely it's not so difficult?"

The expression of concentration faded and she held up her left hand, wordlessly, turning her naked ring finger toward him. Their eyes met once more and he read there what he had suspected earlier in the evening. He wondered if she read it in his eyes as well.

Surely she does. How could she not know by now?

The waiter passed and placed the bill on the table. Faster than Davide would have thought possible, her hand snaked out and snatched it to herself.

"Emilia, *ti prego!*" he extended his hand to her in expectation. "I cannot let you pay for this."

"You can, and you will." She flicked the bill upward in her hand, out of his reach. "You paid for my second breakfast. You paid for lunch and for the train tickets up here. Do you really think I'm going to let you pay for dinner as well?"

She slipped the bill under her plate as the waiter returned.

"*Tutt'apposto?*"

"*Sì, sì.* And could we also see the dessert cart?" She grinned at Davide and he felt a light sweat break on the back of his neck. His hands rested atop the table, willed into stillness while the waiter cleared the plates and silverware.

Oddio... Don't read too much into this. Don't rush out and make a mistake—not now.

"Please, let me do this," she said, putting her hand over his on the table.

Only then did he realize she'd mistaken his desire for something else entirely.

"*Va bene*, Emilia. If it's what you want."

"It is, Davide. *Grazie.*"

If he'd had any resistance left, her smile would have melted it away. As it was, by the time the waiter brought around the dessert cart, Davide knew what he'd suspected all afternoon was now a certainty.

He was lost. Utterly and completely lost.

14

"At what time is your flight departing?" Davide asked, heaviness sitting in his stomach atop the *millefoglie* he'd had for dessert.

"Ten-thirty." Emily frowned. "It's not too early, but having to be there two hours ahead of departure and all that..." She trailed off as they approached the reception desk and Giorgio gestured toward the corner where her suitcase awaited.

"Would you like me to bring that up for you?" Davide asked, ignoring the loaded grin Giorgio sent his way.

"You don't have to," she said, covering her mouth as she yawned.

"I wouldn't mind, Emilia."

"Well, if you're sure..."

In response, Davide grasped the handle and trundled it over to the elevators. He smiled back at her and felt the expression freeze on his face. She stood, twining her fingers in the bottom of her ponytail, a gesture that made her look impossibly young.

In an instant, he saw it all: the two of them in the elevator, his hand stroking her cheek, then reaching and tugging at the elastic that bound back her hair away from her face. He could feel the silken smoothness of her hair beneath his fingertips as the elastic slid down the length of her ponytail at his urging, until it all fell free and loose against his palm.

He imagined twining his fingers in her hair, then, holding her in place and tilting her head back, her mouth opening to receive his, willing, wanting...

"Davide?"

"*Sì, sì...*" He shook his head to clear away the images, although he would have liked to see the vision through to the end.

Emily stroked his arm, clucking sympathetically. "Poor thing— you're as tired as I am, aren't you?"

He nodded, abashed. "I guess it's true, yes. I am quite tired. Let's go..."

The elevator chimed and the stainless steel doors slid open. He dragged the suitcase inside and she followed, almost on his heels. Unable to face her directly, their eyes met via the mirrored walls surrounding them.

Neither of them spoke while they rose to the fourth floor. The only sound was the quiet hum of the elevator itself. When the doors slid open at her floor, Davide's heart sank.

This is it. This is where we say goodnight—and goodbye.

He followed her to her room, the suitcase in his hand seeming to grow heavier with every step, until he considered setting it on the hallway carpet to take a rest. Before he knew it, however, she was moving to slide her keycard and open her door.

With wonder, he watched her miss the slot. Her hands were shaking hard enough for him to see and she took a deep breath before trying again. This time the keycard slid home and the small green light blinked, a soft *click* signaling that the door was unlocked.

"Where would you like this?" he indicated the suitcase following her into the small entryway.

"Anywhere is fine."

He went straight to the luggage rack next to the desk, making a pointed effort to ignore the presence of the queen-sized bed to his left. Placing the suitcase carefully atop the rack, he turned to face her.

She stood by the desk, her arms crossed over her chest and a timid grin on her face while she stared at the floor.

His heart gave a start, a few sudden, powerful beats that rendered him incapable of speech for a moment or two.

Just say it and go. Bid her goodnight and try to salvage a few hours of sleep before the morning.

He opened his mouth to speak but she spoke instead.

"Well…" she began and the rest faded somewhere between a sigh and a laugh.

He could manage only a half-laugh himself. They regarded each other without speaking, the door open onto the hallway somehow making the silence between them larger.

"I should let you rest," he said, barely managing to resist biting his own tongue. He hadn't meant to say that at all, nor anything remotely like it. "I'd better go."

"Are you sure?"

Davide nodded, stopped and nodded again. "*Sì*, I'm sure. Are you?"

"Am I what?"

Permitting himself a shrug, he forced a smile onto his face. "*Scusami*, Emilia. I'm sorry, I'm not making much sense right now. I'm fatigued." He paused, considering how that sounded. "I mean, it isn't that I want to leave, I just…"

"I know. I wish you could stay longer."

"You do?"

She gave him a shy nod. "I've enjoyed this day so much, I hate to see it end. Is that selfish?"

His smile was more genuine now. "It's not selfish. I've enjoyed it very much, too." He cleared his throat and started for the door. Emily reached out to stop him before he could pass her by.

"Davide?"

"*Sì?*" he responded—too quickly, he knew.

"I was wondering if… um…"

"*Sì?*" he repeated, his eyes fixed on her face until she looked away, blushing.

Oddio… Please ask it, Emilia. Ask me to stay. I can't take this much longer, either way.

Her hands were dithering by her sides, then met in front of her waist, one hand pulling at the fingers of the other in an echo of her nervous habit. Davide reached forward and took both her hands in one of his to still them.

"Just say it, Emilia," he said, giving what he hoped was a reassuring smile while concentrating on keeping his own hand from shaking.

"I was wondering: when do you have to return to work?"

Davide stared mutely at her for a moment, processing what she'd just asked. What day *was* it, anyway?

"*Dopo domani,*" he answered at last, releasing her hands and cursing himself for his foolishness once again. Of course she wasn't going to ask him to stay. "I have a meeting tomorrow evening, but that's all." He shrugged to show his indifference at the prospect. "Why?"

"I was wondering if you, um…if you would want to go with me to the airport tomorrow." As if expecting a protest of some sort, she threw her hands up between them and clasped them in a gesture of supplication. "I know it's silly but if you don't have to be back first thing tomorrow, I'd really be pleased if you'd, you know, come with me."

Deep crimson flooded her cheeks once she'd said it, and he raised one hand to press it to her skin. His hands were cool enough that she felt feverish in turn.

This time, she didn't pull away from his touch.

"*Certo*, Emilia," he said, laughing a little at her sigh of relief. "*Certo.* I would be happy to accompany you to the airport. We can meet in the lobby for breakfast at half-past seven."

"That would be great—thanks so much."

"*Di niente.*" He brushed a stray lock of hair back over her ear, his eyes meeting hers fully.

Trying to ignore the flip in his stomach, Davide felt himself drawn to her, recalling their kiss in the piazza and the few small kisses he'd given her on the train. He forced himself to give her a chaste kiss, pressing his lips to her temple as he had outside *Bologna Centrale*, but this time it was much more difficult to draw away.

Emily remained perfectly still beneath his lips, beneath his hand, save for her soft trembling.

Or was *he* trembling?

He inhaled as softly as he could, tasting her scent at the back of his tongue and savoring it as he stepped away.

"*Buonanotte*, Emilia."

"*Buonanotte*, Davide."

By sheer force of will alone, his unsteady legs carried him out the door and down the hall to the elevators. The *snick* of her door closing was a knife's blade drawn down his spine.

My father would be so disappointed, he thought. When the elevator door opened, his own bitter expression greeted him. *Allora... Vaffanculo, Papà...* He punched the button for the lobby harder than necessary and the doors slid closed.

He composed himself as best he could before the elevator opened on the ground floor once again. As he strode toward the reception desk, his friend turned and let his professional mask slip for a moment into an expression of open shock and surprise.

"What are you doing down here? I don't have your name on the reservations list."

"I know. I'm not registered...yet?" Davide asked hopefully but Giorgio shook his head and flung his hands out in a gesture of frustration.

"*Dai*, Davide... You can't be serious! I got your lady friend in by pulling a few strings, but... now we're full." Giorgio leaned against the counter where Davide now slumped and whispered conspiratorially, "Why don't you just *ask* her, anyway? She's kind of cute, in a lonely librarian sort of way."

Davide gave him the most disdainful look he could manage in his state of fatigue.

"I just wanted to be sure that she made it in all right," he said, straightening.

"You could have just *called* if you wanted to check on her."

"I *know*." Davide examined the hotel lobby, seeking an out-of-the-way sofa or chair where he could camp out unobtrusively.

"Don't even think about it." Giorgio shook his head. "If they see you, the management will take you for a vagrant and have you removed."

"What do you suggest, then?" Davide asked over the muted bleeping of the desk phone.

"Just a moment." Giorgio answered the phone, politely explained that the hotel was full and hung up. He looked thoughtful for a moment, scratching his chin distractedly, then gave Davide a half-grin.

"Come with me," he said in a low voice, motioning to the door by the counter where they stood. "I've got an idea."

They passed through a door just out of sight from the lobby, into a tiny room with two sofas and a coffee table filling it.

"Employee lounge," Giorgio explained. "No one else should be in until seven a.m. I'll wake you before I end my shift and you can go out with the early departures."

"Perfect. *Grazie mille.*"

"Just don't come and go too often. The lobby guard will notice if you do."

"He will?" Davide thought of the man who had been sitting in the lobby, engrossed in a documentary on serial killers on the television.

"Well, maybe not," said Giorgio, "but why take the chance?" He hurried back to answer the desk phone again, leaving Davide there alone.

He sank onto a sofa and pondered his rationale for coming all the way to Milano from Bologna. He had *wanted* to stay with Emily in her room but his nerve had failed when she'd practically invited him in.

But there's nothing to stop me now, right? He sighed, knowing it was impossible. *If I show up at her door now, she'll think I'm some sort of madman rapist or something. How else to explain why I would follow her so far? To a hotel* I'd *arranged for her, for that matter. Nothing at all suspicious about that, is there?*

Davide got up and opened the door, cautiously checking that there was no one to see him, then stepped out to ask Giorgio in a stage-whisper if he could get a pillow and a blanket for the night. When Giorgio didn't respond, he came out behind the desk and repeated the question, only to find his friend busy with a customer.

"Oh, *scusate*," he said, blanching and hurriedly stepping back. And then he saw who the customer was.

"Davide?" Emily looked confused. "What are *you* doing down here?"

"I was about to ask you the same," he said and laughed, hoping it wouldn't sound false.

"I left my credit card in the restaurant and they asked me to come down to collect it. Another couple of minutes and I would have been in bed." Averting her eyes, she looked around the lobby for a moment. Davide felt his own anxious flutter, realizing she had found her own choice of words unintentionally provocative.

See? Still more proof that she wants this as badly as I do. So why can't I just act on it?

A weight thudded in his stomach in response. *She's not ready yet. I know it.*

"As for me, well, I came down to… to…say hello to Giorgio. He's my friend, you know, and we haven't seen each other for a while. I haven't stayed here for a while, I mean."

Shut up, shut up!

They fell silent. Davide could feel Giorgio's eyes on them all the while.

"You know the worst part of all this?" Emily asked.

"No, what?"

"I'm wide awake now. The bar closes in about half an hour and I can't sleep. I never can sleep right before a trip, anyway, so maybe I should just stay up all night."

"Do you want company, Emilia?"

He'd spoken without thinking, without even knowing he would until the words had already left his mouth to hang in the air between them. The lightheadedness which followed was so sudden and complete he was unsure if he was still standing.

"'Company,' Davide?"

"I've been told that I could talk all night long, if left to do it. I can guarantee that we'll talk all night, or you'll fall asleep from listening to me, just like my students. One or the other."

I'm blathering. I'm an idiot. And this is where she says something about how sweet or cute I am, then says "No, thank you," in some polite way before she goes upstairs alone.

"I'd like that," she said, her eyes lighting up and making his heart skitter to a temporary halt.

"You would?" he asked, surprised that he didn't have to gasp out the words and actually sounded quite coherent.

"Yeah, I would."

She started for the elevator but Davide stood where he was, with Giorgio making not-so-subtle "Go on!" motions with his hands.

Porca vacca... I don't even have anything to talk about.

15

Although he'd been in the room only a short while before, the act of stepping inside again so soon brought a vague sense of unreality with it. His feet scarcely felt the floor beneath them as he made his way over to the sofa by the window, refusing to permit himself more than a glance at the bed, fearing the thoughts it would bring.

Emily, it seemed, had no such compunction. She sat on the bed and smiled wearily at him.

"It's funny, isn't it? The way we keep bumping into each other?"

He didn't get the feeling she really wanted an answer, so he smiled instead. "*Sì*," he said, after more silence.

"I swear, Davide, this isn't a come-on, but… do you mind if I put on something more comfortable? I've been in the same clothes all day long, and I really need a change."

So do I. He thought wistfully of his change of clothes in his knapsack in Bologna. *I really should have thought ahead. But how was I to know?*

She was watching him with an air of expectation and he realized that he had drifted off.

"Please, do whatever you need to do. I'm fine."

"Okay." She got up from the bed, unzipped the side pocket of her suitcase and took out a plastic bag. "I'll be right back." She disappeared into the bathroom. Davide found himself listening for the *click* of the lock and wondered why he might do that.

No *click* came, though.

"I have a question for you, Emilia," he called to her.

"Just a minute," she said, then came out of the bathroom clad in flannel pajamas, her familiar, shy grin on her face. "See? Nothing too revealing."

His eyes narrowed, trying to make out the pattern. He reached for his glasses before remembering he'd left them downstairs in his coat. "*Che cos'è?* What is that?"

"They're penguins," she said cheerfully. "Penguins holding martinis."

He arched an eyebrow at her and she rolled her eyes.

"It's *cute*, Davide. Penguins don't drink cocktails."

The laugh which escaped him was too large for her small joke but she didn't seem to mind. Davide coughed and rubbed his throat.

"I should get a drink," he said, moving to get up, only to have her push him back down onto the sofa.

"I'll get it for you. What would you like? Something from the mini-bar? Coffee or tea?"

"Water is fine. *Grazie.*"

"Water it is, then."

She disappeared into the bathroom and he could hear the water running for a few moments before she returned, padding across the room in her bare feet. He fought the desire to cringe at the sight.

"I know," she said, proving he'd failed to hide his reaction. "Jacopo used to hate it too. But I don't like wearing socks at the end of the day, even if it's cold outside. I can't sleep if I'm too warm."

"I'm the same, but slippers would be good for walking on a strange floor, no? You have no idea what's on this carpet."

"God, you're being so Italian." She handed him the glass and went to sit on the bed, while he drank the water down in one long draw, grateful for the distraction.

"You said you had something to ask me?"

"*Sì, sì, infatti… Perché non parli italiano con me; non ti piaccio?*" he asked, smiling, though his smile soon faded. The fleeting sadness he'd seen in her eyes and the brief downturn of the corners of her mouth reminded him of her face in Rovigo.

"I'm sorry, Davide. Of course I like you." She looked at the floor for a moment before raising her eyes to meet his again with a discomfiting frankness. "It's nothing personal—I just haven't wanted to speak Italian today, for the most part. I'm leaving, so I won't have much use for it soon. I guess I wanted to try to drop the habit."

"Habit?" he echoed in spite of himself.

"I don't mean to be unfair with you. If you think I am, I really am sorry."

"I don't think you are being unfair, it is just… I don't understand why. I presume you speak it well—*sì*, you even speak with a rather Venetian accent—so I just…"

"I'm sorry," she repeated, cutting him off. There was no unkindness in it, though.

He nodded, trying not to feel rejected all the same. "I must beg your pardon, then, for my mistakes. I am exhausted of speaking English all day."

Her hand went to her mouth and he felt an urge to pull it away.

"Oh, God, Davide, I never thought of that. How rude of me to insist on English."

"No, no, it's okay. I'm just in difficulties now, since it is late." He raised one hand to his forehead and took a deep breath, concentrating. "If I wasn't struggling, I wouldn't ask."

"Still, I should know how that feels. Please, speak Italian if you prefer. But will it bother you if I speak English? I have to get used to it again."

He shook his head, smiling again. "*Prego*, Emilia. I like to hear you speak, regardless of the language you choose."

She waved him off. "I talk too much."

"*Non è vero*," he said, shaking his head and resting against the arm of the sofa.

Emily fussed with the pillows on the bed, then reached up and pulled the elastic off her ponytail. She bent at the waist and flung her hair over her head, massaging her scalp with brisk motions of her fingers.

A small grunt of effort escaped her and Davide bit his lip, unable to take his eyes off this spontaneous display. Her hair was thicker than he'd realized—longer, too—and when she sat up to brush it back from her face, he had to sit on his empty hand to keep from flexing his fingers, imagining her hair tangling around them.

Sono pazzo. That's all there is to it: I'm insane. How am I supposed to…?

"Davide, could I ask you another question?"

"*Certo.* What is it?"

"There was something you mentioned at the bar at the station this evening. I was wondering if you would explain it to me."

"About…?"

"Your father," she said, pausing. "Or, rather, what your mother said about your father."

Davide looked at the empty glass in his hand, wishing he had some water left. "*Sì?*"

"What did she mean when she said she was sure you'd be just like him?"

He rested the glass on the arm of the sofa and trailed his fingertip along the rim, framing his answer.

"If you don't want to talk about it, I understand, of course."

"No, no, *va bene* – it's fine… I am just considering a polite way to say what I am thinking."

Emily's expression darkened. "It's that bad?"

"*Per me, sì.* For many others, not so much. *Mio padre*…was…a bit of a bastard, really."

"How so?" she asked, wary.

"*Lui era*…um…*in italiano?*" he asked, seeking permission to continue in Italian. Emily nodded with a sad smile.

After drawing a deep breath, he pushed the words out all at once.

"He was an unfaithful husband and a terrible father." Picking up the glass, he tapped the bottom of it on the sofa's arm with increasing speed and force until he noted Emily's eyes upon it. "*Perdonami*, Emilia," he said, putting the glass on the table next to him. "I have never actually said that out loud before."

"Davide, I'm sorry—I shouldn't have pried."

"It's okay." He raised his eyes to hers and smiled as best he could. "Really, it is. It's the same old story among a certain class of people here. My father married my mother because of me." He raised a questioning eyebrow and Emily nodded to show she understood. "So, when a little time passed, he found mistresses. For some families this isn't a problem, but my mother responded badly. She did her best to make him miserable and he obliged her by finding women who wouldn't, which she thought justified her being horrible in the first place."

"Oh... Why go through all that? Why not just get divorced? I mean, I know it takes time here but..."

"If I had not been born, maybe they would have gotten an annulment. Since they were Catholic, it was not an option. Especially not then." He shrugged and paused, remembering. "I caught him cheating once. I was twelve, walking home from school, when I saw him in his car with a woman I didn't know. At first, I thought he was with Mamma, but then... I saw her face and I just...knew. He didn't see me, though and when he kissed her goodbye, I had no doubt what was going on."

"Oh, Jesus..."

"Things were never the same after that. I knew too much about him to respect him anymore. The older I got, the more I looked like him – according to Mamma – and the more I was doomed to *be* just like him." He laughed, a slight, bitter edge to the sound in his own ears and a bitter taste on his tongue as well. "It didn't happen, though, like I said earlier. He was disappointed in me, I was disappointed in him and Mamma was disappointed in us both."

Emily piled the pillows on top of each other and leaned against them, propping her head up on her hand. "Go on," she said. "I'm still listening. I just want to get more comfortable."

"Okay, but that is about it, really. When he died, he left the flat in Bologna to me. That was a great surprise, of course. He had never done anything so considerate for me while he was alive."

Emily gave him a soft, sympathetic smile and with that, the bitter taste in his mouth was gone.

Then they were both silent for a while. Davide turned his attention to the furthest corner of the room, pushing away the memories as best as he could. When he looked at Emily again, she lay against the pillows, her eyes closed, her mouth slack in sleep.

He slid down to rest his head on the sofa's armrest and watched her sleep. The idea of getting up and joining her didn't seem quite so far-fetched now. It would be simple enough to do, anyway. If she wanted him to leave, he would. If she wanted him to stay, he would.

It was all up to her, as it should be.

He awoke with a start, recoiling sharply. His lower spine insistently pulled him back down to an uncomfortable position with a hot flare of pain. He pressed his face into the cushioning on the arm of the sofa and drew a quiet, shuddering breath until the spasm waned.

His face and hands were cold, as were his feet. The rest of him was remarkably warm. The weight of a blanket on his shoulder was undeniable but puzzling all the same.

When he tried to sit upright, fumbling to push off the blanket, he remembered belatedly where he was and how he'd come to be there. Now the only light in the room came from behind the almost-closed bathroom door. His eyes were slow to adjust but soon he could see the Emily's outline under the bedclothes. He watched her for a while before he tried once more to get up from the sofa.

He attempted to stifle a grunt and failed. Emily turned over to face him and sat up, leaning forward to see him better in the dim light.

"Davide, are you all right?"

"*Sì, sì.* I fell asleep on this sofa and now…well, it's just my back. I'll be okay, in a few moments."

"Are you sure? You're all bent over and everything."

He sighed; even *that* hurt.

"Davide…don't read too much into this, but why don't you, um…. Why not stay here?"

It was everything he'd hoped to hear, yet it terrified him somehow.

"Oh, Emilia, *sei troppo, troppo gentile.* I could not… *impose* upon your kindness in that way."

Even in the dim light, he could see her disappointment. "Well," she began quietly, while he tried once more to stand up straight, "if you think you can–"

He drew a sharp breath as his back pulled in a spasm yet again and he dropped onto the sofa, awkwardly trying to slow his descent.

"Okay, that does it. If you can't even make it away from the sofa," she said in a clear, skeptical tone, "how do you expect to make it to your room?"

She has a point there. Or, she would, *if I had a room to go to, instead of another sofa.* "If I stay here, though… are you not concerned that, well, *something* might happen?"

Emily put a hand to her mouth and he knew it was to hide a laugh. "Davide, honestly—I think I can trust you, at least for the night. Besides, look at the state you're in."

"It's *temporary*," he insisted.

"It's up to you," she shrugged. "Huddle on the sofa until you feel better and go, or stay here and try to get some rest. You already know what I think." She lay down and turned her back to him with an air of finality.

Davide drew a long, shaky breath, struggling all the while to make it steady. His heart was racing, his hands still trembling with the receding shock of pain in his back. *It's more temptation than any man should be expected to stand, isn't it? How am I supposed to keep turning this down? A soft, warm bed with a soft, warm woman in it?*

He shook his head, his indecision weakening considerably as he viewed her shape beneath the covers. *Nothing has to happen, right? I could just stay with her tonight, no strings attached.* He bit his lip, felt a vaguely pleasant, slow turning low in his belly before he forced himself to stop staring at the curve of her hip. *Who am I kidding? Then again, we're both adults, unattached... and chances are, I couldn't manage anything, even if I wanted to, unless she—*

He bit his lip again, hard enough to worry that this time he might have broken the skin. Raising one hand to touch a fingertip there, he failed to prevent himself from making a soft "hiss" of pain.

"Oh, for Heaven's sake, Davide," she sighed. "Just lie down on the bloody bed and get some rest."

There was nothing for it. He cautiously moved the few paces from the sofa, sat gingerly on the edge of the bed and wondered if she could feel his anxious trembling. He seemed to be shaking all over, so why didn't the bed thrum with his nervous energy?

His lower back made a low, threatening twinge to drag him back to reality. He willed his hands to steadiness, unbuttoned his shirt and removed it with great care before casting it back toward the sofa. He regretted it at once; his t-shirt felt clammy and damp after his brief nap and painful awakening on the sofa and he wished yet again for the change of clothes now abandoned in his office in Bologna.

By force of habit, his hands dropped to his belt and began unfastening the clasp before he paused, uncertain. *What will she think if I strip down like that? Just the belt, then.* He pulled the belt through the loops of his trousers and rolled it up neatly before placing it on the night table. His watch followed a moment later, making a soft *click* in the darkness when he put it down.

Davide swallowed hard, his throat painfully dry. He considered going to get another glass of water, but the idea of hobbling through the room and risking another spasm in his back was simply too embarrassing to contemplate. The air in the room seemed colder and he shivered, ruefully eyeing the heap his shirt had made on the sofa.

It's not too late, is it? I could still.... Oh, to hell with it.

He eased himself down onto the bed, tentatively pulled at the bedclothes to cover himself and lay on his side, his back to Emily. He was still trembling but whether it was from the pain or from being in this rather indelicate position with her, he wasn't sure.

"*Buonanotte*, Emilia," he murmured at last.

She laughed softly in response.

"*Buonanotte*, Davide."

16

He awoke to the soft coming and going of her breath on his chest. He kept still, waited and then felt the touch of her breath once more. Her forehead rested on his pillow, close to his mouth. A few strands of her hair tickled his lips, stirred by his breath in the darkness.

All the while, Davide kept his eyes closed, shaking with awareness of her closeness. The air beneath the bedclothes was a trifle too humid and he could smell a hint of her scent, the salt of her skin.

I really shouldn't...

Then he leaned forward, just enough, and pressed his lips to her forehead in a light kiss. She stirred and he withdrew carefully, touching the tip of his tongue to his lips to taste her salt there. He coughed and she stirred again, her movement permitting their mingled scents to drift out from between them.

She could always ask me to stop.

Keeping his eyes closed, he slowly reached up to touch her hair and brushed it back gently, then kissed her forehead once again, lingering for a moment longer. She sighed, a quiet sound amongst the rustling of the bedclothes, and he let his hand drift slowly, stroking her hair down to her shoulder.

If she asks me to stop, I will. I will.

He placed a light kiss above her eyebrow, then traced her profile tenderly with his nose, breathing in the perfume the hotel soap had left on her skin. He wondered idly when she had washed her face. Was it before he had joined her the second time? Or after he'd fallen asleep on the sofa?

Kissing her cheek as softly as he could, he drew back when she shifted position next to him. She turned her mouth up to his, beckoning with silent want, and he found her lips unerringly in spite of his self-imposed darkness.

Her response was better than he had dared anticipate. Emily received his kiss without any reservation, returning it with gentle eagerness instead. She encouraged more, slipping ever closer to him and moving to accommodate his first, hesitant caresses sliding blindly along her body, over the soft flannel pajamas.

He felt her anxious trembling mirroring his own while they continued their initial timid kisses and explorations of each other. Her pleased shiver when his fingertips grazed the nape of her neck made him smile; when he kissed her ear, she stifled a giggle that made her body quiver next to his.

"Davide," she whispered against his shoulder a few moments later, her breath warming him through his t-shirt. She pressed her lips to the fabric and trailed soft kisses up to the bare skin of his throat, lingering over the hollows pleasingly. He felt her lips vibrate with his own pleased hum before she broke away to kiss his lips again; she permitted his more probing efforts now, her tongue slipping over his in teasing return each time.

Still he kept his eyes closed, unwilling to chance breaking the fragile spell between them. The night air seemed cooler yet, but their arms and legs twining beneath the sheets warmed rapidly from their sweet, inadvertent friction.

Emboldened, he slipped a hand under the blouse of her pajamas and her stomach quivered, ticklish, at his touch. Instead of a giggle or a sigh this time, she gave a small gasp and he hesitated.

Not now, not yet, Emilia, please…

"Oh, Davide…"

The "Oh" undid him. That single soft syllable and the need and want that filled it, coupled with his name. He'd never heard his name spoken in such a way before, not like that, not meant for him alone to hear.

She moved to kiss him once more, her hand over his, guiding him to cup her breast. He exhaled against her neck, unable to help the eager sound that escaped him. He relished the sensation of her breast in his hand, the flesh so warm and supple, filling his palm as though molded to a perfect fit. Her nipple grew erect beneath his caress and her flannel-clad thigh was invitingly soft as well, against his own firming flesh. He briefly regretted that he hadn't taken off his trousers and then she was gently pulling at his t-shirt. Davide drew away from her to tug it over his head and toss it toward the sofa even as she pressed her palms to his chest, her lips following close behind.

Palms flat and fingers splayed, Emily smoothed her caresses over him, warming his skin under her hands. Her kisses, dewy and warm, followed the trails her hands traced. With deliberate care, she slid lower to focus her attention first on one nipple, then the other, nuzzling the hair of his chest in-between. One finger traced downward, following the trail over his waist to the button of his jeans while he twitched in eager anticipation below her touch.

She pushed him to lie back and he did, his hands once more beneath her pajama top, drawing her to lie atop him while he caressed her back and felt her cling to him, kissing deeply all the while. He could feel the warmth at the very center of her, tantalizingly close through what felt like yards of unyielding fabric.

When she slipped a hand between them, stroking where he strained against his trousers, it was all he could do not to raise his hips in a silent plea for more.

Oddio...Will I be able to stop, if she changes her mind...?

Her caresses were maddening, an insistent, adept touch through the fabric of his trousers, her fingers enacting a light and delicate dance over him until he feared things would go too far, too soon. He moved her hand away and she lay beside him while he unfastened and pushed his trousers down, kicking them off his feet and pushing them out from under the tangle of the bedclothes in a clumsy effort.

Soon his hands were in her hair, holding her to his hungriest kisses yet. She eagerly removed her pajama top, guiding his kisses lower and lower. He luxuriated in the lushness of her body, so like goddesses of old, not the mean icons of modern celebrity. He felt drunk and craved more of her, her curves, her full breasts beneath his kisses and caresses, her scent which filled his lungs with each breath. In every possible way, she was utterly unlike any woman he'd ever known before and he was grateful.

Davide tasted the light sheen of perspiration on her skin beneath his lips and breathed against her trembling stomach, trailing his tongue over her slowly, treasuring every shiver. He kissed his way upward, pausing at her breasts to tease both nipples in turn before kissing her mouth once more, slow and deep. She returned the effort with greater passion and he followed her lead. He pulled at the waistband of her pajama bottoms and when he moved to slip his hand beneath, he felt her body go rigid, though only for an instant.

Then he opened his eyes.

Her brow was furrowed in grim determination, her eyes shut tight. Davide swallowed hard, dizzy from this unexpected change of gears, his eyes adjusting in the near-darkness. Emily's expression seemed to soften and she blinked her eyes open, as though waking from sleep.

"No," Davide said wearily, sinking down onto one elbow. *I should have known.*

She looked up at him, her eyes seeking his in the half-light. He moved away to lie beside her, looking blindly toward the ceiling, unable to face her.

"No," he repeated. "I can't."

"Did I–"

"No. Not exactly."

Silence, then: "I don't understand, Davide. If I didn't do something wrong, what's the matter?"

"It's not 'what', it's 'why'."

"Sorry?"

"It's the why that distresses me, Emilia. This isnt about us, its about the two of *you*. I'm not comfortable with that." He breathed in deep and slowly exhaled. "I can't make love to someone who is on display. I never could. I still can't."

"What do you mean, 'on display'? Who would I be showing myself to here, of all places? Who," she asked, her voice catching in her throat, "besides you? I'm not the sort of person who does this lightly, Davide. I thought you understood."

"You know I do."

"So then how could you say something like that?"

He closed his eyes to the darkness. "Because it's true, Emilia. I will never lie to you—especially not about something like this."

"Tell me who, then."

"Emilia…"

"Tell me, Davide."

"You know who it is, who I mean."

"So why won't you say his name? Why must I?"

Davide wondered if she could hear the shrill notes creeping into her voice. "For the same reason you refuse to speak Italian with me." He swallowed hard and waited to see if she would say anything else.

She didn't.

In his peripheral vision, the digital clock ticked another minute past. Then another. In the meantime, the rush began to subside, his body now logy with fatigue mingled with disappointment of different origins. He listened to her breathing, waiting to see if it would waver or catch again.

"Emilia," he said, keeping his voice low, "I know this isn't something you do lightly. I understood that about you early on. You're like me that way. But not doing this lightly is why I can't do this with you now. You're not ready, it's clear."

"How am I not ready? What makes you so sure of that?" Her protest was scarcely more than a whisper.

"I felt you tense just then. When I saw your face, it was plain to me."

"It was?"

"*Sì*, it was. As much as I want this, as much as I want it with you…as much as I want *you*…this isn't the time. It's not right and we both know it." He exhaled, a pained sigh that seemed to come from the greatest depths of him.

"Emilia, when we make love the first time, I want it to be about *us*, for *us*, not to say *vaffanculo* to Jacopo or to make me feel worthy of filling my own needs. I don't want it to be a selfish thing."

She turned to face him, her cheek limned by the light seeping out from under the bathroom door.

"What if I told you that wasn't what was happening here, Davide?"

He reached out and stroked her cheek with his fingertips, still aching to do much, much more.

"I would want to believe you, Emilia," he said, "but I'm not sure I could. I'm afraid I'd be grasping at any straw you're willing to give to permit me to make love with you." He moved closer, pressed his lips to her forehead once more and remained there as long as he dared to. "No matter how much I might want that, this isn't the right time."

He rolled away from her and slid out from under the covers, groping for his trousers on the floor.

"What are you doing?" she asked, as he stood to fasten his trousers.

Stopping short, he turned to face her. "I thought, well… in light of this, you might want me to –"

"Stay."

"Stay?"

"Yes, please."

"I don't know. With what's just happened, I mean –"

"Davide, please." This time there was genuine pleading in her voice. "It would mean so much to me if you would just stay here for the night. Nothing else has to happen, but… I need you."

He sank back down onto the bed, struggling to focus his eyes on her in the dim light. She sat up to face him, wrapping the blankets around her as she did.

"You need me?"

"Yes, I do. When I got on that train this morning, the last thing I ever expected to find was your smile. I tried like hell to ignore you, too, but that didn't work. I could have told you outright to leave me alone, but I didn't and I didn't know why." She shook her head, a wry expression on her face. "You've been the best thing to happen to me in ages, I think. You've made this whole day more than just bearable. You made it enjoyable, and if someone had asked me if that was possible this morning, I'd have said without a doubt that it was absolutely *not*."

Emily slid closer to him and he found himself drawn closer to her as well.

"The fact of the matter is… I don't think I could stand to be alone tonight. That's why I asked you to go to the airport with me. That's why I asked you up here. I didn't mean for this to happen any more than you did, but…I'm so glad for it."

"Emilia." He sighed her name, reaching for her without thinking to do so. He gathered her into his arms, still wrapped in the bedclothes, and held her tight. She tucked her head under his chin and sighed, too; it was a comfortable, relieved sound.

"Please, just don't leave me here alone. It'd feel too much like the first night after…well…at the time, when he left…for good…I would have sworn that night was eternal. It lasted nearly four years." Emily drew away from him, giving a soft, self-deprecating laugh. "You are my sunrise, Davide."

His eyes sought hers in the shadows, trying desperately to read her expression. Not that it mattered. Even if she were laughing outright at him, mocking him to his face, it wouldn't matter. He was still lost and he didn't care.

I'll want her forever. No matter what, I'll want her for the rest of my days.

"I'm sorry, I'm sure that sounded a bit… melodramatic, Davide. But it's true."

"I only wish I had said it first." He reached to brush back her hair and failed to resist the urge to kiss her full on the mouth. "I'll stay, if that's what you really want."

"It is. No question about it." She pressed close again, her face against his chest, and after a moment or two had passed he felt dampness there.

"*Perchè piangi?*" She shook her head and he tilted her face up to his to see her clearly, gently wiping away her tears with his thumbs. "*Dimmi, amore, ti prego.*"

"I was afraid," she said at last. "I was afraid you would go. Now I'm not. *Grazie mille.* This means so much to me."

"*Di niente, tesoro mio...* but you need to rest now. We both do, I'm sorry to say."

She nodded and drew away from him, spreading the bedclothes back out so he could slip under them once again. He pulled her close, held her tight and felt her arms tighten around him in turn. They settled together under the blankets and he knew that sleep would be swift in coming. He hoped the same would be true for her, lest she think him insensitive instead of weary.

To his relief, her breathing evened out almost immediately, the tension in her body dispersing within a few deep, slumbering breaths. His heart was heavy all the same, weighed down now with an undeniable knowledge.

He had no choice: he would have to let her go.

17

Before he knew what it was doing, Davide felt his hand steal out from under the covers to pick up the phone. The unexpected and unfamiliar ringing still echoed in his head, keeping reason and wakeful clarity at bay as he recognized his surroundings. Holding the handset out away from his face, as though it might bite or scratch him if he moved too close, he brought it to his ear in slow increments.

"*Pronto?*"

There was a considerable pause on the other end, then a cautious intake of breath before the caller spoke at last.

"*Buongiorno*, Ms. Spadon. This is Giorgio with your requested wake-up call." Another pause, then: "Davide?"

Chastised, Davide dropped the phone down onto its cradle without responding. The click of the phone settling into place was loud in the silence of the room and Emily stirred, her arm tightening around his waist.

His eyes adjusted to the gray early-morning sunlight seeping into the room from under the curtains and he turned to her. The scowl on her face indicated her childish determination to keep sleeping and he couldn't help but smile.

"Emilia...?" he began, keeping his voice low, reluctant to wake her. "*Tesoro, dai...* It's time to wake up."

She groaned in response and pressed her face to his chest. Distracted by her bare skin against his side, Davide's attention was drawn there. They had both slept naked to the waist, as it had seemed imprudent to suggest she cover herself before sleeping. Besides, her softness at his side had been a fine inducement to slumber.

In fact, he'd had his best night's sleep in a long while.

Now, however, her breasts were nestled against him, distracting and unintentionally arousing. He kissed the top of her head, willing himself to do the right thing, to resist.

Dio mio… How can I focus when she's right here? She's going to see the state I'm in, no matter what I do…

"Emilia," he said, nudging her a little harder, "you're going to run late."

"I'm already running late," she murmured. She rolled over onto her side, away from him, the effort imbued with agonizing slowness, his eyes following all the way. A moment passed before she moved to the edge of the bed to find her pajama top and put it on.

The whole process took much too long. Where the bedclothes had pulled away, Davide's eyes lingered on her pajama-clad full bottom and he was compelled to raise his leg to hide his reaction from her view when she sat up at last.

One hand fumbled with the buttons of her top, the other pushed her hair back out of her eyes so she could make a quick, sweeping survey of the room. She glanced over her shoulder at him, a still-sleepy expression on her face, and his own sincere smile leapt to greet hers.

"Do *you* want to shower first?" she asked him.

He swallowed hard, shaking his head and fighting back the image of her lathering up and rinsing clean. His groin throbbed and his leg jerked protectively to keep her from seeing it.

"*Prego*—you go first."

"Thanks." She crossed the room to her suitcase and dug through it while Davide drew a deep breath, raising his other leg to hide himself from her view. She moved toward the desk and paused. "Did I put my credit card away last night?"

"I don't remember. I think so."

Emily hesitated for a moment before putting the clothes in her hands down on the foot of the bed. Davide shifted his legs yet again, now certain that she hadn't noticed his condition. He sat up while she went to her purse and took out her planner. She flipped through the contents quickly, dislodging a few items which fell to the carpet at her feet.

The photo caught his eye from across the room, as she picked it up and placed it back in her planner. His stomach did a long, cold turn in his belly.

"Emilia, *cara*, what is that?"

"This?" she asked, holding out a ticket. "It's my ticket for the flight yesterday." She looked down at it with an almost nostalgic smile. "I reckon I might need it as proof that I'd booked for yesterday, or something..."

"No, not that," he said, forcing his own stiff smile in return. "The photo."

To his surprise, she blushed and looked guilty. "Oh, that." She flicked through the other papers and documents to look at it again. "It's Jacopo. This is the only picture I have of him now. I don't know why I kept it, really..."

"You don't have to defend yourself, *amore*. I just wondered what it was."

Liar! Oh, you damnable liar...

His stomach twisted again, the wrenching almost painful now as nausea followed close behind.

Emily shrugged and held it out to him. "Do you want to see it?"

Davide nearly reached for the photo but stilled his hand instead. "No, no... I was just curious."

The guilty smile returned to her face and she put the photo back into her planner. "Part of me wants to throw it away, you know? Then again, part of me wants to keep something to remember him by. I have no idea why, though."

"It's only natural. That's a reassurance, in a way." His stomach did yet another roll and he swallowed down another ripple of nausea.

"I suppose it reminds us that this thing really happened, once we've started to forget the pain."

She put her purse on the desk and crossed to the bed, kneeling on it next to him. "You know, if I'd heard that yesterday, I would have thought it ridiculous."

As she moved closer to him, he sat up straight, her dark eyes pushing his fearful thoughts away.

"What do you think now?"

"I'm thinking," she began, then laughed softly before continuing. "I'm thinking, *What a difference a day can make.*"

He reached out and drew her in for a kiss, closing his eyes to savor the taste of her lips. Everything else fell away, save for her mouth on his, the softness of her hair beneath his hand. He lay back and she moved with him to continue their kisses, the effort natural and unhurried.

There was no doubt that now she felt his arousal underneath the bedclothes when she moved against him. Davide considered what might happen if they allowed things to run their natural course. She'd miss her flight, for one thing. Perhaps she'd decide to stay with him, at least for a while, for another.

And the photo?

Irrelevant.

Still, that didn't make it right to keep her there.

As they parted, he sighed into the fall of her hair across his face, trying to ignore the press of her warm thigh against his groin. "*Mi dispiace*, Emilia. I shouldn't have–"

"Stopped?" she interrupted, smiling, and he had to laugh at the genuine playfulness in her smile.

"*Sì*, but you have a plane to catch and not much time to get ready."

"That's true. I'll be quick as I can, then."

Her actions belied her words, though, as she withdrew and gathered her things at a glacial pace. Her eyes held his all the while and his willpower was fading fast by the time she actually disappeared into the bathroom.

Once the door had closed behind her and the rumble of water through the pipes reached him, he blew out a relieved breath and sank deeper into his pillow. The sound of the shower door closing brought him out of the stupor he was threatening to sink into and he got out of bed, zipping and fastening his trousers as he went.

Crossing to the desk, he kept one ear trained on the bathroom door, repulsed by the thought of what he was about to do—but not knowing might well drive him crazy before the day was out. Had he really seen what he thought he had?

He delved into her shoulder bag and pulled out the planner which, thankfully, was resting on the top of the other jetsam inside. The snap popped open with a small metallic sound which made him flinch. Of course she'd never hear it, but he was convinced that she would come out at any moment and discover him going through her things.

I never meant to, not in a million years, not like some common thief.

Still, his fingers were sifting through the loose contents of the planner, seeking that bright blue sky in the photo.

There.

Hands shaking, Davide drew the photo out and edged the plane ticket out to mark the place where she'd put it. Holding it up to see better, he cursed himself for having left his glasses in his coat downstairs.

Not that he needed his glasses to see what he'd suspected.

A sick dread formed in the pit of his stomach. He leaned toward the door of the bathroom and listened to be certain that the sound of the shower was still constant; it was difficult to be sure, over the roaring of his heartbeat in his ears.

He moved closer to the lamp and held the photo of Jacopo directly under the light, hoping his eyes were playing tricks on him but they weren't. Jacopo sat on the Spanish Steps on a bright, sunny day, the sky overhead a pure azure with a single cloud suspended in it. The cloud itself had a shape quite like a horse's head.

There is something too familiar about this man. Have I seen him before? Where? When?

The shower had shut off. Davide carefully returned the photo to her planner. Hurriedly, he put it in her shoulder bag, checking to be sure that everything was in its proper place. He sat on the bed, his hands still trembling slightly as he fussed with his clothes, debating whether he should just finish dressing, or shower as well.

Hearing the sound of the hairdryer a few moments later, he bent over, his face in his hands. It wasn't just Jacopo. There was something about that photo… the cloud. The *cloud* was what was so familiar. The blue sky and the cloud like a horse's head. The image was emerging again in his mind's eye, all the more persistent for the efforts he made to forget.

Non è vero; non è possibile…

"*Cazzo!*" he snarled, standing up just as Emily emerged from the bathroom, already dressed in faded jeans and a misshapen cable sweater that had once been a pale gray.

"Are you all right?"

"Oh, *sì, sì;* I just, how do you say… 'stumped' my toe on the carpet."

"'Stubbed' your toe," she corrected with a small laugh. "You 'stubbed' your toe on the carpet."

He offered her an embarrassed smile in reply. "Right."

"Well, um…the bathroom's free, if you want it."

"*Grazie*, Emilia," he nodded and she went to her suitcase, kneeling down to repack her pajamas and toiletries.

"I hope I left enough hot water for you," she said, her tone surprisingly light and teasing.

"I'll be fine." He went in and closed the door, then braced himself against the vanity to stare at his reflection in the mirror.

You're crazy. You're insane. You're imagining things so you'll feel better about her leaving. Admit it!

He shook his head, the cold lump returning to his stomach already feeling like a permanent fixture. He was growing certain that he wasn't imagining anything, though he wished it were the case.

More than anything, in that moment, he wished it were all in his imagination.

18

When Davide stepped out of the bathroom, Emily was seated at the foot of the bed, waiting. Her suitcase was packed and ready by her side. The sight of her sitting and waiting in this way brought with it the memory of her in Rovigo, when he had first seen her seated on the platform in the station.

His heart constricted with the same realization it had then, even though, for the most part, the haunted look had left her eyes.

She turned toward him smiling, the expression bright and sunny in spite of the fatigued shadows under her eyes. He smiled in return, unable to resist.

"We should go," he said, forcing the words out and praying to whatever merciful higher power there might be that she wouldn't notice.

If she sees it's killing me, she might not go. She has to go, though, if only for herself.

"Okay," she said. Her reluctance was apparent in the hesitation before she responded.

He took her suitcase in hand and went to the door, waiting while she double-checked that she had everything with her. The door latched shut behind them and they walked to the elevator in an almost funereal silence.

"We should stop at your room to get your coat, shouldn't we?" she asked.

Davide stared guiltily at the floor. "I have a confession to make, Emilia."

She hesitated, her finger poised over the elevator call button. "Yes?"

"It's about last night."

Emily pressed the button, her attention seemingly focused on their hazy reflections in the stainless steel doors. "Uh-huh?"

"I, well…"

A soft chime indicated the elevator's arrival and the doors slid quietly open. She stepped inside and Davide followed, trying not to pay much attention to his slightly ragged appearance in the mirrored walls.

He turned to her and focused on the way her light-brown hair framed her face, her eyes seeming especially large beneath the fringe.

"I had never actually booked a room. I know I told you I did, but that wasn't true. I didn't want you to think that I had, erm, designs on you that way."

Cheeks pinking as she grinned, Emily lowered her gaze to the elevator floor. "I thought so."

"What?"

"Last night, when I saw you behind the reception desk, I thought, *What is he doing down here when he should be upstairs, asleep?* Your excuse was pretty lame, too, to be honest."

Heat rushed into his face at the thought. "Yes, I thought you'd see through that a lot sooner. Why didn't you say anything?"

"And make a hash of your '*bella figura*'? That would have been unnecessarily cruel, Davide."

"*Grazie,*" he said, allowing a hint of sarcasm.

Her widening smile proved she hadn't misconstrued his tone.

The doors opened and they stepped out into the lobby, where Giorgio was standing and talking with the morning shift worker. His glance toward Emily and Davide was admirably discreet, as was the tilt of his head toward the coat rack where Davide's coat and scarf hung.

Giving his own subtle nod in response, Davide crossed to the rack and collected his things while Emily went to sign her bill at reception. He bundled up against the cool morning air already seeping into the lobby through repeated openings and closings of the front doors.

"The airport shuttle will be leaving in a few moments, *signora*. I asked him to wait for you," Giorgio said as Davide approached.

"*Grazie*." Emily smiled, then turned to Davide and reached for his hand. "We should go."

"*Sì*, we should. *Grazie*, Giorgio—*a presto*."

Giorgio gave them a too-sly wink, made his way around the counter and disappeared into the office.

"Come on, then. We can't hold the other folks up," Emily told him, tugging on his hand to lead him to the front doors.

Davide followed, his feet growing heavier with every step.

Time slowed to a crawl while he waited for her to check in. He paced by the exit hall, wondering at this peculiar aspect of Milan Malpensa airport. Her airline counter was blocked by security so only passengers could enter. He was reduced to this expectant waiting and watching in the meantime.

He drew a scratchpad out of his coat pocket and scribbled down his address, considered, then added his office information as well.

Just in case she wants it. Just in case...

Watching the exit, he stuffed the paper back into his trouser pocket, feeling conspicuous.

Nearly an hour passed before she emerged, looking a bit frazzled as she made her way toward him. "My flight's delayed," she said with a sigh. "I'm not as pressed for time as I'd thought I might be."

"That's good," he offered and she nodded in response.

"Yes, it is. At the same time, I want to be off, you know? I hate these delays before a big trip. They make something tiring into something exhausting." She looked up at him, her smile fading to a shy grin. "Then again, some delays are nicer than others."

"*Sì, d'accordo.*"

They strolled toward the stairwell leading down to the security check and the gates, her hand snug in his as it had been all the way to the airport. He found himself memorizing the feel of her hand, noting the size and the way it folded securely into his. He was certain he'd remember the softness against his palm; given time, he might even consider the shape of it, too, all the better to remember when she was far away.

They reached the foot of the stairs and stepped to one side to permit other passengers access to the queue. Still hand in hand, they stood in companionable silence and watched countless others go through. The removal of coats and shoes, purses and bags of all shapes and sizes placed into heavy-duty plastic tubs seemed almost choreographed to the murmur of voices and indecipherable PA announcements. Even the step, pause, pass through the metal detectors had a rhythm and he felt her hand twitch in time with it.

He turned and studied her profile for a moment before she noticed his attention and met his eye.

"I'm glad you came to Milan, Davide."

"You said that last night."

"I meant it, too. I wanted so much to say thank you for your help yesterday." She moved closer and lowered her voice. "And now I have to thank you for last night as well."

"Why for last night?" he asked, also speaking softly. "I acted irresponsibly—I shouldn't have done –"

"You didn't, though. Not really, but you could have." She glanced down at the floor a moment before meeting his eyes once more. "Most men would have. I don't know any who would have stopped."

"I didn't want to stop," he confessed, unable to resist. "I wanted to…to…" He gulped quickly. "I wanted to make love with you."

"I know. I wasn't really ready yet, though, even if I wanted to." She smiled, a warm, embarrassed effort, and his stomach flipped pleasantly at the sight. "But I haven't felt that way for a long, long time, Davide. *Grazie.*" She shook her head. "When I think that we met because of your article, the chance that you saw me reading it... Well, I just don't know."

"There was something more, though, Emilia. It wasn't just that I saw you reading my article, although that did pique my interest. It was just that... When the train arrived in Rovigo and I saw you on the platform, I recognized you."

Emily gave him a sideways look. "You recognized me? What do you mean?"

"I'd seen you in my mirror. Rather, I'd seen the expression on your face there. You had the same shell-shocked, fatigued look I'd worn since Letizia left me. I suppose I'm doing better, but when I saw you, it all came back. I thought, *That's me* -- I knew you had been through something big recently. A big hurt, the kind of thing that leaves you wounded.

"Something has changed in you, in just this short time. You seem shaken, but not stunned, not, not...*come si dice*...blindsided. Last night, I let my fear color my perceptions, my fear of *your* fear, and that was foolish of me. I'll never forgive myself for losing the chance we had last night."

She closed her eyes and allowed him to embrace her. "I wish I had known. I wish you had told me."

"So do I. But I'd rather have taken the chance and not have taken advantage. You are such a special woman, Emilia. You are special to me."

"A fellow foot soldier," she said, laughing softly as they drew apart.

"*Sì, è vero.*"

He saw Emily's hands move toward each other in her familiar nervous habit and sadness gripped his heart.

"I should be going," she said. "My flight will be boarding soon."

"*Sì, sì*... I, um... I wanted to offer you this." Davide reached into his trouser pocket and drew out the sheet from the hotel scratch pad. "I don't know if you'll want it, but...if you would like to write me, I'd be pleased."

Emily stared at the paper in his hand for a moment before reaching out to take it.

"It's my home address as well as my office. *Non si sa mai...*" he added, shrugging feigned nonchalance. *I want to kiss her, kiss her, kiss her; maybe if I do she won't want to go. She'll stay and we'll make this work somehow... If I ask her not to go, maybe she'll stay...*

She slipped the paper into her shoulder bag without reading it. "I'd better go," she said softly.

She put her arms around him and he returned the embrace, his leaden heartbeat thudding until he was certain she could feel it this time. He kissed her, a long, lingering effort she seemed equally determined to prolong. He held her close, his arms tight around her as their kisses deepened, and for the moment at least, the echoing sounds of the PA, the beeping of the metal detectors, the murmur of conversations of strangers and the clack of luggage wheels faded into nothingness.

Why didn't I make love with her when I had the chance?

For the first time he allowed himself to look deeply into her eyes and was struck by how dark they were, how familiar and knowing they seemed. He framed her face in his hands, traced one eyebrow with his thumb and felt her smile broaden beneath his palms. He kissed her again and they embraced once more.

"*Forse è troppo presto, ma...*" he began and sighed, afraid of her reaction to what he wished to say. He forged ahead regardless. "*Ti voglio bene*, Emilia."

She nodded and tightened her arms around him. "*Anche io*, Davide. But how is it possible to care so much, so soon?"

"*Non lo so.*" He shook his head in genuine wonder.

"I should go – it really *is* time now."

"Okay." He watched her adjust her shoulder bag and move toward the thinning line to the checkpoint. "Emilia?"

"*Sì?*" She stopped and turned to face him again.

"I think..." he began, "I... *Penso che devi...*"

"*Devo... che cosa*, Davide? What must I do?"

"*Devi essere felice, qualunque cosa accada.* Just be happy."

"*Anche tu*, Davide."

He waited while she joined the queue and filed along silently with the other passengers. She folded her camel-colored overcoat into a bin, placed her bag atop it, then slipped out of her shoes and added them to her things. When she was next in line, she turned to him again and smiled. He smiled back in spite of the heaviness that wrapped around his chest, making it hard to breathe; his heart skipped and stuttered and he wished he could send her the thought repeating in his mind at his heartbeat's pace.

Torna da me, Emilia; return to me.

She started to go through the archway of the metal detector, hesitated, then faced Davide once more before silently stepping through.

Once she'd gathered her things, she looked back for him. He raised one hand in farewell, his heart aching with the memory of doing the same in Bologna and the knowledge that he couldn't give her such a surprise again.

I would if I could – in a heartbeat, I would.

Their eyes met through the Plexiglas wall and he focused all his attention on her, resisting the urge to cross the queue to see her better.

Torna da me, Emilia; torna da me.

The thought was almost painful in its insistence now, pounding along with his pulse, urged faster by a strange anxiety and sensation of loss. *A completely preventable loss, at that.*

The words formed silently on his lips, mouthed as though she were standing right in front of him.

Ti amo, Emilia.

He wasn't sure if he'd imagined the flicker of her eyes upward from his lips or not. He wasn't sure if she understood at that distance. He wasn't sure if he'd mouthed them at all.

What he knew for sure was that she smiled sadly, nodded and walked around the corner and out of sight.

19

Davide waited much too long, just in case. He stayed outside the queue to the gates long enough to notice the suspicious looks from the security guards, then made his way up the stairs to the ticketing level. After a few minutes he went to the arrivals level and waited there.

Just in case.

When he checked the departures board and found that her flight had already gone, he went to the information desk and asked them to page her over the PA system.

Just in case.

When his phone rang in his pocket, he startled and fumbled it out with shaking hands. It wasn't her, of course; just an SMS reminding him about the faculty meeting that evening.

Still, he smiled thankfully at the young woman who had paged on his behalf and left. He bought a ticket for the bus to *Milano Centrale* train station and climbed aboard, his heart sinking with every step. He hadn't really expected her to stay. He'd never actually asked her to, but he knew that if he had asked, she would have.

She'd be here now. Right or wrong, she'd be here now.

He permitted himself to doze off while the bus moved into traffic and made its way to the next terminal. When another passenger settled in the seat next to him, Davide woke to find himself thinking about the photo in Emily's planner.

Jacopo sat on the Spanish Steps, a smug grin on his face, oblivious to the horse-head-shaped cloud in the perfect blue sky behind him. The image took hold of Davide's imagination and the insistent tickle of recognition – but of *what?* – refused to let go.

You're exaggerating and you know it. Just quit thinking about it.

With effort, he turned his thoughts to more pleasant things. Emily, waking that morning next to him, for one; or Emily stepping out of the hotel bathroom clad in her flannel pajamas, for another.

The smile crept onto his face and he turned toward the window to watch the traffic snarls of Milano pass by. He fancied that he could still smell her scent, that warm, musky fragrance which was all hers and not from a bottle.

His smile broadened as he recalled her on the train the day before. Yes, it was purely egotistical, but he *had* gotten a little thrill when he'd seen her reading his article. What writer wouldn't be pleased by such a thing?

Still, what if *that* had been the first thing about her to catch his eye? Would he have been so compelled to find her? To follow her?

Yes.

No doubt about it. No matter how he thought about it, he was drawn to her, for some wonderful and indefinable reason he was caught and pulled happily along in her wake.

Now there was nothing to do but wait.

Almost two hours had passed before the bus pulled up alongside *Milano Centrale*. Davide took his time walking to the ticketing hall, his hands thrust deep into his pockets to hide from the cold afternoon air. He joined the shortest queue he could find and waited patiently for his turn.

The marble architecture all around him kept echoing that of the photo, still scrabbling distractingly at the back of his mind. Time and again he pushed it away, only to have it stubbornly return.

When he arrived to the ticket window, the clerk startled enough to call Davide's attention to his reflection and the scowl he wore.

"*Mi dispiace, signora,*" he said, digging in his coat pocket for the unused ticket from the day before, He hoped the apology sounded sincere.

She relaxed somewhat and conducted the transaction smoothly, making a simple exchange. Ticket in hand, he climbed the stairs to the bar where he and Emily had talked the night before.

Was it only last night? It feels like it was weeks ago.

He entered the bar and examined the pastry case, his stomach rumbling but seeming a million miles away.

"*Buongiorno, signore,*" the barista prompted politely. "*Come posso aiutarla?*"

Davide realized he'd been standing and staring at the pastry case for several moments without even seeing the contents. Other patrons in the line forming behind him were beginning to grumble. "*Oh, sì… Prendo un caffè macchiato e…*" he waved one outstretched finger at a shelf in the case, "*una pasta sfoglia.*"

The barista smiled and gestured toward the collection of pastries Davide had vaguely indicated. "*Quale?*" he asked. "*Ha una preferenza?*"

"*No, una qualsiasi va bene.*" He took out his wallet to pay, feeling a blush creeping out of his shirt collar and into his cheeks. *Anything is fine, just give me anything, for Heaven's sake…*

The barista kept smiling and selected a beignet from the tray. After a knowing nod to one of his assistants behind the counter, he went on to serve the next customer. Davide took his purchases to the tall table in the corner and turned his back to the rest of the bar, resenting the provocation of the barista's perversely-knowing smile.

Why on earth is he acting like that? I'm sure he gets distracted people in here all the time.

Finishing his pastry and coffee, he wiped his fingertips carefully with a small napkin, then took his cup and saucers back to the counter. Davide placed his order ticket and money on the tray at the register and waited for the assistant to give him his change.

He watched her intently to avoid the shrewd expression on the barista's face but again he was greeted with the knowing smile. Davide considered asking the man what was so amusing but decided against it. *I've got a train to catch, why waste time?*

Nevertheless, he spared the man a quick, not unfriendly nod. When he turned to leave the bar, Davide noted that several of the other patrons were smiling as well.

What are they smiling at?

He passed an elderly couple who seemed particularly amused and the old woman turned to the barista to stage-whisper, "*Sì, Antonio, hai ragione; quello è il viso di un uomo innamorato.*"

His steps stuttering, Davide continued out to the tracks, the old woman's words echoing, strangely pleasant, in his head: "Yes, Antonio, you are right; that is the face of a man in love."

Aboard the train, no matter how he willed himself to forget, to rest, he simply couldn't do it. Once the pleased rush from the strange encounter in the bar had worn off, his head became muddled with other concerns.

The worst part was, the smug *bastardo* she'd been married to had actually only been a small part of it all.

His phone beeped again: another SMS, this time from the department head. Davide texted his response as the train got underway:

Will not be able to attend meeting tonight. Am in Milano but on my way back now. Slow train.

With that, he turned off his phone and tucked it into the inner pocket of his coat. He settled back into his seat and stared unseeing out the window, letting his imagination run riot at last.

Davide had never been so relieved in all his life—nor so filled with dread—to see the signs for *Bologna Centrale*. As he made his way through the *sottopassaggio* and out of the station, he swallowed down a distinct sense of melancholy. Almost everything he saw was imbued with a bittersweet memory of one sort or another, all of them leading back to Emily.

He strode swiftly toward home, hesitating for only the briefest of moments before deciding to leave his knapsack in his office for another day. If he went in to get it he'd be seen and his absence at the meeting would be called into question. Bad enough that he'd have to pass so close to the university on his way home. The likelihood was great that someone might spot him and make an innocently incriminating remark later.

All the same, he much preferred to settle the debate between his optimistic and pessimistic sides. He needed to know for once and for all if his memory was tricking him into believing something too inconceivable to be true.

He wound through the labyrinthine streets to his palazzo, the familiar surroundings hardly registering in his mind, so much white noise in the background of the image of Jacopo on the Spanish Steps, the horse-head cloud in the sky behind him.

His face twisted into a scowl again. With grim determination he forced the expression away. The wind cut sharply at his back as he turned the corner under the porticos and flipped the collar of his coat up to shield his neck. Nonetheless, icy fingers needled their way between his skin and his scarf.

Jacopo. A blandly handsome fellow, in truth. Davide didn't understand the hold the Venetian had had on Emily. Had she really felt that way about him? Or had she, instead, shown such dogged devotion in the face of utter rejection because she'd had no say in the end of the relationship—as Davide himself had done when Letizia had gone?

The clapping of his running shoes on the pavement changed timbre and he acknowledged the change beneath his feet. The smooth paving had ended and now he trod the uneven stone-paved lanes adjacent to his palazzo.

His mind turned to his own mistakes. Why hadn't he made love to her last night? What had he been so afraid of? So what if she was doing it to spite Jacopo? If ever a man deserved spiting, it was him.

He shook his head, knowing rationalization when he heard it. It would have been wrong to take advantage last night. It was all over with now, anyway.

That is, unless she comes back.

Davide stood blinking at the top of the four flights of stairs, in front of his door. Disbelieving, he turned to check that he really was there. He glanced down at his keys in his hand, then back to the door with the varnish flaking around the keyhole.

All at once he didn't want to go in. He reconsidered going to his office to retrieve his bag and the clothes he'd worn in *Padova*. It would be good to get the clothes, to wash them along with what he was wearing now, wouldn't it? At the top step, he shrugged and sighed.

No, it's better to see. Better to know.

His stomach turned along with the key in the lock. The sound of the tumblers dropping echoed the thud of his heart in a sickening, dull rhythm before the door swung open. Taking a deep breath he stepped inside, feeling along the wall inside the door for the light switch. A moment later the gray, dusky light was dispersed by the warm yellow cast from the lamp on the end table. The walls and the dark furniture of the living room, normally so welcoming and familiar, now seemed distant and foreboding after only three days away.

He unfastened his coat and shrugged out of it, letting it fall onto the sofa a moment before he sank down beside it. His eyes focused unwavering upon the picture in the frame, brightly illuminated in its own, sunny little disc of light. The photo was the only one he'd kept of Letizia—one which served as a reminder to him each day of the folly of trying to change someone to suit you.

At last he closed his eyes, knowing he'd been correct after all. The details filled his mind's eye and his stomach roiled under his speeding heart at the image of Letizia, seated on the Spanish Steps, the clear blue sky behind her unblemished, save for that distinctive cloud in the shape of a horse's head.

Bentornata a Bologna
Welcome Back to Bologna
(May, 2008)

20

Graced by the touch of a mild May evening breeze, Davide stood by the Neptune fountain, watching the surface of the water ripple. He continued to look for Emily's ring in spite of its apparent absence. It had to have been either found or lost to the filtering system shortly after she'd tossed it in months ago.

He remembered holding her as dusk had deepened into night, while she cried and confessed the truth to him. He'd only known her for a few hours. A divorcee still in denial after four years of separation—one week after the decree of dissolution—she had been returning to the United States, leaving Italy after ten years.

His stomach twisted as he recalled his failure to tell her the truth of how he felt. How foolish and timid he'd been. Even now, it didn't seem possible—it was the stuff of fairy tales or women's romance novels, surely—but now more than ever he was certain of his feelings. The passage of time allowed a more objective view of that night.

He'd felt it first when he'd seen her in Rovigo, waiting for the train. She'd seemed so sad, burdened by melancholy. At first, he'd mistaken his feelings for sympathy—or better still, empathy.

How wrong he'd been not to tell her what had been growing in his heart, wrong not to have acted upon his feelings, wrong not to have confessed straight away that he wanted her to stay with him, for her not to go back to the States.

It had been a bad idea to take her around the city. Now all of his favorite places held memories of her and it was a bittersweet torture to spend any time in those old haunts. Never mind that he'd visited them by himself for years, or that he'd taken Letizia for disastrous visits before she'd left. When he went there now, he thought about Emily all the while.

It was always Emily.

He hadn't intended to stay with her that night in Milano—or had he?—but all the same, he'd found himself by her side. Yes, he'd wanted her; it shamed him to admit such a thing but it was foolish to deny it. In the end, however, he'd rejected her. He'd thought her need for him was fueled by a desire for revenge against her ex-husband and he'd been too hurt by this thought to see beyond it.

Now he understood she'd wanted to be with *him*, not just to strike back at her philandering ex, but to feel loved and needed, to feel *wanted*—and he'd denied her.

Even now, it made him sick to think he'd made such a bad decision.

He loved her. He had from the very start.

Now he wanted to put things right—but how?

Perhaps it would be for the best if he just moved on. There was no sense in pining for someone who wasn't interested in him. Three months was plenty of time to know that she wasn't going to contact him, in spite of his having given her every possible address he had.

I've done all I can do.

Why hadn't he asked for *her* number at the very least? What had held him back?

The final blow had been the photograph of Emily's ex-husband. Not the subject of the photo, or his smug, gratified smile, but the similarity of the setting to another photo Davide knew all too well.

Ma, com'è possibile?

As coincidences went it was unlikely, although the pieces seemed to fit without him forcing them. Letizia had gone to Roma and had taken a married lover, leaving Davide on his own. Jacopo had gone to Roma, had taken a lover and left Emily. Both had left just over four years ago, too, but…?

But nothing. I need to find reasons I'm wrong *about this, not reasons I'm right.*

The sun had begun to set when he found himself in front of *Il Cuore della Grassa*. His stomach rumbled with keen interest at the rich scents wafting from the open window of the kitchen. He hadn't eaten since breakfast.

I suppose it was meant to be, he thought, grasping the door handle and stepping inside.

The waitress sauntered over, placed his order in front of him, and lingered longer than necessary.

"You haven't been in for a while," she said finally.

"No," he said, shaking his head. He stared at the plate, realizing that this dish was what they'd served when Emily was there with him. "No, I suppose I haven't."

"You didn't bring your girlfriend this time," she observed with a probing tone.

Davide looked up at her, his utensils poised over his plate. "Girlfriend?"

"*Sì*, your girlfriend. The dark-haired one who was with you."

He started cutting the meat, forking it into his mouth, chewing and swallowing without really tasting anything.

"She wasn't my girlfriend."

"No?"

"No. She's a friend, nothing more."

As soon as he'd said it, he wished he hadn't. The longing to take it back sat in his stomach, digesting poorly along with his meal.

The waitress' mouth contracted in an expression between disbelief and mild surprise before she turned and walked away.

Much later, most of the bottle of wine was gone when he stood and went to pay his bill. The tiny restaurant was empty save for the waitress, the cook and himself.

He hadn't meant to stay so late, but the more he thought about going home to his empty flat, the more appealing the idea of finishing the wine had become. Now he was vaguely ill, woefully sleepy and much more depressed than when he'd come in.

The waitress rang up the bill and he noted the charge was far less than he'd expected.

"I think you've made a mistake there," he said gently, not wishing to offend her.

"No, I didn't. That's what you owe."

"*Grazie.*" He closed his eyes for what felt like a moment but when he opened them again he found her watching him warily.

"*Scusi,*" she said softly. "*Stai bene?* You looked like you nodded off there for a minute."

"Did I? I'm sorry." He met her pale blue eyes for a moment and managed a smile, hoping it didn't look like a leer. "*Buonanotte,*" he said, going to the door.

"*Buonanotte,*" she called after him.

Stepping out into the fresh air, he drew several deep breaths one after the other, and his head cleared a bit.

Emilia. Dov'è sei, ora? Perché questo silenzio?

By the time he'd reached the next street, he heard the sound of rapid footfalls behind him.

"*Signore? Signore?* You left this."

Blonde waves bobbing enticingly, the waitress hurried up to him holding out a wallet—*his* wallet, as his hand on his hip pocket confirmed.

Oddio! Where is my mind?

That he knew all too well where his thoughts were was no comfort at all.

"*Grazie mille,*" he said, taking it. He resisted the urge to check inside and tucked it immediately into his pocket.

"I could have brought it to you at home," the waitress told him. "Your address is right inside but I thought I'd try to catch you first. I'm glad I did."

"Me, too."

Her smile showed that she'd hoped to hear something like this. "Going home, then?" she asked, tilting her head.

"*Sì*, I am."

"I'm off work now. Would you like to go get a drink?"

He felt himself sway on his feet and he leaned against the building for support. "I don't know... I've had enough, I think."

And I have to work in the morning, God help me.

"Oh. Would you mind walking me home, then? It's late, and I don't want to go home alone."

Davide paused before answering, not sure whether he should read more into her statement. "Sure, I could do that. The fresh air would do me good."

Her flat was just off the *circonvallazione*. The simple, modern building overlooked the ring road and had high fences all the way around, along with a gate one could unlock by reaching through the fence next to it. She let him in with her, unlocked the main door into the lobby and turned to face him in the flickering overhead light.

"*Grazie*, Davide. This was very kind of you."

He tried to remember telling her his name but couldn't.

"You're welcome, uh..."

"Elena."

He blinked. "Elena?" he repeated.

She blushed, or seemed to. It was hard to tell in the flickering light.

"*Sì*, Elena."

"*Buonanotte*, Elena."

"*Buonanotte*, Davide."

As he turned to go, she reached out to snag his arm and pull him inside. The door closed with a solid *whump* behind them before she pulled him to her, wrapping her arms around his neck and pulling him down for a determined kiss.

Startled, he permitted this initial salvo then tried to draw away but the overhead light's timer cut off and plunged them into darkness. Disorientation kept him from getting away in time to prevent her mouth finding his once again. This time, he didn't try as hard to escape. His hands found her hair, holding her in place while he deepened their kiss.

She tasted of wine and smoke from the wood-fire of the pizza oven in the restaurant. Her hair held the scent of the same and he breathed it in when he brought his lips to her neck, the blond waves obscuring what vision he had in the near-dark of the lobby.

Elena pulled at him again, holding him against her tighter than he would have guessed she could. Davide slid his hands over every enticing curve, enjoying the silky-smooth feel of her; what he didn't find on his own, she made a point of showing him herself. He moaned softly when she cupped him through his jeans, her fingers massaging him and manipulating his arousal to greater, more desperate heights.

"Emilia…" he sighed, pressing into her hand.

"Elena," she corrected, without missing a beat. "Come upstairs." Her warm breath tickled his ear.

Realizing his error too late, he pulled away at last, his heart pounding, his stomach turning.

"I'm sorry, Elena. I can't. Really."

"Sure you can." She cupped him again, rubbing him in an insistent caress. "See? You're practically there already." Giggling, she moved to kiss his neck but he shied away, slipping out from under her touch.

"I *could*, but I don't want to. It's nothing personal, I swear. I just can't."

Elena was silent but he could see her eyes, luminous in what light filtered through the thick glass of the doors.

"I thought she wasn't your girlfriend."

"What?"

"I thought she wasn't your girlfriend. The one you came in with."

He sighed, moving toward the door. "She wasn't. She isn't. But I still can't."

"*Oddio...*" she groaned, clearly disappointed. "Just go, then."

"*Mi dispiace*, Elena. *Veramente.*"

She waved him on and he saw the elevator call button light up under her touch. He pressed the door lock and it opened with a loud buzz and a *clack* that echoed through the whole building.

"*Buonanotte*, Davide," she said as the elevator arrived, filling the lobby with light through the glass panel in the door.

"*Buonanotte*, Elena."

Davide stepped out into the night, his head clearer than it had been before she'd pulled him inside.

I must be mad.

Had he really just rejected the advances of a beautiful woman? He'd had the perfect opportunity to get Emily off his mind—if only for a short while—and he'd passed it up. It wasn't like Elena had much more than one night in mind anyway. No strings attached, either, by the look of it.

He shook his head, crossing the road against the light in the absence of any traffic. A wry grin creased his face when he considered how his father would have reacted if he had known about the escapade.

I'd be disowned by now. No doubt about it.

A glance at his watch filled him with dread. It was later than he'd thought. Picking up his pace, he mentally ran through his planned lesson for the first class of the morning but his thoughts returned resolutely to Emily.

He knew he'd dream about her. Why should that night be any different?

The morning class dragged by slower than any in Davide's recent memory. As the students filed out of the classroom, Davide sighed and slouched in his chair next to the lectern, polishing his glasses with his untucked shirt front.

There was a soft knock at the door, the sound almost lost in the sounds of student traffic in the corridor. Glancing up, Davide found a familiar figure in an ill-fitting brown suit leaning in the doorway.

"*Salve, Professore* Magnani," the man said with exaggerated courtesy.

Davide half-grinned. "*Salve, Professore* Lippi. What brings you this way, Michele?" Putting on his glasses, he rested one hand on the armrest of the chair, preparing to stand. His friend waved him back down, already stepping inside and closing the door.

"Davide, *come stai?*"

Shrugging, Davide feigned incomprehension. "*Sto bene*, Miki. How are you?"

"I'm well, actually. But I'm concerned about you." Michele settled into a chair heavily, making it scrape across the floor. "You haven't been yourself lately."

Davide sat up and reached for the sheaf of papers stowed under the lectern. He began shuffling through them without looking at his friend.

"Haven't I?" he asked, a cold ball forming in his stomach.

"*Dai*, Davide. Come on. What's going on?"

"Nothing, Miki. Honest."

"Are you unwell?" Michele leaned toward him, concern etched in the lines of his square face. "Is there something you need to talk about?"

Snorting laughter, Davide shoved the papers back under the lectern and sat back once more. "No," he said, aware his expression had taken on a bitter twist. "*Non c'è niente da dire.*"

"You haven't been the same since you gave that lecture in *Padova*, what, three months ago? *Dimmi, ti prego.*"

"You're sure you want to get into this? When's your next lesson?"

Michele sat back, crossed one long leg over the other and folded his arms across his chest. "I'm free all day. You?"

Davide nodded in response. "Same here." He paused, composing what he needed to say in his head. *Just get it out, then. Maybe it'll feel better once you do.*

Clearing his throat, he mirrored Michele's pose and drew a long, deep breath.

"I met this woman…"

21

Emily stood at the kitchen counter, knife in hand. In the silence hanging between her and her mother, a pot burbled on the stove, the scent of tomato and beef broth wafting through the air.

"Don't you think that if I had known why he left, I'd have done something about it?"

"Well, I have to wonder, don't I? You're here—he's not."

"He cheated on me, Mother, the whole time we were married." Emily moved to face her mother, who turned away.

"Oh, you're exaggerating. Like always." She flapped a dishtowel in a shoo-ing motion. "You've always been dramatic."

Jaw clenching, Emily turned back to the cutting board and resumed dicing a zucchini. Her throat tightening, the taste of salt rose to the back of her tongue while she blinked furiously. She took a deep breath and released it slowly.

A moment later, *his* voice emerged, warm and comforting.

"Don't let her draw you in."

I won't. Don't worry.

Her smile returned as it always did when she thought of him.

"All I'm saying, Emily, is that you seem terribly chipper for someone who's just gotten divorced."

"It's been three months, Mother. Besides, I've had three *years* to get used to the idea."

A disgruntled "Hmph!" was all she got in reply.

"Anyway, it's over and done with." She scooped the slices of zucchini and carrot into the pot of beef stock and hissed when a few drops splashed onto her forearm, stinging.

"I just think it's a shame."

"I know." Emily wiped down the chopping block and the counter before adding the bowl of string beans and peas to the pot.

"I really liked him."

"I did too, for a long time."

"He was a real handsome man. God, he was the best-looking Eye-talian I'd ever seen…" Her mother let out a low whistle that was more of a wheeze. "He was right up there with that Monticello Mastronni fella."

Shaking her head, Emily went to the sink and rinsed her hands under warm water. She'd long since given up objecting to her mother's embellished southern accent, much less correcting her attempts at any sort of Italian.

"He was, at that," she agreed, seeing it was best to be conciliatory.

"I'm still surprised he chased after *you* in the first place."

"Well, gee! Thanks for that." Emily folded her arms across her chest, a dishtowel wrapped around her hand, surprised she was unhurt by the careless choice of words.

"Brava, Emilia."

Grazie, Davide. I know.

"Oh, now… y'know I didn't mean it like that. It's just that he had his pick of women and all."

"Believe me, Mother, I know he did. Better than anyone."

"Well… I just hope this isn't going to make you bitter."

What, like you?

The words remained unspoken but the temptation was remarkably strong nonetheless. Instead, she arched an eyebrow.

"Yes, it'd be a pity if you turned out bitter like your Great-Aunt Frieda. What an old lemon *she* was."

"Mother, she wasn't bitter. She was a lesbian. It's different."

"All I know is she had one bad marriage and she didn't want men no more."

"'*Any* more'," Emily corrected automatically, then bit her tongue a moment later.

"Oh, sorry—I forgot I had Miss English Teacher in the house. Little Miss English Teacher, who dropped out of college to run off and get married."

"Who dropped out of college and ran off to *Italy* to get married, to the best-looking Eye-talian you'd seen, remember?"

Dammit! I walked right into it, didn't I?

With a sigh, Emily replaced her dishtowel and pointed at the white beans in the colander in the sink. "Put those in at quarter to six, okay? The whole pot will be ready at six. If you put the beans in too soon, they'll fall apart."

"Where are you going, then?"

"I've got some errands to run. I'll be back in time for dinner." She got her gray hooded sweatshirt off the rack in the hall and paused in the kitchen doorway. "Do you need anything?"

"No, I'm fine."

"Quarter to six," Emily repeated, then picked up her messenger bag and left.

The coffee shop had an unspoken rule about not using the Wi-Fi without buying something first, so Emily got in line and waited to order. The usual customers were there, all familiar faces to her by now. Since there was no internet service at her mother's house, she'd been coming to *Grab Yer Cuppa!* for the last two months. The mere suggestion of installing a new phone line had thrown her mother into a fit about Emily trying to change everything to suit herself. Regular visits to the coffee shop were the result.

Nonetheless, in spite of her mother's professed distaste of such technology, Emily had noticed tell-tale signs of parental attempts to read documents on the little netbook computer currently tucked safely away in her bag. A document opened more recently than she recalled, for one example; two or three copies of another she hadn't copied herself, for another.

The tiny redhead at the counter was busy counting the change from the previous customer and launched into her greeting before looking up. "Welcome to *Grab Yer Cup*–" She stopped short and smiled in recognition. "Oh, hi, Emily. The usual for you, today?"

"Yes, Gracie. Please."

"Okay. One *caffè latte* coming up." Gracie turned to call to someone over her shoulder. "Latte—make it darker!" She turned to face Emily again. "We'll bring it out to you, if you want. There was a problem earlier, so Travis is still setting up the milk steamer."

"That'd be nice. Thanks." Emily handed over the exact change for her order and crossed the shop to set up her computer in her favorite spot in the corner.

The tiny laptop had been something of an extravagance upon her return to the States, but the purchase had cheered her up. Its size hadn't seemed terribly practical at first but she'd gotten used to the tiny keys. She was especially fond of the small screen that made it difficult, if not impossible, for others to read over her shoulder. It kept her from having to explain why she might sit for stretches of time not writing, not surfing the 'net but reading and re-reading a particular page of the University of Bologna's faculty listings.

She wished his picture had been included, then decided it was just as well it hadn't been.

I'd only sit here pining for him worse than I already am.

Clicking away to her e-mail login, she became aware of someone standing in front of her table. *A rather tall someone*, she amended, looking up at the dark-haired, blue-eyed man in front of her.

"You had a latte, right?" he asked, indicating the tall paper cup on the tray in his hand.

"A *caffè latte*, yes."

His grin broadened at her response before he placed the cup and a few paper napkins on the table next to her computer.

"*Gra—* I mean, thanks."

"You're welcome. I'm Paul, the manager." He offered his hand and she hesitantly took it.

"Emily. Am I in trouble?"

"Why do you ask that?"

"Because the manager just brought me my *caffè latte* and introduced himself. That's usually a bad combo."

He chuckled and shook his head. "No, nothing's wrong. I just wanted to thank you personally for your loyal patronage."

"Uh-huh. Really?"

"Well, I... May I?" Paul indicated the seat across from her and she shrugged in response.

"It's your place, isn't it? Please, go ahead."

"Thank you." He sat down and folded his arms atop the table, leaning slightly in her direction. "Actually, Emily, I just wanted to introduce myself to you. I've noticed you coming in here a lot and..." He trailed off, his face pinking until he looked positively feverish.

She could almost see him gathering up courage like unrolled yarn before he spoke again.

"If you don't think I'm being too forward, uh... I was wondering if you might consider going out with me sometime."

Glancing down at her apparel—gray hoodie, blue t-shirt and jeans, a pair of nearly-destroyed black Chuck Taylors which had been in a closet for the better part of the last ten years—Emily wondered if Paul had been standing close enough to the steamer to unwrinkle his brain.

"Oh, wow... Paul, you know...I really do appreciate your directness with this, so I think I should be direct, too." One look in his wide blue eyes and she knew she had his full attention. She took a sip of her *caffè latte* and continued. "I've, uh, just come out from a long divorce. I'm not sure I'm the best dating prospect you could find in here."

Disappointment furrowed his brow but he said nothing.

"I'm sorry," Emily finished, feeling her skin warming at the base of her throat, the heat threatening to rise to her face.

"'A long divorce'?" he echoed after a few moments and she nodded. "What do you mean?"

"A divorce takes about three years in Italy."

Paul sat back, his eyes widening. "Italy? You're Italian?"

"No," Emily answered and she had to laugh. "My hus– that is, my *ex*-husband is." *Will I ever get used to saying that?* "I've only been back in the States for three months."

"Cool." Paul laughed and relaxed, slouching in his seat. "That explains so much."

"What does it explain?"

"Well, the way you always say '*caffè latte*' for a start. Then the way you say things in another language when you aren't thinking."

"How do you know I do that?"

"Oh, I hear things. My office is right next to the cash wrap." He pointed to the door next to the register. "How about this, then? Don't think of it as a date. We could just see a matinee, maybe get a Coke after, with no pressure. Would that be okay?"

Emily sighed, trying to think of a way to say 'no' politely. She took another sip of her latte to stall a moment longer.

Oh, where's the harm?

"Okay, Paul. Why not?"

"Great. Are you free Saturday afternoon? I have the morning shift here, so I finish at two."

Emily drew a deep breath, swallowing the lump forming low in her throat. Davide's voice was silent, though she'd fully expected him to speak up right about now.

"That'd be nice. I can be here then," she said, hoping he couldn't tell her enthusiasm had already waned.

"Okay. Great. I'll see you then." Paul stood, pushed his chair back under the table and picked up the tray which had held her drink. "I'd better get back to work."

Smiling at him, Emily watched him go, turning her eyes back to her computer screen when she realized she was paying more attention to his retreating khakis than was appropriate. A belated blush finally rose in her cheeks and she gulped down some of her cooled-down drink before logging in to her e-mail.

I don't believe it. I've actually got a date. But do I really want it?

"So it wasn't so bad, was it?" Paul asked, crumpling up the fast food takeout bags and stuffing them into the garbage bin next to the picnic table.

"No, it was quite nice. Thanks for asking me. You know, I haven't been to a movie since I got back." Emily stretched, enjoying the sun on her face.

"No kidding? Wow. I can't imagine not going to the movies. I go every week."

She chuckled at this. "I used to do that, too. I lived for new releases."

They walked along the paved path toward the boardwalk over the lake. Birdsong came and went from the heights of the trees while a soft breeze swept around them to ripple the surface of the water at the shore.

"You know," Paul began, "we could make this a regular thing, if you wanted. A movie, a burger—or a pizza, if you prefer. I dunno, are you homesick for Italy at all? Like, do you miss your friends there and stuff?"

Davide's smile over his *caffè macchiato* in the café came to mind, giving her heart a small twist.

"Yes and no. Some times more than others, you know."

They continued walking, their footsteps making quiet *thuds* on the wooden planks of the boardwalk. The day was cool but the sun kept it from getting too chilly, and now the breeze sweeping over the lake was enough to make Emily zip up her jacket.

Pausing to look out over the water, Emily leaned against the railing and Paul did the same. In her peripheral vision, she saw him watching her. A faint flush crept into her cheeks and she hoped he'd attribute it to the coolness of the day.

"I can't imagine living so far from home," he said, just loudly enough to be heard over the rustling of the trees on the shoreline.

"Neither could I, until I'd done it."

She turned to face him and he leaned in, paused, then kissed her softly. He had to bend to do so and she had plenty of opportunity to dissuade him, but she didn't.

When he resumed leaning against the railing a shy smile played across his lips. Emily looked out at the water while her coloring returned to normal.

Not bad. Not great, either, but still, it's the first kiss.

But would there be more? Did she *want* more?

They'd walked the full circle of the boardwalk and the islands and returned to the path under the trees while Emily pondered this possibility. Paul continued to ask questions about Italy and she continued to answer, until they stopped in a quiet copse of trees where he pulled her to him and gave her a longer, more determined kiss.

She allowed it, waiting for something more to happen. Maybe Davide's voice would speak up, or she would feel that certain, indefinable *something* that would tell her this was right and Paul was the one she wanted.

Neither thing happened.

Paul's kisses were pleasant enough, yes, but they didn't draw her out of herself—out of the world, for that matter—as Davide's had. That Paul didn't notice the lack of eagerness on her part was sad but somehow it wasn't surprising. All she knew was that she didn't feel what she needed to and she'd have to find a way to end this on a good note.

We take from these things what we want to take, I suppose.

With that came a realization: she knew what she wanted. She just had to figure out how to get it.

Or more to the point, how to get it *back*.

(August, 2008)

22

No ghosts should be haunting her. None at all, save perhaps for the memories of her ex-husband and blessedly, he'd already faded into the depths of her daily thoughts. However, that left room for a different type of haunting.

Images, ephemeral and ghost-like, arrived at the strangest times day and night. Davide's gallant offering of his arm when they walked together, his inquisitive dark eyes, his bright smile. His reassuring embrace, his modest laugh, his kisses and caresses in the darkness.

She decided to remember all of these things as long as she could. Recalling them was like having him with her, always. How this could hurt and yet be so wonderful at the same time—six months on, no less—was a mystery, but she wouldn't trade it for anything in the world.

Each morning she awoke expecting to go a few hours without thinking about a certain handsome professor from Bologna. Each morning she realized, in having had that expectation, she'd already thought about him, so the point was moot.

So he crept into her thoughts throughout the day with the same gentle, subtle tenacity he'd shown her in Italy. Still, it was difficult to say for sure, since she'd only known him for one full day.

One full day which had proven the highlight of the last five years.

One full day about which she had never spoken a word to anyone.

One full day which had given her a cluster of memories to cling to and which soothed her to sleep each night, a pale substitute for his affection and tenderness in the darkness.

Window down and driving on autopilot, she continued over to Ann Arbor, heading to her lunch date with Jenn, who at one time had been her best friend in the world. Although they'd drifted apart over the years, after Jacopo's departure Emily had made a point of getting in touch with her again.

Ten years had passed so quickly and so much had happened to both of them—in her friend's case, marriage, a new career and kids were now all in the picture. Jenn's eagerness and excitement at Emily's call earlier that week had brought the old rush of friendship along with it.

Nonetheless, Emily's thoughts drifted resolutely to Italy, to Bologna, to Davide.

What is he doing now? Is he working? Eating? Sleeping? Making love?

This last drove a tiny spike of jealousy into her heart, although he wasn't hers to claim. That she fantasized he had mouthed the words *"Ti amo,* Emilia," to her before she walked to the airport gate was her problem, not his. Still, did he think about her at all, as she thought about him?

She pictured him walking down one of the streets they'd strolled together, perhaps turning to enter the bookshop he'd pointed out to her, telling her of his fondness for it. She imagined it being sunny, raining hard and foggy all at the same time, her mood flickering from one setting to another with a pleasant capriciousness.

Her desire to see Davide in all sorts of weather was, by now, nothing new. Was that strange? A small part of her feared the answer.

Thinking of the slip of paper in her purse, she smiled. Though she'd written all the information down in her planner, she still carried the sheet from the hotel notepad where Davide had scribbled down his addresses. When she was stressed out—which was often, since she was still staying with her mother—she took it out, read it and re-read it until she felt calmer.

The thought of his spidery, almost indecipherable handwriting made her flush with tenderness, as it had the first time she'd ever seen it. She pictured him writing, scrawling the notes on his lecture pages, or on the slip of paper he'd given her with his addresses, and a physical ache to hold him close would grip her.

However, she had yet to contact him. She resolved that she would, though. Soon.

Jacopo's e-mail that morning had made certain of that.

"Please, Jenn! If you keep squeezing like this, you're going to break me!"

With a final *squee!* Emily's friend released her at last, holding her by the shoulders and turning her from side to side.

"You look great, Em. Seriously, seriously great."

"Thanks." Emily's eyes skimmed over Jenn's now slightly rounder figure. Naturally, she couldn't age like everyone else and look dumpy—instead, she'd taken on Marilyn Monroesque measurements. "You're looking pretty good, too, you know. Marriage agrees with you."

Jenn shrugged. "After the fourth year, I guess it started to take."

"Or after the second kid, maybe?"

"Maybe. But, damn, Em, look at yourself!"

As Emily waved her away, Jenn pulled her in front of the door of the restaurant, pointing to their reflections in the glass.

"Honestly… you look stunning."

Emily took a moment to sort out that it was, indeed, her own reflection she saw in the glass doorway. *God, she's right. Have I really changed this much? I look better than I thought.*

"Let's just go in, okay?" she huffed. "I didn't have breakfast this morning; I'm starved."

"Fine, then, let's go." Shaking her head, Jenn blew out a sigh. "You still can't take compliments, can you?"

"I guess not." Emily gave her friend a grin. "But thanks for trying."

Once they'd placed their orders and been served their drinks, Jenn leaned across the table and whispered, "So, did you hear about Jason?"

"No, what about him?"

"He heard you were back. He called me and wanted to know if you really were back in Ypsi."

"*Fuck.*" It came out louder than she'd meant it to and Emily clapped one hand over her mouth. Jenn's snorting laugh didn't help dispel the impression that all eyes in the restaurant had turned their way, either. Folding her arms on the table, Emily buried her face for a few moments, trying to keep a fit of giggles at bay. "You're not serious," she said, at last, dragging herself upright once more.

"I'm dead serious."

Emily bit back the Italian curses that threatened to flood out, although the whole litany would have been immensely satisfying to say.

Drawing a deep breath, she refocused on the matter at hand. "Why did you tell him I was here?"

"I *didn't*. I don't know how he found out. Hell, I don't even know how he got my number in the first place."

A pause, then they spoke at the same time.

"Your mother."

"Mom."

The server passed and Emily reached out for him. "Are you serving alcohol at lunch?"

Jenn waved the server on, shaking her head. "She's joking," she said, then turned back to Emily. "I thought you didn't drink."

"Looks like a good time to start, doesn't it?"

"Em…"

"I know, you're right. Dang, he's got a nerve!"

Jenn slapped the tabletop lightly with one hand, raising her glass with the other. "And she slips back into the vernacular in record time!"

Emily laughed and took a sip of her cola. "I can't avoid it, living with Mom."

"Good Lord, why don't you move out? You said in the e-mail the divorce settlement was generous enough."

"Yeah, well… I don't want to, not just yet. I don't even know how long I'm staying here."

"Where were you thinking of going, Mouse? I mean, Em. Sorry."

"It's okay, Sissy. I've kinda missed being the Mouse."

They both laughed and the server arrived with their appetizer orders. Emily eyed the basket of fried mozzarella and potato skins with a guilty grin. She thought of Davide and the look of horror which would surely cross his face if he saw her eating such a thing. She wanted to laugh and cry at the same time.

The sensation passed quickly but not quickly enough.

"What was that, then?" Jenn took a few samples and put them on an empty plate, eyeing her.

"What was what?"

"That look on your face just now."

"I don't know what you're talking about." Emily plucked a couple of mozzarella sticks out of the basket and put them on her plate. Using her knife, she cut one into three pieces. The hot cheese collapsed and oozed out of the breading in a somehow saddening way. "Somewhere, an Italian is having a stroke over this. Not from eating it, though."

"Answer the question, Miss Mouse."

"It's nothing. I don't think so, anyway."

"I'll stop pushing, then. But I will say this," she paused, waiting for Emily to look her in the eye before continuing. "Quite frankly, divorce seems to be agreeing with you. If I didn't know better, I'd be willing to swear you were in love."

Emily let herself smile at this. "Would you really?"

"Yes, I would. So, where are you thinking of going?" Jenn gasped. "Are you going *back*?"

"To Jacopo? Lord, no!"

"Well, to Italy, then. Is that it?"

"Not exactly. Jacopo wrote me an e-mail this morning. We might have a buyer for the house."

"Oh." Jenn paused, considering. "You have to go back for *that*? Can't you get your lawyer or whoever to take care of it?"

"Do you think I'd really just trust him to give me a fair deal? Besides, I own half that house--I need to be sure I get my share."

"Yeah, but...to go all the way back there. To, you know, to *see* him again? Won't that be painful?"

"I'm sure it will be, but what else can I do? He said it's going for almost half a million euro—can you believe it? I can't take a chance that he'll find a way to screw me out of my share of that. It's more money than I'll ever see for the rest of my life!"

Jenn nodded, focusing on the potato skin on her plate. "I guess I can understand that. All the same, you've got to find a way to stick it to him, you know? Some way to show him you've so moved on, that he doesn't have a prayer at all."

"He doesn't want *me*. That's plain enough. He's even got a fiancée."

"That sure didn't take long. Jesus, the ink is barely dry on the papers."

Emily speared a piece of mozzarella, which had already congealed to an unappetizing heap on her plate. She ate but didn't really taste it. "It doesn't matter to me. Really," she insisted.

"I can't figure you out, Mouse. The last letter you sent me before you came home sounded like you'd never get over him. Then you get back and I don't hear from you for six freakin' months and when I finally do see you, I find...this!" She spread her hands out as if revealing the conclusion of a magic trick. "What happened to you?"

Emily shrugged again, meeting her friend's gaze fully. "I had an epiphany: *Life goes on.*"

The server arrived and cleared their old plates, setting their entrees before them. "Do you ladies need anything else?" he asked, smiling at Emily.

She smiled back, tilting her head just so, the way she'd always seen Jenn do it. "I'm good, thanks," she said and the server's smile broadened with genuine pleasure.

The server looked at Jenn, who merely nodded and then turned back to Emily. "Well, then. Someone's got a secret, eh?"

"Maybe. Maybe not."

"I'll get it out of you, you know."

"Uh, huh. I'll bet you will. It's not much of a secret, though. I don't think so, anyway." Emily sipped her cola and put it back on the coaster with over-cautious precision. "First, though, you've got to finish telling me about Jason."

"Ugh..." Jenn shook her head and busied herself with her meal. "Not much to report there. Like I said, he gave me a call and asked if you'd really come home. I said I had no idea and could he do the planet a favor and just fuck off. He didn't come right out and say it, but I'm pretty sure your mom told him you were here."

"So why didn't *she* tell me he'd called? Why send him to you?"

"I don't know. Maybe she thought it would be better if I told him? That way you wouldn't be as angry with her."

Emily bit her lip, considering the possibility. "Either way, I'll have to discuss this with her. Crap."

"Get your mind off it for now. Tell me what this secret is."

"There's nothing to tell, really."

Jenn stared at Emily, deep in thought. "It's a man," she said, sounding like she was in a trance. "Holy shit! Did you meet someone?"

"Sort of," Emily said, focusing on cutting several pieces of steak.

"'Sort of?' What does *that* mean? How do you 'sort of' meet someone?"

Her stomach twisting anxiously, she weighed her options. She could keep evading until Jenn wore her down, or she could just plunge on in and tell her best friend all about her encounter with the Bolognese professor.

It'll be just like taking off a bandage. Just rrrrip! *and it's over. Done.*

She decided to take the plunge.

Her story didn't take as long as she'd thought it would, in part because she chose not to tell everything there was to tell. Those thoughts she carried with her into sleep remained private, along with all the most personal details. Still, Emily was compelled to mention the one puzzling part of the whole evening in Milan: why had he thought she was acting out of revenge against Jacopo?

They had moved from the restaurant to sit in Jenn's minivan, both of them filled to the brim with the addition of dessert and coffee, which Emily had consumed without being fully aware of what she'd had. The need to keep her hands busy, to occupy herself somehow while she explained that day in Bologna and that night in Milan, had been surprisingly strong.

Jenn's eyes were focused somewhere in the middle distance, occasionally flicking away to follow a vehicle passing on the road in front of the restaurant. Emily watched her watching the road, noting the way her friend's perfect profile had softened over time.

We've both changed so much, haven't we?

"So he just stopped all of a sudden?" Jenn asked.

Emily nodded. "Yeah, he did. Things were going right along, but then he stopped and said he couldn't be with me if I was going to be 'on display.' I still don't know what he meant by that." She sighed heavily, recalling his troubled face and the way the white of the pillow seemed to glow in the half-light. "He thought I was trying to get back at Jacopo somehow—sure, why not?—but that wasn't the only reason I was with him."

"Could I ask you a really...*nosy* question?"

"Sure, I guess so."

"Precisely *when* did he stop? What was happening?"

Emily swallowed hard, thinking back. "He was about to, um... he was about to, you know, *touch* me."

"How? Where?"

"Come on! You know…" Emily could feel the blood rising in her face and was grateful for the tinted windows around them. "He was putting his hand under my pajamas and…" She mimed the action over her stomach and paused, her blush fading faster than it had come. "Oh…"

"What is it?"

"My scar. It was because of my scar."

"He stopped because of your scar?"

"No, no, he didn't." A tear slipped down her cheek and Jenn reached forward quickly, resting her hand on Emily's arm.

"Mouse? Are you okay?"

"I'm fine. Really I am, but oh, God what a stupid mistake." Emily wiped her face with the back of her hand and more tears fell. "I don't believe it. I froze up a bit when he touched my scar, but he thought it meant something else. He probably didn't even notice the damned thing."

She read the clock on the dashboard and faced Jenn again. "All this time, I've been too scared to really think about it. I reckoned it meant that he'd changed his mind, but it just didn't sit right with me, you know?"

Jenn smiled sadly. "Well, now you know better."

"Yeah, I sure do." Emily thought of the piece of paper in her purse and smiled too. "And so will *he*, very soon."

23

O ne, *two, three, four—one, two, three, four...* It was unclear when
exactly the numbers had become a mantra.

One, two, three, four—one, two, three, four...

Each number corresponded with the pounding of Davide's
running shoes on the asphalt as he climbed the hills outside the city.
Odd numbers for the right foot, evens for the left, breaths drawn and
expelled with each four-count.

The August heat was peaking, sauna-like in its intensity but he
kept pushing forward. It was the only way to empty his head of any
distractions. He'd lost track of how many kilometers he'd biked, he'd
run as far and as fast as his legs would carry him yet he couldn't
outrun the empty flat which awaited him in the city center. He
couldn't outrun the memory of her face in slumber, or the sound of
her sighs that night in Milano.

One, two, three, four—one, two, three, four...

Emily was a ghost persistently haunting him and he couldn't
shake her. He'd given her every possible means to contact him—
home and work addresses, e-mails, phone numbers. Six months had
passed since he'd bid her farewell at the security gate in Milan
Malpensa Airport and he'd heard nothing from her. Only her voice
whispered in his head, in his memories.

When he biked or ran, however, her voice quieted. It never stilled; if it did, he would have been sorry to lose it—but it subsided, drowned by the rhythm of his pacing.

Every once in a while, however, she broke through.

One, two, three, four—one, two, thr–

He stumbled over a break in the asphalt and went sprawling, cursing as he fell. For better or worse, he'd mostly landed in the dirt alongside the shoulder. Still, he'd managed a fair amount of road rash on his way down.

Now that he wasn't running, his breath came in great, heaving gulps, his heart pounding painfully. It was probably too hot for this; common sense said he should have gone out earlier in the morning, or late in the evening. However, the impulse to run had come when it had come and the need to—God help him—forget her for a while had been too strong.

After checking his pulse, he set about picking the bits of gravel and assorted detritus out of his knees and the heels of his palms. Shaking his head to dislodge the sweat threatening to drip into his eyes, he noted the cyclist coming his way, one of several who had been descending the hill he'd been climbing.

He continued brushing off the dirt and stood when the cyclist slowed and circled back in his direction.

"Davide?"

Merda. He raised one hand in belated greeting, recognizing his colleague's voice. This figure clad in multi-colored spandex looked nothing like the shambling professor of humanities he knew at the university. However, the voice like grinding gears was unmistakable.

"Corrado? *Ciao, come va?*"

"*Va bene...* Better than you, I think. What happened?"

"I fell," Davide answered, looking back toward the city beneath its shroud of heat-haze. "You've had a good ride?"

"Not too bad." Corrado nodded and cycled past, fishing in the pocket on the back of his cycling jersey. He tossed a tiny first aid kit to Davide and looked out at the city too, circling slowly. "It's quiet already—lots of folks heading out on holiday early, I guess."

Davide opened a tiny bottle of peroxide and rinsed his cuts. Finding a small gauze pad, he daubed carefully at the scored skin, swiping the blood and dirt away. "You're going away at *Ferragosto*, too?"

"*Sì, sì...* Only for two weeks this time; one week in the mountains, one week at the sea. Maria's convinced the boy needs both this year. *Gesù*, that woman is draining me dry..." Circling around to make another leisurely pass, he took the kit back from Davide and tucked it in place. "What about you? Is it sun or sea for you this year?"

Davide shook his head, tugging his shirt up to wipe his face dry. "I hadn't planned anything, to be honest. Holidays just got past me this year."

Corrado rode away and then returned, precariously maintaining his balance without dislodging his feet from the bike pedals. "That's no good. Why don't you take my place for a while?"

"I don't think Maria would like that very much," Davide said and laughed, knowing that wasn't what Corrado had meant.

"*Bravo*, Davide. *Sette più.* Still, why don't you? I've paid for two weeks in both cases already and the places will be sitting empty for half that."

"I don't know. I appreciate the offer, though."

"Think about it, then. Let me know by next Thursday and I can get you the keys for the mountain house before we leave Friday afternoon."

Davide paused, considering this.

The last thing I need is two weeks without anything to do anyway. I'll go crazy—and how will I know if she's written me?

"I'll think about it," he said, more to placate his colleague than anything.

"Do that. I had better get back now. Call me."

"Sure, sure..." Davide nodded and waved him on.

He knelt to tighten his shoelaces and felt the slow pull and tear of the fresh wound on his knee as he did. The heels of his palms throbbed, finally subsuming the sting of the peroxide, and he shook his hands to dull the pain further as he stood up again. He arched his back with care, stretching before he resumed running, this time for home.

There wasn't even a breeze as he headed downhill, carefully picking his way and gaining speed.

One, two, three, four—one, two, three, four…

Soon the soothing repetition was back in place and he concentrated on that for a while. The closer he got to the city, the hotter the day became, and he reduced his pace to a quick walk by the time he reached the center of town. Winding back to his palazzo, the idea of a shower and a nap to escape the heat had already taken on an irresistible appeal.

Stepping inside the lobby area of his building, he paused to check his mailbox, even though he could see the space behind the narrow Plexiglas window was empty. Glancing down he found a jagged thread of blood trailing down from his knee to soak into his sock. With a sigh, he turned to ascend the stairs and tugged his shirt up to wipe his face again.

"Eh, Magnani!" an elderly voice called. Davide paused halfway up to the first landing to see who it was.

"*Sì?*" he called back, before understanding he'd have to go back down to find out what they wanted. Once in the lobby, he braced himself for what he knew would be an unpleasant encounter. "*Signor* Montanari, *come sta?*"

"*Prendi la tua posta.* Your mail was in my box again," the old man scolded, as though Davide had done it himself.

"*Mi dispiace*; I've told them several times they're putting it in the wrong box. I don't know why they do."

Mr. Montanari grunted in response and looked Davide up and down, wrinkling his nose in obvious distaste for the younger man's unkempt condition. Annoyed, Davide again pulled up the bottom of his t-shirt and wiped his face with it, exposing his stomach, well aware this would lead to even more unpleasantness in the future.

For now, his neighbor did his best to turn on his heel—a shuffle step punctuated with the rubberized *thump* of his cane—and pretend to ignore him.

Summoning the last reserves of energy he possessed, Davide hurried up the four flights of stairs to his flat. He prayed his legs would hold out until he at least got past his front door.

As soon as he stepped inside his flat, his knees threatened to give out, but not from fatigue. The address on top of the stack of mail the old man had given him, now smeared by the sweat on his hand, was in Ypsilanti, Michigan.

Emily.

His first instinct was to tear into the letter right away. Instead, after putting the letter on the telephone table by the front door along with the rest of the post, he forced himself down the hallway, stripping as he went.

A shower first. Clear my head, clean these scrapes and wash these clothes. Then I'll read it. A few more minutes won't kill me.

He piled his damp, dirty clothes into the washing machine and added soap, then turned to wash his shaking hands before he removed his contact lenses. The desire to retrieve the letter stronger than ever, he closed the door of the bathroom and, as an additional absurd touch, locked it.

In the shower, the shock of cold water on his back made his breath freeze in his chest. After a moment or two it ran warmer and he struggled to concentrate on something, anything, besides the letter in the hallway.

The water-softened scab on his knee broke once more and a thread of blood smeared and diluted into the slow drain of water on the shower floor. It stung when soap seeped in and again when he rinsed the soap away. His palms still throbbed, too, but that pain ran much, much deeper—almost distant, really.

His running mantra seeped into his consciousness, thrumming away in a tick-tock rhythm in his head. The throbbing in his hands and knee kept time while he toweled off.

One, two, three, four…

Never mind...

With another push of will, he managed to tend to his knee and his hands, cleaning them with great care though his eyes watered. Soon he made his way to his bedroom, pulled on fresh clothes and sat on the bed, now strangely afraid to see what Emily had written.

The phone rang and he jumped up, stuffing his feet into a pair of disintegrating house slippers before he shuffled down the hall to answer.

"*Pronto?*"

"*Signor* Magnani?"

"*Sì?*"

"This is the Biblioteca Sala Borsa. The books you requested have arrived. As we're closed next week, you may wish to collect them by this weekend."

A wave of relief washed over him even as he looked at the letter next to the telephone. "*Grazie.* I'll pick them up today," he said, picking up Emily's letter and putting it in the book bag next to the table.

"They'll be at the desk."

Upon arriving at the Biblioteca Sala Borsa, Davide went directly to the first floor. He strolled the perimeter of the atrium, watching the other patrons, thinking all the while to Emily's letter. Finally, he pulled the letter out of his book bag as he settled into a vacant seat to examine it, feeling a smile tug at his mouth. Her handwriting was very neat; he thought he could see traces of where the ink had bled under whatever she'd used to make the straight-edge lines at the bottom of the letters.

His hand shook lightly and he rested it on his lap to still it. He hadn't felt like this since the first time he'd ever kissed a girl: nervous, exposed, even transparent.

He held up the envelope and with a keen eye, he studied the stamps, the return address, even the watermark on the back, above the seal. He resisted the urge to smell the envelope but knew that had he been at home, he would have done it.

Fingers tapping an ever-changing rhythm against the seal of the envelope, he turned his gaze back to the expanse of Plexiglas flooring of the *piazza coperta* two stories below and the Roman ruins visible underneath it. Carefully slipping his finger under the flap of the envelope, he tore the top edge open. *I'll just read it quickly, then go collect my books at the front desk.*

He thought there was a hint of her scent on the pages inside.

No—she didn't wear perfume...did she?

He shook his head and unfolded the airmail pages with care. Here her script wasn't as neat or controlled, but it certainly was small. He fished out his glasses and put them on to make out the tight loops and tiny fragments of thought. To his great surprise, he found she had written in Italian and his nervousness returned.

"Caro Davide," the letter began, *"I am writing this in Italian for a simple and ridiculous reason—my mother keeps looking through my things and if I don't send this letter right away, I don't want to face another Inquisition like I did when I got home. I'd have sent an e-mail, but I think she might have my passwords and is, in her inept fashion, snooping on my computer.*

"'Home,' what a word. House and home are the same on this page, in your language, but my reality is so different. I love her—my mom—but I just don't like her very much right now. She is convinced I ran Jacopo off, that I didn't fulfill my end of the marital bargain somehow. No matter what I say, it's my fault he left. So what can I do? What do I do?

"I argue, I cry and then I go out or lock myself in my room like a sullen teenager. How is it our mothers can manage to reduce us to this?"

Davide grinned and allowed himself a small chuckle. He glanced around the Sala Borsa and then resumed reading the letter.

"I'm very lucky, though. I have something that she doesn't know about—not yet, maybe not ever—which makes me feel happier than she believes I have any right to be.

"I have an exquisitely happy memory tucked away like a precious jewel, all my own. It's still quite new, the color and clarity are positively radiant and I can adore it whenever I wish.

"I hope you do the same."

Davide looked up again and noted the light fading from the high windows overhead. He folded the letter and put it away, then went to the stairs. *I've got to get my things and go.*

Heat bounced off the paving stones to greet him when he stepped outside, the piazza filled with more sun than he'd expected. He moved to one side of the doorway to permit himself a moment to adjust, then walked toward the fountain, Neptune standing tall and proud in the midst of it.

So, old man, did you appreciate her sacrifice? Davide watched the rippling waters, squinting against the sun reflecting off the surface there. *Did you decide to give her a break now that she's gone?*

"What should I give you to bring her back?" he asked quietly so passers-by wouldn't hear. "Another ring? Blood? A limb?"

He looked toward the church and sighed.

Santo Giuda Taddeo? Sant'Antonio? To whom do I make my supplications, then? In the end, is she a lost person or a lost cause? For that matter, is she even mine to claim?

The letter was maddeningly vague on that point.

He turned for home, shuffling through the piazza on leaden feet.

At the edge of the piazza, he stopped and looked back at the fountain. In his memory, he felt the cold February night descending, her arms warm around him and his mouth on hers while they stood next to the sea god.

It was too distracting to permit himself to recall much more.

At home, he continued reading.

"I hope you do the same and that the memory means as much to you as it does to me. Davide, you stood out to me from the very first moment, the first time I saw you, on that train. At the time, I wasn't sure why.

"After our talk in Milan, I think I understand what it was which caught my attention. Two things, actually: one was a look of understanding you had in your eyes. You were a wounded person and I was, too. I sensed some of myself in

you and you said you did, too. Once I got past my fear and my trained distrust, I saw it much more clearly—but I guess I didn't recognize it right away."

Davide slumped against the arm of the sofa. Had he really said these things to her that day? He must have. If he hadn't, it was eerie how she'd described precisely what he'd felt at the time. It was surprising to find he'd forgotten even a single moment of that day.

"The second thing which caught my attention was more obvious. Your shoes. I've never seen an Italian man with such scuffed shoes before, even though they were running shoes."

He had to laugh at that.

"That was all the evidence I needed that you were different from the crowd, from the others—most especially, from Jacopo. The two of you couldn't be more different, or have less in common. Even now that reassures me."

His stomach roiled in protest.

My God, she couldn't be more wrong.

24

The handwriting on the envelope almost made her heart stop before she'd even read what it said. The loose, loopy scrawl was as familiar to her as her own writing, after months of having read the notes and corrections on his lecture over and over again. It was all she needed to see to know the letter was from Davide.

How her mother had missed the Italian postmark in the rest of the mail was a mystery, but she wasn't about to call it to her attention. Although her mother's purse and car keys were gone from the hall table, Emily slipped the letter into her own bag. The urge to sit down and read it right there and then was almost overwhelming, but she resisted.

After a glance out the kitchen window to reassure herself that her mother was indeed out, she went to the kitchen and got a soda and a packet of saltine crackers. Making a mental note to get a post office box, she climbed the stairs to her room and locked the door behind her.

She placed the letter on her desk, sat down and ate two of the crackers, willing her hands to stop trembling.

When she'd sent the letter to Davide, she'd made note of the date on the desk blotter calendar. A comparison of that date to the postmark on his letter proved, surprisingly, that only two weeks had passed.

Which means he mailed this the day after he got mine. Maybe even the same day.

The realization gave her heart another hopeful jolt.

With trembling fingers, she slid her father's letter opener under the gap at the top of the envelope. With a careful, swift slice, she opened the top and then placed the blade on the desk.

The scents of paper, ink and something more elusive emerged as she pulled out the folded sheets of stationery and smoothed them under her hand. When she brushed her fringe out of her eyes she caught the smell again. This time she recognized it: his cologne. She breathed deeply to catch the scent again and felt a sharp pang. Hadn't she admired his cologne in the café that morning, and savored the day's last traces of it that night when they'd curled up together to sleep?

She focused on the pages before her, ignoring the tightness in her throat. As always, the shapes of his letters were soothing, visible echoes of his voice on the page.

"Cara Emilia,

"I respond in italiano *as per your request.*

"I am sorry that you are struggling so, at home. It was my sincerest wish that you would be happy there, after what you went through here. You are right, however, in saying that our mothers possess a special gift for reducing us to our place as their children, no matter what our ages might be. For some, this must be a wonderful thing. (Perhaps not so much for us, eh?) Still, I trust that you will find strength and solace somewhere."

Emily smiled, nodding. "I do," she told him. "I only wish you knew where I find it."

"I also trust that your mother does not mean to hurt you. She probably doesn't understand what transpired between you and your husband. I am sure that you, like many children, sought to hide the worst of your own pain in order to protect her from worry.

"Still, it cannot be easy to endure. And for this reason, I feel responsible for some of the hurt you carry."

"What?" Emily asked aloud, glancing around the room, as though she would find Davide there, waiting for her response. She stared at the page before her, her vision blurred in confusion until she concentrated on his writing again.

"I must have hurt you further with my actions in Milano. I sincerely wish I hadn't acted so rashly, Emilia. That this must distort your fond memories of our time together is something I fear.

"I see now what you wanted from me was not collusion in any sort of vendetta against your husband. You only sought comfort and I denied you this, out of my own foolish pride. Truly, this is something that I regret like nothing else I've ever done in life.

"Emilia, if you can forgive me, it would be the greatest gift I could ever receive."

"Oh… oh, my God…" Her hand went to her abdomen, her thoughts flashing back to that night in Milan and his last-minute change of heart. "You thought…? You didn't notice at all, did you?"

An unexpected tear slipped down her cheek and she drew a shaky breath. "You silly man—you *still* don't get it?" She held the letter up and shook it as she might shake a particularly obtuse friend by the shoulders, then placed it on the desk. She pushed the letter away before her tears could fall and smear the ink, then stood and crossed to her nightstand to get a tissue. A sudden laugh escaped her and she shook her head, returning to her desk to pull out fresh paper to write her response.

As much as she loved seeing his messy handwriting again, she longed to be able to sit down and write him a simple e-mail. Not for the first time, she resented her mother's refusal to get a proper Internet connection. Even more so, she felt a fresh surge of anger that the woman had made those fruitless attempts at reading files on her computer.

"I guess I have to spell it out better, then." Her stomach flipped unpleasantly and she sighed, considering what she'd have to tell him. "Everything," she said. "I have to tell you everything. But…damn it, it wasn't you, Davide—it wasn't *you!*"

Feeling a momentary foolishness for speaking out loud—some habits were harder to break than others—she bent over the sheets and began scribbling her response.

By the time she'd finished, evening had fallen and the room was nearly dark. She heard her mother downstairs, preparing dinner in the kitchen, the TV blaring one of the evening news programs.

Re-reading her letter in the glow of her desk lamp, a sense of lightness overcame her. The all-over feeling was similar to the one she'd had in her hand after she'd tossed her ring into the fountain in Bologna. She closed her eyes and saw Davide's perplexed expression in her memory, as clear as on the day it happened.

Her throat tightened once more, the longing for him pulling at her deep inside until it was a physical ache. She rubbed her arms until the numb, tingling feeling ceased. Then she stood, put the letter into an envelope and sealed it before she tucked it into a drawer.

She'd mail it in the morning and she'd dream of him that night. That much, at least, was given.

The last light had gone from the sky, leaving the living room in darkness. Davide placed the letter on the end table and switched on the light. He had no idea how long he'd sat in the dark, reflecting on what she'd written, until he was unable to see what was on the page.

He'd been even more wrong than he'd thought that night. In his determination to impose his own feelings on their encounter, he'd misread everything.

It all made sense, in retrospect. Her body language hadn't spoken of determination, but of fearful expectation.

Judging by the letter she'd sent, she wasn't unduly hurt in the end. There was a small sense of relief with the realization, but it came with a new species of regret: that of having lost an opportunity to convince her to stay. *The* opportunity, perhaps.

The rest of the letter had its own intrigue. The house in Rovigo, the one which she partly owned, was up for sale. An interested buyer had put in a bid a few weeks ago and there was a chance she might have to come back to Italy for the sale.

The idea gave him a glimmer of hope. If she came back to Italy, she might return to Bologna. And if she returned to Bologna...

Davide pulled off his glasses and pinched the bridge of his nose, his thoughts stubbornly returning to the other topic of the letter. He'd had no idea of her history, that she'd experienced such a loss. She'd mentioned her father was dead, that her mother was distant, but she'd never mentioned anything like this.

A miscarriage at seventeen? Dio bon...

He picked up her letter and read the passage again.

"...I guess it all happened because I was lonely. My father was gone, my mother and I rarely spoke now that our 'buffer' wasn't there to keep us from hurting each other anymore. The first boy to give me attention got all he wanted in return. I didn't want to drink, I didn't want to get involved with drugs and I thought I was being careful enough. I did what I could, anyway.

"I didn't take the pill regularly enough, so I used other methods and thought that would work. I didn't know anything had happened until it was all over. My mother hadn't had any idea I was doing anything sexual until that morning in the hospital when the doctor told her what was happening to me.

"She was there when I woke up. I woke up to disapproval, plain and simple, in her eyes. I'd gotten a punishment I must have earned. The look on her face told me that she knew I'd been fooling around with boys. What it didn't tell me was that I'd nearly died, that I'd lost about two days and my uterus in the bargain."

Davide looked up from the letter, catching his reflection in the window across the room. The expression on his face was a surprise to him and he stared at the image of himself staring back. In time he was able to wipe away the grimace of pain he saw there, the sadness that replaced it feeling somewhat more acceptable.

"So," he murmured to the empty room, his eyes straying back to the letter in his hand, "what does this change, then?"

Absolutely nothing.

Fatherhood had never been high on his list of priorities. So he wouldn't be able to have children with her—so what? Besides, what was the guarantee that he'd make a better parent than his own father? There wasn't one and he knew it.

The point was moot, anyway.

So why does this hurt so much? Is it for her pain, or for mine?

He'd never given it much thought before. All he'd wanted was for Emily to return to him and give him the chance to…

To do what? To be her friend? Her lover?

Her husband?

He startled at this last, looking around the room. Now he was getting ahead of himself and he needed to get this under control. She hadn't even said that she'd be coming back, only that she might have to, if the house sold.

And yet it almost made sense. She might stay with him; wouldn't that be the logical thing to do? Although he doubted she'd want this, after her disastrous first marriage and all she'd gone through.

But this is different, no? Jacopo was worthless. He cheated on her. He lied to her.

Davide saw the photo of Letizia, still on the table by the lamp. He stood and crossed to it in a few swift steps, snatching it up. He carried it back and sat on the sofa again, studying it carefully.

That cloud was the same. He no longer questioned the similarity, but accepted it as fact. The man reflected in the mirror in the photos Letizia had hidden had been Jacopo. He knew this with a cold certainty which turned his stomach and brought the grimace back to his face.

I'll have to tell Emilia, won't I?

But what good would that do? Wouldn't it hurt her again?

Won't it hurt her if she finds out I knew? Won't that be worse?

He shook his head and put the photo on the sofa cushion, face down. It was too surreal for words.

He swiftly re-read the letter, his eyes skimming over her perfectly-shaped cursive writing. She'd written slowly, it was clear—the words were too well-formed to have been written at speed.

And yet they weren't all perfect, were they? There was a noticeable change where she'd written about Jacopo's new marriage. What emotion had taken her at that moment? Anger? Sadness? Jealousy?

His bile rose with a mix of those same emotions. If Jacopo had married the woman he'd left Emily for...

Davide shook his head, dismissing the thought. It didn't matter. If Jacopo had married Letizia, they were well-matched and deserved each other. They could make each other happy or miserable and it meant nothing to either Emily or him.

Except that it did. Somehow it did and Davide couldn't pin down just why that was for the life of him.

All things in time.

Sighing, Davide sank back against the arm of the sofa and rested his hand over his eyes. He imagined Emily—young, scared and confused—waking in a hospital room to her mother's cold disapproval and sutures on her abdomen; knowing something had happened, but unaware of how bad it truly was. Not knowing how close she had come to losing everything.

He sighed again, a shaky, watery sound. A painful catch in his throat made his eyes water.

He'd never thought her loss was so great. Not like this.

Now it was his loss, too.

(February, 2009)

25

The thuds of books on desks and the shuffle of feet over worn ceramic tiles eventually quieted. After stepping up to the lectern, Davide took a few moments to sift through his notes until the chirp of a mobile phone distracted him.

Glancing across the classroom, he noticed the student slipping one hand into her purse. She retrieved the offending object and read the screen before reflexively lifting it to her ear.

"*Spegnilo*, Alessia," he said, wishing he could make a more forceful command.

A few of the students snickered while she murmured a hasty goodbye to her caller and switched off the phone.

"*Scusi*, Prof." She gave a shrug. "I forgot it was on."

He narrowed his eyes, nodded and went back to his notes. A week into the second semester and they were still "forgetting" at least once per lesson. Never mind they should have figured it out during the first semester.

I could paint a notice on the wall behind my head, Turn off all mobile phones or I'll toss them out the window, *for all the good it would do.*

"All right then," he began, pulling a page of notes out from the stack in front of him. "Who wants to summarize Monday's –"

A tweeting tone in the far corner of the classroom interrupted him. Davide turned in time to catch another student fumbling with a tiny mobile. "*Scusi*, Prof!" the boy said, cutting the phone off mid-tone.

At least he actually sounded guilty. That's a step in the right direction.

"Anyone else? Shall we all check to be sure our phones are off?"

In spite of his aim to sound sarcastic, it had come off as a polite request. A handful of students actually double-checked, however, and he was gratified to see them turning off the phones and putting them away.

"*Va bene*... If there won't be any more interruptions...?" He paused, scanned the room and tried to ignore the sniggering of some of the students. As a class they knew him too well. He was no disciplinarian, no stern lecturer, but he would have liked not to have to work so hard at maintaining order.

"Okay. Who wants to summarize Monday's high points, then?"

As expected, Mohal's hand was the first in the air. The boy rose to stand next to his desk, reading his notes aloud in a melodic accent. Davide only half-listened, his thoughts already turning to the day's planned topics and the inevitable questions that would follow.

When Mohal finished reading, Davide nodded in his direction and offered a slight smile. "*Grazie*, Mo. Now, picking up where we left off, I –"

A distinct, melodic beeping sounded and he grasped the edges of the lectern with both hands, scanning the class.

Oh, for...

"*Santo Cielo*..." he groaned. "Whose is it *this* time?"

There were no furtive shufflings, no patting of pockets or digging into rucksacks or purses. A few students exchanged sidelong looks, with some turning around in their seats to seek the guilty party.

The beeping continued. Davide's eyes took another sweep across the room before Mohal raised his hand shyly.

"*Sì*, Mohal?"

"Prof? Forgive me, but I think it's *yours*." The boy tilted his head toward Davide's desk, across from the lectern.

Davide turned to his desk. Indeed, the next salvo of beeps came from there and he glanced shamefaced at the class.

"*Scusate…*" He crossed to his desk and opened the top drawer. The beeping obligingly grew louder.

No one ever calls me. Everyone knows I'm working at this time.

The screen bore a long string of numbers looking like so much arithmetical nonsense. Nothing of the sequence was familiar. He shrugged toward the class and flipped the phone open, ready to tell his caller that he was working and couldn't talk.

"*Pronto? Chi parla?*" he answered abruptly, an instant before realization struck him.

001—that's a country code.

A muffled scratching followed by a clearer "*Pronto? Davide? Sei tu?*" made his breathing shorten around his racing heartbeat.

"Emilia?" Without a second thought he abandoned the classroom, hurrying out into the corridor to hear her better.

"*Sì*, Davide, it's me. *Come stai?*"

"Never better, believe me." Closing his eyes, he leaned against the wall and pressed the phone to his ear, as if to bring her closer. "*E tu come stai*, Emilia?"

"*Sto bene.*"

A silence followed, long enough for him to check his phone to be certain he still had a signal. As he raised the phone back to his ear, her voice returned to the line.

"Could you repeat that?" he asked, as a door at the end of the hall swung shut with a *bang.*

"I'm coming back next week."

Gripping the phone tighter, he gingerly adjusted its position while his other fingers grappled for a hold on the smooth plastered wall. "Next week? *Veramente?*"

"*Sì, sì*—I arrive Tuesday evening. I've already booked the hotel and everything."

"*Ma…perché?* On such short notice?" *I have so much to do, so much to get ready…*

"Well, you remember I wrote you about the house—right?"

Davide nodded before realizing she couldn't see the gesture. "*Sì*, I remember."

"It sold. The paperwork is going to be signed a week from Thursday and I want to be there."

"You still don't trust him."

"Not even as far as I can throw him," she said in English and Davide dwelled on the strange turn of phrase for a moment. "Could I ask you something?"

"*Certo.* What is it?"

"I was hoping you could give me a ride, to be honest. My hotel will be in the city center and I don't know my way around, so…"

"*Allora…* Why don't you send me your flight information? I would be happy to pick you up."

"*Grazie*, Davide. Thank you so much…"

"*Di niente*, Emilia. You know it is my pleasure." He sighed, turning to look over his shoulder through the door of the classroom. "Unfortunately, now I must get back to work."

"Oh, no! I didn't realize—I messed up the time, didn't I? You'd think I'd have gotten it right after living there so long… I'm sorry."

"It's no problem. Aside from some teasing from my students, it should be fine. Call me any time you need to, please."

"Okay. *Ciao.*"

"*Ciao.*"

Davide switched the phone to silent and slipped it into his pocket. He remained outside a few moments longer, trying to fix a neutral expression to his face. It was already proving more difficult than he'd anticipated.

Emily was coming back. After nearly six months of letters and an occasional e-mail, she was returning to Italy. Better still, she was staying in Bologna.

What more could he want?

Easing the receiver down onto the cradle, Emily stepped away from the telephone table, her eyes never leaving the phone.

I could have sworn I'd planned the time correctly.

All the same, had she imagined the eagerness in his voice when she'd told him she was coming back? Surely not. In his letters and e-mails there was always a sense of guarded expectation—as though he wanted to say something more than might seem appropriate.

He was tenacious and cautious at the same time—just as he'd been in Bologna. A smile creased her lips and she tightened the sash of her robe as she walked into the kitchen to put the kettle on. Her mother wouldn't be up for a couple of hours at the earliest. There was plenty of time to enjoy the start of the day over a cup of tea with the newspaper spread out on the table.

As quietly as she could, she set about preparing her tea, then went out onto the front porch to collect the day's paper. Wrapped in a plastic sheath, it rested in its usual place within easy reach, on the hedge next to the steps. Though retrieving it only took a few seconds, she had to rub her arms vigorously to fight away the cold seeping through her flannel pajamas and heavy robe. Her toes in fuzzy slippers complained of the frosty air before the warmth of the house got through to them again.

She recalled her refusal to wear slippers in Milan and how Davide's typically Italian mortification had followed. Emily smiled again, rubbing her hands over her cheeks to warm up. Slipping the paper out of the plastic, she spread the pages out on the table and went to the boiling kettle before it could start to whistle and wake her mother.

As she poured the hot water into her mug, a crystal-clear image filled her mind. While she prepared tea, Davide sat opposite her, his warm smile greeting her over the steam before he turned back to whatever paperwork he was reading and revising.

It was so real, so *tangible*, that she reached out to touch his arm before the image faded and the empty chair and dimly-lit kitchen once again filled her vision. She wasn't surprised by this, considering how vividly she recalled much of their day together—never mind the night.

After retrieving the small milk pitcher from the fridge and her Italian cookies from the pantry, she sat in front of her newspaper and tried to turn her thoughts away from Davide. She inhaled the rising steam of her mug, the moist, soothing vapors of Yorkshire tea loosening the tightness in her throat while a few deep breaths eased the constrictions of melancholy gripping her chest.

I've missed him so much more than I'd have thought possible.

Though she'd lived in Italy for ten years, it still seemed strange to say she was *homesick* for the place. Yet the whole time she'd been in Ypsilanti, she'd missed Italy. Then again, that wasn't quite right, either: she wasn't homesick for Rovigo, where she'd lived for nine years. She didn't really miss Venice, either, for all the romantic foolishness that had gone on there.

No, she missed getting up and going out for a coffee at the bar, shopping for her daily groceries or going for a stroll when everyone went out, virtually *en masse*, to do the same.

Though it was hard to believe, she missed some of the inconveniences of life away from her home: not having a clothes dryer; shops being closed on Sundays, Monday mornings and Thursday afternoons; even recalling the transportation strikes which the transit workers planned with such precision and held according to schedule brought a fresh sense of nostalgia.

Emily smiled at this last memory. The most recent such strike she'd experienced had actually paid off rather handsomely for her, hadn't it?

Without a doubt, she missed Davide. In turn she found she missed Bologna—at least the version he'd shown her. If she were practical and thought hard enough, she knew she'd thought about both the man and the city every day since she'd gotten home.

Was it surprising to find she wanted to return? But what if things weren't quite how she recalled them? What if she were setting herself up for another huge fall, as she'd done with Jacopo?

The similarities were only on the surface, but were there nonetheless. It would be foolish to dismiss them too easily. And yet...

Davide was different. In every way possible, in every way she could see, he was different. Wasn't this the reason she'd fallen in love with him?

She gasped into the early morning silence of the kitchen, a momentary vertigo sweeping through her and leaving her disoriented. There it was: she'd been completely unable to sidestep it this time around. The knowledge came with a certainty and a rightness she'd never felt before in her life. She was in love with him, a man she hardly knew but believed she knew completely.

The humming of the fridge switched off a moment later, plunging her into an even deeper quiet, through which a come-and-go snore drifted down the stairs. Taking reassurance from the evidence that her mother was still sound asleep, Emily sat back and breathed a slow sigh.

She folded her hands around her mug and stared at the brown mass of the tea bag at the bottom.

There. I've thought it for real this time. I've danced around it in our messages long enough and here it is. I love him. But is it possible? After such a short time?

Yes, it was true that she'd only known Jacopo for about a week before she'd agreed to stay in Venice. That had been lust pure and simple, which in short order had become genuine affection. Unfortunately, it had been enough to convince her that his proposal of marriage six weeks later was sincere. *Love*, though? Perhaps not so much. She'd convinced herself she'd loved him and once he'd gone, she'd convinced herself he loved her, still.

She was good at that. Was it any wonder she was afraid to believe it of Davide now? No matter what she wanted to believe, she tried to be rational and clear-headed this time around.

Not that it was working.

The very thought of him sent her body into a tizzy. A giddy, schoolgirlish anticipation greeted every letter and every e-mail she discovered waiting for her. She liked his letters best, since she could pore over them and study his handwriting and smell the little bits of him the pages contained.

She was trying to be levelheaded, but was failing miserably. What was worse was that she didn't really *care*. It felt good to have something to look forward to, to have some reason to smile. Davide gave her that. Effortlessly.

Now, because circumstances gave her the perfect opportunity to do so, she was returning to Italy.

Back to Bologna.

Back to Davide.

She was, it seemed, returning home.

26

None of the people streaming into the terminal was Emily. Davide watched closely. Each time the sliding doors opened, he caught a glimpse of activity beyond. But it was never a long enough look for him to see if she was there. Lines of people gathered around the conveyor belts, trundling baggage carts from one place to another or waiting for their bags to arrive.

Checking his watch told him an hour had passed since her flight had been scheduled to arrive. He'd certainly shown up with plenty of time to spare—he'd already been waiting in the arrivals area for nearly two hours.

The stream of traffic slowed and stuttered, then stopped. One or two passengers came through the doors every few minutes or so and then the hall was quiet. Looking around, Davide saw he was alone. His heart sank.

She said she was coming today. She said she'd be here.

He looked at his mobile phone to see whether he'd somehow missed a message from her, but found none. The chair creaked as he sat back, his gaze still fixed on the doors.

Any moment now. Surely she's coming.

The rustling of the ribbon on the gift-wrapped package in his hands seemed loud in the not-quite-silence of that part of the airport. Two *carabinieri* passed by, giving him a cursory examination from beneath the low brims of their uniform caps before continuing on their patrol of the hall.

Again he checked his watch. Almost time for dinner. Surely Emily would be hungry, but she might be too tired to go out. The name of her hotel had slipped his mind for the moment, but he knew he'd recall it soon enough.

I'm sure it's close to Pino's. I could take her there, maybe…

The sliding doors opened and his heartbeat quickened as he straightened in expectation. An older Italian couple passed through, grumbling and pushing a nearly-empty baggage cart ahead of them.

Maybe she took another flight? But why didn't she call to tell me?

He fiddled with the ribbons on the gift, fluffing them where they'd become crushed in his pocket.

I'll try to call her, if she doesn't get here soon.

Nodding to himself, he tried to relax and continued to monitor the entrance. Any minute now, she'd be there.

At last.

I can't believe that I forgot my cellphone. Again. This is getting to be some kind of ridiculous habit.

Emily fidgeted, her restless hands twitching with the desire to dial Davide's number. If only she'd remembered her phone, she'd be able to call and tell him she'd been delayed and was now stuck just inside the baggage claim area, waiting in a line for the airline's lost luggage office. Why one bag had arrived in Bologna from London and the other hadn't, she couldn't figure out on her own. It was unlikely the frazzled desk clerk currently enduring several angry Italians, one rather haughty Swede and herself would be of any help.

All she wanted was to fill out the requisite paperwork and get out of there. Knowing that Davide must be—surely he still was?—on the other side of the doors at the far end of the hall, made the wait all the more frustrating.

Then again, it gave her time to think. Not that she hadn't had plenty of time to think either on the eight-hour flight to Gatwick or during the seven-hour layover there before her connecting flight to Bologna.

Her stomach twisted with the realization that she was about to see him again. It had been nearly a year since their night together in Milan, which had been filled with so much promise until that misunderstanding had come between them.

How should she greet him, then? A hug? A kiss? What kind of kiss? A friendly one? A *very* friendly one? What was he expecting, with her just off the plane?

Shaking her head, she stepped forward in line. *I'll just have to play it by ear, I reckon. No sense in getting all worked up, anyway.*

Their hands flailing, the Italians concluded making their collective point and signed the paperwork anyway. Still gesturing and bemoaning the inconvenience of their misdirected bags, they walked toward the doors at the far end of the hall.

Frowning, she turned back to face the desk and found the Swede was already signing his paperwork.

"*Signora?*" The harried clerk gestured to indicate Emily should come forward. She stepped up to the desk, her carry-on bag and one suitcase in tow.

In a remarkably pleasant surprise, she made it through the whole process of describing her bag—the size and contents, color and style—with no trouble.

"*Quando arriverà qui?*" she asked, vaguely entertaining the thought of waiting for it to arrive.

"*Ci vorranno ancora delle ore, signora.* I'm very sorry for such a delay, of course."

Funny, you don't really sound like it.

"Do you wish to collect it here tomorrow morning," the clerk continued, "or would you like for us to have it sent to you?"

"Send it, please."

"*Va bene...allora.* Please fill in this form with the address where you'd like it sent." The clerk slid the paper forward and turned to key something in on the computer.

Emily stared at the sheet with something like horror, her mind blank. She had no idea what the address of the hotel was. Digging out her planner, she thumbed through it without finding her reservation form.

Oh, no. Don't tell me I've forgotten that, too?

Biting her lip, she continued paging through, wishing she was better organized. The only addresses she found were her old Rovigo address and Davide's home and office.

I doubt he'd mind, though…

Quickly she copied his home address onto the form and turned the paper so the clerk could read it. He nodded, his fingers moving smoothly over the keyboard without pause while he squinted at her handwriting.

"*Va bene…* Your bag should arrive in the morning, first thing." He handed Emily her information on a slip of paper and she put it in her planner with exaggerated care. The last thing she needed was to lose something else, particularly of such importance. "Make sure that someone is there to collect it when it arrives."

Emily barely managed to avoid rolling her eyes at this last comment. "*Grazie.*"

"*Prego. Buonasera, signora.*"

"*Buonasera…*"

The walk to the sliding doors seemed much longer than it should have been. Her legs were suddenly unsteady and she paused out of range of the electronic eye which would trigger the doors to open, her heart and mind both racing.

Eagerness overcame her at last and she took a step forward, bracing herself for her return to the two things she'd missed more than she'd ever have believed possible:

Davide and Italy.

The soft *shump* of the doors opening drew Davide's attention up from the floor. He blinked to refocus his eyes and his heart stammered to life at the sight of her. Rushing to his feet, he was made aware by her rather amused expression that he'd moved too quickly. Her hair hung limply, almost obscuring the circles under her eyes and the lines lightly etched into her face.

Oh, no… Something's wrong.

"Emilia?" he said, his voice trembling into a questioning register. It was as though he hadn't spoken in ages.

A smile wavered but held firm on her lips and his heart sped faster still. He ignored the wave of dizziness and unreality which washed over him. When his legs seemed steady enough, he put the gift in his coat pocket and started toward her.

"Davide…" Emily's voice shook too and he pulled her into his arms. He buried his face in her hair, breathed in her scent and the sterile airport smell that surrounded them.

Her arms tightened around him and he held her tighter too, his eyes shut to everything around them. The tension in her shoulders was made clear by how they started to relax beneath his hands, her deep sigh against his neck.

"*Bentornata a Bologna,*" he said, as he chuckled and pressed his lips to her temple. *Welcome back to Bologna.*

"*Grazie, Davide. Sono contenta di essere qui.*"

He pulled away from her and met her eyes, startled. "*Stiamo parlando Italiano?*" *We're speaking Italian now?*

"*Sì. Perché no?*" she asked, smiling. "*Stiamo qui, vero?*"

Smoothing her hair back from her face, Davide smiled. "*Sì. Siamo qui, finalmente.*" His eyes met hers while his fingers continued touching her hair, her cheek, as though verifying she really was with him. When he moved closer to her, she tilted her face up to his.

Seeing the invitation in her gesture, he twined his fingers in her hair and brushed his lips over hers in a light caress. She pressed closer, deepening the kiss without hesitation until they parted at last.

"I gave them your address," she said, still speaking Italian.

"Eh?" Davide's eyes narrowed. "You gave *who* my address?"

"The airline. One of my bags didn't make it from London and they're delivering it in the morning. I couldn't remember the hotel's name or address, so I gave them yours." She bit her lower lip, shyly meeting his eyes. "I hope that's okay?"

"*Certo*, Emilia. But do you remember the hotel name? If I'm to take you there tonight, I should know which one to take you to."

"Well, I thought I had my reservation sheet here in my planner, but..." She shrugged and began fishing through her shoulder bag. Flipping her planner open, she paged through it from the front, pausing to wet her fingertip with the tip of her tongue from time to time.

Davide, too aware of his interest in the flicker of pink each time she did this, tried to concentrate his interest on the objects flashing past in the planner. After a moment he realized he was watching for the photo of Jacopo she'd kept there a year ago.

Why worry about that? She's not here for him this time. Our kiss was proof enough of that.

"I don't believe it." Emily groaned and took out a folded sheet of paper. "I had it right here all along. Why didn't I see it before?"

Davide grinned and reached to stroke her hair. "I suppose you didn't really need it."

"But now my bag is going to your house. Should I tell them the hotel's address?" She looked over her shoulder at the sliding doors and started to turn in that direction before he touched her arm and turned her back.

"I don't think you can go back in. *Non ti preoccupare*, I will bring it to you in the morning."

"Aren't you working?"

"Not until after lunch. Besides, it's a perfect excuse to come see you."

Not that I needed an excuse...

Emily nodded silently, but Davide thought the look in her eyes said she felt the same.

"I thought if you're not too tired, we'd take your things to the hotel and I would take you to dinner to welcome you ho– back."

She seemed to consider this. "That'd be nice. *Grazie*."

He took her bags and started for the exit, Emily trailing behind, looking around dazedly.

The doors opened for a group ahead of them, letting in the odors of engine exhausts, cigarette and pipe smoke, all of it somehow metallic and frosty with winter air.

He pushed her bag to one side away from the doors and pulled the package out of his pocket. Shouldering her carry-on bag with one hand, he presented the slightly crumpled gift to her.

"I forgot to give you this."

"Oh, Davide..." Her smile strengthened as she accepted the gift. "You didn't have to get me a present."

He shrugged, pleased. "What good is a homecoming without a gift?"

She didn't acknowledge his choice of words and he was grateful.

"Should I open it now?"

He nodded toward the package. "*Sì, prego.*"

Her fingers delicately undid the ribbon, carefully tearing the shiny paper where it was taped together. He thought her hands were trembling as she opened the box to reveal the contents.

"Oh...!" she sighed, appreciative. "Gloves! You got me gloves?" Her voice trembled and he reached for the box.

"*Sì*, Emilia. I recalled that you didn't have any last time."

"They match my coat," she said, grinning.

Davide's cheeks flushed and he shrugged again. *No need to tell her I've held onto them for a year, that I bought them the day after she left.*

Without meeting his eyes, she shyly pulled one glove on, then flexed her fingers.

"They're too small," he said, questioning.

"No, they're great. Leather stretches." Emily flexed her fingers again and pulled the other glove on. "See?"

She turned her hands over, admiring her gift in the fluorescent light of the hall. At last she met his eyes again. "This is, without a doubt, the most considerate gift I've been given in a long, long time. *Grazie ancora.*"

Grabbing the lapels of his coat, she pulled him down for a swift kiss on both cheeks. Absurd as it seemed, his heart raced with these chaste, polite kisses. The thought of gathering her to him and kissing her again briefly flashed through his mind.

"Come, let's get you settled in. You need some food and some rest." He picked up her suitcase and turned for the door.

"I'm afraid you're right. Davide?"

"*Sì?*"

She started to say something, but shook her head instead. "Never mind. Let's go."

27

Another hotel lobby, another check-in—and again, Davide was by her side. In a way, Emily couldn't help feeling her life was on a continuous loop, but at least this time she was coming to him, not leaving him behind. Collecting her key from the desk clerk, she indicated the back of the lobby. "The elevator's this way," she said, leading but watching him over her shoulder.

Picking up her bags, he followed quietly. She stifled a yawn behind her hand and glimpsed amusement in his expression.

"Give me a break, would you?" she said, speaking English for the first time that evening. "I'm exhausted."

He nodded and she pressed the call button, suppressing another yawn at the same time. "Thanks for your help, by the way. I don't know if I could manage that bag right now." She laughed quietly. "I'd probably curl up on it and sleep, right here in the hallway."

"*Lo sai*, Emilia, if you are this tired, perhaps I should leave you to rest this evening."

"No," she said, too quickly, but Davide didn't seem to mind.

"I want to see you. Besides," she began, stepping into the elevator, "I have to try to stay awake if I'm going to get over my jet-lag."

"Okay." He trundled the bag into the elevator and there seemed to be a hint of relief in his voice.

At the top floor, they made their way down the hall to the room. Opening the door, Emily slid her other hand along the wall, seeking the light switch.

The light revealed a study in pale pastel greens. The ceiling sloped down at the far side to end just above the doors of a built-in closet. The satiny bedcover was striped with green and gold, matching exactly the colors—though not the pattern—of the carpeting. Emily hung her coat on the hook and put her purse on the marble-topped desk while Davide opened up the luggage rack and placed her bag on it.

"Where's the window?" she asked through a yawn.

"There," Davide said, pointing over her head.

I must be tired. How did I miss that?

Emily looked up at the inset of the ceiling over the desk. She studied the glass pane and the shutter slats closed to the night, puzzling over the mechanics of it.

"How do I open it?" she asked at last. "The shutter, I mean. Do you know how?"

Davide shrugged, then went to study a panel on the wall. "Maybe it's this?" he said and pushed a button. A sudden loud rumble overhead showed he'd guessed correctly.

Or, rather, he had *almost* guessed correctly. The window itself opened but the shutter remained closed. Cold night air, carrying a hint of snow, blew in through the gap between the window and the casing before he found the button to close it again. Another switch slid the shutter open and Emily stood beneath the window, gazing up at her reflection against the night sky.

"*Grazie*, Davide. At least I'll have natural light in the morning." Looking around once more, she smiled. "It's quite nice, really. I kind of like it."

"How did you come to choose this hotel out of all the places to stay in Bologna?"

A flush crept into her cheeks while she considered her reasons. "Well, I wanted to be in the city center, for one."

"Okay."

"And this is close to *La Finestrella*, remember? It's right around the corner."

Davide's grin broadened. "You took a room here because of *that?*"

"Well, that, and it was just about the only place left in town this week. It's really hard to get a hotel here, you know."

"*Sì, lo so….*" He seemed about to say something more, but fell silent instead, his dark eyes meeting hers steadily. "I'm so glad you're here, Emilia," he said at length.

"*Anche io,*" she said, her voice low in the silence of the room.

If I weren't so tired, I think I'd throw myself at him.

She covered her mouth to hide a yawn and Davide looked away, examining the room again.

"Are you hungry?" he asked. "I know a nice place near here. It's nothing fancy, but the food is good."

Still yawning, Emily nodded, then wiped her eyes. "I'm very hungry, actually. They fed us on the plane, but that was a while ago."

"Let's go, then. Pino's fills up quickly." Davide took her coat off the hook and held it out for her to slip her arms into the sleeves. When she did, he put his arms around her from behind and gave her a gentle squeeze.

She leaned into his embrace with a soft sigh. She wanted to close her eyes to feel his embrace better, but that was a bad idea.

I'd probably fall asleep in his arms. Not that it would be a bad thing…

Instead, she smiled back at him and began fastening her coat for the walk to the restaurant.

Davide poured water into her glass before he filled his own. "So, can I ask what your schedule is like? Perhaps we'll be able to meet while you're here."

"Yeah, I'd like that. Let me think… Tomorrow I'm basically free. I figured I'd need to recover from jet lag and…" Emily yawned, covering her mouth and turning away from him for a moment. "I guess I got *that* right."

He chuckled and sat back from the table when the server approached to give them their entrees.

"I think you're right," he said, reassuming his forward stance as the server departed. Picking up his fork, he assessed the *tortelloni alle noci* on his plate, then tilted it toward her. "Do you want to try?" he asked, but she shook her head, already twirling her own fork in her *tagliatelle*. "What about the day after tomorrow? You're going to Rovigo, *sì?*"

"*Sì, sì.* I'm leaving here around ten a.m. It's supposed to be a brunch meeting." She shrugged, but her nonchalance wasn't convincing.

"I wish I could go with you," he said, then took a bite of his pasta. He swallowed it along with the sinking feeling in his chest. "I couldn't find anyone to take my lessons for the day, though."

"I know, Davide. I'll be okay. I'm just not looking forward to seeing him again."

"*Mi dispiace*, Emilia."

"It's not a problem, really. I guess I'm worried about what I might say to him."

"What do you mean?"

"Let's just say I've got some choice words for him, if he says the wrong thing."

The notion of Emily letting her anger loose upon her ex-husband leapt to mind, and Davide failed to resist the smile playing at his lips. Too late, he raised his hand to cover his still full mouth and she arched an eyebrow at his reaction.

"What?"

He shook his head, trying to swallow his mouthful without choking on laughter. "*Niente*," he managed at last and covered his amusement by taking a sip of his water. "Just a silly thought."

She eyed him with suspicious amusement, shook her head and resumed eating.

"So you'll be back in the evening, then?"

"I think so," she said in English. "Unless he tries to screw me or something."

The unexpected switch in language threw him almost as much as the words themselves. Unwanted, unbidden, the image of Jacopo seducing and humiliating her yet again formed in his mind. Davide's hand clenched into a fist and he moved it out of her view. He sat up straight, squared his shoulders and stared intently at her face. "*Cosa? Non ho capito*—I didn't understand."

Emily looked at him, her expression blank save for her fatigue. "What?"

"'Unless he tries to *screw* you?'" He shook his head to demonstrate his incomprehension. "Do you really think he would do that?"

"Oh, Davide... *Mi dispiace*... I'm really tired." She wiped her mouth, her face pinking drastically. "I didn't mean... I just meant I have this concern he'll try to get away with more than is fair. You know?"

"It's okay, *amore mio*. Don't worry." He paused, realizing how he'd addressed her. She didn't react, but twirled her fork to gather more pasta instead.

Did she not notice, or is it that she doesn't mind?

"Emilia," he began, directing his eyes toward his plate and pushing a *tortellone* around with the tines of his fork. "I know you didn't mean it that way, but...isn't that a possibility?"

"What do you mean?"

"Jacopo," he said, forcing himself to say the name before he stuffed the *tortellone* into his mouth. Emily's questioning gaze followed the gesture and focused on him until he'd swallowed and had to continue speaking. "I'm thinking that maybe it's something that's possible, no?"

"What is?"

"Have you given any thought to what could happen there? When you see him again?" It was his turn to blush now, for having inadvertently broached this subject in the first place. "It happens all the time with divorced couples when they see each other after time has passed."

Emily took a drink of her water, her eyes meeting his over the glass. "I hardly plan on talking to him, much less sleeping with him."

Nodding, he focused once more on his nearly-empty plate until she leaned forward to rest her hand over his on the table. Raising his eyes to hers, he was transfixed by the intensity of her expression. She shook her head slightly, her cool fingers grasping his hand.

"That will *never* happen, Davide. It simply won't."

Heart racing, he nodded again. The effort required to do so was astounding. He'd never seen her like this—was it a result of her fatigue and her determination to get through the evening before succumbing to her exhaustion? Or did she feel this passionately about the situation—and about him—after all?

Dare I to hope?

A new image sprang to mind—infinitely more pleasing—and his determination revived.

Not tonight, but soon. As soon as possible, I have to act.

But when?

Davide had fallen strangely silent on the walk back to the hotel through the dark, meandering streets. Emily considered that perhaps he was tired too, but her own fatigue actually seemed to be fading the closer they got to the hotel.

His hesitation at the door caught her attention, but she didn't want to embarrass him by reacting to it. For much the same reason, she hadn't reacted when he had called her "*amore mio*" in the restaurant.

And oh, how nice that had sounded when he said it.

A little flurry of excitement erupted low in her belly at the thought, warming her in spite of the cold.

She collected her key and smiled at Davide, hoping he would recognize it for the invitation it was.

He did.

They walked silently to the elevator and she frantically tried to think of something to say. Everything sounded like a cheap come-on, loaded with suggestions she didn't quite intend.

But if he wants to stay, I'll let him. I should just ask, though, shouldn't I?

She toyed with the key while they walked toward her room and Davide paced a half-step behind her the whole way. The urge to turn and look at him was almost irresistible. His presence at her shoulder was somehow reassuring.

He paused in the doorway while she stepped inside and turned to face him.

"I should go," he said. "But I'll be back in the morning with your bag. Is there anything you need?"

Besides you?

Banishing the thought almost as quickly as it came, she watched him for a moment before speaking. "No, I think I'm fine. I always make a point of packing a few second-day things in every bag I have, just in case," she said, hiding her cringe as best she could.

"*Davvero?*" He chuckled softly. "I do the same thing." He leaned against the doorjamb, his dark eyes watching her with a soft, studious expression.

"*Sì?*" She laughed too and stepped closer to rest her hand on the frame, next to his shoulder.

"*Sì...*" He gestured over his other shoulder shyly, half-nodding. "I should go," he repeated, hesitating where he stood.

"Okay." She didn't even try to keep the disappointment out of her voice. "I'll see you tomorrow, then."

"Right."

His eyes met hers, held her gaze in the silence. Her heartbeat moved to resume its frantic pounding just beneath her throat, her pulse filling her ears until she wondered if he might be able to hear it. There was just enough time to wonder if she might faint from a combination of anxiousness and exhaustion before he leaned in and brought his mouth to hers in a light, barely-there kiss.

For a moment she wondered if she had imagined the kiss, as he seemed not to have moved from his place in the doorway. But the next left no doubt.

Davide gently slipped his arms around her, his lips meeting and parting hers with soft, unhurried intent. Emily pressed closer, sliding her hands up to touch his face before she wound her arms around his neck. His arms tightened around her until she felt the buttons of his shirt through her light sweater. Her fingers itched with the desire to undo each button slowly and with great care.

When the kiss ended, Davide touched his fingertips to her cheeks, his lips alighting just behind his caresses. She savored the solidity of him pressed against her chest, the heat of his body seeping through his shirt to warm her. She eased her hand down from his neck to his heart, felt it speeding under her hand, and smiled.

Breathing deep, she relished his scent—not his cologne, but *his* scent, salty-sweet beneath the clean-laundry smell of his clothing. Emily wanted to curl up under his chin and nest there, in the hollow of his throat, were it only possible.

I should ask him to stay. What's the harm? Why wait?

Before she could speak, he drew away, his hand still resting on her cheek.

"*Buonanotte*, Emilia. I'll see you in the morning."

He's right. I don't know why, but he's right.

"*Buonanotte*, Davide. *Grazie per tutto.* Thanks for everything."

Another swift kiss, a chorus or two of "*Ciao-ciao*," and he was walking toward the elevator while she closed the door and let loose a long, unsteady breath.

28

Still feeling Emily's lips on his, her arms around his neck and her body pressed close, Davide sank onto his bed. The readout on the alarm clock flickered over to one a.m., the hazy green glow illuminating the bedside table.

He'd spent nearly an hour at a nearby bar, sipping a Crodino, trying to decide whether he should go back to the hotel and declare his intentions. In the end, common sense had won out and he'd returned home, determined to sleep before her suitcase arrived in the morning.

Undressing slowly, he closed his eyes and replayed their kiss over and over in his mind. Her scent seemed to carry on every breath he drew. He fancied he could still feel her hand on his heart and he remembered her doing the same thing while boarding the train to Milano a year ago. A small gesture, performed so carelessly, yet she had no idea she possessed him utterly each time she did so.

If she'd asked me to stay, I would have in a heartbeat.

Heaven knew he'd done his best to provoke her into doing so. He couldn't ask to stay, because he feared she'd acquiesce only to please him. It had to be her decision, completely and totally hers. And so he'd kissed her and held her so close he could feel her heartbeat in the press of her body against his.

Pulling on his pajamas and slipping under the covers, he tried not to dwell on this last memory. Helplessly, he found himself unable to stop reflecting on their stay in Milano and all that happened there. It was too easy to recall the softness of her skin, the scent of her hair, the fullness of her breasts, her hips...

He rolled over, breathing out hard, careful to keep the covers spread evenly over the bed as he turned onto his other side. The king-sized bed was always far too large for one person, but tonight it seemed larger than ever. It had been another one of his father's ill-afforded extravagances and Davide wished yet again he had disposed of the thing before he'd moved in nearly twelve years ago.

He felt hollow, each heartbeat seeming to echo in his chest. He considered how many times his father must have brought women to this flat to "entertain" while Davide and his mother were home in Riccione. For that matter, how many times had his father had strange women in this bed while Davide was in class, just a stone's throw away?

The usual sea of anger raged in his stomach before he suppressed the thought.

Think of Emily instead and deal with the consequences, if you must. There's no use going down this road any more. He's gone and all that is over with now.

For a moment he feared it was easier said than done. Then, blessedly, memories of their kiss a couple of hours before returned to him, trailing sweet frustration in their wake.

By now, the mere thought of her caused an ache deep within him. It was no longer want but need—pure and simple need. Had she not been so exhausted, had her trip not been so difficult, he had no doubt he'd be making love with her at that very moment.

Excuses, excuses... What's the real reason, then?

He cowed as though menaced and the answer to his own question came to him.

I'm scared. Simple as that. I'm scared she won't really want me.

It was utterly ridiculous, but there it was. Never mind she'd done everything but throw herself at him in Milano and never mind that she'd shown nothing but interest in the hotel a short while ago; the fear of her possible rejection still loomed in his mind.

If he were being honest with himself he'd have to admit that on the occasions he'd shown interest in a woman, she'd generally reciprocated—at least, since he'd become an adult. The nightmare of his teenage years had ended on a slightly positive note—although his mother's doomsaying had tainted everything somewhat.

Oddio... How our youth haunts us all...

He turned over again, flinging one arm out across the length of the bed and picturing Emily in her hotel, asleep under the green-and-gold bedclothes. Almost able to feel the rise and fall of her breathing, he curled his arm and imagined her in his embrace, pressed warm and close. He recalled her curves in the modest flannel pajamas she'd worn in Milano and the physical ache returned low in his belly, more focused than before.

Breathing slowly he felt her beside him, soft, warm and inviting, reaching for him and drawing him closer still. His ache changed, became more difficult to deny as his dream evolved with each breath. She was there with him, moving her body against his, her hands delicately stroking him with the most provocative caresses possible.

Surrounded as he was by her warmth, her softness, her scent, there was nothing to do but to give in to it all and allow her to envelop him. They were in Milano again, alone in her room, but this time there was no flight waiting, no departure looming in the first light of dawn. There was only her.

She lay on top of him, fitting him perfectly, her hips rolling slowly and guiding him along until they were joined at last. He matched her rhythm and rocked up into her with a low sigh before she spread herself over him, her mouth firm on his own, her hand reaching back to stroke him inside her...

Davide awoke gasping, his face burning with awareness and a vestige of shame dredged up from his teenage years. The bell in the hallway trilled, no doubt the sound that had woken him to the evidence of his dream in the first place. Mortified, his first instinct was to burrow under the covers and wait the visitor out.

Emily's suitcase!

He hauled himself out of bed, stepped into his slippers and forced himself to ignore the cold air chilling the wet spot on the front of his pajamas.

"*Chi è?*" he called loudly into the handset of the *citofono*, convinced that they'd already gone.

"*Signor* Magnani? We have a delivery for a *Signora* Miller here. Will you accept it?"

"Of course, I'll, uh… I'll be right down. Bring it inside, please." He hung up the phone and buzzed the *portone* open before hurrying to put on his clothes from the night before.

He snatched his keys from the telephone table and tried to smooth his mussed hair with one hand, then rushed down the stairs to the front door, nearly losing his slippers a time or two in the process.

The corridor was freezing cold, untouched by the heat of the radiators in the flats. The front door was propped open by a rather large man, himself bundled up against the February cold in a puffy coat and a skullcap which made his head seem absurdly small.

"*Signor* Magnani?" the man asked, his voice surprisingly soft in the quiet of the main lobby.

"*Sì, sì, sono io.*" Davide crossed to him and took the pen the man offered, signed the slip on the clipboard and handed them back. The man slid the suitcase toward Davide, spared a brief glimpse at his slippered feet and gave him half a smile.

"*Buongiorno, Signore,*" he said, already turning to go and pulling the door closed behind him.

Davide waved distractedly in his direction and bent to grasp the suitcase handle. The shuffle of feet behind him got his attention and he turned to find Mr. Montanari eyeing him suspiciously.

"Going somewhere?" the old man asked.

"No," Davide said, working to keep his sudden annoyance out of his voice.

He sidestepped around his neighbor, dragging the suitcase along, the wheels leaving wet, gray tracks as he went.

"Watch that, Magnani! They don't come to clean the floors again until Tuesday."

Davide arched one eyebrow and then shook his head, deliberately stepping closer to the old man and continuing to drag the suitcase behind him. "*Mi dispiace, Signore*, but it's too heavy to lift."

"*Va bene, ma –*" Montanari cut short his blossoming tirade, nostrils flaring. He regarded Davide's slippered feet with a scowl of profound distaste which contorted his wrinkled features, then huffed again. Without another word, he stumped away toward the door, his cane making rubbery *thuds* on the tiles as he went.

Stifling laughter, Davide crossed to the stairs and started up, the suitcase much lighter than he'd expected.

If anyone had told Emily she would sleep soundly after Davide left, she'd have thought they were insane. However, the anticipated tossing and turning hadn't come and she'd drifted off into a deep and contented rest. Regardless, when the alarm went off at 8:00 a.m., her whole body complained that it was only 2:00 a.m.—and why was she being so disagreeable about staying under the covers, anyway?

The fleeting recollections of the dreams she'd had of Davide didn't make waking up any easier. Even fighting the temptation to perhaps drift back into the dreams where they'd made love much of the night seemed like a pointless waste of energy.

She dragged herself out from under the plush and cozy bedclothes and squinted up at the gray sky visible through the skylight. She refused to grumble and moan any further. It was time to get ready—there was no way to know when Davide would arrive with her suitcase.

After a quick shower, she dressed in the clothes she'd stuffed into her carry-on bag: a pair of jeans and a hooded blue sweatshirt. For a few moments, she sincerely regretted not packing something a little dressier. To compensate, she dug in her shoulder bag for a tube of tinted lip balm and swiped it across her mouth.

Nothing too fancy, but at least he won't think I'm a complete slob.

The hair dryer the hotel provided simply wasn't up to the challenge presented by thick hair. Giving up on the underpowered little wall unit, Emily put down her hairbrush and toweled dry her hair, stopping when she heard a gentle knock at the door. After one last look in the mirror, she took an elastic band and pulled back her hair before stepping out of the bathroom to answer, her heart already skipping in anticipation.

Davide.

Just in case it wasn't him, she left the chain locked as she peered out into the corridor. She smiled on seeing him, his back to the door while he looked out the window across from her room, down to the courtyard below. A flood of excitement swept over her as she watched him.

When she cleared her throat to speak, he turned to face her and his name didn't leave her lips. Instead, her breath caught in her chest and she gawped at him for a moment before she closed the door to unlatch the chain, her heart pounding.

This is ridiculous...

"*Buongiorno,* Davide." She swung the door open and he trundled her bag into the room.

"*Buongiorno,* Emilia." He paused at her side, returning her smile with an unexpected radiance which made her knees go weak. "*Hai dormito bene?*"

"*Sì,* I slept very well, *grazie.* And you?"

He hesitated briefly, a flare of deeper color rising in cheeks already reddened by the cold. "*Molto bene, grazie.* I hope I haven't disturbed you too early?"

"No, not at all. In fact, I wanted to ask you something."

He turned to face her, his glasses flashing in the brightening light of the overhead window. "What's that?" he asked, folding his arms across his chest and tilting his head, his eyes fully on her.

"You're wearing your glasses today," she said, though it wasn't what she'd meant to say at all.

"*Sì...* I'm working this morning—my contacts aren't good in the light there. I get headaches."

"Aww…" She reached out to stroke his arm, an automatic show of concern. "Anyway, I wanted to ask if you'd had breakfast yet…?" she asked leadingly.

"No, I haven't. I normally get a *caffè* and a brioche or something near work. Why?"

"I thought maybe you could join me downstairs. I asked at the desk and they said you could." He started to speak and she rushed to continue. "Besides, I've already had them add it to my bill. So now you have to."

"It would be my pleasure, Emilia."

It was all she could do to keep from doing a little dance on the spot. "Great! I'll get my shoes and we can go down." She went to sit on the bed and pulled on the sneakers she'd worn the day before. "I understand that they have a nice selection here--not just bread and coffee, but other things, too."

Davide's eyes flicked over her before he turned his attention out the skylight. She knew he'd just taken in her entire outfit in a single glance and she wondered what he'd made of it.

"You know," he said, stretching as if to see out the slanted window better, "I have a sweatshirt just like that. For a moment I thought yours was mine, but I remembered you've never been to my flat."

"You do?" For some reason she had to grin at this and she looked up from tying her shoes.

Davide nodded, then faced her again, his grin matching hers perfectly. A slight tingling warmth rose in her cheeks before she could look away.

"Emilia, if we're only going downstairs, do you mind if I leave my coat here?"

"Please do," she said, standing up. The urge to throw her arms around him as he slipped out of his wool overcoat and hung it up wasn't easily stifled, but she balled her hands into fists and managed. "Shall we go?" She tucked her room key in her pocket and Davide hung back to let her leave ahead of him.

"So, what are *your* plans today?" she asked once they'd made their selections from the buffet bar and had found a table apart from the other guests.

"*Niente di speciale*... I have two classes and a department meeting this afternoon. *Sfortunatamente*, this means I can't ask you for lunch today." He sipped his tiny cup of espresso then picked pieces off his chocolate croissant. "What are *you* going to do?"

"Oh, I don't know," Emily said, shrugging, her hands busily tearing small, sticky pieces off her pastry before she popped a piece in her mouth. "I might take advantage," she continued, then licked a bit of icing off her finger, "and spend the day in bed."

Davide hesitated in raising his cup to his lips again, then took another small sip. She noted that he blinked furiously for a moment or two, his dark lashes fluttering tellingly behind his glasses.

I just embarrassed him, didn't I? With that innocent little remark?

It wasn't intended to be provocative, even if he'd interpreted it that way.

"So what about tonight?" she asked in order to change the subject. Davide gulped the last of his espresso down before responding. She could tell by his next flurry of rapid blinking that his thoughts must have taken another off-color turn.

She feigned obliviousness and attempted to compose herself as modestly as was possible. It shouldn't have been difficult, considering she was bundled in a bulky sweatshirt and a pair of faded jeans, but no matter how she tried, she found a suggestive subtext to every gesture she could make.

Davide looked around the lobby and focused on the front door for a moment. Emily struggled to resist the giggles following her next thought:

If he had his coat, he'd be flying out of here by now, I bet.

"Would you come out for dinner with me?" Davide asked at last, and Emily nodded with more enthusiasm than was necessary.

Now she saw it was *his* turn to restrain himself. He slid one hand over his mouth, but not before she spied the wide grin which settled there. His gaze strayed around the room and returned to her, striking and direct in a way it hadn't been earlier.

Emily took a sip of her *caffè americano* and swallowed hard, aware the *gulp* could be heard in the silence between them.

It's obvious: we're both insane.

No sooner had she thought it than he began to chuckle softly and she followed suit.

"What are *you* laughing at?" she asked.

"I don't know. Something in your eyes," he answered. "I've never seen you look this happy."

She looked down at the table, considering this. "Wait 'til you see me after Rovigo," she said softly.

"Why is that?"

"Because," she said, raising her cup to her lips and her eyes to meet his, "I'll never have to see *him* again."

29

"You said something interesting at breakfast this morning. I'd like to ask you about it if I may."

Davide held the door of the hotel open and Emily preceded him, loosening her scarf as she went.

"Okay, *spara.*" She mimicked firing a gun before she stepped up to the desk.

When she glanced back at him while she collected her key, her dark eyes left him momentarily speechless. The desk clerk asked a question, she answered, and Davide understood none of it, regardless of which language they had spoken.

He waited until they were moving toward the elevator before trying again.

"You said this morning that you would be happier after you settle this business in Rovigo, because you'd never have to see him again."

"That's right."

"Is there a reason for you to be nervous about seeing him? Has he said or done anything to make you worry?"

Emily shook her head as they stepped inside the elevator and the doors closed.

"No, not really."

"*Not really*," Davide echoed, mistrusting the vagueness of her reply.

"I mean no, he hasn't. Sure, he's written me more e-mails and letters since I went home than he did the whole time we were together, but that doesn't mean anything."

"No? Doesn't it?" He stiffened and folded his arms. "I would think the opposite."

The doors opened and they stepped out into the corridor. Emily rested her hand on Davide's arm, tugging lightly until he relaxed and walked beside her toward her room.

"I thought the same thing at first. However, he was engaged—married now, actually—and I was reading too much into it. I don't mean anything to him, Davide. Not any more, if I ever really did."

"He *did* marry you, Emilia."

She sighed, not looking at him. "To make his mother happy, yes. Not because he ever loved me."

Davide fell silent, keeping pace with her while processing this last bit of news. "I don't understand," he said at last, though he feared he did.

"She was dying." Emily unlocked her door and turned to face him. The door bumped gently against her foot but stayed open. "By all rights she should have passed long before I arrived on the scene, but she kept holding on, insisting that he marry and give her a grandchild before she was gone." She leaned against the doorjamb, gave him a wan smile and made a small flourish with the hand that held her room key. "Enter one gullible American girl—who can't have babies, besides—and he's hit the jackpot, hasn't he?"

I think I'm going to be sick...

"That's horrible," he managed at last and she shrugged once more, her false smile fading away.

"That's life, I guess. He got what he wanted and for a long while I thought I had, too. I worked overtime at that delusion, though—I see that now." Looking up at him, her eyes filled with concern. "Are you all right, Davide? You look a little ill."

"Perhaps I shouldn't have had that dessert," he said, trying to grin. It felt genuine enough and he persisted with it until her concerned expression lightened.

"Would you like some water or something?" Emily stepped back and opened the door, indicating with a tilt of her head he should come inside. "Sit down for a minute and relax. See if you feel better before you head home."

He nodded, distracted as the sound of the opening theme of the late news caught his attention.

"Your television's on?"

"I turned it on before I left. I hate coming back to a silent hotel room. I don't know why, but the quiet depresses me if I'm alone."

"I do the same thing." The phrase was becoming habitual, by now, but it was true. "Well, in hotels I do. At home it doesn't bother me to have quiet."

Emily smiled and hung up her coat and scarf, indicating Davide should do the same. "I'll get you some water."

"I think I'm fine, Emilia. It was perhaps just a momentary indigestion." He hung his coat on the same hook by the mirror that he'd used that morning, then stood in front of the television to watch the tickertape scroll at the bottom of the screen. "You watch the Italian news? Why not CNN?"

"It's good practice for me, I guess. Besides, I'm used to *your* Italian," she said, pouring him a glass of water from the bottle sitting on the desk. "I need to be able to follow everyone else's, too."

He nodded and turned his attention back to the program, not wanting to think about what lay ahead of Emily the next day.

I'm more nervous about it than she is. I don't know why that is—she seems confident enough that she can handle it.

Still, it was worth noting she had changed since she'd arrived. It wasn't just in her voice—although that was softer, more hesitant than when they first met.

He wondered if perhaps this was because they spoke Italian almost exclusively when they were together. In the rare instances where they spoke English, she sounded different, more self-assured.

For a moment he considered if the same was true for him. Was *he* different when he spoke her language instead of his own?

But it wasn't just a matter of language. Her posture, her gestures, even her facial expressions were just a little different in Italian, too.

"It's funny you should say that," he said when the program went to a commercial.

"That I should say what, exactly?"

"You're used to *my* Italian. Is it so different?"

"Not exactly, it's just... There's a way you speak to me and a way you speak to, well, just about everyone else."

"I didn't know I did that. I'm sorry."

"Don't be, Davide. I think it's normal, you know? On some level, you're bound to be aware that I'm not a native speaker, so you address me differently. I kind of like it."

"You do?" He leaned against the desk and faced her, his hands flat on the tabletop. "Why do you like it?"

"It's kind of like there's a version of you that's just for me."

He laughed in spite of himself. "Like there are two versions of you?"

"What?"

"It's something I noticed before. Nothing bad, it's just that, when you speak Italian, you seem more...*timida* than you do when you're speaking English."

"I never thought about that. I guess there sort of *are* two 'me's," she said, suddenly thoughtful. "There's an American version of me, when I'm home or even sometimes back when I was teaching." She smiled, pondering the question. "Yeah, there's an Italian version of me, too. It's hard to explain it, but there really is a point when I'm traveling where I kind of switch over from one to the other."

"But is it a conscious decision? I mean, do you say 'Now I'll be the Italian me'?"

"No, not quite. Sometimes I'm aware of it later, but usually I just go from one 'me' to the other." She drew a quick breath, glancing around the room. "Once I'm halfway home, somewhere below Iceland, I guess, it's like a switch sort of...flips. If I'm going to the US, when I get to that point, I suddenly start missing Italy and everything about it.

"And, yeah, it's the same when I come home. I miss the US and *it* suddenly becomes home."

"I'm confused. Which place *becomes* 'home'?"

"What?"

"Which place suddenly becomes home for you when you come to Italy?"

Emily fell silent, clearly thinking hard.

"Emilia, this is something you should consider: which place is truly 'home' for you now? Where do you most want to be?"

"To be perfectly honest, I have to say I'm not sure."

Davide's face fell momentarily, but he recovered.

"But," she continued, "I have to say this, too: Bologna seems even more beautiful this time around. Has it always been this way?"

"No," he said, his heart lightening. "That's a pretty recent development. I only really noticed it a short while ago."

Color rose to her face and she pressed one hand to her cheek as though to wipe the ruddiness away.

"Anyway, every time I come back to Italy, I dread it. Just a little, but I *do* dread it."

"Why is that?"

"Oh, it's just... I don't know. Even this time, I had a little feeling of 'Ugh, here I go again' before I got on the plane. I couldn't wait to get back and I was looking forward to seeing you, but I still felt that 'Ugh' feeling."

"*Dimmi*: exactly what do you dread so much?"

"I guess it's the whole mixed bag. It's a beautiful place and it's full of beautiful people. Sometimes, that makes me feel like maybe I don't really belong here. Then there's that whole different rhythm of life to readjust to every time." She shook her head and shrugged. "Sometimes I can just jump right back into it—like this time, I got over the jet lag pretty quickly, my Italian hadn't suffered too much and it wasn't so hard.

"Other times, I hate even getting on the plane. I start thinking: 'Oh crap, I'm going to be surrounded by *them*'."

"'Them'?" Davide asked, half-laughing already.

"Italians." Emily laughed too. "I know it sounds absurd, but sometimes I feel like Italy would be exquisite if it weren't for some of the people I meet here." She held her head in her hands, groaning in mock pain. "I sound positively xenophobic, don't I?"

Davide laughed out loud. "No, just American." She groaned again and he thought the tone seemed momentarily defensive. "Lucky for you, I know you well. Besides, I think I understand. Sometimes I have a similar feeling."

"You do?" Emily looked at him through her fingers. "Really?"

He nodded again. "*Sì*, more than I care to admit. Tell me, does Italy feel different for you compared to, say, ten years ago?"

Surprised, she nodded slowly. "In some ways, yes, it does."

"Then you're not alone. I, and several of my colleagues, feel the same way. Perhaps you can take solace in this fact."

"I'm just happy to have met one of the good guys."

He looked away modestly for a moment and picked up his glass of water at last, hoping the gesture might hide his embarrassment.

"And then," she continued, "there's the fact that once I'm here, I'm thrilled to be here again. Almost every time I've come back, I've had another little 'honeymoon' period, you know? Where everything I see just seems so beautiful, I can't believe I wanted to leave it in the first place.

"I fall in love with this place every time I step out of the airport. Even the people who drive me crazy make me want to grab them and give them a hug. Well, except for the guy peeing under the overpass."

"Who is that?" Davide laughed harder than ever and Emily did the same.

"Seriously, you haven't noticed? There's always a man peeing under the overpass—especially when you leave the airport."

"*Oddio*, Emilia. This is too much."

"It's *true*, Davide! Watch the next time you go to the airport— I'm telling you, you'll see him! It might even be same guy."

"So you think there's a serial overpass pisser? Really?"

"Well, okay. I'm not sure it's him *every* time. I don't look that closely, to be honest." She shook her head. "Listen to me going on... Sit, sit..." she said, waving a hand toward the desk chair, then toward the bed. "Make yourself comfortable—I need to brush my teeth, if you don't mind. I had no idea how potent that bit of onion on my pizza would be."

"Oh, um... Okay." Davide spotted the remote control for the television. "Do you mind if I...?"

"No, go ahead. I'll be right back." She disappeared into the bathroom and closed the door.

Already flipping channels, Davide sat at the head of the bed and leaned back against the headboard, his glass of water still in his hand. He drank the water down in a few quick swallows and put the glass on the nightstand, then shifted position and continued turning the channels, looking for something else to pass the time until she came back out.

Finally he settled on the news program he'd begun with, though the newscaster's droning proved dangerously soporific. He straightened up, shifted position a couple of times until the ridge of the headboard pressed against his back, and settled in to watch the program again.

There. At least I won't fall asleep this time.

Emily stepped out of the bathroom, her lips and tongue still tingling from the mouthwash and toothpaste she'd used. The peppermint scent was pleasant enough, though the mouthwash was stronger than she liked.

If it cuts through that onion, though, I'll sleep a lot better.

"Davide? What time is your class tomor–" she stopped short, finding him leaning against the headboard of the bed, remote control grasped in one hand, his glasses knocked askew where he'd curled up to press his face against a pillow.

"Well, heck," she muttered. "I was only in there about ten minutes, tops."

A soft, atonal snore was his response.

Shaking her head, she smiled in spite of herself and crossed the room to peer down at her sleeping guest. His glasses were pressing hard against the bridge of his nose, the skin there paler where the frames pinched.

Ouch.

Reaching gingerly for the edges of his eyeglasses, she paused to be sure he wouldn't startle awake before she tried to take them off him. She had to press her hand against the pillow to get the lower part free, then they slid off easily. Davide swallowed and turned his head slightly as though listening for something, then nestled against the pillow once more, still grasping the remote.

Emily folded the earpieces back and set the glasses on the nightstand, eased the remote out of his hand to switch off the television and then pondered her options.

She could wake him up, but it seemed cruel just to send him back out into the cold at that late hour.

She could get ready for bed and see if he woke up. She considered making a little noise, so it wouldn't be like forcing him to leave.

Or I could just give him a blanket and let him stay. We both have to get up early-ish anyway.

She looked through the closets and found an extra duvet, which she folded in half and draped over him. Her thoughts drifted back to Milan, how she'd done the same when he'd fallen asleep on the sofa in her room.

After getting her pajamas out of her suitcase, she went to the bathroom and changed quietly, the door cracked open just enough to hear the occasional snuffle from the bed.

She switched off the other lights and slipped into bed with care, not wanting to disturb him. Before shutting off the light on her nightstand, she watched him sleep for a few minutes, a tenderness aching in her chest. The strength of her desire to reach out and stroke his hair, to touch his cheek, took her by surprise, though she resisted as long as she could.

Oh, the hell with it.

She slid closer, the covers bunching up between them, and she placed a soft kiss on his cheek, followed by another on the edge of his mouth. She breathed in the last traces of his cologne, making a mental note to use his pillow the next night. Her fingers quivered, yearning to caress the shadow of stubble along his jawline, and she moved away to keep from doing so.

If I wake him, he might leave. That's the last thing I want, isn't it?

Nodding in response to her own question, she snuggled down into the covers, still watching him. Finally, she reached back and switched off the last light in the room, tensing to see if that would wake him.

It didn't and she was grateful.

She listened to his breathing in the darkness. The soft regularity was soothing and familiar, and soon she lay drifting on the edge of sleep. This was what she'd wanted since returning home, what she'd longed for every night for a year.

For heaven's sake, why are we dancing around this, anyway? What are we so afraid of?

When she turned onto her side, he snuffled again, sounding close to wakefulness. Emily froze, waiting to see if he would wake up or not, trying to formulate an explanation to give as to why she hadn't woken him in the first place.

I'll tell him the truth. I didn't want him to go.

Davide shifted position, the bedsprings making soft, squeaking protests. A fluttery, ticklish sensation emerged low in her belly as Emily considered the noises the bed would make if they made love on it. She clenched her thighs together, which only made the warm flutters worse, then tried to distract herself, hoping to lose her focus on the pleasant frustration persisting there.

Unable to see the clock, she had no idea how long she lay there, her imagination running wild, before he turned over and draped his arm across her waist. Even with the bedclothes piled between them, the intimacy of this contact was enough to send a shudder through her body, a bright flare seeming to flash and extinguish itself all at once.

With Davide's breath warm against the nape of her neck, his arm snug around her waist, she was almost able to ignore the tickle of the few tears that traced her nose to fall onto her pillow.

She counted four silent drops before she fell asleep.

30

T he scent of her hair was the first thing he recognized in his surroundings. The industrial "clean" scent of the pillowcase beneath his cheek told him nothing. Then he realized he didn't care about anything but the scent of her hair.

Her skin smelled lovely too, a hint of her soap remaining there along with something earthier, more natural, underlying it. The salt of her skin or the oils of her scalp, perhaps.

He wondered how long his arm had been around her waist, since it had been long enough for him to perspire from the unbroken contact.

The blue-gray light from the skylight was growing brighter; surely she'd wake soon. Davide breathed deeply, slowly, hoping to avoid disturbing her.

What day is it? He blinked once, twice, then shut his eyes. *Is it Wednesday? No, it's Thursday. Merda. I have a lesson this morning. What time is it? I'll have to go home and change clothes before I go in.*

Instead of looking for a clock or glancing at his watch, he tightened his arm around her and pressed closer. With the duvet between them, he couldn't feel the curves of her body any better. He sniffed her hair again and moved closer to enjoy it, before brushing his lips across the back of her neck until she stirred awake.

"Emilia…?" He kept his voice low and quiet, hoping to ease her out of sleep. "What time is your train to Rovigo this morning?"

"Ten-fifteen, I think." She rolled back to look up at him and then returned to lying on her side. "What time is it now?"

Davide moved to read his watch over her shoulder. "It's almost eight," he said, regretting the late hour. He considered apologizing for falling asleep there, but pushed the apology aside.

"When is your lesson?"

"Eleven, but I have a quick meeting before that."

"Ugh."

"*D'accordo.*" He sighed, unable to put off what was inevitable. "I should go. I have to get ready for work."

"You could shower here," she said, her voice muffled by her pillow. "Go on, I'll get mine after you're done."

"My clothes are wrinkled."

"You're wearing a sweater and jeans. No one will notice."

"They're what I wore yesterday."

Emily moved to face him again, smiling. He smiled too, taking in her sleepy eyes and the tangles of her hair. She *looked* as though she'd spent a rather contented night and he wished it were so.

"Ah," he said. "I see. So at this stage of my career, I should be creating small scandals?"

"I'm sure the students would enjoy it."

He chuckled and gave her a swift kiss, the effort so spontaneous and natural he didn't give it a second thought until he'd rolled away to get up from the bed. She hadn't objected, which was nothing short of encouraging.

Mindful of time slipping away, he hurried through his morning routine, still entertaining the notion of a quick trip back to his flat to change clothes before work. People *had* noticed changes in him; Miki had said so months ago, hadn't he? Best not to rock the boat more than was strictly necessary.

When he stepped out into the room, Emily was standing at the desk, sipping a glass of water. She turned to him with a smile and he felt the floor drop out from under his feet.

Her hair was tousled, her childish flannel pajamas rumpled and mussed. Still, the soft flush in her cheeks sealed the impression of someone who had just been tumbling around in bed with her partner, he thought, though he had no earthly reason for it.

This is how she'll look after we make love.

"*Hai finito?*" she asked.

He nodded wordlessly, not trusting himself to speak. Not yet.

"I'll be quick—maybe we can get some breakfast?" she said, disappearing into the bathroom and freeing him to think clearly.

"*Forse, sì…*"

A plaintive chirruping rang from the folds of his coat and Davide crossed to it, fumbling through the slack pockets to find his mobile phone. He'd barely extracted it before flipping it open to answer, a maddening tickle at the back of his thoughts.

"*Pronto?*"

"Davide? It's Miki. Where are you?"

Oddio… What did I forget?

"Why?" he asked and then it hit him in a rush—the staff breakfast meeting. He'd agreed to attend the evening before, when he was rushing out to meet Emily. "*Merda…* Miki—I don't think I'm going to be able to make it."

"Well, see if you can get here before it's over, eh? There're some important things to discuss, you know."

"*Sì, sì… Lo so.* I'll be there as soon as I can."

"*Ciao.*"

"*Ciao-ciao…Ciao…*" He flipped the phone closed, still saying goodbye. *Now what?*

He sat on the edge of the bed for a moment, then stood up in order to resist the temptation of lying down to wrap himself in the sheets once more.

I'll wait for her to finish, then explain why I have to go. I can't believe I forgot that meeting this morning, but we've just had one yesterday, so… Never mind, it's not important. If I miss it, Miki can fill me in. But then he'll want more details about why I'm late…

Davide shook his head, sighing. It wasn't really so complicated, but at the moment, it certainly seemed that way.

Lost in thought, he didn't notice she was next to him until she rested one hand lightly on his shoulder, startling him out of his contemplation of the roof just visible through the skylight.

"Is something wrong?"

"Not terribly so, no. I have to leave right away, Emilia. I forgot about a department meeting this morning."

"I thought you had one yesterday."

"We did. This is rather an informal one. They asked me last night and it slipped my mind completely."

"Oh." Her disappointment was plain. "I guess you should go, then."

"*Sì*... This is not how I wished us to part." He pulled his coat off the hook and put it on, his eyes never leaving hers. "Be careful in Rovigo, eh? Don't let him get away with anything."

She gave a little laugh at this as she walked him to the door. "Don't worry about a thing, Davide. I won't."

He bent and gave her a swift, gentle kiss, his hand stroking her hair back over her shoulder as he did so. A damp strand wound around one finger, cool against his skin, and he took his time untangling it.

"I should go," he said, the words dull on his lips.

"I'll see you soon."

He paused in the doorway and turned to face her once more.

"Call me when you get in, okay? We'll have dinner."

"Sure. I'll do that."

He nodded, still picturing her with her hair mussed, her pajamas in disarray. "*Va bene*. I'll see you later, then."

There was nothing provocative about her in that moment, and yet he couldn't stop looking at her, couldn't bring himself to leave the room and go to work. Without thinking, he reached for her and she stepped readily into his embrace, tilting her face up for his kiss.

It was too much. As his lips touched hers the gentle caress he'd intended became something vastly different. She yielded to him and returned the kiss with equal fervor, her body pressed to his, her tongue meeting his in flickering strokes which sent flashes of heat to his core.

He pushed back into the room, fumbling the door closed behind them as they went. Her arms slipped around him beneath his coat while his hands sought her breasts through the fabric of her blouse, cupping them to feel her nipples rigid against the soft flesh of his palms.

Without ending their kisses she sighed deeply, shuddering into his touch, openly eager for more. She slipped one hand under his sweater, pulled his button-down shirt out from the waistband of his jeans and slid her hand from his belly to his back, drawing him closer to her.

I want you...

He swallowed the words before he could speak them, aware it would be the last straw. He wouldn't part from her from that moment on if the sentiment were breathed into life. The timing was always just a little bit off somehow. The unfairness of it brought a surge of anger and his hands dropped to grasp her hips and draw her roughly to himself. If he couldn't say it, he would demonstrate it instead.

Her soft, yearning sound of want proved his point was made, and she understood. Her other hand rose up to twine in his hair, holding him firmly for another kiss, this one slow and deep as their frantic energy ebbed away.

As he trailed his lips along the curve of her throat a few moments later, she wrapped her arms around his neck. He held her close, luxuriating in the length of her body along his, every curve fitting perfectly to him while they calmed together.

"I'll call you as soon as I get back..." Though she hadn't said anything explicit, he nodded his understanding, his complicity, and held her tighter. In the span of a heartbeat he was filled with desperation and longed to beg for her promise, then was reassured once more.

She would call him when she got back from Rovigo.

When she got back from Jacopo, and when she would never have to see him again.

31

As far as Emily could tell, the station in Rovigo hadn't changed. It was still a postage-stamp-sized stop on the way to somewhere else, a moderately charming city hidden behind the start of urban sprawl alongside the railway. She managed not to dwell too much on the memories lurking all around her there: the platform where she'd waited, or the newsstand where she'd bought the magazine containing Davide's article. In spite of her efforts, anxiety underscored her mood.

Tugging at her gloves, Emily snuggled her hands inside them as she came out of the station, remembering the night Davide had given them to her. The bite of the wind soon diverted her attention from this pleasant memory. She pulled her bag more securely onto her shoulder and made her way toward the taxi stand. With every step in that direction, she cursed Jacopo and his *notaio* for having arranged a lunch meeting.

No doubt about it: he did it so it would take forever. I know how Jacopo takes his time eating.

A fresh gust of wind swept around her, lifting her hair and toying with her scarf while she waited for a taxi to arrive. She had plenty of time to get the *notaio*'s offices, but her impatience built with every second.

I just want to get this over with. Is it too much to ask?

A white station wagon with a "Taxi" sign on the roof pulled up alongside her. She checked the station to reassure herself she wasn't poaching someone's ride.

"*Vai in centro?*" she asked when he rolled the window down.

"*Sì, certo…*" he said, waving her inside, and she slipped into the backseat, grateful for the warm interior as she gave him the address in the city center.

Luckily, the driver was the quiet type. No questions about where she was going or why and no monologues or rants about tourists, foreigners and immigrants, and why the country would be better off without them. As soon as her Italian had been up to the task, she had enjoyed debating these topics with her students and work acquaintances, asking whether they would have *her* thrown out of Italy as well.

Yet she'd never had those debates with Jacopo. She'd quickly found he held a rather conservative opinion, but she'd never felt comfortable challenging him. Frankly, she had been afraid of how he'd answer.

For the duration of the taxi ride to the city center, Emily was determined to push aside thoughts of Jacopo and concentrate more on Davide. More to the point, she concentrated on his kiss that morning, before he'd left her room.

Even now, hours later, she shivered a little at the thought of it, a fresh rush of excitement flooding through her. There had been something so different in his kisses and his touch that morning. There had been a greater passion, a greater urgency in their farewell than she'd ever felt before.

This is going to happen. Soon.

Emily closed her eyes and pictured his face before he'd left her. The almost plaintive expression in his eyes had alarmed her, had almost made her call out to him when he'd finally turned to go, but she'd let him leave. If it hadn't been for his meeting—if not for her meeting, too—they might have stayed and seen things through… She couldn't bear thinking about it for long. The opportunity had come and gone, but there would be another. Perhaps even tonight.

A little quake of anticipation ran through her at the idea. She smiled, looking down at her gloves. A perfect fit, though he'd had no idea what size she wore. They were an exact match for her coat, too, just a shade deeper for a stylish contrast. She flexed her hands and watched the leather stretch, the quiet, supple sound just audible over the road sounds in the taxi.

"*Eccoci arrivati, signora!*"

She fumbled out the cash and told him to keep the change. He nodded his gratitude and she got out, checking the address of the building against the one in the e-mail she'd printed out. Her smile faded away. When this was over, she'd go straight to Davide and whatever might happen, would happen.

The reception area appeared quite modest: framed prints which hung on pale blue walls, gleaming marble floors, dark wooden furniture everywhere. Even the receptionist wasn't particularly notable with her heart-shaped face, long dark hair with a hint of a wave, businesslike dress and demeanor.

Emily explained why she was there and the girl pointed to a sofa along the wall.

"*Prego, si accomodi. Il dottor* Fontana will be ready for you shortly."

"*Grazie.*" Emily crossed to the sofa and sat, then checked her watch. If she had to wait more than forty-five minutes, she'd leave and take her chances with the whole mess. Maybe.

Oh, who am I kidding? I'll stay here all day, just to be sure it's done.

Then the door opened and Emily went cold when she saw him come in. She swallowed hard, the sound in her ears almost covering his softly-spoken question to the receptionist.

Her throat went dry, clenching hard enough for her to worry she might not be able to breathe. His back to her, she knew all-too-well the shape of his shoulders, the tilt of his head, the soft wave in his blond hair, every gesture he made while heedless of her attention.

Just like always.

Even his leather briefcase was familiar, though the canvas shopping bag in his other hand was not.

The receptionist's professional manner had evaporated completely. Now she leaned on one hand, laughter in every word, her eyes focused on the man while she looked up at him through lowered lashes.

Emily rested one hand over her stomach, momentarily sickened that she would have reacted in much the same way if taken unaware. She sat up straight, smoothed her coat over her lap and ignored him, to no avail. Her eyes seemed to return to him with a will of their own.

At last she focused on a real estate magazine and picked it up from the side table to leaf through it. She refused to glance over toward the receptionist's desk when the girl let out a squeal of laughter. Keeping her hand still, Emily turned the page and stared at the photo of a pop singer's refurbished home theater, trying to direct her thoughts forty-five miles away to Bologna, to Davide.

"Emily?"

She hated herself for the small thrill at the "Emmy-Lee" pronunciation of her name. She closed the magazine and looked up at him, her heart speeding.

A beard. That's new.

"Jacopo," she said with a calm she didn't quite feel, a flicker of pride following close behind.

"You made it," he said in English, a sincere smile on his lips. She couldn't tell if it reached his eyes or not; she couldn't bring herself to look.

"*Sì, sono qui. Come stai?*"

His pale blue, summer-sky eyes sought hers relentlessly until she met his gaze. "I'm very well…now."

"*E perché?*"

"I'm glad to see you," he said, insistently continuing in English.

Emily said nothing, hoping she looked as cool and disinterested as she wanted to.

Puzzlement flitted over his face as he cleared his throat, looking around the reception area. He turned toward the girl at the desk and

Emily knew he was giving her a flirtatious smile. The girl's flustered fussing with her papers was evidence enough.

With a roll of her eyes, Emily sat back and turned her attentions to her magazine again.

"Emily." Jacopo turned to face her and she drew her focus from the magazine to meet his eyes. "Could we talk privately?"

"Why?" she sighed, relenting and speaking English as well before dropping the magazine on the table in a show of annoyance. "What is it?"

"Please?"

Davide's entreaties came to mind and Emily willed her racing heart to slow. Was there any harm in such a request? They were in a public place, both of them due to meet with the lawyer in a few minutes. Jacopo wasn't foolish enough to try anything overt.

"Where?"

"Come with me." Jacopo walked down the corridor to the meeting rooms, leaving her to follow. Her resentment flared at his presumptuousness, so she took her time standing and following a few moments later. He stopped at one of the empty rooms, held the door open and gestured for her to precede him.

Emily tossed her coat over the back of the nearest chair and faced him, folding her arms defiantly across her chest. "What is it, then?"

"I have something for you." Jacopo placed the canvas bag on the table. "You left a few things at the flat last year. I found them when I was going over the properties a couple of weeks ago."

Emily turned and looked inside the bag, a lump forming in her throat. She recognized the cell phone and the leather gloves immediately, but the small mailing tube shoved in the bottom of the bag turned her stomach.

Proserpina.

She bit her lip and closed the bag, not looking at him. The memory of him giving her the print of Prosperina accepting the pomegranate seeds, the act which had started their relationship so sweetly, threatened to leave more unpleasant memories strewn in its wake.

"Thanks, I guess."

"You can use the phone now. I charged it for you—the charger is there, see? I loaded the minutes, too. I couldn't believe you'd forgotten it."

"Me neither."

"Emily…" he began, stepping closer to her.

Here it comes… She refused to look at him, her hands starting to shake from his proximity.

"I want to ask you if we could go somewhere and talk after this meeting today."

"Are you kidding me?" His cologne, the one she now knew he had custom-blended at a *profumeria* in Rome, danced enticingly along her tongue, leaving elements of bergamot and sandalwood behind.

He was near enough to lean in and kiss her, if he wished. For a moment she wondered if his neatly-trimmed beard would be ticklish on her lips. For the briefest possible instant, she wanted to find out. The thought of kissing him thrilled and terrified her, as it had in his palazzo on the Grand Canal so many years before. Had something happened with his wife, then? This wasn't the behavior of a married man.

Not that he's ever behaved like a married man.

"No, I'm serious. There is much I'd like to say to you, Emily. Much I'd like to apologize for."

She was unable to stop her small gasp at this. His cell phone rang in his pocket and he withdrew it, examining the number for a moment before he flipped it open.

"*Scusami*, Emily, please."

He moved to the corridor and Emily rummaged in the canvas bag for her own phone. True to his word, it was fully charged, the minutes loaded.

Incredible.

Emily put it in her purse and turned to face him when he came in again.

"*Era mia moglie…* My wife gets nervous when I don't call on time."

"I can't imagine why," she said, the words out before she'd realized it.

Jacopo nodded, the gesture remarkably humble. "This is why I hoped you'd stay here tonight. I wish to talk to you."

"What do you mean, *tonight?*"

"I've reserved a hotel room for you. I thought perhaps we might have dinner and discuss things."

She was about to reply when the receptionist pushed the door open and peered inside. "*Scusate.* If you're ready, *Il dottor* Fontana will see you in his office."

"*Prego*, Emily—could we discuss this afterward?"

"I don't know, Jacopo. We'll see."

32

As stalling tactics went, it proved a spectacular failure. The meeting moved from *Il dottor* Fontana's office to a restaurant across the street. They met the purchaser there, a rotund and unremarkable man named Moretti. Emily nursed her single glass of wine for the entire meal, but drank a small bottle of mineral water on her own—the amounts were reversed for the others.

Still, when the paperwork was handed around, inspected and signed nearly three hours later, Emily hadn't been so blindsided since Jacopo left for Rome five years ago.

It can't be right. It just can't be.

Jacopo explained with an almost unsuitable tenderness that the funds were already in her account, the proof in her hands in the form of copies of the bill of sale. It served as a receipt, as it were, with a number she hadn't expected to see, because it was for a far larger amount than what he had told her was due. Her share of the house had doubled, seemingly overnight.

When he asked again if she would stay in Rovigo so they could talk, she numbly agreed, reaching for her cell phone.

"Who are you calling?"

"I was supposed to meet someone tonight. I need to let him know I won't make it."

"'Him?'" Jacopo asked, raising one eyebrow and tilting his chin toward the phone in her hand. "Who is this?"

"A friend," Emily smiled, knowing no matter what she said, he would read much more into it. She walked a few paces away, listening to the ringing of the phone.

"*Pronto?*"

Emily sighed in relief at Davide's voice. "*Ciao. Sono io…*"

"*Come stai*, Emilia? Is everything all right?"

"Everything's fine. I just, um… I'm not going to make it back in time for dinner. I'm so sorry…" For a moment, her throat tightened and her eyes burned with tears. She swallowed hard and continued, determined to keep her voice steady so he wouldn't worry. "I have a few things to discuss with him, so I'm going to be late."

There was a long pause on the other end of the line and she held her breath, waiting for his response.

"Oh. Well…call me when you get in?"

"I will, I promise. I'll call you as soon as I get back," she said, a deliberate echo of her words in the hotel that morning.

"Emilia?"

"*Sì?*"

"Be very careful, please. Don't trust him."

"Not even as far as I can fling him," she said in English and was reassured by Davide's soft chuckle.

She snapped her phone closed, returning to Jacopo. "So. What do you have to say to me?"

"I have an appointment in an hour," he said and raised one hand to stay her protest. "As I said, I've reserved you a room, so if you would wait for me –"

"I have other ways to spend my time, thanks. I'm not going to sit around while you're doing *business* anymore." She spun the word as hard as possible, filling it with every lurid inference she could manage.

Amazingly, he looked chagrined.

"Emily, I'm supposed to appraise some properties for the bank, here in the center. It'll take a couple of hours at most, but I can't—I *won't* let you leave without talking to me."

"You don't have a choice." She turned and began walking toward the station, ignoring the wind which numbed her face as she went. The winter sunset cast deep red shades along the street, darkening fast.

The sound of Jacopo's footfalls caught up to her in no time. "Don't do this, Emily, please." He grasped her arm and pulled her to a halt. "It's not safe to walk to the station at night. At least let me take you, or something."

"What happened to not letting me leave?"

Jacopo shook his head, his complexion ruddy in the late afternoon light. "I have no right to ask this of you."

"No, you don't."

"But I'm asking anyway. Emily, please."

"Fine. Which hotel is it?"

"The Crown," he said, hailing a passing taxi and then opening the door for her. "I'll be there in a few hours. Just go to the desk and give them your name, okay? They're expecting you."

Jacopo handed the driver cash for the trip without even consulting him about the cost. Emily stared out at him from the back seat.

What could be so important he'd go to this much trouble?

She watched him through the window until the taxi turned the corner and he disappeared from sight. Melancholy washed over her while she turned her attention to the city itself, hoping to forget the lost look in his eyes.

"Before you start, I want to know—why didn't you tell me the truth about the house?"

After Emily's prolonged refusal to accept the menu, Jacopo lowered it to the table. He shook his head, a half-smile on his lips. "I promise, it wasn't deliberate. I made a mistake when I sent you the information on the price, that's all."

"Really? That's a pretty big mistake."

"I know. I copied the wrong part of the document when I sent the e-mail to you. Instead of the full price, I sent you your share, after expenses. Should I apologize for that?"

Emily laughed and Jacopo visibly relaxed. "No, I guess not. It made for a nice surprise."

"A nice surprise?"

"A *very* nice surprise," she amended, picking up the menu at last.

"Will you join me for a glass of wine, Emily? I feel as though we should celebrate this."

"Celebrate what?"

"The sale of the house, for one thing. That we are here together is worthy of a toast or two, isn't it?"

"I don't know about that," she said, conceding a smile.

The server arrived to take the orders and disappeared into the depths of the kitchen with such efficiency that Jacopo didn't have the chance to remove the befuddled expression on his face.

Emily sipped at her water, her eyes never leaving his. "I'm being civil, Jacopo. That doesn't exactly mean I'm *enjoying* your company."

His eyes narrowed in what appeared to be genuine puzzlement. Emily took another sip of water to cool the heat raging in her stomach. *My God, he really doesn't understand, does he?*

"Do you think what you did to me is so easily forgiven?" she asked in Italian, knowing her voice would carry to the closest tables. "Do you think one year is enough to forget ten years of lies?"

He made a *tsk* sound, shaking his head in a dismissive gesture. "You exaggerate, *tesoro mio*."

"I don't. And don't call me that. You lost that privilege a long time ago."

Jacopo fell silent, staring at the empty dishes on the table before them. "Circumstances changed," he said after a few moments.

"Indeed, they did." Emily picked up her water glass and didn't drink. She was far from thirsty. It was something to do, to keep her hands busy so they couldn't, say, grasp a fork or knife and fling it at him.

She stilled her trembling hand in her lap and feigned calm as the server arrived with a bottle of wine and two glasses. He poured a small amount in one glass and waited while Jacopo assessed it. At his nod, the young man disappeared once more.

"I never wished to hurt you," Jacopo said, in English yet again.

"*Hai fallito, spettacolarmente.*" Emily drew a deep breath, ignoring the bile rising in her throat. "You hurt me more than you could ever understand. Knowing the whys and wherefores doesn't change anything."

Jacopo said nothing. The entrees arrived and Emily stared at her plate, certain she couldn't eat any of it. Eventually the mechanics of eating filled the long silence between them.

"*Dimmi una cosa,*" she said, when the dinner dishes were cleared and the dessert served. "I'm begging you, please, to be *honest* with me now."

Jacopo looked up from his plate to meet her eyes. It seemed to take some effort. "I will."

"Did you *ever* love me? Or was it always just for your mother's benefit?" She sat up straight, steeling herself for whatever response he might give, and refused to let his eyes stray from hers.

He swallowed hard, blinking rapidly, and for the first time Emily realized his eyes were red. After a pause he spoke so softly she had to lean closer to the table to hear.

"I did. But not at first."

Instinctively, her hand went to her throat. Blinking tears back, she desperately wished she'd never asked. Had she really wanted to know? Was he telling the truth now?

"I thought," Jacopo continued, his voice still scarcely audible in the murmurs of conversation around them, "if I hurt you enough, you'd leave and it wouldn't be up to me to break things off. I thought you'd leave before Mamma died and she'd think I'd at least tried... But you refused to *go*. I had to be obvious about things, and you *still* didn't go, didn't get angry—*niente*. I was going out of my mind until I realized that *you* cared for *me*. You didn't care about money, or where we lived or anything else."

"I didn't."

"When Mamma died, I thought I'd let you go then. I thought you'd understand what I'd been doing, who I'd been seeing…and yet, you never seemed to. If you did, you never said anything. That's when I fell in love with you."

"And that's when you left."

He nodded in response and a small laugh forced itself out of Emily's throat. His eyes narrowed in confusion and she poured some of the wine into her glass.

"Jacopo," she began calmly, "it seems to me that you're a little unclear on a few concepts."

The rest of dinner passed under a strained air of civility.

"It's late—I have to go." Emily pushed her chair back and stood up. Jacopo rushed to do the same, signing the check and handing it to the server.

"It's only ten o'clock, why the hurry?"

"I have to catch a train," she said, going to the alcove near the entrance to retrieve her coat.

"Which one?"

Emily shrugged. "Whichever one is going to Bologna next, I suppose."

Jacopo withdrew his cell phone from his pocket and began scrolling through pages on the touch-screen. "I'll see what the schedule is."

"You don't have to do that."

"Please, I insist…" His words trailed off and he gave her a nervous look, tapping at the screen all the while.

"What's the matter?" Emily froze, her arms halfway into her coat sleeves. "Is something wrong?"

"I…" Jacopo gave her a plaintive look and resumed scrolling. "I had no idea, I swear."

"What is it?"

"There aren't any trains until one a.m."

Emily pulled her coat on and grasped his wrist to read the screen for herself. Her stomach rolled unpleasantly and she bit back the first word that rose to her lips.

Davide.

"This is ridiculous. That can't be right—it's not even ten-thirty."

"*Sì*, but this is Rovigo. The next train is at 1:19 a.m., after that, the next is at around six a.m."

"I can wait there, then."

"*Sei pazza?* You can't hang around the station or take a train at that time of night."

"Why not?"

"It's too dangerous. How will you get from the station to, uh, wherever you're staying? At two in the morning? No, Emily, you can't do that." He grabbed his coat and put it on, following her out onto the sidewalk. "Just stay here. You can leave in the morning."

"I'm supposed to meet –"

"You can call your friend and tell him what happened. I'm sure he'll understand."

God, I hope so.

"Listen," Jacopo said, gently taking her by the arm and leading her toward the hotel, "I'll walk you up to your room and you can call your friend, okay?"

Emily turned her head sharply toward him and he released her, his hands up in a gesture of surrender.

"I just want to see you there safely, that's all."

"Damn it…" She groaned, one hand rising to her forehead while she closed her eyes. "You never fail to screw up every plan I make," she muttered, not caring whether he heard or not. "Fine, fine—let's go. I want to get as early a start as I possibly can in the morning."

True to his word and to her immense surprise, Jacopo was a perfect gentleman. He matched her pace as she walked swiftly along the sidewalk to the hotel, held the door when they arrived and even summoned the elevator on her behalf.

He accompanied her to her room and waited quietly while she unlocked the door with a swipe of her keycard. She propped the door open with her heel when she turned to face him, thinking how she'd done the same with Davide just the night before.

That turned out so nicely, too.

"Well, this is it, I guess," she said, the first words they'd spoken since leaving for the hotel.

"I guess so. Emily, I..." Jacopo exhaled slowly, his sentence unfinished. "I don't know what to say now."

"Neither do I." A lump formed in her throat and she tried to swallow it down. "Tell me something, Jacopo."

"What?"

"Are you happy?"

He tilted his head, then gave a half-shrug. "I think so, yes."

"Good," she said, nodding. "I am, too."

Jacopo smiled, a genuine effort that seemed to light up his face. "I'm glad to hear it, Emily."

She nodded again and he leaned in to kiss her on one cheek, then on the other. Emily returned the familiar, habitual gesture, taken by surprise with the press of his lips to her own.

His hand twined in her hair, holding her gently in place while he deepened the kiss. She closed her eyes, remembering how it had felt with him the first time around.

His beard does tickle, then...

He pulled her closer, trailing soft kisses back to the tender flesh behind her ear. She raised her hands to his shoulders, grasping him and drawing him down so her lips met his temple in a slow, gentle caress.

"Go home to your wife," she whispered, pushing him away with a tenderness that made her ache deep inside.

With three short steps, she was in her room, the door closed between them.

33

In spite of the cold, Davide was already sweating. When Emily's call didn't come by ten a.m., he gave up and went for a run. Though he hadn't given up completely; his mobile phone jounced in the front pocket of his sweatshirt, fastened to a cord to keep it from falling out. His chosen route would only take him about halfway around the *circonvallazione*, not into the hills outside the city.

If Emily called, he could be home in roughly half an hour. Less, perhaps, depending on where he was. Enough time had passed, however, for him to think this was unlikely.

To be fair, he had received a call the night before. She'd rung from a hotel in Rovigo, telling him she would be in Bologna in the morning. With considerable reluctance, he thought, she'd told him about Jacopo's last-minute kiss, and her refusal.

He wished this information did more for his spirits.

Emily had also said there was more to tell him, but it would be best to talk in person, in the morning.

Now the morning was nearly over and no calls had come. He'd only brought his phone because he hoped to hear from her— normally, he ran without it, hating the distraction. The bouncing in his pocket made him wonder whether he'd felt the vibration of an incoming call. After checking five times in fifteen minutes, he resolved to hold off until he'd covered a quarter of the ring road.

After an hour he completed the circuit, slowing his pace as he entered his street. As he cooled down his clothes clung to him, the brisk winter air prickling at the perspiration on his face and in his hair. By the time he arrived at his building, he felt as though he'd stepped out from a sauna and into the snow.

His breath misted around his face while he fumbled out his keys and unlocked the *portone*, then went inside to collect his mail. For what seemed like the first time in ages, Mr. Montanari wasn't there to complain about Davide's mail being in the wrong box. He was tempted—albeit briefly—to leave some of his junk mail in the old man's cubby.

Grinning, Davide took a deep breath and made a run at the stairs, intending to jog all the way up without pausing. It was getting harder to do that lately. His footsteps resounded on the marble steps, slapping out a weakening rhythm as he went, and he checked his watch as he approached the next-to-last landing.

Pretty good time, there. I'll just —

Vaguely aware of someone at the top of the stairs, he looked up and stumbled, barely managing to avoid barking his shin on the rounded marble edge of the step.

"Emilia?"

"Davide." She smiled and his weary legs threatened to give out altogether. "I guess I'm a bit early. Sorry."

"No, no… Perhaps I'm just late?" He dug in the pocket of his sweatshirt to retrieve his keys, his eyes never leaving hers even as he stabbed the key blindly at the lock. "You were leaving?" His mobile phone buzzed silently and he took it out with his other hand, wondering why it hadn't rung.

"I thought maybe I'd confused the time or something," Emily said, her voice echoing in the corridor. "I didn't sleep well last night."

He read the text message aloud as he swung the door open. "'I'm at the hotel now. Should be there around noon—is that okay?'"

"You just got that?" Emily's eyes widened.

"It happens sometimes. I don't know why. Come in, please. I'll be ready in a few minutes."

"All right." She stepped inside and hung her overcoat on the coat rack next to the door.

Another buzz of his phone followed while he held the door open for her. Reading the next text message quickly, he switched off the phone and dumped it in the basket on the table by the coat rack.

"What was that?" Emily asked.

The light filtering through the glass panels of the doors along the hall gave her skin almost the same pale gray tone of her sweater.

Davide switched on the hall lamp and warm yellow light touched the walls. "I've just been informed that you called. I'm so sorry, Emilia... I don't know what's wrong with my phone."

"Don't worry. I'm here now, right? I still feel bad about last night, though."

"*Di niente*," he said with a dismissive wave. "*Non importa.*" He unzipped his sweatshirt and quickly zipped it up again before running a hand through his sweat-dampened hair.

Oddio, I reek.

"Listen, ah... I'm sorry, but I need to make a shower, before –"

"Take a shower," Emily said, her tone gentle.

"What?"

"You need to *take* a shower. Or *have* a shower." She blushed deeply and raised one hand to her face as if to hide. "Sorry. It's a reflex."

"Oh, okay... Um, I need to do that before I can do anything else. Would you like something to drink? I have water and juice, or I could make you some tea, or –"

"Why don't I make the tea while you have your shower? I'm pretty sure I could find the kettle if you point me to the kitchen."

Davide paused, thrown. "Well, I... You wouldn't mind that? It seems terribly rude for me to ask."

"It isn't, I promise. Just tell me where the tea is and I'll figure out the rest."

"*Va bene...* This way. The kitchen's in the back, there," he said, pointing to the door as he stepped toward the bathroom. "The tea should be in the second cupboard from the door. There's sugar and honey there, too."

"Great, I'll get it started."

He took off his sweats and checked the pockets before tossing them into the washing machine on top of the towels. A nagging feeling of having forgotten something lurked at the back of his mind while he undressed.

I'm just distracted because I didn't expect her to be here.

With every clammy layer of clothing he removed, his skin grew colder. Harboring greedy anticipation of a steaming hot shower, he piled each article into the washing machine until he peeled off the last of his underclothes and realized he hadn't brought any clean clothes in with him. Worse still, his bathrobe was still on the drying rack in front of the balcony windows, in the living room.

A sensation like ice water trickled down his spine and he shivered.

I'll wrap up in a towel and grab something from the bedroom, then.

When he turned to the towel rack, he found it empty. He hadn't put any on the shelf, either. There were plenty in the *armadio* in the hall, of course, but he couldn't reach it without risking running into Emily.

With no towels left and his bathrobe in the other room, his only option was to pull his sweaty clothes out of the washing machine and put them back on.

No, I'm going to have to ask her... He opened the bathroom door a crack. "Emilia?" he called.

"*Sì?*"

"Would you do me a favor?"

"Sure."

"Would you bring me my bathrobe? It's on the rack in the living room."

"Oh... Yeah, okay."

Hoping to preserve some sense of modesty, he pressed against the door and reached one arm out to take the bathrobe when she arrived a few moments later. *"Grazie,"* he said, hoping his uneasiness wasn't obvious.

"Prego," she answered, turning her face away and hurrying back toward the living room.

It took a moment before he understood her hasty departure: he'd pressed himself against the glass panel of the bathroom door. She'd had a rather thorough, if blurry, view of his body.

Maybe she didn't see? It is possible that she didn't notice, surely... He hung his robe on the hook, obscuring the glass panel. The more he thought about it, the more certain he became: she *had* seen, no doubt about it.

Non ci posso credere...non ci posso credere...

Shoulders slouching, he turned on the shower and stepped in while the water warmed.

Non ci posso credere... I cannot believe it... He hoped vaguely that she wouldn't hear the thumping of his head against the tiled shower walls, again and again, as the steam rose around him.

Emily sat on the sofa, hunched over, her face in her hands, torn between two wholly separate urges—to whoop with exhilaration, or to swoon with embarrassment?

He couldn't have intended the show he'd just given her—he wasn't the brazen sort. *But he should know — my God, could I have been more obvious about looking at him? At* it?

It had only been a moment or two, but those moments felt like an eternity. He reached for the robe, she gave him the robe and she left. Simple, right?

No.

Her memories of him from the hotel in Milan were still quite clear—and that glimpse just now had proven her case. She had only caught a hint of his sweat when they met on the stairs; she'd had a much stronger sense of him at the bathroom door.

And damned if it wasn't all I could do to keep from joining him.

Desperate for some sort of distraction, Emily walked around the living room, crossing to the window that led onto the balcony. As she stepped out into the afternoon sunshine, her arms tingled with gooseflesh beneath the knit of her sweater.

Breathe, then—breathe deeply.

After a few minutes her mind felt clearer, but she kept drawing deep breath after deep breath, her fingers fiddling with the tab of her sweater's zipper until she shivered and rubbed her arms. "Now what?" she muttered, closing the balcony door behind her. She glanced down the hall to the bathroom before perching again on the sofa. "Lunch, maybe, and then…?"

When the shower shut off she got up and walked quietly to the kitchen. She kept busy, filling and starting the electric kettle, choosing mugs from those resting in the rack above the sink, taking the tea and sugar out of the cabinet he'd mentioned.

The burbling of the kettle peaked a few moments before the sound of Davide's hairdryer ceased, the two shutting off at almost the same time. Emily stood at the tiny kitchen table, its leaf folded down and out of the way. There was just enough room for two people to pass each other in the tight space left. One café-style chair was stacked atop another and she separated them, placing one on the opposite side of the table from the other.

He never sits in here. I bet he rarely even eats here.

While she poured the hot water into the mugs, she listened keenly and was rewarded with the sound of him passing through the hallway and into another room. His bedroom, most likely, since the quiet *thump* of a closing door followed.

A short while later the faint creaking of an opening door caught her attention.

A pause, then, from the hallway: "Emilia?"

"*Sì?*"

The approaching sound of his footsteps made her heart race. She breathed deep, willing herself to calm. When he stopped in the doorway she turned to face him, opening one of the tea packets and taking out the bag without looking at it.

"The tea will be ready in a couple of minutes," she said. "I didn't add any sweetener; I don't know which kind you like best."

"*Grazie.*"

Her hands were suddenly too heavy, too clumsy, under his watchful eyes. It took effort but she was able to still their shaking before she put a tea bag in each mug, swirling them around to color the water more quickly.

"You're not wearing your glasses?" she asked.

He shrugged, the gesture somehow a response in the negative. "I don't need them at home unless I'm reading or watching TV."

She couldn't help smiling at his "tee voo" pronunciation of "TV."

"Are you hungry?" he asked, his eyes flicking to the refrigerator at the end of the narrow kitchen. "I could make something."

"That would be nice. Could I do anything to help?"

"Please, sit." From the rack next to the sink he took a pot and filled it with water, then placed it on a burner, turning the fire on high. He tossed a handful of coarse salt into the pot before going to the refrigerator. After a moment, he took out an unidentifiable object in plastic wrap and a single clove of garlic. From the cabinet over the countertop he withdrew a small bottle with a cork stopper and another bottle of some sort of spice.

He took spaghetti from another, taller container, made a circle with his finger and thumb and measured a portion out before chucking it into the boiling water.

"Five minutes," he said, holding up an open palm before retrieving and setting out plates, forks and knives. He gulped down some of his cooled tea before he unwrapped the plastic-wrapped item. Emily saw it was a huge hunk of hard cheese—*Parmigiano Reggiano*, by the scent of it.

Davide took a small knife with an oval-shaped blade from a drawer and worked it into the hard surface of the block until a few small chunks broke free. He repeated this before placing several pieces on a small plate and rewrapping and putting the cheese away.

Emily watched, fascinated by the efficiency with which he worked as he stirred the pasta, then brought out a pan and drizzled olive oil into it. After adjusting the flame under the pan, he opened the spice bottle, sprinkled some of its contents into the oil and stirred it around with a wooden fork. With quick, careful movements, he sliced the garlic clove and tossed it into the oil, tilting the pan to and fro for a moment.

The aroma of browning garlic and red chili pepper drifted through the kitchen and Emily sat back, inhaling the scent contentedly.

"I had no idea you could cook, Davide."

"This isn't cooking," he said glancing over at her with a grin. "It's survival. I don't have much in the house, so this will have to do."

"Wow…"

He put a colander in the sink and dumped the spaghetti into it, shook it once, twice and then poured the pasta into the pan on the stove. A few deft tosses with the wooden fork and a wooden spoon and he carefully served out portions onto the plates.

"*Aglio, olio e peperoncino*; garlic, oil and chili pepper pasta," he said and she nodded to show her familiarity with it.

From the refrigerator he took out a bottle of mineral water and a half-empty bottle of Lambrusco, which he placed in the middle of the already overloaded kitchen table.

"It's *amabile*," he said, indicating the wine. "I think you could drink it, if you want to try."

"*Grazie*, Davide."

"*Buon appetito*," he said and nearly dropped his fork when he went to pick it up.

They ate in silence, with only the clinking of glassware or silverware between them. Whenever she looked up from her plate, Emily caught Davide's eyes glancing down to his own, or to the side—anywhere that was away from her. At first he merely seemed nervous. By the time they finished the pasta and he collected their plates, nervousness had given way to outright agitation.

He brought the small plate of *Parmigiano Reggiano* to the table, along with a bottle of deep brown liquid. "*Aceto balsamico di Modena*," he said, drizzling the tiniest amount over and around the cheese.

Emily nodded and Davide sat down, plucking a piece of the cheese from the plate and popping it into his mouth.

"*Sei arrabbiato*," she observed, abandoning any prelude.

Davide shook his head and turned to look out the window.

"You're upset, then. With me."

A pause, then he shook his head again.

Emily watched him intently, his leg bobbing alongside the table, his hand fidgeting with the paper towel he'd used as a napkin, his eyes still averted from her. The memory of arriving in Bologna to find the strike had halted the trains, came to mind. This was how she'd behaved with Davide then, in the *sala attesa*, when she'd been so anxious to leave. *So anxious and so…what else?*

"You're scared," she said, her stomach hollow in spite of their meal.

His eyes flicked from the window to her face and back again. After a few moments he closed his eyes and rested his forehead against the windowpane.

"*Ti ha baciato*."

"*Sì*," she said, helplessly watching the shuffling of emotions across his face which went from fear to anger to hurt, only to finish at fear once again. Fear didn't bother her, she could dispel that; anger she could deal with, too. But hurt? Seeing such an expression on his face twisted her heart so hard she could scarcely breathe.

"He kissed you." His voice had weakened with the repetition.

"*Sì*," she said, more clearly this time, with an air of defiance. "He kissed me and I felt absolutely nothing. It meant absolutely nothing to me."

"No?"

"No. Because of you. I felt nothing because he wasn't you."

"*Io?* Me?" Davide turned to face her, his eyes seeming to lose focus and then regain clarity.

"*Tu*, Davide," she said and smiled. "*Tu*."

34

The meal over, Davide silently set about preparing espresso in a small *Moka* pot on the stove. Emily sat at the little table, now cleared and wiped down, the extra leaf folded away again.

"Why don't you have a seat in the living room?" He turned to face her, his hands never pausing in their task. "I'll bring these in a few minutes."

Her dark eyes sought his in the fading light. The room seemed to be graying as the corner windows fell into afternoon shadow.

"You're sure?" she asked.

He nodded in response. "*Sì, sì.* It won't take long."

She waited a moment longer before getting to her feet. He met her eyes and offered a smile before she passed through the doorway and out of his sight.

Three steps took him to the door where he tapped the light switch; the fluorescent tube overhead flickered to life a few seconds later. By the time he placed two mismatched espresso cups and saucers on a tray, the thick, bitter scent of the coffee filled the space around him. He warmed a minuscule pitcher over the steam of the *Moka* and added a little milk to it, then placed it on the tray with the cups, a small sugar bowl and two teaspoons.

That done, he allowed his mind to wander until the espresso was ready. He crossed to the window and looked outside. The shadows had already swallowed his building, but long fingers of yellow-orange sunlight still withdrew slowly from the street. All the better to disguise the rush of heat rising to his face.

How foolish he had been to worry about Emily's dealings with Jacopo. How could he entertain—even for a moment—the thought that she'd give in to any advances from the man? After what he'd done?

Her explanation had covered everything: missing the train because she'd agreed to dinner, Jacopo's apparent sincerity, his failed attempt to seduce her yet again. Davide admired her strength. He understood what it had taken for her to resist such charms; he'd known someone like Jacopo all his life, and hadn't his mother feared he'd be the same?

He put the *Moka* on the trivet and carried everything to the living room. Emily stood at the window, quiet, focused on the street four stories below. Davide watched her, noting how she remained so still, so silent. He placed the tray on the table against the wall, not wishing to disturb her.

"I always love the way the storefronts look at this time of year," she said, breaking the silence. "There's something so cozy about them, isn't there?"

"I've always thought so," he said, pleased. He scooped sugar into the cups and poured espresso over it.

"That's the bar where you took me that morning, isn't it?"

Davide nodded. "*Sì.*" He added a few drops of the milk to each cup and stirred it in. "That's right, it is."

"Why didn't you tell me then you lived so close by?"

"Well, I..." He shrugged and stepped closer to her, offering her a cup. "I suppose I was afraid of how it would sound."

"What do you mean?" She took a sip and nodded her satisfaction before turning back to the window.

"If I'd said, 'You know, you can see my flat from here', you might have thought I was flirting with you in the worst way." Davide looked down at the lights of the bar and the reflections in the wet street. He paused to drink half his cup in one go. "At the very least, I thought you'd think badly of me. 'Oh, he brings me to a bar right next to his flat, eh? Very convenient.'"

"Would you have mentioned it if you hadn't been afraid of scaring me off?"

"I don't know. It just seemed too forward at the time." He drank down the rest of his espresso and she did the same.

Emily turned to face him, her face almost unreadable in the half-light. "Did you want to, though? Then?"

"*Sì,*" he said and it felt like a confession. He yearned to read her expression, but it wasn't possible in the growing darkness. Instead, he took her cup and placed it on the tray with his own. "I wanted to, very much. I wanted many things that day."

"What were you afraid of?" Her soft question seemed to surround him.

"Of wanting." He turned and drew her closer to see her face at last. He touched her cheek lightly and smiled. "Because you wore your ring, because you were so anxious about traveling alone, I thought you were still married. I was afraid of wanting a married woman, of wanting someone else who would reject me."

The edge of her mouth quirked beneath his fingertips. "I wouldn't have rejected you, though."

"I know. Then I would have been afraid of your acceptance and of what it said about me. What kind of man would I be if I propositioned a married woman, anyway?"

"Hm... Things changed, though."

"*Sì, è vero.* Some things changed; others did not."

"Such as?"

He framed her face in his hands, seeking her eyes in the ambient light from the street.

"I still want you, but now I'm not afraid."

"You're not?"

"I'm not," he said and brought his mouth to hers in a light, gentle kiss.

Emily closed her eyes, savoring the sensation of falling although she kept on her feet. Davide's fingers slipped along her neck, tickling the sensitive flesh behind her ears and she shivered, the movement bringing her closer to him.

Each kiss was slow and soft, his lips pulling and parting hers and sending a sweet glow coursing through her with every touch. She drew away to trace her lips over the tender skin under his jaw, touching her tongue to him for fleeting tastes of the salt of his skin. He clutched her closer in response, bringing his mouth to hers again for a deeper, hungrier kiss.

A hint of the sugar he'd used to sweeten his coffee was still on his lips, the dark bitterness of the espresso still on his breath, and Emily drank this in with every stroke of his tongue on hers. She shuddered deeply, moving against him to urge him on, and he led her away from the windows toward the sofa along the far wall.

His kisses trailed to the soft skin behind her ear, down the curve of her neck into her shoulder where he paused, tasting her with quick little flicks of the tip of his tongue. Her hands twisted in his sweater at the shoulders, drawing him closer as she sought his mouth with hers.

When he sank down onto the sofa, he drew her down with him, his hands deftly guiding her to sit astride him. She was aware of her own warmth and knew he felt it too when he grasped her hips and pulled her against him. Now her hands wound in his hair, holding him in place while she kissed him, enjoying the fantasy of being in control for the first time.

Davide unzipped her sweater and slipped his hands inside, smooth palms and fingers sliding over her too-warm skin, tickling her back and belly with each caress before sliding up to cup her breasts. He sat up to bring his mouth to one nipple, sucking gently through the fabric of her bra.

Emily groaned softly, her hands resting at the back of his head and pressing him closer. His hands slipped to her back, seeking the clasp that wasn't there.

"Davide," she murmured, pulling away and showing him the front clasp between her breasts. His expression of delight as he reached up to fumble open and pull off her garments gave her a momentary youthful thrill.

"*Che meraviglia*," he sighed, his fingertips tracing the outline of her bare skin with a sweet dedication until Emily plucked at his sweater, wanting his skin against hers. Belatedly comprehending, Davide grappled with it, finally tugging it over his head and frantically unbuttoning the shirt he'd worn beneath it.

Unable to help herself, she began to giggle at this display of eagerness, and he followed suit, chuckling deep in his throat as he held her to himself, kissing her with a cheerful passion.

With some surprise she recognized the feeling: elation. Absolute elation. For the first time she was with him and there was no train waiting—no train, no plane, no specter of an ex-husband hovering over her shoulder. There were only the two of them this time, in this place—in the entire world, for all it mattered—and there was nothing else she wanted or needed.

Davide slipped his hands along her sides to the waistband of her jeans, moving forward to unfasten them and gently tug down the zipper before he smoothed his fingertips between the denim and her skin. He caressed the curve of her hips, slid his touch back to the roundness of her bottom and groaned softly when she rolled her hips slowly forward to allow him to go lower still. Her own quiet sound of contentment was low in her throat, just above his lips, and he opened his mouth to breathe it in.

Her anxious shudder when he brought his hands forward to her belly again wasn't unnoticed. When he drew away to face her, her expression was hidden in the shadows, her profile limned by the light from the windows.

"Emilia?" he whispered and she shook her head in response.

"It's a reflex, I guess," she whispered back, one hand rising to her face; whether the gesture brushed her hair back or swept away a tear, he couldn't quite be sure.

"I'd like to see," he said, his voice low and soft.

Her shaking sigh clutched at his heart. "Okay..."

Yet when he reached to switch on the lamp on the end table, she reached to stop him. Through the shifting of her weight atop him he felt, more than saw, her reluctant retreat an instant later.

Vision reduced to a squint in the sudden yellow light, Davide closed his eyes for a moment or two, then opened them to Emily's face. Shadows nestled in the lines of discomfort he found there and he reached with both hands to stroke them away with the lightest touch he could manage.

"*Amore, ti prego*... I'm sure it's not so bad as this."

"That's the problem. I honestly don't know."

In the warm yellow lamplight, her skin glowed with a beautiful peachy cast. As his hands moved down over her neck, her shoulders, the fullness of her breasts and the sweet roundness of her belly, he watched her try to control the anxiety that played over her face before she looked away.

At last, he looked down at the source of her agitation. A thin pale line threaded from beneath her navel to disappear under the waistband of her panties. The skin around it appeared slightly stretched and puckered, but only if he really focused on it; otherwise it was almost invisible, unless the light touched it just so to reflect with a slight plastic shine.

It was difficult to comprehend; all this emotion over something one could hardly notice now? Of course, for her it was something that marked her, something "other," and that was enough to have it prey on her serenity.

"Emilia, *tesoro*... *Non c'è niente*. There's nothing there."

"I know... That's the point, isn't it?"

A weight settled dully in his stomach, leaden and burning. "Oh, no... No, Emilia, it isn't the point."

She turned slowly to face him. "No?"

Davide shook his head. "I don't love you for *this*," he said, pressing his fingertips flat over the scar and pushing lightly. "I don't love you for this," he smoothed his hands over her belly, "or for this," his hands slid over her jeans-clad thighs and up again, "or for this, or this…" he grazed her breasts and cheeks with his fingertips, his eyes meeting hers all the while. "I love you for all of this and none of this… *Amore mio*, you mustn't ever doubt that."

He drew her down for a kiss, turning them over so she lay on the sofa beneath him. "I love *you*, Emily Miller," he said, brushing his lips along her throat until she gave a soft shudder.

"But *why* do you love me, Davide?"

He paused and pulled back to look her in the eye. "Why do you love *me*?"

Her lips parted, ready for her response, but she fell silent. Her eyes met his steadily and he waited for her to understand. When the smile creased her lips once more, he kissed her, slow and soft.

She slid one hand between them in an eager caress and he moved reflexively toward her touch. Emboldened, she unfastened the top button of his jeans, then made a more timid effort at the next when it didn't undo easily.

"Like this," he murmured, his hand over hers, guiding her. "Just like this…" The delicate, tantalizing touch of her fingers was almost too much to take. "*Aspetta, tesoro*… This is all wrong."

"What? Really?"

"I don't want this to happen here. Come with me." With some difficulty he managed to get to his feet and take her hand, leading her out of the living room.

With every few steps they took, he was compelled to stop and kiss her again. The air was cooler in the hall than in the living room. His caresses gave her shivers with each glancing touch.

"Davide," she began softly, "I know this isn't the best moment to ask, but… do we have any, you know…?"

He could just make out her questioningly-raised eyebrow in the ambient light of the hall.

"Any…?" he echoed and belatedly understood. "Oh, right." *Gesù, I hadn't even thought about that.* "Maybe," he shook his head, resisting the urge to panic. "But the ones I've got are bound to be expired. I haven't, ah, since…you know. I've given blood since then, though." He shrugged and Emily giggled, drawing him closer for another kiss.

"That's okay. I know I can trust you," she whispered against his mouth, and the rush of relief which followed nearly made him dizzy.

Almost giddy with curiosity, Emily entered his bedroom. His king-size bed was stunning in its uniqueness—and not just for its size. The headboard was remarkable, a framework of dark, heavy wood, shelves and carvings spread over its surface. As they crossed toward the bed, which rested on a wide, faux-oriental carpet, she saw that the headboard was actually a part of the wall itself—a set of bookshelves with the bed placed carefully in front.

Davide stood silently next to her, allowing her to look.

Turning to him in the near-darkness, Emily saw a glimmer of his anxiety, his eyes moving to the headboard and back to her again. She put her arms around his neck, holding herself against him as firmly as possible before she pulled him down for a kiss.

His eager embrace followed, his mouth seeking and finding hers, his tongue slipping past to toy with hers, and she encouraged him with her echoing responses.

"*Amore…*" he whispered against her skin, sending another surge of gooseflesh along her body before his hands warmed her anew. "*Ho voglia di te…*" He spoke so softly, if she hadn't felt his breath on her skin, she'd have sworn she'd imagined it.

"*Anche io…*"

He knelt before her, helping her out of her shoes and her jeans, handling her with the utmost care and attention. She felt precious, fragile even, beneath his gentle touch. His hands strayed upward in a warm and ticklish caress, up over her calves, the sensitive skin at the backs of her knees, the cool thickness of her thighs.

He lingered at her hips, sliding his hands back to her bottom and forward again, and though she flinched at the light and ticklish touch, she didn't pull away. He raised his eyes to meet hers and she shivered, partly from the cold, but also from the depth of his gaze. This was somehow more than she'd expected.

This is what devotion looks like.

Then his hands slid forward, his fingertips just grazing her flesh, dipping between her thighs and parting them gently. His gaze lowered and she shivered again, embarrassed by his new focus in spite of the dim light, but unwilling to try and shift it away from herself. Losing her balance, she was compelled to take a single step outward, and he slipped his thumb between her thighs, tenderly seeking her pleasure.

She gasped, a brief, clarifying intake of breath, when he found her center and stroked gently with the pad of his thumb. She gasped again, dizzy, her hands gripping his shoulders when he pressed his lips to her in a soft kiss, his tongue delving, searching, finding.

It was too much. Her knees gave and she had to support herself with an awkward hand on his shoulder, fearing the humiliation which would follow if she fell upon him and turned this unspeakably erotic gesture into a farcical event.

She didn't fall. He supported her with willing and apparent ease, even as his tongue stroked her to a raging ache, almost fulfilled, then slid deeper still.

He felt her shudder around him, tasted her earthy musk as he lapped her in. The gesture felt greedy, his need for her immense, and he ached for his own release even as he gave her this one. He refused to hurry, though.

He withdrew and trailed kisses up to her belly, lingering briefly over her scar on the way. He'd thought her a goddess once before, or some sort of siren, perhaps—now she was a work of art in his hands, pliable and taking shape, emerging from the clay.

Her curves slid under his hands, her breasts warm beneath his lips, until at last he kissed her mouth once more and felt her body arc into his, eager, wanting.

Divine.

He eased her onto the bed before he finished disrobing and felt a flash of timidity for his own evident desire as he lay naked next to her. Her hands strayed over his skin, cool but warming with her caresses, growing more insistent by the moment. He kissed her again, pressed against her fleshy thigh and moved against her, his ache flaring into a sweet beseeching for relief.

Not yet.

Fingers twining in his hair, she guided his mouth to hers again and again, her lips pulling at his and causing a fresh pulse of agony to sweep low over him each time she did.

Not yet, he thought again, pulling away.

Dropping his mouth to her neck, he felt her pulse racing beneath his lips and he moved downward, exploring, tasting, savoring all of her. He took her in with his mouth, his hands, relishing and reveling in her and her giving of herself.

Hesitating once more over her scar, knowing the muted pinkness beneath his mouth was scarcely noticeable, he felt her shudder and sigh, and he understood. His lips caressed the reed-thin line, slipping downward into the thatch of curls, and he knew she was nervous by the peculiar trembling that took her then.

"Emila..." he whispered and she stilled under his hand. "*Tesoro mio, ti amo...*"

She sighed—a light, wordless sound—and that was all.

He moved to kneel on the bed, his hand slipping between her thighs once more, meeting resistance, but only for a moment. When he moved to kiss her, she opened to him and he sensed her shyness in doing so.

Softly, gently, he pursed his lips around tender flesh and she made the least little flinch at his touch. "*Mi dispiace...*" he murmured against her and kissed her again.

She drew out a long, slow breath and his warm lips caressed her until she trembled, helpless, beneath. It was completely different than before, with his mouth full upon her and her hips rising to meet each wet caress of his tongue as he drank her in. Every stroke brought her closer to the edge, his hands grasping her hips as he delved deeper into her, slight stubble on his cheeks and chin rasping over too-tender flesh to create a tantalizing friction.

It seemed to last forever. When she began to fear this was too soon since the last and she wouldn't be able, he flicked her with the tip of his tongue until she called out in surprise and release. Her hands sought his hair, her hips rose and fell to meet the rhythm of his tongue and she heard his own pleased murmurs breathed out against her. While she calmed, he trailed kisses across her shaking thighs.

And then he was moving up over her, still delirious with her salty-sweet musk and the warm, silken slickness of her flesh that had welcomed him. Mere intoxication wasn't as liberating as this, his lips and tongue moving over her body until he brought his lips to hers once more. He kissed her and she didn't resist, though her scent was heavy on his lips, his chin. She welcomed him anew, her tongue teasing and receiving, as sweet and slick as where he'd kissed her before.

He nestled against her, not entering, but feeling the delicious wet heat spread over him with each languorous stroke. His ache was now an insistent throb, keeping time with his pulse, and she raised her hips to his, her hands sliding down his back to guide him into her.

Then he was inside her and she rolled her hips to meet him, struggling to hold back her own relieved cry. She ground against him, desperate to feel him closer, deeper. She pulled him down to her for another kiss, frantic, pleading, and he met her with equal fervor.

"Oh...," she whispered, the last of it a light, surprised squeak as he thrust harder into her.

Soon, words failed her. She was falling into darkness and letting herself go, her cries fading and becoming distant in her own ears.

Clenched between her thighs, while her whole body matched his pace and coaxed him further, he felt her fingers skate down his back to grasp at his hips. They moved back to dig deeper into tender flesh, spurring him on. His name had faded to a guttural, keening cry in her throat, the sound rocking out of her with each thrust.

He was dangerously close now, fighting to keep his own cry from emerging.

And then her body arched to align with his, trembling around him, grasping and holding tight to him and pulling him in ever deeper.

He gasped out her name into the curve of her neck, her hair caressing his face as he shuddered inside her, his whole body thrumming with the energy of release and submission. Nothing else existed; there was only her, the depths of her holding him tight.

He found his voice in the darkness and she echoed his words in return.

"*Sono qui, amore mio.*"

"I'm here, my love."

35

The rise and fall of Davide's chest under her hand was hypnotic. Slowly Emily flexed her fingers, stroking the hair on his chest, feeling his heartbeat beneath her touch. When she thought of how his heartbeat had felt against her own, a fresh craving trembled deep inside her.

She grinned, knowing he'd never believe it if she said she still felt him within herself. Her hips twitched in anticipation of another delicious, slow connection, the longing intensifying to a sweet ache before it faded out.

Their scents mingled underneath the bedclothes and as she moved, she caught the warm, earthy perfume as it drifted into the cool air of the room. Burrowing deeper to nestle against him she inhaled, slow and deep, acknowledging the delicate scent and what it meant.

She could taste him still: the salty, musky fragrance of his skin remained on her tongue and she considered allowing herself another taste, if she could do it without disturbing him while he drowsed next to her.

It wasn't until his hand covered hers that she realized she'd closed her eyes and had begun to doze instead. The weight of his fingers sent her mind wandering pleasantly to his touches and caresses from before.

She opened her eyes at last to find him peering at her, the light from the windows making his eyes glisten. His hand slid up her arm to her shoulder, never leaving the cocoon of heat the bedclothes made, yet raising goosebumps as it went.

He moved closer, bringing his mouth to hers without speaking, and she yielded to the kiss with a sense of relief. A new anticipation tickled maddeningly and she twined her legs with his to move against him, seeking to temper it for a while longer. She traced her tongue teasingly across his lips when they parted and he pressed closer, avidly seeking more.

"Davide...?" she murmured against his mouth.

"Sì, Emilia?"

Threading her fingers into his hair, she waited until he drew away to look at her before she spoke.

"I want you," she whispered. A frantic energy infused his kisses while his arms slipped around her and held her tight against him. His lips parted hers roughly and his tongue slipped past to challenge hers with deft parries and thrusts, inciting her to follow suit. She did, the thrill from before flowing swiftly to her center, setting an aching pulse in motion where he'd eased between her thighs but not yet joined her.

She gasped when their mouths parted at last; another gasp followed when his fingers found her, stroking eagerly and then sliding inside her with a matter-of-fact urgency. Her hips moved to the rhythm he dictated, his slick motions hastening her pulse faster still until she sucked harshly and had to clench her thighs around his hand to stop him touching too-sensitive flesh.

Oh, God...I don't really want him to stop.

He withdrew his hand slowly, leaving slippery trails along her thigh as he rolled away from her. Grasping gently, he pulled her astride him, adjusting the bedclothes so they stayed covered and warm against the evening air. She nestled atop him, her mouth finding his in the near-darkness while his caresses strayed over her back and hips, seeking and probing gently as they went.

She gasped again and his murmured apology warmed her cheek before his caresses resumed, sliding forward and down to stroke her as before. Finding the rhythm again, she rolled her hips in time to his touch until the ache demanded more.

So close...so close...

She had never been so ready.

He moved to embrace her and she lay atop him, his own readiness evident in his hardness pressed to her belly. The undulations of her hips worked him closer and closer and finally brought him inside with long, languorous strokes.

He raised himself to her, ascending into her warmth as she rolled back to meet his efforts with growing excitement. Soon she was rocking her hips with the enthusiasm of single-minded pursuit, driving hard upon him, muffling her cries against his shoulder.

The sounds which accompanied her exertions were rousing in their own ways: each soft sigh or groan of pleasure carried Davide closer to his own end—a little too swiftly for his liking. His hands strayed down her back, over the smooth skin of her waist to the lush swell of her hips. His own low sigh blossomed into a long moan as she pulled away to sit up, the bedclothes falling away from them and the cold air chilling their skin in a rush.

He brought his hands to her breasts, cupping them and stroking her nipples until she sighed and covered his hands with her own, her hips slowing to a calmer measure. The beckoning sway never stopped altogether; each slow roll drew him closer to the point of no return.

"Emilia," he whispered, but had nothing more to say—there *was* nothing more. "*La mia* Emilia..."

She eased herself down to lie on top of him again, her mouth hard upon his, her tongue seeking, thrusting in cadence with her hips.

The low creaking of the wooden slats beneath the mattress seemed to urge her on, the protests growing louder and more frequent as she hastened her pace, crying out again. He felt her getting closer to her release and he prayed silently that he would—at the very least—accompany her there.

Her frenzied tempo faltered and she shuddered, grinding hard against him. A soft moan escaped her and Davide shivered, fighting the urge to give in and follow her right away.

Oddio...

Seeing her expression fade from determined to sated, he nearly succumbed. Even more arousing was the knowledge that her cries were genuine and meant for him alone.

Emily allowed herself to sink down onto him, her heart racing, her breath shallow. Moments passed while her body pulsed, snug around him. She stayed there, nearly drowsing, until the fresh distraction of his grasp on her hips stirred her and he thrust into her from below.

With fresh energy she eagerly met his efforts as a new, more elusive ache demanded relief. They kissed briefly until he pulled his mouth away, exhaling his own low sounds of endeavor while he held her in place and moved forcefully against her.

Her attempts to move with him were futile, such was the strength of his hold on her, but the beautiful fierceness in his expression was unexpected, sending fresh heat through her. The scowling set of his jaw and the narrowing of his eyes spoke of pleasure near to pain. She felt him swelling within her, his thrusts quickening until his pace stuttered to a shaking halt.

Once more, she eased herself down onto him and found his heart racing beneath her own. Nestling in the curve of his neck, she felt him throbbing inside her and it was enough to unleash a final, sharp thrill through her.

"*Ti amo...*" he murmured, his voice only just audible over her own heartbeat.

She kissed his neck softly, her hand pressed to feel his heartbeat between them. "*Anche io ...*"

His quiet chuckle shook them both and then subsided into the darkness.

He touched her cheek with tenderness unlike anything she'd ever known before and gratefulness wrenched her heart. Failing to blink fast enough to fight back the tears which welled in her eyes, she felt the cool trails they left on her skin in the darkness.

Davide held her tightly while she sobbed against him, brushing his fingertips over her face to wipe the tears away. He smoothed her hair back from her face, his eyes seeking hers in the dim light before he pressed his lips to her temple in a soothing kiss.

"*Dai, dai...perché piangi?*" he whispered, his fingers seeking delicately across her face for more tears and wiping away those he found.

"*Non so...*" she whispered back, shaking her head, holding him tighter. "I guess I hadn't realized how much I wanted this."

He kissed her, his lips brushing over hers until she returned the gestures with a greater strength. "And you cry because...?"

"Now that I've got it, I'm afraid of losing it."

Another kiss, stronger than the last, and he whispered against her lips, "You won't. *Lo giuro.* I swear it."

She started to move away and he reached to stop her.

"Stay, Emilia, if you like."

"I'll squish you," she said, swallowing a reluctant giggle at the thought.

"No, you won't. *Dai, stai con me...*" The fingers of one hand tangled in her hair, drawing her down for another kiss while the other grasped her thigh and held her to him.

"Okay, I will."

She nestled against his neck again, rising and falling with his breath, feeling something beyond the hazy shine of afterglow. The sensation started deep in her chest and grew bigger, wrapping her up and tying her directly to him.

He tugged the bedclothes up over them, the cool fabric warming slowly all around. His hands caressed her back in slow, soothing strokes which simultaneously warmed her and gave her little chills.

Safe. I feel safe here.

Determined not to cry again, she shut her eyes tight and willed the looming tears away. When the sense of safety returned, Emily reached out with her mind to pull it closer still.

Davide moved to kiss her forehead, then the tip of her nose and he resumed his caresses, savoring her skin beneath his hands. He felt himself growing soft, slowly slipping out of her warmth, and he waited for it to happen before he eased Emily over to lie beside him.

Already sleeping, she turned onto her side and curled with her back against him. He adjusted the blankets carefully and aligned himself with her.

When his stomach rumbled hollowly, he turned and read the digital clock with some surprise. It was half past seven in the evening—still quite early, really—but he didn't have anything to make for dinner.

He smiled to himself and nuzzled the skin at the back of her neck. Emily twisted away sleepily, then returned and he touched his lips to her shoulder in an airy kiss.

"Emilia?" he said quietly and she shifted away. Placing his hand on her shoulder, he stroked the bare skin beneath the blankets. "Emilia, *amore*…?"

"*Sì*…?"

"I'm going to the kitchen to see what we have for dinner. Do you want anything?"

She shook her head in a sleepy, petulant protest. Then, after a pause, once Davide had turned to go: "Water."

He wondered if she was even awake. Taking no chances, he slid out of the bed carefully and fumbled around for his robe on the chair in the corner. Glancing over his shoulder, he found Emily completely hidden beneath the bedclothes, save for one foot which she had freed from the tangle to expose to the night air.

A wave of tenderness swept over him at the sight and he paused in putting on his robe to stare at the plump, pink toes, curled up in the duvet.

"*Ti amo*, Emilia," he whispered, grinning, before stuffing his feet into his slippers and shuffling out of the room.

Pale morning light shone through the windows, turning everything in the room to shades of blue and gray. Emily lay quiet beneath the heap of bedclothes, blinking awake and taking a few moments to be sure that she wasn't dreaming. Davide's soft, even breathing behind her was further proof and she closed her eyes for a moment, grateful.

I wouldn't have been surprised if last night had been a dream.

Peering out from under the covers, she found her clothes folded neatly on the chair by the windows. Davide must have awakened in the small hours of the morning and done this while she slept, as she had no recollection of the clothes being there when they'd last made love sometime after midnight.

He turned and reached for her as she shifted position and his eyelids fluttered, then opened wide, his mouth curving into a smile.

"*Ciao*," he murmured, drawing the word out to several syllables.

"*Ciao*," she whispered back, pressing close. The feel of his skin on hers was too wonderful for words; she nuzzled closer still and tucked her head under his chin, savoring his scent while he rubbed her back with slow, lazy strokes.

"Do you have any lessons today?" she managed at last, fearful of falling asleep from the hypnotic repetition of his touch.

"No, I don't. I'm free the whole day." He reached up and brushed her hair away from her face, moving to place a slow kiss at the curve of her neck. His hand slipped down to cup her breast and Emily arched into his touch with a low sigh.

At the gurgling protest from her empty stomach, Davide chuckled and drew away.

"I see I need to take better care of my guest," he said, still laughing. "I'm depriving her of basic courtesies."

"I wouldn't take it that far…" Emily drew him back, pressing her lips to the hollow of his throat for a moment. "Besides, I've never been so well attended to."

"You flatter me. Anyway, it's later than it seems, I'm sure." He twisted away and then returned to gather her into his arms, obviously hesitant to leave. "It's nearly seven. Why don't we get up and have breakfast? It's been quite a while since dinner, such as it was."

"I'd like that," she said. "Let me get ready first." Emily got out from under the covers and the carpet felt pleasingly soft beneath her feet when she stood beside the bed. Feeling foolish, she found herself trying to face away from Davide in a senseless show of modesty. What was there to be embarrassed about now? He'd known her as intimately as possible, hadn't he?

The marble-tiled floor was absolutely freezing. With a quick, almost silent hiss of surprise, Emily stepped back onto the carpet that surrounded the bed. Davide chuckled again, sitting up to grab his slippers off the floor and offer them to her.

"Take these."

"No, I can't. You'll need them."

"Okay." He got out of bed, apparently free of any modest impulses of his own, and crossed to the bureau along the wall. It was hard not to watch him, not to observe the way the light caressed him and settled into soft shadows which accented the muscles of his legs and the lines of his back. A soft shimmer centered itself in her and negated the chill she'd gotten from the floor.

"Here, try these." He tossed her a pair of thick athletic socks and returned to the bed as she sat to put the socks on. "We'll get you some slippers today, if you like."

"Maybe," Emily said with a small shrug, her eyes straying wantonly once again. Didn't he have any idea how beautiful he really was? Couldn't he at least cover up a little? Act a little self-conscious? "We'll see."

This time, when she walked away she picked her steps carefully to be sure she wouldn't slip on the tiles in her stocking feet. She had to force herself to concentrate on the task at hand and keep her thoughts from straying to how she probably looked from behind.

Yes, it was better to think of *him* in the early-morning light, instead. Much better indeed.

In order to hide his amusement at Emily's over-cautious departure, Davide raised one hand to his mouth as he watched her go. Once her ample bottom had disappeared through the doorway and out of sight, he rubbed his aching cheeks and wondered how long it had been since he'd smiled hard enough to have it hurt.

It had been much too long. At the very least, it had been long before he'd met her.

How things had changed—literally overnight. Had he ever been so content with Letizia? It was difficult to remember, especially now, what the first days with her had been like.

He thought to the photo with the horse-head cloud, now stashed in a drawer in the sideboard in the living room. When Emily told him she was coming to Bologna, putting it away was the first thing he'd done upon arriving at home that afternoon. That had been enough to set his mind at rest, at first.

But no longer.

How many times had he thought the photo was still in its former place on the table and had gone to remove it? Like a close whisper in a crowded room, it spoke to his conscience on a level he couldn't avoid, insisting that Emily should know. The knowledge of the photo's existence was frustratingly difficult to negate and more than once he'd considered simply destroying it to be done with it. It lurked at the back of his mind whenever he passed through the living room, although he'd completely forgotten it the night before. Hardly surprising, really, considering he'd had a much better distraction close to hand.

Though Emily was so much more than a mere distraction.

Still, he'd had so many opportunities to tell her and had yet to take any of them.

His restless hands fussing with the bedclothes, Davide watched the bedroom door for her return. Already his thoughts were taking more lascivious turns and his face warmed with a modest shame.

I'm behaving like a horny teenager. Shouldn't I at least try *to have some dignity about this?*

No, never mind any of that. This was something to enjoy, right here and now, and he was determined to.

36

It took a week before Emily grew accustomed to waking up beside Davide. Each time she opened her eyes, she felt a fleeting moment of disorientation before her surroundings became familiar. This Thursday morning, however, the disorientation didn't come. His soft breathing beside her was expected, his presence beneath the covers reassuring.

The expectation of waking alone faded like the uneasy shades of a bad dream in the morning light. She lay quietly, enjoying the difference. Though he had a lesson in the late morning, she didn't want to wake him.

How quickly things had changed. Granted, it had taken them a year to reach this point, but now she was here, with someone she loved and trusted and her life had never seemed so settled, so safe, so...perfect.

A memory of Jenn crept in, the overly-dramatic way she would gasp and then persuade Emily to say something, anything, in an effort to remove the jinx created with such wishful thinking.

Then another incomplete memory stirred, leaving Emily inexplicably uneasy.

Asleep, Davide turned onto his side and put his back to her. Still, his movements didn't allow even a hint of the cold air in the room to seep under the sheets.

The deep cold of a night without heat was something she'd forgotten after a Michigan winter with all the central heating she could hope for. She'd found it difficult to readjust at first, but now she'd come back to the old routines for keeping warm: slippers for one, using a terrycloth robe to dry off after her shower for another.

There were the newer routines, too, since she'd been with Davide. She'd found while watching the vaguely purple shadow on the ceiling a couple of mornings ago that the red and blue sign of the coffee bar across the street cast its glow onto the street at precisely 5:30 a.m. With the first gentle *ping* of the radiator near the window, she didn't have to check the clock to know it was 6:00 a.m. She could set her watch by the precision of the radiator, as well as the street cleaner, the garbage truck, even the bells which rang in the *campanile* a couple of blocks away to call the faithful to Mass at 7:15.

Small wonder Davide rarely consulted a clock once the day began. Emily's initial self-consciousness at intruding upon his schedule had vanished after their first morning together. Since then he'd made a point of showing her the closest shops to his home and the shortest route he took to work.

The surrounding neighborhood was fairly quiet for the most part, except when the occasional teenager-driven scooter blatted by, or when the delivery trucks for the bar or the small grocery shop on the corner arrived with a pneumatic sigh and double-blast of the klaxon a couple of mornings each week.

Most of the sounds she found idyllic, in their way: the pleasant greetings of a group of elderly women to one another on the street outside, or even the intermittent *zing-zing* from the bells of cyclists passing pedestrians on the uneven street, gave her a sense of contentment she couldn't quite explain.

If she stepped outside early enough, she sometimes caught the smell of bread and pastries baking in the *forno* down the street, or the scent of a neighbor's near-constant cooking for her family, which started in the morning and didn't seem to stop until well after the dinner hour should have been over.

By Sunday night, she already knew the layout of his neighborhood quite well. The nondescript faded umber façade of his building soon ceased to blend in with the surroundings. The labyrinthine streets were no longer nearly so daunting; the mix of medieval and modern architecture painted in varying shades of yellow, red and umber provided easy landmarks for orienting herself.

Turn left at the yellow three-story building, then right at the graffiti that says "SIB".

"All roads don't necessarily lead to *Roma*," Davide had said. "Most of them here go to the *circonvallazione*, or to Piazza del Nettuno. Once you get the towers in sight, navigation is easy enough, no?"

When she'd noted something in a shop, he'd made a point of buying it. He wouldn't let her pay for the slippers there on the floor on her side of the bed, either. This was difficult—coping with his generosity was something she hadn't anticipated. Somehow, she hadn't yet gotten around to telling him about her good fortune with the sale of the house. The truth was rather simple: she had enough money to live independently for quite a while. No problems, no pressures. She didn't even have outstanding bills to pay. If she continued living modestly, she wouldn't even need to work for a long while.

When she thought about her sudden, surprising wealth too long, it made her dizzy, almost fearful of hyperventilating. While Davide didn't seem the sort of man who could be emasculated by his partner having more money than he did, it was hard to be sure. Men were so unpredictable when it came to their earnings and how well they provided for their partners or families—Italian men even more so. Whenever she'd tried to broach the subject of money, he always steered the discussion to a different topic. Sometimes he'd managed it so skillfully she didn't realize until later what he'd done.

If nothing else, he certainly had a talent for talking. She'd never been so truly 'engaged in conversation' with anyone before. Not even Jenn had been quite so verbose.

Wind him up and let him run, Emily thought, recalling his impromptu lecturing on the day they'd met and how much she enjoyed it. Other women would have run screaming in the opposite direction once he'd started dissecting a subject, labeling the parts and digging to get at the deeper truths within.

When one such prolonged discussion wound down and she'd said, "We're both such geeks, aren't we?" he'd almost seemed hurt in spite of her reassurances that she'd meant it as a compliment. His hurt didn't last and soon they were both engrossed in a new discussion which didn't end until she'd spontaneously thrown herself at him—literally—and they'd made love on the sofa in the living room.

That had been the night before.

The soft *ping* of the radiator sent Emily deeper under the covers to snuggle next to Davide and slip her arm around his waist. He stirred as though waking, then placed one hand over hers and settled back into deeper sleep.

She closed her eyes and breathed in his scent. Then, lulled by the slow and steady rhythms of his breathing and his heartbeat beneath her hand, drifted off once more.

"You lied to me." Emily stood at the gate, her suitcase on the floor next to her, her eyes red and puffy in her drawn face. "I can't believe you would do that."

"I didn't lie, Emilia, you know I didn't."

"You did. You knew and you didn't tell me. It's the same thing, isn't it?"

"Not at all." Davide shook his head emphatically, raising his hands in front of himself as though to ward off the objections which would follow. "It really isn't the same thing."

"It is. You let her go to Rome alone. You let her steal my husband. How could you do that?"

He focused on the crowd behind her, milling through the gate to board the plane. A tall, blond figure was watching them with seeming disinterest, his hands busily roaming over different women as if inspecting them, assessing them as they passed to board the plane.

Sudden and unexpected rage surged through Davide and he fought against the crowd which now flowed around him, a sea of faces, each indistinguishable from the other. Except for the blond man by the gate who waited patiently while the crowd parted to permit Emily to pass.

"Emilia, amore—ti prego, no!" Carried away from her by the human tide, a sickness filled his stomach. The sickness filled his mouth so he couldn't speak, couldn't cry out to her any more, couldn't plead for her to stop, to reconsider what she was doing.

Her head hanging low, she shuffled toward the gate, toward the plane.

Toward Jacopo.

Before Davide opened his eyes, he reached out for Emily. Her absence was enough to drive a cold spike of fear straight through him, his eyes snapping open to be sure she actually wasn't there. He sat up quickly, looking around the room for a sign of her presence—any sign would do—but it wasn't until he'd gulped several shallow, panicked breaths that he smelled coffee warming on the stove and heard the water running in the shower.

Gesù, it was only a dream...I still haven't told her, though.

A recurrence of the sickness from the dream made his stomach turn. He'd considered telling her about Jacopo and Letizia so many times in the past week, it was no wonder it preyed on his sleeping mind now. It was a lucky thing she wasn't here to ask what was wrong, or what he had dreamed which so disturbed him.

Sinking back down onto the pillow, he pulled the covers up to his chest and stared at the ceiling. A childish urge to curl up in a ball and wish the feeling out of existence followed and he willed it away with some effort. The urge, not the feeling.

It's not my fault, though, is it? Even if I'd gone to Roma with Letizia, Jacopo would still have left Emily regardless.

And weren't Letizia and Jacopo a perfect match? All along, Emily had needed so much better than what he'd given her.

Sure, there had been a lot of pain all around, but in the end, it had worked out for the best. Letizia had found her counterpart; Emily, hers.

"*Basta, scemo*," he scolded himself in a whisper. "There's no use in dwelling on it in this way."

In the silence which followed, Emily's humming carried to him, her slightly off-key rendering of some pop song coming and going in the splashes from the shower. He smiled as a sense of reassurance took hold.

Everything would work out. He just needed to be patient—that was all. When the right time came, he would tell her and she would understand.

It would be all right.

As Emily got dressed, Davide returned to the bedroom and crossed to the window. He stood and watched her finish, his sweet smile even lighting his eyes.

"Why don't you come with me today? I have only two lessons, with a lunch break between. It'd be perfect. If you like, you could come with me to my lesson."

"Really?" Emily glanced at Davide, pulled her sweater over her head and tugged it into place. "Your students won't notice the middle-aged American sitting in the back of the room and get all self-conscious?"

"If one shows up, I'm sure they might, if they aren't distracted first by the beautiful woman who comes in with me."

He smiled and the butterflies in her stomach did their usual dance in response.

"They won't notice, I promise," he said, reassuringly. "I'll tell them you're auditing the class and they'll ignore you like they do everyone else."

Davide stepped over to her, reached out to smooth the line of her sweater. His hands glided up over the soft cable-knit to her breasts, cupping them gently until she pressed closer, her arms slipping around his neck with familiar ease. The warm, bittersweet coffee taste on his lips and tongue was too enticing to resist and she drew him down for a long, slow kiss, breathing in the rich espresso scent.

They parted with some difficulty and Emily blinked hard to focus. He licked his lips and shook his head, turning away from her for a moment to unplug his cell phone and put it in the pocket of his coat, before draping the coat across the foot of the bed.

"If you kiss me like that again, I won't make it to work," he said and she noted the almost wistful tone in his voice. "So what do you say? Will you come with me?"

"As much as I'd like to do that, I'm afraid I really should go to the hotel this morning," she said, sighing. "I need to call my mother and let her know I'm doing all right. If I don't call once a week, she starts to worry."

"Really?"

"Hard to believe, but yeah, she does. She convinces herself something horrible has happened if I don't call by my deadline."

"Oh," he said, not meeting her eyes.

Emily moved in front of him and brought her fingertips to the downward crease of his mouth. His frown disappeared at her touch. She smoothed down a stray lock of his hair, then wrapped her arms around him again.

"Why don't I meet you for lunch? Then we could do something after you finish work. Does that sound okay?"

"*Sì, sì.*"

"Maybe we could meet at the hotel after your last lesson?" she asked, nuzzling his throat.

"*Certo, tesoro.* That sounds wonderful." He bent and brushed his lips over hers, his hand on her cheek.

One more kiss, then, she promised herself. Just one more kiss and then she'd be on her way to the hotel to change clothes and call her mother.

Then his hands were in her hair and his mouth was hard on hers and she was fighting not to give in, forcing her hands to relax and stop pulling him closer, commanding her feet to stop leading them both to the bed.

By the time his lips were grazing her bared belly, she decided in the future she'd have to pick her battles more carefully.

When Davide reached for Emily while she dressed again, he received a slap on the hand. It took real effort to resist her, though she did nothing at all provocative. Just the sight of her peaked color and her tousled hair, now pulled back into a loose ponytail, was enough to rouse him.

"You have to get going," she scolded, "and so do I. I'll see you at lunch, okay?" She made for the door.

"Of course," he said and tried for a kiss anyway.

After indulging in a single swift peck, she barely managed to get away from him. "*Ciao, bello,*" she giggled, heading for the door.

"*Ciao, bella,*" he called after her and then the door closed and cut off the sound of her footsteps bounding down the stairs.

A glimpse of the clock spurred him to a quick wash before he dressed again, humming to himself and occasionally singing under his breath: "*Una mattina…mi son svegliato…bella ciao, bella ciao, bella ciao, ciao, ciao…*"

He paused in front of the mirror in the hall and ran his fingers through his hair once more, knowing it was quite hopeless. Without another shower, he'd never get the mussed waves back into any semblance of a style and there simply wasn't time.

Not that he'd ever pass up *this* sort of delay.

Smiling to himself, he slipped into his coat. He should already have been well on his way. He patted his pockets, checking he had everything he needed: wallet, keys, spectacles, mobile phone. Yes, everything was present and accounted for.

No sooner had he swung open the front door than the phone on the table shrilled, echoing in the corridor. Out of habit, he dug out his mobile phone and checked it.

No calls, no messages; he hadn't missed anything.

He looked at the phone on the table, still shrilling away. It surely wasn't Emily calling; she'd only just left and she knew he was supposed to be out by now. Curiosity won out and he closed the door behind him to answer.

"*Pronto?*" Silence which wasn't quite silent followed. "*Pronto?*" he repeated, letting agitation slip into his voice. These sorts of calls were the worst and they always came when one was heading out for an appointment of some importance. "*Chi è?*"

"Um, hello? Hello?" a distinctly American female voice queried as Davide moved to put the phone down. "Hello, who is this?"

"Hello?" he answered, the word feeling more foreign than ever in his mouth. The demanding tone of the caller had already set him on edge and his suspicion of her identity was fast-forming.

"Do you speak English?"

"*Sì*, I speak English. *Parli italiano?* I'm guessing not, so who is calling?"

"Is this…Dah-veed Mag-nan-ee?"

"Davide Magnani," he corrected, twirling one hand in an impatient *let's-get-this-going* gesture. "*Sì*, you've called the right number. How can I help you?"

"Is my daughter there?"

Oddio…the infamous Mamma. "No, *Signora* Miller, she isn't. She is at her hotel."

"No, she isn't. I just called there."

"She's on her way then. I'm sorry, but she isn't here."

"Oh, right. Listen, I have an idea who you are—I couldn't read your letters, but I copied some of them into the interwebs and I know that you must be Emily's new boyfriend or whatever they're calling it nowadays –"

You did what *with her letters?* he thought, shocked at the off-handedness of her admission.

"*Signora*," he began, struggling to keep his tone civil in light of this news, "*mi dispiace*, but I'm on my way to work. If you would like to speak to your daughter, you must call the hotel. Give her time to get there and call again."

"What time is it there? It's early, isn't it? You don't fool me, young man," she said and the combination of her insinuating tone of voice and condescending choice of words was enough to raise his hackles. "I know she was there last night. She didn't go to the hotel—I spoke with the clerk."

"I'm not sure what you want me to say, *Signora* Miller. Your daughter is not here...now. Why don't you call her mobile? I'm certain she has it."

"I don't have that number."

"Oh, well, I'm sure she'll give it to you later. *Buongiorno, Signora* Miller. Have a good day."

"Wait a moment," she said quickly and Davide paused before setting the phone down. "I'd like to ask you a few things."

"I really don't have much time for –"

"I won't take long."

"*Va bene...* Okay. What is it you wish to know?"

Contrary to her previous statement, there was a considerable pause before she spoke. Davide checked his watch, listening keenly to be sure the connection hadn't fallen.

"Who are you?" she asked, finally.

At least she's direct.

"I am Davide Magnani. I'm a professor here at the university."

"I know that, I figured it out from those letters. I mean, who are you to my daughter? How long have you known her?"

"I don't have to answer that."

"Ah, I see. Are *you* the reason she got divorced? Admit it."

He felt his eyes widen in astonishment. *Sei pazza?* He wanted to shout down the phone. *Are you crazy? Who asks that?*

"Of course not," he said, struggling to keep calm. "I met her after that was finished. If it reassures you, I had nothing to do with it." *At least not directly*, he amended to himself.

"Well, then," her voice softened somewhat and Davide leaned against the wall, resigned. "At least tell me your intentions with her. If you're after her money, you can just forget it."

Money? Is there something Emilia hasn't told me?

"I have no idea what you're talking about, *Signora*."

"Sure you don't. Just don't get any big ideas, young man, I'm telling you—because I'll tell her myself."

"*Senza dubbio.*"

"What was that?"

"Never mind. I'm putting the phone down now, since I have to go to work and you've already made me late. *Grazie* for the call, *Signora* Miller. When I see Emilia, I'll tell her you tried to reach her. Oh, one more thing?"

"What?"

"Don't call this number again, *per favore*, unless someone has died. *Buona giornata.*"

With that, Davide set the phone in its cradle and checked his watch one more time. *I'll take the bike—I should just make it.*

37

A soft staccato tapping pulled Davide's attention away from the pile of papers on his desk. He looked up to find Emily's shy smile in the narrow gap between the door and the frame and he waved her in, relieved. Another ten minutes and there wouldn't have been time for them to go out for a relaxed lunch. He hated thinking he might have had to take her to a bar for a sandwich and a soda, or something equally unimpressive.

After all, he had something of a culinary reputation to maintain.

Emily stepped inside the office, picking her way with care through the chaos of boxes and papers. "I'm sorry I'm late..." she said, trailing off as she took her coat off and draped it over the chair. "Wow, I see nothing *here's* changed," she added with a laugh.

"No, I'm afraid not. I'm still digging out from under this mess. I want to discard or burn most of it, but the department head says I can't." Davide stood and came out from behind the desk, stepping around a stack of boxes to slip his arms around her waist. "He promises someone will collect it all and sift through it but I doubt it'll be anytime soon. Is everything all right at home?"

"*Sì, va bene.*" She returned his embrace with a soft sigh of satisfaction. "There was just the usual merriment. Mom was stressed since I hadn't called her and, evidently, she had a little run-in with a particular Italian..."

Davide groaned, unpleasant heat spreading over his cheeks. He started to speak and Emily pressed close to touch her lips to his mouth. The pull of her lips on his curtailed his memory of the phone call. The softness of her mouth on his was much more pleasant and he relished it until she drew away to trace a few light kisses up to his temple.

"Don't worry, *amore*," she murmured, her breath tickling his ear. "She deserved it, I'm sure. I know how she can be—the third degree Jacopo got when we met was the stuff of horror films."

He swallowed down his aversion to any comparison to Jacopo and gave her another kiss. "Our conversation wasn't so bad as that, I don't think," he said and tightened his embrace.

"Oh, but you gave her such drama to play with!" Eyes alight, a delighted grin on her face, Emily pulled back and clapped her flattened palms against his chest. "You made her day," she said enthusiastically. "You were—until I spoke to her, anyway—the callous stranger who seduced her daughter and now stands between us, jealously guarding his prize."

"No…" Davide groaned, suddenly seized with regret. His hands fell to his sides, his whole body slumping under the weight of disappointment. He sat on the edge of his desk, shaking his head, unable to meet her eyes.

"*Sìì…*" Emily stretched the word out and laughed again, settling onto the chair where she'd draped her coat. "Never mind. I tried to set her straight, but from here on out, she won't be calling your number anymore. I told her, 'Unless someone is dead or dying, you call only the hotel and you leave a message there for me. I'll get it there.' She wasn't too happy about *that*, I'm sure."

"I told her something similar," he said, wincing. "I'm sorry."

"Don't be. As long as she's miffed with me, she won't make any more phone calls. I don't think so, anyway." She glanced around and again met his eyes. He remembered the first time she'd sat in the same chair, amidst the disorder of this room.

The memory brought with it the tumult of emotions he'd felt at the time, along with the sensation of how his heart had raced while sitting across from her, how torn he'd been between his inexplicable desire for her and the need to maintain a respectful distance.

Even more frustrating, there had been signs she was attracted to him as well and the idea that he might attempt to seduce a married woman wasn't nearly as repulsive as he'd thought. The only thing which had stopped him then was the thought that his father would not have stopped.

Yet even today there was a quickening of his pulse, a need to control his breathing, to still his nervous hands. They'd last made love a few hours ago and still his head was full of images of having her here and now in this office, amongst the dusty books and stacks of papers which surrounded them.

"What are you thinking, Davide?" she asked softly.

"I'm thinking about when you were here before," he said. "I'm thinking how much I wanted you then."

"You are? You did?"

A smile, unbidden, creased his lips. "*Sì*, I am and I did."

Emily shifted position just the least bit. Something in the gesture betrayed her surprise.

"I thought you were married, so I didn't try, but I wanted to. Very much."

She dropped her gaze and seemed to study the floor for a few moments. Davide wondered what she watched so intently. Was it bits of shredded paper from the edges of a notepad? Dust gathered into tendrils of fluff, which crept and twirled on the slightest breeze? Pencil shavings which had missed the dustbin and had drifted onto the floor?

"When was the first time, then?" she asked.

"The first time *what*?"

Emily looked up and met his eyes. "The first time you wanted me."

"Honestly?"

"I'd prefer an honest answer, yes—but aren't you always honest with me?"

His thoughts flashed briefly, guiltily, to the photo in the drawer in the living room.

"Of course, *tesoro*. I know what it means to you." *And I don't really care if* you're *keeping something from me, do I?* "The first time was when I sat next to you in the station."

Her eyes widened. "Really?"

Davide nodded, focusing on meeting her eyes. "You smelled so good, I just wanted to get you somewhere I could find out if it was you, or your perfume, or what."

"I don't wear perfume."

"I know that now. Then we came here and when we were talking, I had this image of us in my mind…"

"*Davvero?*"

"*Sì, davvero.*" Now it was his turn to shift position, to ease his discomfort. The room seemed warmer, too. Perhaps he should open the window for a few minutes?

"I'm intrigued," she said, her voice barely carrying to him. "Do go on."

"*Francamente*, no, I don't think I should."

"*Perché no?*" Emily stood and crossed the two paces to him. "Can't I know what you were thinking about me at the time?"

"It's not so much what I thought about you. It's what I wanted to do with you. Or more to the point, what I wanted to do *to* you."

He moved to sit directly facing her and she stood with her hands resting lightly on his thighs. Her fingers traced abstract shapes over his jeans and his muscles quivered beneath her touch. She moved closer to him, bringing her mouth to his, as though for a kiss.

"'*To*' me?" she echoed, her lips brushing over his as she spoke. Her breath was fresh, almost cool, with the mint from her toothpaste. "Really?"

"*Sì*," he said, resisting the urge to nod. Resistance kept his tone neutral as he sought to maintain their closeness without touching. "I had no idea how you'd react, so my imagination was rather one-sided."

"Oh." Her fingers trailed higher, the loops and swirls she drew leading slowly inward. An aching pull low in his belly acknowledged every curve her fingers traced. "I wish I had told you the whole story sooner."

"Me, too. It would have saved us a lot of time," he said, trying not to grin and failing.

"That, and you could have had me here." Her fingertips skimmed over his crotch, barely there, deliberate enough to show the contact was anything but accidental. "What did you want to do, Davide? How did you want to do it?"

When he started to answer, her lips met his, her tongue darting out to seek his own. He deepened the kiss, his tongue stroking hers in a long, slow echo of her caresses as he wound his hands in her hair, holding her in place. Her touch was clearly intentional now, stroking him until he stood and pulled her close, her hand still cupping him through his jeans.

Withdrawing her hand, she aligned her body with his, her hips moving against his with the same maddening rhythm her hand had traced moments before. His hand slid under her sweater, downy knit above, supple skin beneath, the soft heat of both making him ache for her even sweeter warmth.

It would be so easy, wouldn't it? To clear the desk and just take her here and now—God knows she's willing.

The knock at the door seemed impossibly loud, the hollow wooden boom filling the tiny office as though descending from above. They pulled away from each other so swiftly his head swam. He sat down hard on the edge of the desk while she spun away from the door, her hand over her mouth.

It would take too long to move to his chair and sit, and his vision had tunneled, making it difficult to know how much time had passed between the knock and the present moment. Belatedly realizing that Emily's hand was suppressing a fit of giggles, he drew a deep breath to clear his head and desperately hoped his visitor would say his piece and leave.

"*Avanti,*" he called and the door swung open easily.

Merda... Was it open the whole time?

"*Ciao*, Davide," Michele said, stepping inside. He stopped short upon seeing Emily and smiled. "Ah, *scusate*. I'm sorry, did I interrupt?" he asked, looking at Davide again.

Davide cleared his throat and prayed Michele wouldn't notice his condition. He shook his head and Michele gave him a sly, knowing grin.

"Emilia, please allow me to introduce my friend, Michele." Davide gestured from one to the other. "Miki, this is Emily."

"*Piacere*, Emily," Michele said, taking her hand. "It is a pleasure to meet you."

"*Piacere*, Michele," Emily said, bending to take her coat from the chair. "I'll just step out for a moment and let you two talk." Her pink cheeks flared a brighter red as she and Michele turned in a slow circle in the tight space, his hand still holding hers. "Call me when you're ready for lunch, Davide?" she asked.

"Yes, just give us a minute, *va bene*?"

"Okay. *Ciao.*" She withdrew her hand and gave a little wave before she went out.

"*That's* the one?" Michele tilted his head toward the door and Davide nodded. "Wow," he said, pursing his lips in appraisal. "*Che bel tocco di —*"

"She speaks Italian, Miki," Davide interrupted, knowing where the next words were likely to lead.

"*—ragazza*," his friend finished. "What a sweet girl she seems to be—that's what I meant to say."

"She's a woman, Miki. Not a girl."

"And an attractive woman, at that."

"You thought she wouldn't be?"

"*A volte si fanno trottare anche gli asini,*" Michele said, making a gesture as though pulling back on reins.

At times, even donkeys can trot. Davide sighed. *There goes Miki with his charming sayings again.*

Arching one eyebrow, Michele chuckled. "I'm just teasing, you know that."

"Of course. What brings you by, Miki?"

"At such an inopportune moment, you mean? Nothing, really. I just thought I'd drop by and see how you were doing and..." Michele paused, turned to look out the door and then turned back to Davide. "When did she get here? To Bologna, I mean."

"About two weeks ago. Why?"

Michele looked at his watch, then grinned at Davide once again. "I should have known. She's why you were late to the meeting, am I right?"

Davide tried to maintain a neutral façade but instead felt a flush in his cheeks betray him. His friend chuckled long and low, nodding sagely before grasping Davide's shoulder and squeezing hard.

"I knew it. Obviously, you two are... well, I don't need to say it, I can practically *smell* the pheromones flying around in here."

"*Porca vacca*, Miki. Must you?"

"Must I, what? *Non sono io quello che sta andando in bianco qui, amico mio.*" Michele made a blocking gesture in front of his crotch.

I'm not the one who's practically blue-balling here, my friend.

"Miki..." Davide's face burned hotter than ever. Such an open reference to his obvious physical frustration was simply mortifying, even though Emily wasn't around to hear it.

"No," his friend continued, picking up his previous theme. "No, that would be you. If I'd been a couple of minutes later I'd have caught you two at it on the desk, no? I'd have loved to see that." Michele laughed heartily. "Not that I blame you at all. If I'd seen her on her own, I'd have a go."

"You're married." Davide suppressed a sigh. His friend could be so trying sometimes.

Michele shrugged. "Eh, I'm not dead. Besides, I like a woman with a little cushioning. How the hell do *you* manage it, though?"

"Manage what?"

"You go from Letizia, who could bring a government to its knees, to someone like *that*," he said, gesturing out the door, "who is just so damnably *ripe* you want to squeeze —"

"Stop," Davide said, raising one hand and standing up. "Stop now. Not another word, *per favore*. Not about Emilia. Not about my..." He trailed off, uncertain how he'd meant to finish the sentence.

My what, *exactly?*

Michele stopped, his hands still raised in a dual cupping gesture until he shook them into loose fists and dropped them to his sides. "*Mi dispiace*, Davide. I got carried away. I would just like to know how you get such beautiful women. Honestly, I meant no disrespect."

"*Lo so*, Miki."

"I see why your mood has changed for the better. I'd be a very happy man with a woman like that in my bed, too."

"*Miki…*" Davide put as much warning as he could manage into his friend's name, but feared it wasn't terribly convincing.

Michele gave him an apologetic look and raised his hands in a gesture of surrender. "Right, right… I should let you get out for lunch, then. You have a lesson this afternoon?"

"*Sì, sì*. And you?"

As usual, a noncommittal shrug was Michele's response. Davide stood, got his coat and ushered Michele out into the corridor where Emily waited nearby.

"*Dimmi*, Emily," Michele began, "how are you enjoying Bologna?"

"I'm enjoying it very much, thank you," she said, giving both men a smile which made Davide reconsider leaving the privacy of his office.

"He's showing you the sights, *sì?*" Michele swung open the heavy door at the bottom of the steps and held it while she and Davide passed through.

"*Sì, certo*. It's a beautiful city," she said and Michele took her hand.

"If you find he's neglected giving you a proper tour, I hope you'll call on me." Michele bent and gave her a swift kiss on each cheek, and Davide noted the surprise in her eyes. "It's nice to have finally met you," Michele said and tipped a wink in his friend's direction. "I'm pleased to find he didn't either exaggerate or downplay your beauty. *Ci vediamo!*" he called back, already strolling away.

"So he knows, eh?" Emily asked.

Davide nodded. "You don't know the half of it, *amore*. By this afternoon, everyone in the department will know."

"How do you feel about that? Do you want them to know?" She hugged herself in a gesture which suggested she was uncertain of what his answer might be.

"It spares me from climbing a tower to shout it myself, so I guess I should be grateful."

"You'd really do that?" she asked, her mouth quirking up on one side.

"In a heartbeat." Davide gathered her into his arms and softly kissed her. "I think *le torri* are open at this time of year—we could go up, if you wish. I'll proclaim in every language I know from the top of the Asinelli."

Emily giggled playfully. "And what would you say?"

"I will say, 'I love Emily Miller!' And I will say, '*Io amo* Emily Miller!' And I will say, '*J'aime* Emily Miller!' If I'm feeling especially bold, I might even say, '*Eu amo* Emily Miller,' but my Portuguese isn't very good."

"What would be required to convince you to do that?" She giggled again, reaching up to touch his face, her fingers lightly tracing the shape of his smile before he pressed close and kissed her once more.

"*Chiedimi di fare così, e lo farò,*" he said, then repeated himself in English for emphasis: "Ask me to do so, and I will do it."

He didn't give her the chance to say anything more. He lost himself in the warm, eager yielding of her lips and tongue to his. Her arms wrapped tight around his neck while his hands sought out her curves through the heavy material of her winter coat.

They stood at a distance from the sidewalk in a recessed doorway beneath the porticos, yet the feeling of exposure persisted, as though they were in the middle of a piazza. The sound of passing footsteps echoed, twanging off the concrete-and-plaster of the archway over their heads and the wooden door at their shoulders. The frosty air he tasted between kisses was slightly metallic, sharp and mixed with a hint of snow. There were no distinct thoughts in his head, only the recollection of their kisses from before in his office and a silent plea for more of her than he could legally ask in public like this.

As though of its own volition, his hand sought a gap in her coat, seeking the warmth of her skin against his own, if only for a moment.

"Prof?"

Davide quickly withdrew his hand and straightened up as best he could with Emily's arms still wound around his neck. Together, they turned toward the speaker and found a number of students looking on, several with expressions of surprise on their faces, some self-conscious grins scattered throughout the group. One in particular stood out and Davide was compelled to address him directly since he'd been the one to speak.

"*Ciao*, Mohal, *come stai*?" He then directed his attention to the group at large. "*Ragazzi*," he said with a tilt of his head.

One of the girls in the group nudged another girl, stage-whispering, "*Hai visto? Te ho detto che era lui.*" Davide's first instinct was to shush her until he recalled they weren't in class.

Might as well let them have their fun.

"*Ciao*, Prof. Sorry to interrupt. Really, very sorry."

"It's not a problem, believe me."

Losing interest, the group had already begun drifting away, some of the students laughing, some still with looks of disbelief. Mohal hesitated, a questioning look on his face, before he turned and walked away with the others.

"I do believe he was blushing," Emily said softly and Davide nodded agreement. "Why do you think that is?"

With a shrug, he turned and slipped his arm around her, leading her along the portico. "I don't know. I guess he's just embarrassed to see a teacher acting like one of his classmates."

"So are you enjoying a second adolescence, then?"

"More like my first, Emilia," he said with a soft laugh, squeezing her closer. "I wouldn't have it any other way."

"Is it wrong to enjoy a hotel room so much?" Emily asked when Davide rejoined her on the bed and bent to tie his shoes.

He chuckled and shook his head, still fussing with his shoelaces. "I think it's only natural." He sat up again and turned to face her. "Besides, I enjoy it too, especially in the middle of the afternoon like this."

"It's too bad you have to go back to work..." Emily's hand rose to Davide's chest through his unbuttoned shirt, stroking there and then trailing downward. His belly twitched under her touch as she pressed her hand against him.

He leaned in for yet another kiss, his own hand tracing down from her face to caress her bare breast. "I really must go. I'm late as it is."

"I'll be there when you finish. I need more time to get ready."

"*Va bene.*" He hurried to finish dressing and examined himself in the mirror. "I'll see you in a couple of hours."

Emily nodded, sweet anticipation flowing through her at the thought of what they would do after dinner. Davide paused, watching her closely before his mouth crooked slyly and he crossed to her once more.

The bed creaked ever-so-slightly under his weight as he sat down next to her and pulled her to him for a long, slow kiss. "*Ti amo, Emilia,*" he said quietly when they parted. Folding her hands between his he kissed the tip of each finger, then gently released her.

"*Anche io ti amo,* Davide." How good it felt to say it, too.

"Rest, *tesoro mio.* I'll see you very soon."

"Okay."

With that he stood and put on his glasses, quickly checked his hair in the mirror and put on his coat. He was still shrugging into his sleeves as he blew her a kiss and went to the door, disappearing from her sight.

No sooner was he gone than Emily felt the weight of his absence. She snuggled down into the bedsheets, tugged closer the pillow he'd used and breathed deep to inhale his scent. A moment later she almost wished she hadn't done so, as her yearning for him increased immeasurably. A quick glance at the clock showed she had two hours to wait until she could see him again.

Still feeling his kisses on her fingertips, she raised them to her mouth and brushed them over her lips. She pictured his face, the look in his eyes as his lips had touched her fingers, his hands holding hers.

Soon her thoughts drifted to their lovemaking, how lighthearted and playful it had begun, how warm and tender at the end when they'd settled into one another and drowsed without parting first.

It wasn't necessary to look in a mirror to know that a broad, cat-in-the-cream smile was on her lips; the solid *rightness* it made told her so. With a long, languorous stretch, Emily spread herself out beneath the sheets and considered where they should stay that night. She could bring him back here and experience the vaguely-illicit sense of having him in her hotel room or she could go to his flat and enjoy the comforts of being in his home, safe and warm.

"What to do, what to do…"

Surely it wasn't such a difficult decision?

The old-fashioned, bell-like ring of the phone broke the dozy silence settling around her and she rolled over to answer, trying to wake up before she lifted the receiver.

"*Pronto?*"

"Emily, is that you?" Her mother's voice doused her sleepy ease with icy efficiency.

"Yes, mother, it's me. Who else would answer in my room?"

"Am I interrupting anything?" she asked pointedly.

"No, sorry, we're finished. He's already gone," Emily answered with a forced cool.

A long silence followed.

"I can't believe you can be so crude. Then again, I can't believe you'd take up with some stranger so soon, either, which just goes to show how well I know my own daughter."

Emily said nothing, preferring to let the silence spool out once again.

"Are you there?" her mother asked, sounding distracted.

"Yes, I'm here. Is something wrong? It's not like you to call so many times in a day." *Or ever, for that matter.*

"I'm just concerned, is all. You take off to go over there to collect some money from your husband –"

"My *ex*-husband," Emily interjected, knowing her mother wouldn't slow her budding tirade.

"– and take up with Professor Smartypants, who I don't like in the least –"

Emily bit her tongue to keep from laughing. *Professor Smartypants? Oh, that's too good!*

"– and now I'm wondering if you'll come back or what?"

"Mother, I'll let you know as soon as I decide."

"And when will that be?"

"I have to be honest: I don't know."

"Emily, has he asked you for any of the money? You know, to finance some sort of scheme or something. I mean, he *says* he's a teacher or something but how can you be sure?"

"For Heaven's sake, Mother…" Emily pressed her fingers to her eyes and restrained a sigh. "I'm not an idiot. But, for the record, no, he hasn't asked me for money or anything else. And he *is* a professor here at the university. I've been in his office."

"Then what on earth could be keeping you there for so long?"

Emily bit back her next retort, aware that telling her mother what she'd just been up to would hardly be diplomatic.

"Like I said: as soon as I decide when I'm coming home, I'll let you know. Okay?"

"I can't wait around forever, you know. There are things I'd like to do but instead I'm on hold until you figure things out. I have a life, too."

"Then live it. I'm not stopping you. You can even have boys over, okay?"

"Your sarcasm is unappreciated, young lady."

Young lady, she says. Like I'm fifteen all over again. "Mother, I know you've been seeing Mr. Hendrick from the grocery store. It's okay. Have fun—why not? I am."

"Fun? Is that what you call it? Running around with rude, uncultured, money-grubbing —"

Now Emily did laugh out loud, not bothering to cover the mouthpiece of the phone. "Oh, you see? There it is. If you met Davide, you'd see he's one of the kindest, sweetest, most polite and intelligent people I've ever met. Never mind that he's completely uninterested in money—mine or anyone else's. Besides, you hated Jacopo before you met him, too, remember?"

"And look how good your judgment was then, Emily."

Her laughter faltered, then stopped altogether. "You've made your point, Mother. Don't worry about me, okay? I'm a big girl and I've gone into this with my eyes wide open. All right? Incidentally, the only person even mentioning money lately, is you."

"Just what are you insinuating, Missy?"

"Nothing. Nothing at all. Listen, I'll call you next week, all right? I have to go now. Goodbye."

Without waiting for a response, she dropped the phone back onto its cradle and fell back onto the bed with a soft *whump*. A scowl etched itself onto her face—until the phrase "Professor Smartypants" came back to mind.

With a snort of laughter, she got up and untangled herself from the bedclothes.

"I have *got* to find a way to use that one," she said and laughed again, brushing her hair in front of the mirror. "Poor misguided Mother..." The woman was so off the mark it almost wasn't funny.

Honestly, I'm insulted on his behalf.

Her mother had no idea how hard it had actually been to get used to Davide's honesty. His refreshing willingness to answer any and every question kept her from asking in the first place. Whatever she wanted to know, he'd tell her. Knowing that was enough to sate her curiosity.

What had her mother called him? Rude? Uncultured? Money-grubbing? Emily paused, staring at her reflection. *Money-grubbing? Why does she keep bringing up money? Did she tell him about the profits from the sale?*

She narrowed her eyes focusing on the reflection of the bed, imagining him there. He hadn't said anything to her about it, so maybe there was a chance nothing had been said. Surely he would be curious about it after her mother had provoked him, though?

Another few strokes of the brush and she put it down, turning to face the bed as though the answer was there in the mussed sheets and crumpled pillowcases. She knew he really didn't care about that sort of thing, so why was she bothered all of a sudden by the fact that he might know?

Because I've had plenty of time to tell him and I haven't?

Fine, no big deal. I'll tell him tonight.

But how to explain the delay?

It'll come to me. It has to. He won't care, anyway.

How can he not? I've got more now than he'll earn in the next ten years, probably.

She shook her head, went to collect the clothes from the floor and piled them on the bed. Honesty would be the only approach, of course. She'd just have to open up to him and tell him the rest of what happened in Rovigo.

Simple enough, right?

Still, as much as it pained her to do so, her mother's sentiments still echoed in her head. She'd trusted Jacopo, and she'd trusted Jason before him, and both times she'd been devastated by their betrayals. How could she be so certain Davide wouldn't hurt her, too?

God knows I'm probably not the best judge of character, as it happens.

"No," she murmured quietly, crossing back to the bed to sort through the clothes pile. She couldn't start thinking like that again. She'd made the right choice when she'd trusted Davide a year ago and she was right to trust him now.

Her phone rang from the pocket of her coat, which lay on the bench under the coat hooks by the mirror. She took it out, checking to see who her caller was—if only out of habit. Naturally, it was Davide. There was no one else who would call her on this number.

"*Ciao*, Davide. *Dov'è sei?* You aren't at the restaurant already?" She glanced at the clock with mild alarm. More time had passed than she'd expected.

"*Ciao*, Emilia. No, I'm still at work. Would you mind joining me directly at the restaurant?"

"Of course I can meet you there."

"*Bene.* I'll wait for you outside, okay? *Ciao...*"

He was clearly still distracted. Emily couldn't help smiling, though she suspected his distraction meant she'd be at the restaurant well before him.

"Okay. *Ciao-ciao.*"

"*Ciao-ciao*," he echoed, then closed the line.

With that, she closed her phone and tucked it away in her pocket again. By the time she'd dressed, left the hotel and made her way to Piazza Maggiore, the sun was slanting across the city, casting the paving stones in a reddish-orange glow.

She stopped on the corner and watched the fountain in the center of the square; the figure of Neptune atop his pedestal standing tall in the lengthening shadows. From this vantage point, she couldn't see the water or observe the play of light across the surface of it. Only the thin streams spraying from the mouths of the fish held by the cherubs at his feet, or from the mouths of the faces along the base, or from the cupped breasts of the female figures astride arcing sea creatures were visible. It was tempting to stay there a while to watch until the shadows climbed higher and higher, until they would finally swallow the very tip of the trident in his hand.

The memory of her first kiss with Davide, there at Neptune's feet, warmed her in spite of the chill of the coming evening air.

I'm in the right place. Maybe for the first time in my life, I'm really where I'm supposed to be.

Hugging herself, she set off across the piazza, heading for the restaurant where— if she was lucky and he'd managed to get away from the office—Davide waited.

38

The server had barely left the table before Davide spoke. "Mohal has asked me for advice on women."

"Who? Is that the boy we saw today?"

"*Sì, lui.* He stopped me after class and asked to speak with me privately. Naturally, I assumed he wanted to discuss the lesson. Instead, he asked me for advice on getting a girl to notice him."

Emily smiled, thinking of Davide's initial overtures on the train and in the station when they'd met. Not that his efforts had been much of an approach—at first.

"Well? What did you say?"

"What *could* I say? I told him to be himself and to be honest with the girl he likes about how he feels." He shook his head wearing an expression bordering on dismay. "*Santo Cielo,* I'm no expert, anyway. I felt like a fraud."

"Why do you say that? You did that with me, didn't you? Honesty is good. Women like honest men. Take it from me: liars are vastly overrated."

His eyes darted away from hers, his expression tightening, growing even more serious as he sat up straighter in his chair. Emily turned her attention back to the basket of *grissini* on the table before fumbling out a packet and tearing it open

Is he thinking about what Mother told him? Should I tell him about it now?

"I don't know," he was saying. "The whole situation made me uncomfortable. I wanted to send him to the counselors at Student Services but he looked so, so…I don't know…*convinced*, I think is the word. He looked so convinced that I could help him, I was afraid that if I'd sent him away he'd have never come to me again for anything else."

"You want him to come to you, then?"

"Well, yes—about lessons, my lectures, research, that sort of thing. His personal life, though? That's not exactly a good idea."

"Why? Do you think your opinions are useless?"

"Of course not. After all, I'm the natural choice to come to for advice on women. Look at all my years of experience."

He said this with an ironic curl of his lip, Emily noted. She grinned again taking a bite of a crispy breadstick and crunching thoughtfully for a moment. "What is it that makes you so nervous, then?"

"Well, unless he actually *wants* to remain unmarried until he's nearly forty, I'm not sure I'm quite the font of knowledge he's seeking." Davide chuckled, then fell quiet suddenly before he shrugged it off. "It's a gray area, I'm afraid. If something went wrong based on what I told him and the university found out? It could be a bad thing in the end."

"Well," Emily took a sip of her water, "I think it's great he came to you, and I think your advice was perfect. Sure, he's probably heard it a thousand times before, but maybe now he's heard it from you, he'll do it."

Davide gave her a hopeful look. "You really think so?"

"*Sì, certo.* I do. I think it's possible you were the final nudge he needed to do what he wanted to do. Did he say why he wanted your advice and not one of the counselors?"

Davide shook his head, his lips holding a thin, straight line. "No, but he did say he'd seen us."

"Today, I know."

"No, another time. He saw us at the bookshop, too, and he guessed you were the person who called me at work that day. Seeing us together today was only what motivated him to ask me." He smiled. "He said we looked so happy, I must know something about relationships."

"At least you know something about honesty. That's enough and that should have helped him. You'll see—everything will be fine." Emily gave him a smile of her own and reached out for his hand.

Davide leaned across the table, took her hand in his and kissed the air over her fingers, barely brushing her skin with his lips. When she shivered he grinned releasing her only when the server arrived with the *antipasti* and set them on the table.

"So what did you do while I was giving advice to young would-be lovers?"

Emily sighed, picked up her fork and poked at a bit of *lardo*, then spread it over a piece of bread. "I talked to my mother."

"Again?" Wine glass in hand, Davide watched her carefully. "Is everything okay?"

"Oh, everything's fine. She's just upset with me as usual. She says I'm keeping her from getting on with her own life, because she doesn't know when I'm coming home. It's ridiculous, really, but there it is."

"I should apologize to her for how I addressed her this morning," he said, nodding affirmation as he put his glass down.

"No, you shouldn't. Look, Davide, my mother is not the most endearing person around. Even if she met you, she wouldn't like you." Emily took a bite of her bread and *lardo* and resisted the urge to sigh with pleasure around it.

"Why not?"

"Because you're not Jacopo," she said, wiping her mouth with her napkin and placing it back in her lap.

Davide's brow creased in puzzlement. "I don't understand."

"Somewhere along the way, my mother became convinced that he was perfection itself. Frankly, I think she got snowed by the looks and the money, just like I did. Now she thinks I'm the reason things didn't work out." Emily reached for her own glass of wine, only half-full, and gulped down a mouthful. "It'll always be *my* fault now."

"But how can she not take her daughter's side?"

Emily shrugged and met Davide's eyes.

"I don't know, *amore*. To be honest, I don't know if I really care."

Mohal's questions had planted a seed which needed little encouragement to grow. Sure, the question had been on Davide's mind for some time, but to take such a leap so soon into their relationship required an impulsiveness he didn't know he possessed.

Which made the idea all the more sensible and he'd come to want it more than ever. But was it only a machination to keep Emily near? A ploy to keep her from changing her mind and running away?

He'd never considered that their time might be limited. The idea she might not have a choice in whether she stayed or went certainly played a part here, fanning the flames of panic at the possibility of losing her. Some unforeseen legality could easily bring the flowering of their relationship to an early frost.

Since her divorce, was she now limited to a tourist's visa? Would they be doomed to three months together, then three months apart? How long could that work before she got tired of coming and going? How long before someone "back home" suddenly started to appeal to her more and more, and convinced her to leave behind Italy—and himself—forever?

Che melodramma, he thought with a sigh. *There's an easy solution to this and I've just got to make up my mind to do it.*

Emily's lack of costume jewelry was frustrating. No amount of subterfuge gave him the "in" he needed to determine her ring size, no trickery succeeded in subtly teasing the information out of her either.

It's just my luck to fall in love with a clever woman.

Asking her mother wasn't an option—not by any means. He didn't know Jenn's number and, anyway, he wasn't sure how likely she was to be of any help. He staunchly refused to go through Emily's things to find out the names and numbers of any other girlfriends who might be able to tell him. The memory of going through her bag in Milano still weighed on his mind as it was.

The next two weeks passed faster than Davide had dreamed possible. More often than not, he woke to find Emily by his side in the early hours of the morning. With each morning he found her there, he grew more convinced that he'd made the right decision.

And so he lay awake, listening for Emily to slip into a deep, sound sleep in the small hours of the night after they'd made love. He fought the fall into slumber himself, almost succumbing more than once, until the reason he wanted to stay awake occurred to him again.

Finally, convinced she was sleeping, he took the length of thread off his nightstand and fished her hand out from under the bedclothes as gently as possible. She stirred and tried to pull away and he froze, his heart thudding so hard his whole body shook with each beat.

Emily settled once again, her breathing soft and even, her hand atop the covers and within easy reach, lit by a square of moonlight through the window.

Grazie a Dio…

With exaggerated care, he slipped the thread around her ring finger and pinched where the end would make a loop. He slid out from under the covers and, still pinching the thread as though it were a grenade which might explode if he released the least amount of pressure off it, he hurried into the hallway to switch on the table lamp by the door. He pulled out the cuticle scissors he'd stuffed in the drawer beneath the lamp and snipped precisely where his fingers clamped the thread, before allowing himself a quiet sigh of relief. The tiny envelope from the drawer seemed comically huge compared to the thread inside, but he solemnly sealed it and tucked it away.

After a few moments, his heartbeat calmed and the cool night air frosted over the perspiration on his skin. He had no idea how long he'd been there but he'd gone cold and clammy all over. The warmth of the bed, with Emily in it, beckoned from down the hall and he made his way quietly toward the bedroom.

He'd go to the *gioielleria* in the morning on his way to work. And as soon as he had the ring, he'd ask her.

On the first try, he found the perfect poesy ring: a white-gold band with a setting in the shape of two joined hands holding delicately detailed flowers, in the midst of which sat a modest ruby. On either side, a scattering of tiny diamond chips glittered, set into the band itself. It was anything but ostentatious, yet he was sure that few women would turn their noses up at it.

Certainly, it didn't compare to the ring Jacopo had given her but few could—and on Davide's modest salary, such an investment would prove devastating.

On Friday evening at the flat, after dinner, they settled on the sofa to drink their espresso. He did his best to steer the conversation around to her stay in Italy and she'd managed, somehow, to dodge his questions and follow different tangents instead.

Why couldn't she just let him ask his questions? Was she avoiding something? What was it her mother had said? Something about money—presumably the money from the sale of the house—but Emily had yet to acknowledge anything unusual had happened.

And hadn't she said she had news for him when she called that night from Rovigo? Had she changed her mind about telling him?

Finally, he resigned himself to being blunt with her about what was on his mind.

"You have your *Carta di Soggiorno, sì?*"

She seemed surprised by the question and—if he wasn't misreading things—also a bit relieved.

"Yes. I have dual citizenship, actually. I don't know why, but Jacopo insisted on it after a couple of years, once I was eligible. Seeing as how I wasn't exactly deported after the divorce, well…I guess that's *one* kindness he gave me." There was just enough sarcasm in her tone to make him cringe. Perversely, it also fueled his hope.

"So you can stay as long as you wish."

Emily nodded, an inquisitive arch to her brow.

"I was thinking, then…" Davide began, but faltered.

"…*Sì*…?"

"Maybe it would be a good idea… Only if you really wanted to, that maybe you might consider, um…"

She leaned in closer, her eyes meeting his until he looked away. "Yes?"

"Why don't you just… Why not just stay here, with me?"

"Really?"

"*Ma… sì.*" He was unable to face her for a moment and when he met her eyes once more he was pinned, helpless, waiting for her answer.

Emily's eyes widened, her surprise written plainly in them. "I'm sorry, Davide… I just want to be sure I understand this. Are you asking me to move in with you?"

"*Sì.* That is what I want. Or even–"

"You realize I can afford the hotel, though. In fact—"

"*Naturalmente, sì.* That's certainly true, but don't you think it's silly to keep spending money on the hotel room? You're here much of the time anyway, so I should think this is the logical, erm… progression of things. I have plenty of space—you could have your own room, if you wish."

"Well, that's a hard offer to resist, Davide."

"Why resist, then? It makes sense, no?"

"*Sì*, of course it does. Not that I'd need my own room."

"Well, you know…" He put his hand to his pocket again, hesitated and then resumed gesturing as he spoke. "I meant you could make the other bedroom an office, or a studio or something. Whatever you want, we can do that."

"I don't know…" she said, trailing off.

"I'd like to have you here with me."

Emily smiled. "Say that again, please."

"What?"

"Say that again, that last part."

"I'd like to have you here with me?"

"Not like a question. Say it again."

"I misspoke."

"Oh."

"I *want* you here with me, Emilia. I *need* you here with me."

"Davide?"

"*Sì?*"

"*Chiedimi se sono felice.* Ask me if I'm happy."

"*Sei felice*, Emilia?"

"*Sì, sono felice. Non sono mai stata così felice.* I'm happier than I've ever been."

"*Amore, ascoltami…*" Davide's hand returned to his pocket in a glancing touch before rising to fold with the other in a gesture of supplication. He couldn't meet her eyes, it seemed. Instead, his focus shifted from one spot to another, all around her face, the sofa where she sat, the living room itself. When at last his gaze held hers, he blinked so fast she wondered if he had something in his eye.

In short, all his usual nervous tics were present and accounted for. Emily tried not to grin at this, her heart warming at the thought she might know him so well now.

But did she? Really? She certainly hadn't seen *this* coming.

I'll tell him about the money tonight. He should know, if we're going to live together.

He cleared his throat and stood. His hand dipped toward his pocket before he spoke again. "*Penso che…* I mean," he said, switching to English, "I think that I should ask you something else."

A thrill shot through her, shivering down and heating up her spine with alternate heartbeats. If she didn't know better, she'd have sworn he was about to…

No, no, surely not…

She imagined she saw the faintest bend in his knee before the phone rang and he turned in that direction instead. A deep breath cleared her head. Of course she was overreacting—he was going to ask something about her moving in, *that's* what this conversation was about.

The phone rang again and he snatched the handset up off the cradle with an air of annoyed distraction.

"*Sì, pronto? Pronto...? Chi–?*" At once his back straightened, his shoulders squared. She could sense his tension from across the room.

With that, a sudden *wrongness* seemed to fill the air around her. Emily forced herself to breathe deep, willed her hands to stop shaking and watched Davide.

He turned toward her with obvious reluctance, his expression somewhere between concern and frustration. "Yes, *Signora* Miller, your daughter is here."

Mom. The muscles in her legs turned to jelly as a peculiar relief flowed through her. Nothing was wrong with her mother, if she was the one calling. What nerve she had to call like this, if Davide had told her not to!

A flash of guilt twisted her stomach when she considered that she hadn't called the hotel to see if she'd had messages for the last couple of days. All the same, she was obliged to tell her mother not to call here again.

"Yes, of course." Davide's tone was remarkably civil, his expression now more neutral, almost unreadable. "Just a moment," he said and folded his hand over the mouthpiece holding it out toward her. "Emily, it's for you."

"I'm so sorry, Davide," she said, crossing to him. "I'll tell her not to call –"

"It's all right." He handed her the phone and before she'd raised it to her ear, she realized he'd called her "Emily" and not "Emilia."

Silence hung between them, heavy and oppressive. As Emily brought the phone up to speak to her mother, Davide had to fight the desire to curse his ill fortune.

The little box in his pocket, now hidden by his sweater, could wait. But for how long *this* time? He wanted to rail against the bad luck that plagued them but suspected it would be incredibly petty to do so.

Especially now, if the somber tone of her mother's voice was any indication.

"Hello, Mom?" Emily's eyes focused on him, so Davide steeled himself to keep a neutral expression on his face. He noted the puzzlement in her face, the inquisitive rise of her brows, the confused pursing of her lips. "What's going on? You aren't supposed to…"

The silence deepened, broken by the faint rush of steam in the radiator next to the window. Emily's face went slack, stunned. If he listened hard, he could hear the murmuring of her mother's voice on the receiver, indistinct and yet full of consolation. The words didn't matter; he got the gist, regardless.

"How?" Emily asked, one hand reaching out toward Davide. "When?"

He stepped forward and took her hand guiding her as though she were blinded by this news, whatever it was, and helped her settle onto the sofa. Her mother's murmuring was louder, easily heard now, but still unclear.

"Oh… Ohhhh… God…"

Emily shook her head and Davide wondered what he should do. Put an arm around her? Wait for the call to end first? Touch her to let her know he was there for her? Leave her alone? What?

"I don't believe it, Mom… I don't understand. Why did he do that? What good does it do? It has to be some sort of mistake, it has to be…" A strange, choking sob shook her but no tears were in her eyes. "I'm sorry, Mom. It's okay, really. I understand, and he does, too. No, I'm sure he does. Yes. Yes… I'll call you later, when I find something out, all right? Okay. I'll talk to you later. Okay. Bye. Bye-bye…"

The silence returned, following the quiet *beep* of the phone disconnecting. Davide reached to take the receiver from Emily's limp fingers before it could fall to the floor and he put it quietly on the end table before turning to face her again.

The silence grew deeper still, until he spoke softly to dispel it. *"Che è successo?"*

"It's, um… It's Jacopo," she said in English.

Coldness formed in Davide's chest, sinking lower and lower before he could speak. *"Sì?* What did he do?"

She continued staring into the middle distance, her face still expressionless. She seemed about to speak, but fell silent again.

Davide waited.

She took another breath and exhaled slowly.

"Jacopo is dead," she said, her face twisting in an expression of confusion which would have been almost comical any other time. "He died and my mother says he named me in his will." She turned abruptly toward Davide. "Why would he do that? It makes no sense at all, does it?" She turned away before he could answer, shaking her head. "No, it doesn't make sense. None."

Davide was silent, too stunned to speak. Jacopo had *died?*

"He was driving back to Rome on the A1 and flipped his car. Can you believe it? I bet he wanted to drive because he had that new Z4. I saw it when I was in Rovigo—he loves driving, always thinks he's better than everyone else on the road…"

Icy tendrils wrapped around Davide's stomach squeezing and twisting slowly. *Flipped his car. Was he alone, or was* she *with him?* He shook his head, a momentary disgust sweeping over him. It didn't matter.

"Emilia…"

"Mom said the lawyer called there to speak to me. He wanted to know if I could come to Venice." She shook her head. "I'll have to call him. The lawyer. Maybe I can get out of it?"

"If that's what you want, *tesoro*," Davide put his arm around her shoulders and she accepted his embrace without encouraging it.

"Should I? Go, I mean."

"Perhaps you should give yourself some time to consider it."

"I'll have to go soon. They tried to reach me last Tuesday. It happened last weekend." She raised one hand to her face.

"I'll take time off work and go with you, if you want," he offered quietly and she turned to face him again.

"You will?" Her hand dropped to seize his squeezing tight. "I *need* you to do this, Davide. I can't do it if you don't go with me."

Her face twisted into a grimace and for an instant he wondered whether his face mirrored hers, whether she felt ice water trickling to fill her stomach, too. His hand was numb when she released it.

"My God, this is so strange... We're divorced, we sold the house...I'm not supposed to have anything else to do with him. Why was I in his will, for fuck's sake?" She spat this last out as though it left a bad taste in her mouth.

Davide shrugged silently and grasped her hand. She shuddered under his touch and leaned against him burying her face against his neck. A small strangled sound escaped her, fading into a long sigh which warmed him through his sweater and shirt.

"The worst thing is, I'm not sure how to feel. Do I mourn him? Do I feel indifferent? What?"

When she drew away to look at him, her eyes were too bright, too wide. There was just enough time for him to wonder if she was about to cry before she wrapped her arms around his neck and clung to him as though to life itself.

39

onday morning was cold and clear. Emily waited silently on the furthest platform from the station building of *Bologna Centrale*, her eyes unseeing, fixed on the wall beyond the track. Though Davide's hand—warm, ever-present and reassuring—was closed over hers, it could not fill the hollowness she'd felt inside since her mother's call.

She swallowed with a dry throat. Her eyes were achy and tight from crying. This was the hardest thing to understand, the persistent need to mourn a loss she wasn't even sure was hers. How much mourning was appropriate? Why was she so disturbed?

Before this, she'd honestly believed she was finished with Jacopo for good. Instead, even though he was dead, she had to deal with him yet again. Would this be the last time or was there another strange circumstance waiting to force them together again in the future?

She shivered and Davide squeezed her hand in reassurance. The smile she wanted to give him in return remained trapped somewhere inside her, unable to rise to the surface.

It was impossible to ask him for more than he'd given her so far. When she'd cried, he'd held her without asking questions. When she had been silent, he'd let her be silent. He'd seemed to know what she needed before she had, bringing her a cup of tea here, a light snack there. He'd cooked her favorite meal on Sunday afternoon while she'd napped in the bedroom, the shutters closed to block out the light.

He'd even gone to the grocery store on Saturday morning just to find a jar of American peanut butter and then made peanut butter pancakes for her. This, after he had declared them a culinary abomination the week before. She had no idea where he'd found the recipe.

And still she mourned Jacopo, the man who had lied to her from the start, had cheated from the beginning of their marriage and had left her for another woman. Not to mention that he'd tried, just shy of a month ago, to seduce her once again in Rovigo.

Guilt tickled at the back of her conscience with the memory: for having let him kiss her, even though she had turned him away; for not having told Davide about her profits from the house sale; for her current curiosity as to just what Jacopo had bequeathed her.

An unexpected tear slid down her nose and its path told her that her head was down. Davide's arm lay tight around her shoulder as though he were holding her up. His effort wasn't quite necessary but it helped.

One look at his face was enough to tell her he was troubled, but she lacked the courage to ask what bothered him so. When he noted her watching him, his expression always changed to sincere concern but she didn't forget the thin-lipped, drawn look it had replaced.

He hadn't slept well, either. She'd lain awake the night before, on her side, eyes wide open and staring at the wall and she'd often felt him awake beside her. He'd feigned sleep, of course. Perhaps he hadn't wanted to add to her worry but she couldn't help thinking she would have preferred him to hold her and to talk to her instead.

From overhead, the loudspeaker announced the arrival of their train. Davide squeezed her hand again, drew her close and placed a gentle kiss on her temple, his lips warm in the cold air which blew past while the train slowed to a halt in front of them.

"You should have worn gloves," she said, noting the shaking of his hand before he released her. It was a rare thing for him to forget something so simple, so basic. He pulled the door open and then offered his hand to help her aboard the train.

"*Sì, hai ragione*," he said, his voice thin and somehow distant. "I forgot them in my other coat."

She ascended the stairs and entered the carriage, Davide's hand at the small of her back steering her to their seats.

"*Siamo qui, amore*," he said when they had reached their row and she settled into the window seat without a word.

Lifting his glasses, Davide pinched his nose and rubbed his eyes trying to relax the muscles twitching in his eyelids. He was far more tired than he'd expected to be and the day had hardly begun. Unbuttoning his coat he sat beside Emily resting his hand over hers and watching the other passengers board and find their seats. He sat straight and tried not to stare openly at anyone in particular. He didn't really see them, anyway.

Emily had called the lawyer on Friday evening, expecting to leave a message with his service or on his answering machine. Instead, she'd reached him directly, but had been unable to elicit any information about the bequest. After nearly half an hour, she'd succumbed and agreed to go to *Venezia* to find out what Jacopo had left for her.

Davide's eye twitched again. Grateful that Emily hadn't noticed, he raised his hand to rub it.

I should have ignored the phone. I should have asked her to marry me before answering it. I should have done everything differently.

Of course, it was pointless to wish for such things. He'd answered the phone, she'd gotten the news and the weekend had passed in mourning instead of joy. Instead, Jacopo and Letizia had somehow managed to disrupt his and Emily's life once again.

The train left the station, gradually gaining speed along the track into the morning sunshine. It would have been a beautiful day, if not for where they were going, or more to the point, the reason why.

They would have been home, planning a happier future already, had things gone the way he'd anticipated.

Suppressing a rush of resentment, Davide wondered if Emily had noticed his anxiety, whether anything he'd done so far had betrayed it. He'd felt guilty for not telling her about Letizia and Jacopo, for having kept it to himself all along and now in one horrible, terrible blow, it didn't matter anymore. Somehow the loss of the burden made it worse. He still needed to tell her, but what was the point now? Why rub salt in the wound?

Worst of all, part of him was relieved to have everything settled so decisively and it sickened him to find any sort of relief in something which could devastate Emily like this. He'd lain awake the night before, desperately trying not to disturb her with his restlessness while he went over the events again and again.

The previous afternoon, an undeniably morbid impulse had compelled him to go online and find out what had happened. He'd found a photo of the accident scene. There was precious little left of the car; it was difficult to tell where the car ended and the lorry it had collided with began. It was obvious no one could have survived. At once, he'd closed the page and erased the history of his browser, deleted all the temporary files—everything to be sure no trace of what he'd seen was left on the computer in his study.

An urge to cry from a combination of twisted gratitude and shame had come and gone. Afterward, he'd gone to the bathroom and been quietly sick while Emily napped in the bedroom. Once the nausea had passed, he'd cleaned himself up, gone into the kitchen and prepared dinner, taking care not to wake her until it was ready.

He'd never kept such a secret before. Now that he no longer had to, he felt worse than ever. How the hell had his father done it? How did *anyone* do it, if they really loved someone?

And why do I give a damn if Letizia is alive or dead? After how she handled things, I should be glad to be rid of her. So why is it that I'm not? Why do I want to be able to say goodbye?

Reflexively, his jaw clenched and his hand tightened over Emily's on the armrest. She turned to him, her eyes red-rimmed and shining, dark shadows puffed underneath, and still he found her beautiful.

Gratefulness swept over him and he leaned toward her to press a soft kiss to her forehead. He thought of the velvet box tucked away in his bedside drawer and felt a small flicker of hope.

I will ask her, as soon as we've got all this business behind us and the time feels right. There'll be plenty of time to sort it all out and then we'll get on with things, just the two of us.

"*Ti amo*, Emilia," he murmured, just loud enough for her to hear.

"*Ti amo*, Davide," she murmured in response, and rested her head on his shoulder, her eyes slipping closed for the first time that day.

There was no relief, even in her self-imposed darkness. So Emily sat up and watched the scenery pass by, the rubble of construction sites and crumbling farmhouses fading into the fog, her stomach roiling uneasily all the while. As they left the station for Rovigo behind without stopping, she understood what she needed to do.

I can't take it any more—not today, of all days.

"Davide?"

"*Sì?*"

"There's something I've been meaning to tell you."

Davide straightened beside her and her first thought was that he was bracing himself for something. Cold certainty filled her stomach and the sensation of flipping came to a halt.

"What is it?"

"I never told you about what happened in Rovigo."

"What do you mean?" His arm tensed alongside hers on the armrest of the seat. "You told me what Jacopo did. Was there more?"

"Not about *him*, not exactly. There was more to that visit than I'd expected." Emily directed her attention out the window to the brown and gray landscape fading away into the fog.

"I see."

343

"When Jacopo wrote me in the States and told me that the house was selling for around half a million euros, he had made a mistake. A pretty significant mistake."

"*Sì?*" Davide nodded and then crossed his legs stiffly. "Did he not give you what you'd hoped for, then?"

"Actually, I got more than I expected. Much, *much* more." She turned to face him, meeting his eyes with some difficulty. "Davide, the half million is what I came away with. It was my half of the proceeds."

His expression didn't change in the least. He'd gone rigid, as though steeled against this revelation. The only indication her words had made any impact was the slight raising of one eyebrow.

"Really?" he asked, his voice low, disbelieving.

Emily nodded, her cheeks heating with shame. *I should never have waited this long. Maybe this was the wrong time to tell him?*

"I'm so, so sorry I didn't tell you before this. I was going to say something when I got back but then so many good things were happening—it just didn't seem so important, somehow..."

He reached over to grasp her hand and then gave it a small squeeze.

"I don't care about this. Do you understand that? It changes nothing between us."

She nodded again, swiftly, her eyes burning with new tears. "I didn't mean to lie to you, though."

"You didn't. You never have. That's all I've ever asked of you and that's all I'll ever ask of you. Just be honest and direct with me, always."

"Of course. But still –"

Davide shushed her gently and she fell silent wrapping her arm around his and pressing her face against his shoulder as though to hide.

There. That wasn't so difficult, was it?

Warm comfort filled her at his calm acceptance of this news, but something wasn't quite right, not yet. The tension in his arm remained, a faltering tremor in the muscles which came and went.

We're both so tired, though. I'm sure that's all it is.

Davide's mind reeled from the monetary figure she'd named. In all his life, he'd never earned that much money. He sincerely doubted he ever would.

Half a million *euros. No wonder her mother was so convinced I was after money.*

He couldn't help wondering if perhaps other men would be thrilled to learn that their girlfriend/fiancée/lover was so wealthy because frankly, it made him sick to his stomach. If this was her idea of a big secret, then his secret seemed much worse in comparison.

Not that it mattered now, with Jacopo and Letizia out of their lives for good.

Upon stepping out of the train station, Emily stopped short at the top of the stairs, her grasp on Davide's arm tightening. The view of the canal and the dock for the *vaporetto*, crowded with tourists even at this chilly time of year, was unexpectedly familiar. The feeling of returning home was frightening, especially since she'd never planned on coming back.

Davide rested his hand over hers in the crook of his arm, a tender, reassuring gesture as he led her quietly toward the dock. She followed, trying not to see the city around her, trying harder not to think too deeply—not yet. She only surfaced in her mind for the briefest possible moments in order to choose which boat to take, or to determine the right route to follow to reach the lawyer's office.

The damp odor of the narrow alleyways brought countless memories rushing back, almost too quickly for her to contain them. She recalled Jacopo strolling through them during his leisurely pursuit of her, followed by his swift, almost frantic seduction of her once they'd both succumbed to their desire to be together. Every dark doorway seemed to reach out to her in an attempt to draw her deeper into recollections which had become infinitely more painful in his now-permanent absence.

The lawyer's office was much too ostentatious for such a somber occasion. Emily had been there with Jacopo years before, after his mother had passed and she'd thought the same then. The tapestries adorning the walls were too colorful, the chandeliers too opulent, the hallway too grand and the marble floors too clean and shiny. Not that it would make any difference if the opposite were true. If the building had been shabby, decrepit and dank, Emily still would have been uncomfortable and utterly out of her element.

However, if her familiarity with the place and the people meant this would end any faster, she'd take it.

The secretary, a slender redhead with blonde highlights and an expensive tailored suit, smiled solicitously and explained that *Avvocato* Trevisan would see Emily in a few moments. She indicated a leather sofa along the wall with one elegant hand and Emily went there to sit down.

Davide followed silently reaching for Emily's coat when she took it off. The sofa creaked a little as they sat down and Emily looked around, amazed even more by the sumptuousness of their surroundings.

His eyes scanned restlessly from place to place and she knew he was assessing and appreciating the art and décor in ways she simply couldn't.

She pressed her shaking hands to the cushion beneath her, willing the tremors to stop. Waves of nausea rippled and rose in her throat until she raised the backs of her fingers to her mouth, their coolness soothing against the heat of her lips.

"This isn't a reading of the will," she said, her words reflecting warm off her fingers.

"*Come?*" Davide inquired softly, as if the office itself were a museum.

"I said, this isn't a reading of the will. They only do that in movies. I still don't know why it was so important for me to come here."

"It was probably a requirement of some sort. Could Jacopo have wanted you here for some particular reason?"

Shrugging, Emily stared at the Oriental rug beneath their feet. "It'd be just like him to force me to do what he wants from beyond the grave." Her voice rose shakily to break on the last word. "Sorry..." She wiped at her eyes with a tissue and stuffed it back into her bag.

Davide took her hand in his and held it tight. "Do you want me to come in with you?"

"I don't know..." she said, thinking for a moment. It *might* be easier to have him there, but at the same time, this felt somehow...what was the word? *Private*. "I don't think so, Davide. No. But if I change my mind, I'll come get you, okay?"

"*Certo, amore. Come vuoi.*"

A few minutes later a soft buzz from the desk drew her attention. The secretary stood and crossed to Emily, the businesslike smile still on her lips.

"*Avvocato* Trevisan is ready for you, *Signora*."

"*Grazie,*" Emily said, already standing. Davide held her hand, steadying her until she stepped away from him. She followed the secretary around the corner and into an office, where the woman held the door for her before silently leaving a moment later. The scent of books and old leather filled the room and Emily's vision tunneled for a moment.

"*Signora* Miller," the man behind the desk said, rising to his feet and extending his hand. "It is good to see you again. I am only sorry it is for another sad occasion."

Stepping forward, Emily took his hand, belatedly registering the blonde woman seated in one of the two leather armchairs in front of the leather-topped desk. "*Anche io, Avvocato,*" she said. "A sad and rather confusing occasion, I must say."

He released Emily with an indication that she should sit. She did, giving the blonde a nod and felt an icy stab in her stomach.

Oh, my God... the widow *is here?*

"Yes, it is rather a confusing event, I'm sure." He nodded in deference to the blonde and faced Emily again. "And all rather unorthodox as well."

"So, what is this about? I mean, I can't understand why I've been included in this."

"*Neanche io,*" said the blonde, her voice frosty. *Nor can I.*

"*Signora* Costa, now that *la Signora* Miller is here, I can explain." Trevisan's eyes shifted from the blonde to Emily and back again. "The deceased –"

Signora Costa winced visibly and Emily looked away. What a cold term that was.

"Forgive me, ladies. *Il Signor* Spadon has made some unusual bequests. While they are perfectly within the parameters established by Italian law—which is to say that *la Signora* Costa has received all that is due to her, legally speaking—*il Signor* Spadon also left a letter to explain the reasoning behind the distribution of his estate." Trevisan took a business envelope out of a manila folder and held it up for them to see. "If I may?"

Signora Costa gave a curt nod and Emily echoed the gesture more gently. Trevisan cleared his throat and began to read:

"It is my hope and wish that this will be enough to prevent difficulties from erupting between my heirs. I say 'between' because there are only the two of you, Emily and Letizia. You are the only loved ones I have left in the world and I hope that what I have left behind is enough to ease your days in my absence."

The icy roiling in Emily's stomach chilled again. *Her name is Letizia?*

"Letizia, I leave you my home in *Venezia,* as we spent many wonderful hours there together. The fund I have established should pay for the upkeep for another fifteen years, if you budget wisely and keep your spending modest. I know you can do this, as you've proven able to do so since we married. I also leave you the flat in Roma and the properties in Treviso. These you must fund on your own or sell when you need money. I leave this up to you. I also leave you a letter which *Avvocato* Trevisan will give you today."

Trevisan took out another envelope and slid it across the table to Letizia, then continued reading.

"Emily, to you I leave my share of the proceeds from the sale of the house in Rovigo, as this was our home and where you worked so hard to make it one for the both of us. I also leave you the apartment building in Rovigo and all the remaining profits from the rents collected there over the past ten years. I also leave you a private letter."

Trevisan handed this to Emily and sat back in his chair scanning the rest of Jacopo's message.

"While I understand there may be animosity between the two of you, it is my utmost hope that you will both rise above this and cooperate, one with the other, in these matters. I have given much thought and consideration to the above distribution and I believe it to be fair to both of you.

"You have my love."

Emily smiled in spite of things. Typical Jacopo, assuming they'd fight like cats over the spoils in his absence. He'd probably never imagined that such a gift would feel more like a burden to her.

But do I have to accept it?

Letizia straightened in her chair, her eyes narrowing, her lips pursing and then flattening into a long, thin line. A single blonde curl fell to brush her cheek and she tossed her head moving it back without touching it.

"Is that all he has written?" Letizia asked, her voice trembling. "Is that all he has to say?"

"Except for the private letters you both hold, *sì*, there is nothing more."

Emily raised her head and sat up straight as well, meeting Trevisan's eyes when he looked at her again.

"What if we disagree?" she asked.

"I don't understand."

"What if we disagree with Jacopo's bequests?"

A hint of annoyance flitted across Trevisan's face; he'd obviously expected this. "If you disagree with the apportionment, then you will have to go to probate court and –"

"No, I mean… I don't want it. *Any* of it."

Though Emily sensed Letizia turning sharply toward her, she kept herself focused on Trevisan instead.

"Are you saying you don't want the property?" he asked, raising one hand as if to silence the other woman.

"Yes, that's what I'm saying. I don't want the money, either. I don't want any of it."

Trevisan shifted through the paperwork on his desk, shaking his head. Emily had to fight the urge to smile openly. Clearly her move was out of left field, utterly unanticipated. She had gained plenty from her life with Jacopo and generous though this gesture was, it was completely unnecessary.

Besides, this was a tie to him she could sever, if she tried. One less connection to a life she wanted to put behind her for good. The profits from the sale of the house had been fair and she'd taken those willingly. It had been her home more than his, anyway.

But this?

No. Let la Signora *Costa have it. May it do* her *some good.*

"This may provide some difficulties, actually." Trevisan scanned one document, then another. "A portion of the funds has already been transferred. The properties, of course, await your approval."

"How much of the funds, percentage-wise, have transferred then?"

"Approximately fifty percent, *Signora* Miller, making roughly two hundred thousand euros."

Emily was quiet for a few moments. The house in Venice was worth much, much more than this. Surely Letizia would be satisfied if she took this result and went?

"Is it possible to stop the rest of the transfer?" Emily asked at last.

Letizia stood and walked out, her heels clacking noisily on the marble flooring, silenced only by the slamming of the door behind her.

Out of the corner of her eye, Emily watched her go.

In other circumstances, I'd be inclined to call her a bitch but I suppose I should let it slide.

Trevisan turned his own attention back to Emily. "It should be," he said, continuing as though there had been no interruption at all. "I will, of course, need you to sign some documents in front of a witness to show you renounce the rest of the bequest."

"Of course," Emily said and managed a weak smile. "Whatever it takes." *I want him out of my life for good.*

Startled by the slamming door and the sound of rapidly clicking heels across the marble floor, Davide stopped studying the pattern of the Oriental rug and looked up. His mouth went dry at the sight of Letizia crossing to the secretary's desk, her long legs in her short black skirt scissoring decisively along in too-high heels.

No, it's not possible.

Helpless to stop, he shivered, knowing if anyone were watching him, they'd see it plainly. *But how else does one react to a ghost standing before them?*

He couldn't hear what she said to the secretary, as her words were too soft-spoken to be heard over the clanging chaos of the heartbeat echoing in his head. She looked the same as she had the day she left, save for a tendril of hair which had worked free of the too-severe twist at the nape of her neck.

He was gripping the armrest of the sofa hard enough to leave sweaty grooves in the leather causing a twinge of pain in his hand. With effort, he managed to release his grasp and flex his fingers until the feeling came back to them, though his eyes never left her.

When at last she turned away from the secretary's desk, she froze seeing him there.

"*Santo Cielo*, what next?" she said with a sigh and clacked across to where he sat, before her footfalls dulled on the carpet. "Davide?"

She was still stunning. Even in mourning, with dark circles and drawn features exaggerated by her drab clothing, she radiated a glamour he'd never seen elsewhere.

"Letizia," he said at last, standing on shaky legs and praying his voice wouldn't betray his shock at seeing her here.

The gold bracelet on her wrist clinked softly as she raised her hand to her forehead in a gesture he remembered well. "What are *you* doing here?"

"I, uh..."

"I mean, surely you're not here to see me."

Che arroganza!

"No, actually, I'm not."

"Then what business do you have in *Venezia*, in the offices of my husband's *avvocato*, days after his passing?"

"I have my own reasons, Letizia."

"I'm sure you do, Davide." She didn't look at him. Instead she focused on adjusting her bag and taking out a tissue to dab at her eyes, careful not to smudge her makeup. *"Come stai, allora?"*

"Until this moment, I've been well, *grazie*. And you?"

"Blessed. Until..."

"Blessed?" *What a curious choice of words*, he thought.

"*Sì*, blessed. I've been very happy with my husband."

"I see."

Without prelude, Letizia's eyes filled with tears. They spilled over, carrying traces of mascara and clearing faint trails through her makeup. She belatedly raised her tissue to dab away the imperfections. Her shoulders slouched and she lowered her head, moving toward the sofa. The leather creaked beneath her as she sat down and Davide sat beside her, his hand going to her shoulder in a sympathetic effort.

"I've been very happy with him..." she repeated, her voice so soft Davide had to lean closer to hear, "...and now he's gone."

Without thinking, he reached up to brush the stray tendril of her hair back behind her ear, the gesture filled with a tenderness he hadn't anticipated. She looked up at him with a gratitude he'd never seen in her eyes. Her hand moved to rest on his knee, the effort natural and unaffected even as his own hand still rested on her shoulder.

The gray-blue of her eyes held him fixed firmly in place, just as it always had, drawing him in to contemplate the many different shades in such light colors.

"*Stai bene*, Letizia?"

"*Sì, penso di sì*." She paused, pressing her lips into a tight line before she spoke again. "Why *are* you here, Davide?"

"I'm here with Emilia."

"'Emilia?' You're here with the *ex-wife*?"

"Yes." Emily appeared then by the other armrest of the sofa. "Yes, he is."

40

Arching one elegant brow, Letizia stood slowly, her cool gaze moving over Emily like an alpine wind. At one time, such a look from such an elegant woman would have cowed her, but not anymore. Emily straightened and met Letizia's appraisal even as a chilled sweat broke along her spine.

Letizia. Davide's *Letizia. I can't believe it. What a twisted, screwed-up world this is.*

Behind the realization came a wave of vague nausea and Emily rested her hand over her stomach in an effort to quell it. Davide was on his feet in an instant to stand at her side, his arm around her waist, guiding her to sit on the empty sofa.

She recalled him doing something similar in Bologna on the day they met, when she'd let him lead her then, too. A lump rose in her throat and swelled, refusing to allow her to swallow it down and she regarded Letizia again.

"Emilia? *Tesoro?*" Davide stroked her hair, brushing it back from her face with a gentle touch. He moved to meet her eyes and she tried to focus on his concerned, troubled face.

"I'm fine," she said reaching out for his shoulder. "Really. It's just a lot to take all at once."

Something like guilt flashed across his face and she averted her eyes wishing she hadn't seen it. The clacking of Letizia's high heels as she left the reception area drew Emily's attention for a moment, while Davide sat beside her on the sofa, taking her hand in his.

"Are you certain you're okay? You looked as though you might faint." He pressed his hand to her cheek, and she thought his palm felt strangely warm. A moment later he pressed his lips lightly to her forehead, his kiss feverish against her cool, damp skin.

Her mind raced, as though fleeing connections she didn't wish to make. Better to be numb, to be confused, not to allow the pieces to click into place. Surely they'd do so soon enough and then she'd deal with the situation.

Just not now—not yet.

The landscape passing by the windows was nothing special, yet Emily could hardly bring herself to meet Davide's eye. To come out of *Avvocato* Trevisan's office and find Davide sitting with his arms around Letizia had been shocking enough, but finally comprehending that she was *his* ex-fiancée was beyond belief.

It was absurd but she kept seeing him with his arms around Letizia, kept hearing her say "You're with the *ex-wife?*" as though it were somehow shocking and unthinkable, an impossible step down from some great height or other. An unacceptable demotion from herself, perhaps—even though *she'd* been the one to leave.

Seeing the look of shame on his face at her discovery, and wondering what it meant, had been the worst part of all.

She wanted to believe he had acted on instinct, kind-hearted as he was. Letizia had a moment of vulnerability and he'd put aside his own bitterness to try to offer her comfort. It was a little hard to swallow, though, since this woman was the one who had devastated him with her departure some five years ago. Could he really show her such tenderness, after all of that?

Then again, hadn't Emily felt a stirring of her old affections when Jacopo had said her name in the *notaio's* office in Rovigo? Hadn't she let him *kiss* her? Which was worse?

She didn't know what to think. She couldn't think. So much had happened in one day and the day wasn't over yet. There was no chance for coherent thought in all the chaos in her head.

As the train slowed to a halt, a passel of passengers stood to disembark. Emily swallowed hard, unable to look away from the blue-and-white sign reading ROVIGO in rounded capital letters. She'd once stood on that same platform convinced her world had ended, only to wind up on a completely different course than the one she'd charted.

A few weeks ago she'd stood there after having spurned her ex-husband's advances the night before, filled with the strongest confidence she'd ever felt. When she returned to Davide, they'd begun their life together at last.

One hand went to her mouth, her fingertips brushing over her lips distractedly while she remembered Jacopo's kiss. It wasn't possible, was it? Was she actually missing *him* now? If there had been no Davide, if she'd returned for the sale of the house and Jacopo had done the same, what would have happened then?

We would have made love—or at least, we would have done something close to it.

Her hand dropped to her lap and she closed her eyes while the train pulled out of the station. Her thoughts drifted aimlessly, projecting an alternate version of the events in Rovigo: their lovemaking; his profession of his true feelings for her; his heartfelt, remorse-filled apologies; his leaving Letizia to be with her again.

Would he still be alive?

Hadn't Jacopo said he'd fallen in love with her at the end? Over dinner, just a few weeks ago, he'd claimed it was the reason he'd left. He'd fallen in love with her at last, and so he'd left her for Letizia, so as not to hurt her any more.

For a moment, she felt his hands in her hair, holding her in place for his kisses, his mouth soft upon hers at first, firming as his insistence grew. Over the years they were together the intensity of his lovemaking hadn't changed at all—he was always as passionate as he'd been the first time, which was how he'd fooled her into believing he was faithful. She'd never doubted for a moment in all that time.

But oh God, how he'd fooled me with that.

Tears sliding down her cheeks brought her out of her reverie and she opened her eyes to find Davide watching her, ready with tissue in hand as needed. She accepted it from him and turned away again, wiping her eyes delicately and trying not to wince at each touch of the tissue on her over-sensitive skin.

Still, she couldn't look him in the eye.

As the sky darkened, the reflections in the window became clearer. Emily could see Davide without looking directly at him, so she didn't fear him taking any false cues to start talking.

Not wanting to hear him speak was another shock in a weekend full of them. Silently, she prayed there would be no more surprises. She wasn't sure she could stand another.

Davide cursed himself at least a thousand times as the train moved toward Bologna. Again and again he bit his tongue, desperate to maintain his silence and give her the space she needed until she was ready to talk. Each time she glanced his way, he found himself leaping forward mentally—eager, hopeful, a faithful hound seeking to please his mistress.

Was it ironic that this was precisely the nature of his relationship with Letizia years ago? To see himself behaving this way once again was mortifying. Never mind the innocence of his consolation; he'd seen the silent exchange between the two women and he'd seen the toll his actions had taken. The expression on Emily's face in the reception area was another shade of what he'd seen in his mirror when Letizia left him, and it was the same one Emily had on her face in Rovigo when they met: betrayal.

Resentment stirred deep inside him. How could she simply assume he'd behaved improperly? He'd done nothing—absolutely nothing—improper or unacceptable and yet she'd already seemed convinced he had. God knew he hadn't begrudged her Jacopo's kiss at her hotel in Rovigo—what was a hand on the shoulder, a momentary kindness, compared to that?

He wondered if she'd put it all together, whether she'd fully comprehended what had come to light today. He had a suspicion she hadn't—not yet. Not everything.

A cold, uneasy twist of his stomach made him shift in his seat. For a moment his thoughts turned to ulcers and how quickly one might develop.

She was looking out the window at the lights flashing past, as though the answers to the mysteries of life lay among the farmland and industrial parks looming in the darkness, and he wanted to move forward to take her hand in his, to draw her close, kiss her and promise her everything would be all right. It was the sort of promise which always led to trouble but he still wanted to be able to make it.

Now we've got this behind us, we need to move forward.

Outside there were more lights. Factories and warehouses lay bathed in orange-yellow arc sodium light, the occasional lone guard or dog pacing along empty yards of machinery or stacks of building materials.

Emily sat up and rubbed her eyes, like someone waking from a restless sleep.

"Emilia?" Davide ventured softly.

She turned to face him. "*Sì?*"

"*Tutto bene?*"

She shrugged and turned to watch out the window again. "*Più o meno.*"

They passed a warehouse, the wall along the tracks adorned by the names and logos of different automobile manufacturers. Davide watched them slide past: Mercedes-Benz, Jaguar, Land Rover, BMW.

"We'll go home and you'll get some rest, *sì*? Let's keep dinner simple tonight. We can get a pizza on the way, maybe."

She nodded and Davide fell quiet while the train slowed to a halt.

When they walked out of the station, she curled her hand into the crook of his arm and allowed him to lead her back to the flat. He rested his other hand over hers and placed a quick kiss on her temple, inhaling the honey-vanilla scent of her hair before they continued on their way.

It took some effort to keep from wolfing down dinner. Davide was surprised at the size of his appetite in spite of the stress and worry of the day, but considering how little they'd had for lunch, he supposed it wasn't particularly strange.

The spurts of conversation here and there had helped slow him down and fed his sense of relief at being home. Emily wanting to talk was perhaps the most reassuring thing of all.

They used the pizza plates he'd had for years, the ones with cartoon *pizzaioli* on them, tossing dough into the air with ecstatic expressions on their faces. Letizia had hated the plates with a passion, declaring them childish and tacky before banning them to the nether regions of the china cabinet in the living room.

One of his first acts of rebellion after her departure had been to bring them back into the kitchen and put them in the drying rack. He'd rarely used them since but Emily had insisted on serving their pizzas on the plates tonight.

"Are you at all curious about what he left me?" she asked at last, while he gathered the dishes and utensils to wash them.

"I didn't think it was my business," he said with a small shrug and went to the sink, his curiosity nevertheless piqued.

"Of course it is. We're together now. You're entitled to know you don't have to support me."

"Not that I'd mind if I did."

"If you did what?"

"If I had to support you," he said, turning to face her, his back to the sink. He thought of the poesy ring in its velvet box in his nightstand drawer.

In a few days, when the dust settles, I'll ask her.

"I guess you must have been quite surprised to see Letizia today."

Davide nodded and dried his hands on a dishtowel. "'Surprised' isn't quite the word I would have used, to be honest."

For the first time that day, a small smile creased her lips.

"I guess it wouldn't be," she said.

"*Caffè?*" he asked, gesturing toward the *Moka* on the stove.

"Not tonight. I want to try to sleep."

"*Va bene.*"

"I just can't believe it," she said, standing and walking out of the kitchen. He followed behind, switching off the lights as he went.

"Neither can I."

"I thought Trevisan wanted to see me alone. He never mentioned that *she'd* be there."

"I doubt there was any malice intended."

"No, evidently it was what Jacopo wanted: both of us there, so there couldn't be any confusion or sniping later."

Davide half-laughed and Emily turned to face him.

"Why do you laugh?"

"Because I have to imagine that was precisely the idea but the precaution would be meant for her, not you."

Dio mio, what an ego the man had...

"Is she really *that* bad?"

Davide raised an eyebrow in mild surprise, but said nothing. Emily sighed and went to the window.

"I just don't get it. How does she manage to get all the men she does if she's so catty? You saw how she was with me, right? Or did I dream that?"

"I wish I could say you had dreamed it, Emilia. I'm sorry, too." He put his arms around her and held her tight, loving the feel of her against him.

"For what?"

"For letting her treat you like that," he said and kissed her cheek. "I should have spoken up."

She shrugged and squeezed him in response. "It's not your fault. It's in her nature and you were probably too flustered to respond."

"It was such a shock —"

"I can imagine."

"–I thought after Jacopo's accident that she was gone, too."

Spoken before he could stop them, his words carried an implication too clear to ignore. For a moment he prayed Emily hadn't heard, that when she'd spoken, she'd missed what he'd said.

His arms tightened instinctively, even before she'd begun to withdraw from his embrace. Emily's eyes narrowed when they met his and she pushed harder, stepping back from him. Helplessly, he reached for her again.

She sidestepped his grasp easily, moving farther away.

"What does *that* mean?"

"I, er…" Everything was swirling around him, a whirlpool sucking him downward. "I just assumed that she was with—I mean, I never expected her to be there when we were."

"So you expected her to be there…when? At some other time? Why?"

Her words were lost to him. Panicked, he sought a way to turn what he'd said in a different direction, to cover his tracks and find safer ground.

Oddio… What have I said? What have I done?

"Emilia, I–" he began and then fell silent, only to see understanding light her eyes an instant later. Emily moved farther away from him as she wrapped her arms around herself.

"Why wouldn't you tell me you *knew* Letizia was Jacopo's wife?" Her voice trembled to a high, panicky register. "You *knew* your ex-fiancée ran away with *my* husband but you didn't think you needed to tell me."

It was a statement, not a question. Hearing the words spoken so bluntly only spurred his panic further.

"I *didn't* know, not for a fact," he said, a pleading tone creeping in. "I was never certain."

"But you *suspected?* Based on what?"

Davide moved past her toward the sideboard. Her eyes followed him so intensely he was certain they were boring holes in his back as he went. The drawer squeaked as he tugged it open and he reached in to take out the photo of Letizia, still in its frame.

"When I saw that photo you had of Jacopo," he said softly, trying to slow his panicked heartbeat, "I thought of this one right away. I convinced myself it was probably just a coincidence."

Liar!

He turned to Emily and unsteadily passed the picture to her. She grasped it hard in one trembling hand, her knuckles turning white while the color seemed to drain from her face in kind. He wondered whether the shock of recognition alone would be enough for such a reaction.

"What are the odds?" she asked, sounding winded. She continued studying the picture. "It's almost exactly the same. She looks as happy as he did in *his* photo, too."

While Davide said nothing, he did consider the weight of her words. It was true; Letizia had looked incredibly happy in that picture. And only now did he understand why that was. She'd found the love of her life in Jacopo and, presumably, he had found the same in Letizia. It was almost as if some cosmic matchmaker had gotten his wires crossed along the way.

When Emily spoke again, her voice had strengthened, taken on a harder edge: "You didn't tell me. Why?"

Her eyes met his. Instead of the incrimination he feared, he found only hurt and disappointment.

"I didn't hear from you for so long and then... I was afraid if I told you..." His throat aching, he faltered again and she stepped closer to him.

"You were afraid...what?"

"I was afraid you would blame me."

"Blame *you*? For what?"

"If I'd gone to Roma with her in the first place, Letizia would never have run off with him. All of this, the whole damnable mess— it's all my fault."

"Don't be ridiculous, Davide." Her tone was curt and impatient. "You should have told me. I mean, what's the point of hiding it?" She held the photo up between them in an accusing gesture.

"I thought about it, but I didn't know you well enough at the time to know how you might react. Then you didn't contact me and by the time you did, so much time had passed.... The more time passed, the harder it got. You know how it is."

"Sure I do. But it still doesn't feel right to me. I still don't understand why you didn't tell me when you first knew." She walked to the sofa and dropped down onto it, folding her arms across her chest with an angry huff of breath, the photo still clutched in one hand. "If I didn't know better, I'd think you didn't trust me."

Davide bit his lip, trying not to grow impatient himself. *Gesù, didn't I just explain this?*

"How would that have sounded, Emilia?" He crossed the room and sat at the opposite end of the sofa. "Honestly. How was I supposed to bring it up?"

He snatched the photo away from her, holding it before him as though he were seeing it for the first time.

"Should I have said something like, 'You know, I'd like a better look at that picture of your ex-husband, because it's very much like one taken by the man who stole my fiancée. Never mind that I've fallen in love with you already, I'd just like to rip open any wounds you've got before they've had a chance to heal so you can leave me too.'"

"Don't be so melodramatic."

"I'm just trying to make you understand why I didn't tell you then."

"There was plenty of time *after*, though. You had nearly a whole year of letters and e-mails and phone calls—what more did you want? A choir of angels to accompany you?"

Stung by her sarcasm and with a sickening coldness filling his stomach, Davide stood and walked to the window, his gaze dropping to the photo in his hand. It was uncanny. How many times had Letizia said this same sort of thing to him?

"It's hardly the sort of thing one discusses via *e-mail*. Besides, I didn't mean to hide anything from you."

"Yes, you did."

For the first time, her sentiment had a ring of truth to it and he flinched inwardly. Had he really been as straightforward with her as he could have been?

Of course I was. What other choice did I have?

He turned to face her. "No, I didn't. I wouldn't lie to you."

"You know what? One time, I was sitting in a cafe in Venice, watching the sunset reflect on the face of a palazzo across the canal, thinking about the fact I now lived there. My new husband sat across the table from me and he reached out and took my hand, and in that moment, I was absolutely, indescribably happy. I realized then that I'd never been so content. My luck had finally turned and my life was something I actually *wanted*.

"But then, a little over five years ago, I understood that moment—and so many more which followed it—was a *lie*."

Emily looked him in the eye, her expression devoid of warmth or trust.

"It wasn't until last year, when you and I met, that I found someone I really believed I could trust. I thought I'd found someone who would create memories that would remain true, too." She shook her head, letting her gaze drift around the room as though she were lost, a sleepwalker waking in unfamiliar surroundings. "But now I see that's not the case and..."

She shrugged and released a soft breath, her eyes already reddening, though no tears fell.

"You say you wouldn't lie to me. So why did you? I know a thing or two about lies. My whole marriage was based on them, though there were none on *my* account."

"Are you sure about that?"

"What do you mean?"

"*Francamente, amore*, it seems to me that you lied to yourself all along. Men like him don't lie; they simply are what they are."

He'd only wanted to make a point and now his heart twisted in his chest at the shift of her expression from anger to something closer to hurt.

"And how would *you* know this, if you're so honest?"

"I'm the son of a liar, remember?"

"Well, you know what they say, don't you?" Standing, Emily went to the door, leaving the sentiment unfinished.

Davide hurried to catch up to her as she took her coat off the rack in the hall and opened the door. "What is it they say, Emilia? Finish your thought."

"'Like father, like son,' Davide. *That's* what they say."

41

Davide reached out and slammed the door. The sound, angry and hollow, echoed outside in the corridor and down the stairwell.

For a moment he remained speechless. Her words sank deep. She knew how he felt about his father, how much he'd struggled to stand apart from that loathsome man. Did she really think he was the same? Was what he'd done just as bad?

When he finally spoke, with considerable effort he managed to keep his voice level and steady. "When you speak of family resemblances, *amore*, you should know you're on very shaky ground."

Beside him, Emily froze, her hand clutching her coat, her gaze fixed on the doorknob. She didn't raise her eyes to his. Instead, she continued looking at the door as though waiting for him to move away.

"Emilia..." He trailed off, a heavy, regretful sickness filling him inside. He hadn't meant to say such a thing to her, knowing how delicate her relationship with her mother was. He'd never permitted himself to give in to such a knee-jerk reaction before, had he?

"I can forgive a lot of things, Davide. Really, I can. The only thing I can't bear is a liar."

"I'm not a liar," he managed, finally. "I didn't lie to you."

"Then why did you feel so guilty?"

"I felt guilty because I knew I should have told you sooner. But I didn't lie about anything."

"A lie of omission is still a lie."

"Like you not telling me about the money? How long were you going to keep *that* little secret?"

Emily paled briefly before a rush of color filled her cheeks. Her hands fluttered restlessly for a moment before wrapping around the strap of her purse and holding tight, but she said nothing.

"And don't forget, when we met, you didn't tell me the whole story about you and Jacopo."

"That's different."

"How? *How* is that different?"

"I'd only just met you."

"And I'd only just met *you*. I had no idea how you'd react to knowing I thought Letizia was Jacopo's mistress."

"But you had time to tell me, just like I told you. The difference is I waited a few hours—you've waited more than a year!"

"What difference does it make? You know *now!* It changes nothing either way."

"It does, Davide. It changes everything."

"*Come?* How does it change anything?"

"You've lied to me. That's how."

Dio Santo, we're just going around in circles here.

"What's more, you only told me because we saw Letizia today. If you hadn't seen her, if we hadn't both been there, would you have told me the truth?"

"Of course I would have."

"When?"

The simple directness of the question threw him. He started to answer and stopped short. While he sought a response which wouldn't incriminate him, silence filled the space between them and screamed his guilt nonetheless. When *would* he have told her? After asking her to marry him? No, of course not—that wouldn't have been the right time, either.

"You're doing it again." Her voice was weighted with disappointment.

"Doing what?"

She said nothing. He moved away from the door and put his back to it. She stepped quietly past him to open it and step out into the corridor. Cold air crept into his flat, icy fingers slipping around him before the door closed, the soft *click* of the latch cutting them off.

He became aware of the photo in its frame, still in his hand. With a disgusted sound, he threw it back into the living room, the gesture followed by a tinkle of broken glass.

The echo of Emily's footsteps on the stairs had scarcely faded before he snatched his keys out of the basket. The door slammed shut behind him as he raced down the stairs, intent on catching her before she could leave the relative warmth of the lobby.

No such luck. He reached the last step and rushed around the corner to the empty lobby. A sharp, frigid wind blew along the street as he saw her walking away huddled against the cold. No matter what she'd said to him, no matter how much it might have hurt, his heart went out to the small, lonely woman making her way along the street.

He jogged after her, doing his best to ignore the chill, his footfalls clapping noisily first along the rough paving of the street and then the marble floors of the portico.

"Emilia, *ti prego, fermati.*"

"No." She didn't look back.

He stayed next to her, shivering but warmed a little by the swift pace. "*Dai*, Emilia. Come back to the flat and let's talk."

"No. I want to go to the hotel." She was speaking English again, her tone indicating she wouldn't switch to Italian anytime soon. "I want some time to think…alone."

"That's a terrible idea," he said, resigned for the moment to speaking English as well.

"What is? Thinking?"

"Being alone. Right now that's the worst thing you could possibly do."

She stopped short; he went a few paces without her before stopping, too.

"Why is me being by myself such a bad idea? Do you think I'll do something stupid?"

"No, no. It's just…listen. If you go to the hotel, it's just going to be you and maybe the TV. If you're sad, it'll make it seem worse. If you're angry—same thing, and with no one else to talk to, you'll just dwell on the negative until everything seems hopeless and a waste of time."

"Uh-huh…"

"By morning, you'll convince yourself of the worst and then that's it for us." He almost wished she would start walking again, if only so he could warm up again. He rubbed his arms quickly, the friction giving little comfort against the wind.

"And what do you propose instead? That I come home with you and…what? Everything will magically improve? I'll forgive you, just like that?"

"There's nothing to forgive!" His shout echoed along the portico and he fell silent, embarrassed. "For the last time: I didn't lie to you."

"I know. You're *San* Davide, patron saint of good guys. Incapable of telling lies to anyone except those he loves."

Davide flushed with a rush of anger, the skin at the back of his neck prickling.

"And who are you, then? *Sant'Emilia?* Patron saint and martyr of women who lie to themselves and run away from everything?"

"Excuse me?" Her eyes narrowed, her brows knitted together in puzzlement.

"That's what you're doing, Emilia. You're running away. This is a simple argument but you're making it into something else. Why?"

"I'm not –"

"Yes, you are. You're running from the last person on earth you should be running from. I love you. I don't know how many times I've told you that but I've meant it every time."

"So had I."

Had?

All at once, the cold night around him seemed impossibly distant. *Everything* felt somehow false, painted onto a paper-thin reality which he might accidentally punch through without meaning to. He forced himself to speak again, desperate to make some sense of what was happening.

"Yet you're willing to let this...*misunderstanding* come between us?" His shaking hands gestured in a wide arc, as though trying to take in everything surrounding them, then drew inward, closing to the space between them. "How is that fair to me—to *us?*"

"How did hiding something from me bring us together, in your opinion?"

"You're overreacting. I understand you're stressed and upset after this weekend, with all that's happened, but you've got to think rationally."

"I do? Wow, what a surprise." She shook her head with weary disdain. "Good God... You're so used to deciding who's right and who's wrong you can't take a moment to see this from any perspective but your own, can you? Don't you understand if you lied to me about that, then I have to wonder what else you lied to me about?"

"No, I don't understand that. I *should* have told you, it's true. I haven't denied it, but I haven't *lied* to you about anything. Ever."

"Are you sure?"

"*Sì!*"

"Really?"

"For once and for all, I haven't lied. Do you know why?"

"Why?"

"Because I've loved you from the day we met," he said, his voice rising, "and most importantly, because I'm *not* Jacopo!"

Emily stood blinking up at him, saying nothing. Then she turned on her heel and started away. Swiftly, Davide reached out and grasped her arm.

"We need to talk this through," he insisted, but she tried to wrench out of his grasp.

"Let me go."

"No, Emilia," he said, tightening his grip. "Come back to the flat. I meant what I said about being alone."

"What you meant is that *you* don't want to be alone. I'm perfectly fine with it myself."

"Emilia –"

"Let me go!"

"No–"

She spun around toward him and stumbled and he bent to catch her before she could fall. Instead, her raised hand met his right eye, knocking off his glasses and connecting with a bright flash of light and pain.

"*Ahia!*" Davide clapped one hand over his eye and released her.

"Oh, my God…are you okay?" Her words were muffled by her hands, cupped over her mouth beneath her disbelieving eyes, but he'd heard her clearly enough.

"You…hit me?"

"Not on *purpose!* I've never hit anyone before." She reached to pull his hand down and he pulled away from her only to bump against the window of a shop. "Are you okay?"

"I don't know—I've never been punched before."

"I didn't punch you."

"Are you sure? It certainly feels like you did… *Vacca boia*, it hurts."

"Let me see. Please?"

Davide slouched against the wall next to the shop window and let her pull his hand away. While her hands fluttered around his face and brushed his hair back, he breathed a heartfelt and resigned sigh. "At least you weren't wearing the ring."

"What ring?"

"'A' ring, I mean. At least you weren't wearing *a* ring." He looked around, eyes narrowed to see better. "*Dov'è sono i miei occhiali?*"

Turning sharply on her heel, Emily took a few cautious steps, half-convinced she'd crush his glasses underfoot before she'd seen them. Then, with a sigh of relief, she bent down and picked them up from the sidewalk. She checked the lenses for scratches in the light from the window display before turning back to him.

Silently Davide reached for them, a vaguely resentful scowl on his face. He also checked the glasses for damage before trying to put them on and made a small hiss of pain as he set them back on the bridge of his nose.

"I am so, so sorry," Emily said, contrite.

"Never mind that—how does it look to you?"

Emily frowned. The skin around his eye already had a slight puffiness. "I think you'd better get a cold compress on that."

"*Oh, Dio…*" he groaned, but didn't move from his place against the wall.

"Come on, if you wait too long you'll get a shiner."

"*Cosa?*"

"*Un occhio nero.*"

"*Ma, va…* Okay." He got to his feet and folded his arms across his chest, rubbing them for warmth. Shaking his head, he spared her a glance and headed back the way they had come, seeming to trust her to follow.

She hesitated for a moment before walking beside him, her hands stuffed in her pockets while she sneaked a few looks at him. Her stomach roiled at the thought of going back to his apartment. The desire to go back to her hotel hadn't gone away—if anything, it was as strong as ever—but her responsibility for his injury seemed to demand at least she make sure he was all right.

I can't believe I actually hit *him.*

After the cold night air, his apartment seemed unusually warm. The skin of her face and hands tingled before she'd even taken off her coat and had hung it on the rack by the door.

Sounds from the kitchen drew her attention and she stepped inside to find Davide rummaging in the freezer with a dishtowel in his hand.

"*Non abbiamo ghiaccio. Devo usare qualcos'altro...*" he said, raising his voice over the crunching of frost in the freezer. In the absence of ice cubes, he drew out a blue freezer pack and wrapped it in the dishtowel, then slammed the door of the freezer shut, shivering.

Emily's heart sank at the sight of him awkwardly holding the square bundle to his eye. There was something pitifully endearing about him in that moment forcing her to bite back a small smile before guilt overtook her. When she rested her hand on his arm as he passed, she pulled away in surprise at how cold he was. She followed him out of the kitchen and across the hall to the bedroom, where he put down his makeshift ice pack and began disrobing, paying no attention to her.

"Davide?"

"*Sì?*"

"Are you okay?"

He paused in unbuttoning his shirt and half-turned to face her. "*Sì, sì, sto molto bene.* I've just been punched in the eye by my girlfriend, who would rather stay alone in a hotel than be near me, who refuses to listen to reason and who refuses to accept my apologies for the mistake I've made."

He shook his head and sighed, then took off his shirt.

Emily couldn't help but feel he was milking the injury just a bit, but the slight swelling around his eye sufficiently pushed more teasingly scornful thoughts away.

He put on his pajamas and got into bed, warily watching her all the while, as if she might lunge at him at any moment. "Are you still going back to the hotel?" he asked.

She took a deep breath before crossing to the other side of the bed, shaking her head as she went. "Not tonight," she said, lest he think she'd changed her mind altogether. "I'm staying here, if that's okay."

"Of course it is." His tone was gentler, relieved. "I'd hoped you would."

Her pajamas were on the chair by the window, neatly folded even though she didn't remember leaving them that way.

He must have done it before we left this morning.

A stab of guilt lodged in her stomach, keeping her cold under the warmth of the flannel as she slipped under the covers. He moved nearer to her across the expanse of the mattress but she stayed close to the edge on her side, lying with her back to him.

She felt him hesitate before he lay down. A look over her shoulder found him on his back with the ice pack obscuring his face from her view. Another flare of guilt shot through her as she pressed her cheek to her pillow and took a slow, deep breath.

She'd try to talk to him in the morning, to explain better. That, and she'd apologize again before she went to the hotel. Time alone was what she needed, no matter what he said, and she would find it however she could.

Even if it meant going away.

Emily awoke blinking and disoriented, shaking all over. Davide was awake too, already rolling out of bed by the time she understood where she was.

"What was *that?*" he asked, going to the window and peering out through the curtains.

"I don't know—I was asleep."

A moment passed before he nodded, still looking out. "I see now. Someone drove into one of the *cassonetti* on the street."

"Really?"

"*Sì*, but don't worry. They're already out of the car. They're fine. Drunk maybe, but okay. Left another dent for the garbage collectors to find."

He chuckled and got back into bed, bringing a small rush of cold air with him. Emily shivered and snuggled down under the covers, grinning to herself. "Does that happen often?" She'd noticed the dents in the dumpsters before, but hadn't realized they were a frequent, if inadvertent, target of any cars.

"Enough, I suppose. It's usually the same person. I think he lives at the end of the street and tends to get a little off-course when he comes home." He chuckled again, going deeper under the blankets.

The glow of the coffee bar's sign tinted the curtains a pale, mottled violet.

Davide slid closer to Emily and she kept her eyes closed, her breathing even, anticipating.

"*Tesoro?*"

"Hm?" she asked sleepily, hoping to deter him. He stroked her hair with a light, gentle touch and her heart clenched.

"*Vuoi fare l'amore?*" he murmured, his breath tickling her ear.

She drew a deep breath and rolled toward him, finding his dreamy, hopeful face in the half-light.

"*Sì, lo vorrei,*" she whispered, her throat tight around the words.

He twined her hair between his fingers and traced her profile with his lips, slowly bringing his mouth to hers for a long, questioning kiss. She answered readily, letting him part her lips with his to touch his tongue to hers in an anxious, teasing caress.

His hand slid down to cup her breast through her pajama top, his thumb seeking her nipple and stroking it until Emily curled to press into the palm of his hand to ease the ache he created.

Encouraged, Davide strengthened his grasp, kneading her flesh in his palm and pressing closer to deepen their kiss. Emily flinched away and then pulled him to her, arching upward to wrap herself around him. His fingers fumbled at the buttons along the front of her pajama top, clumsily undoing the garment before he trailed open kisses down her throat to her breasts. She tangled her fingers in his hair, holding him in place and concentrating on the feel of his lips and tongue, warm and wet in the cold air as he sucked greedily at both her nipples in turn.

When she released him, his kisses returned to her mouth with a ravenous fervor she could only succumb to, helpless to resist. His hands seemed to be everywhere at once: in her hair, roving over her breasts and belly, holding her hips tight as he moved against her.

The numbness of the past few days persisted, slowly giving way to an intense, demanding ache deep within. A need for contact—

anything, any kind—filled her. She pushed for more, frustrated and desperate to feel his skin against hers, and struggled to slip her hands between them, to try to touch him, to caress him in return. His pajama buttons were unwieldy beneath her fingers which were somehow distant, not quite a part of her. Finally, she pushed the fabric up and out of the way to feel the warmth of his belly on hers.

The ache grew, pushing her awareness of Davide further away.

His hand slipped beneath her pajama pants to stroke her with fevered insistence and he'd scarcely touched her before she found herself rising to him, moving in tandem with his efforts. Gooseflesh rose over her chest and belly while heat flashed into her face and throat and under his fingers. Emily grasped his arm, the flex and release of his muscles there driving her even faster toward their goal.

With a gasp and gulp of breath she shuddered against his palm, her thighs clenching tight and holding him fast in place. The evidence of his own excitement rested hard against her thigh and once she'd released him, he moved to push her pajama bottoms down and off. A moment later, he fumbled his own nightclothes out of the way—if only just—and pushed between her thighs.

Even as they joined, she'd never felt more distant from him. All that mattered was how he felt inside her, atop her. His heat and desire and need were all she was aware of and with a sickening dread she understood he could have been anyone—anyone at all—and it would have been the same for her in that moment.

This wasn't making love—not as they'd done before—this was frantic, fretful copulation and nothing more. The passion, the hunger, the desire were all there, but their private, personal connection had been lost. Her eyes burned and she closed them to the tears which threatened to come in the midst of it all.

He was getting close; she could feel it in his rhythm, in the labor of his breath. She kept her eyes closed and concentrated on how he felt, above and inside her, listened keenly to the staggering of his breath. When she felt him reach his shuddering climax it was enough to drive her to her own. He exhaled a long, low moan against the curve of her neck and sank down onto her, his breathing shallow and slowing to a deeper, slower rate.

They parted and he moved to lie next to her with a soft, satisfied sigh. For Emily the hollow feeling returned, hitting her so hard she was sure he must have felt it, too.

Instead, he pulled the blankets up and readjusted his pajamas without a word.

Hurt by his silence, Emily turned onto her side, putting her back to him while Davide settled down to sleep again. She dressed with almost furtive care, trying not to disturb him, trying not to acknowledge the coldness which had risen inside her, now gripping her chest.

She drew a shaky breath and released it in the growing light, the tickle of a tear slipping down her nose soon following.

I need to think, to be alone for a little while. Just for a little while and with as much distance as possible.

With the absence of the warmth of his touch, the rush of being close to him, she couldn't escape what had risen to replace them. The soft rhythm of his sleeping breath, normally so reassuring, brought instead a profound loneliness which wrapped around her heart and held fast.

42

avide felt her tremble around him, heard her quiet sounds
of satisfaction mingling with his own and wished it could
last forever. Emily's warmth beckoned to him in the
aftermath of their lovemaking and he could not resist the siren song
of her softness beneath him.

He was lost in the feel of her around him, holding him close and
inside her until he couldn't remain any longer. He withdrew slowly,
moving to lie alongside her with a contented sigh. She had accepted
his explanations, had made love with him and everything in his world
had been put right at last.

Now that she knew the truth, everything he'd feared had faded
away. The relief of forgiveness was enough to show him how foolish
he'd been from the start.

From this moment on, I will be honest with her: absolutely and totally
honest.

His injured eye gave a sharp throb, a reminder of what it had
cost to get her to change her mind. He reached for the ice pack but
found it had gone lukewarm after having sat out for much of the
night. The ache gradually ceased and he drifted in and out of a weary
doze.

Emily lay next to him, snuggled down under the covers and
dressed in her nightclothes again. The thought of the curves of her

body, hidden under the duvet, was too distracting to permit sleep for a while. He ignored this as best he could, forcing his mind to go blank so he could drift off at last.

Instead, he pictured the velvet box in his nightstand drawer and smiled in the gray early morning light.

No sense waiting any longer. I'll ask her in the morning.

She wasn't beside him when he awoke. Davide sat up slowly in bed, listening closely for any sound of activity in the flat. There was none.

He threw back the covers and stuffed his feet into his slippers, hurrying into the hallway to listen again. "Emilia?" he called and got no response. Heartbeat racing, he moved through the flat forcing himself to go calmly and resist the urge to panic.

"Emilia? *Tesoro mio?*"

How foolish will I feel when I find her, if I let myself believe she's gone?

Of course, that foolishness would be preferable to the swiftly-building dread filling him as he called her name without any answer.

She *was* gone.

The silence in the flat seemed to drown out his thoughts, resounding around him and rendering his slippered footfalls distant and muted on the marble floors.

How could she? After last night, how could she still want to go?

He stood listening in the hallway, unbelieving. He willed himself to breathe, to move, to shower and dress with a forced, mechanical calm. With a mantra-like prayer repeating in his mind, he got his coat and left his flat, moving in slow-motion toward Emily's hotel.

Numb fingers dialed her number and it was without much surprise that he listened to the message telling him that her mobile phone wasn't available. The hotel phone rang once, twice and he was momentarily confused by the deep male voice which answered.

Oh, right. It's the front desk.

"*Pronto?*" the clerk repeated with a hint of impatience.

"Ah, *sì, c'è la Signora* Miller in—"

"*Sì, sì;* are you *il Signor* Magnani?"

Davide's heart lifted. "*Sì, sono io.*"

"*Mi dispiace*, sir, but she isn't taking any calls. I was asked to let you know."

The icy efficiency of the response was tinged with a hint of genuine sympathy. Davide seized it with both hands. "*La prego*, couldn't you just 'forget' and put me through?"

"I'm sorry, sir, but no, I cannot."

The throb of his heart was enough to make his eye ache again. He put one hand against the wall of a building and leaned heavily on it. "*Ho capito. Grazie*. I'll try to reach her another way."

His strength fading, he ended the call and tried to still his frantic thoughts. There had to be a way to get through to her, to talk to her and try again.

Sheer persistence had paid off once before. Surely it would be enough now?

More phone calls to her mobile went without a response. When he found himself in the street in front of the hotel, it was no surprise. If anything, it was inevitable.

If she ever believed that I'd give up so easily, she's sadly mistaken.

But was it worth it? To work so hard to break down a barrier she'd put up for no valid reason?

She thinks *it's valid, though. She's convinced it is, and if I let this go, I'll lose her forever. I can't go through this again. I won't.*

If she'll just agree to stay, I'll give her all the space she wants. But she's got to stay.

A rush of heat flowed out through the automatic door of the hotel brushing his hair back as he crossed the threshold. The clerk at the desk gave him a disinterested glance before focusing with a glimmer of recognition.

As Davide passed the desk, he heard the man sigh, then clear his throat.

"*Scusi, signore?* Can I help you?"

"I'm just going up to see my friend."

"*La Signora* Miller?" There was no doubting it now. The clerk recognized him from his previous visits. "She asked us to inform any guests that she didn't wish to be disturbed. I'm sorry. Would you like to leave her a message? We'll see that she gets it."

Davide crossed to the desk, his eyes on the clerk all the while.

"*Certo, grazie.*" He leaned closer under the guise of accepting the pen and paper the clerk offered. "Couldn't you just let me by? Please?"

"I'm sorry, sir, but we cannot." The clerk leaned closer, pretending to file some paperwork. "I cannot risk my job," he said quietly.

Davide nodded, finished writing his note and folded it in half before sliding it over to the clerk. It was a simple enough plea, on paper: "Please, let's talk this through." No name, no endearments. There was no need for either, was there?

The clerk put the note in the slot for Emily's room. "*Signore,*" he began in a low voice, turning toward Davide again, "if you were to go to the table in the corner there, I might not even notice you."

"*Davvero?*"

"*Sì.* Sometimes it happens our guests have guests of their own, and we miss them when we go into the office."

"Oh, I see." Davide picked up a brochure and examined it while the clerk busied himself at the desk. A few moments later, the man tapped some papers into a neat stack and put his back to Davide before disappearing into the office.

Gratefully taking his cue, Davide hurried to the chair at the table in the corner of the breakfast nook. He sat quietly and waited for the clerk to return, then realized that he had a clear view of the elevator and stairwell, side by side.

A smile rose to his lips, unbidden and sincere. Across the room, the clerk cleared his throat and nodded conspiratorially.

Nothing left to do but wait. No matter how long it takes.

Three hours later, he was still waiting.

Each time the quiet tone of the elevator's arrival pinged, each time the sound of footsteps thumped mutedly along the carpeting of the stairwell, Davide watched expectantly to see if Emily would emerge.

The desk clerk passed by and nodded in Davide's direction, raising one hand in salute. As he returned to the desk, the sliding doors opened and Davide caught a glimpse of a white taxi parked in front of the hotel. The elevator chimed again and Davide turned his attention toward the sound.

Emily stepped out, pulling her suitcases along behind her. She hesitated on seeing him, her expression swiftly changing from recognition to resignation before she made her way to the front desk. She didn't look his way even when he stood and crossed to the desk to stand next to her there.

"Emilia?"

"My cab is waiting," she said as though to no one in particular. "I'm checking out today, Francesco." The clerk gave Davide a quick look before accepting her key and going to print out her bill. He took the note from the slot for her room and gave it to her along with the printout.

"*Firmi qui*," he said, indicating where she should sign. He caught Davide's eye, his grim smile purely sympathetic.

"Emilia, please," Davide said quietly. "Can't we talk about this?" She shook her head, still silent.

"*Ti prego*, Emilia… Let's just go somewhere and talk."

Emily bit her lip and again shook her head. He reached out and touched her shoulder, only to feel her stiffen beneath his hand.

"Davide, I've made up my mind, okay? I just need some time by myself."

"But where are you going? I said I'd leave you alone if you wanted me to and I meant it."

She turned toward him, her eyes narrowing. "And yet here you are, clearly a man of his word."

Stung, he glanced at the clerk and felt his face flush. "Okay, you're right, but can't we –"

"No. I'm going home now. I need distance and I need some time. This is obviously the only way I can get it."

"But –"

Pushing the bill back to the clerk, still looking at Davide, Emily stepped away from the desk. "I'll call you in a few days, all right?"

"Well, then," he began, turning away from the desk so only she could see his face, "at least let me take you to the airport myself. Please?" he added, before she could protest.

After a long moment, she sighed and nodded wearily. "Okay, fine. Come on."

Suitcases in hand, he led her outside to the waiting taxi. The driver got out and opened the trunk, tending to the bags while she and Davide got inside. They sat in silence for the duration of the ride and when he pulled out his wallet to pay, she indelicately pushed his hand aside.

"I can get this, remember?" she mumbled, and he put his wallet away without speaking, pretending he hadn't heard. He slipped his hand into his coat pocket and drew out the small velvet box, keeping it hidden in his palm. While she leaned forward to pay the fare, he slipped the box into her purse, saying a silent prayer as he did so.

If nothing else does, please let this work.

They entered the airport in silence, the only sounds between them those of their footfalls on the pavement, which were soon lost in the confusion of the departures hall.

With a distinct sense of dismay, he saw she already had her boarding pass in hand.

Damned online check-in.

She led him to the counter and turned in her suitcases, smiling and chit-chatting with the clerk who attached the tags and stickers and sent them on their way. Davide watched quietly, biting his lip to keep from speaking, never mind how much he wanted to try to persuade her to stay.

It wasn't until they approached the queues to the gates that he found his voice at last.

"Emilia, please reconsider. This doesn't have to happen."

She said nothing, her gaze locked straight ahead and focused on the lines passing through the security checkpoint.

His hands were shaking, his stomach churning until he thought he would either be sick or pass out from anxiety.

"*È ridicolo*—Emilia, *per favore... Non lasciarmi così.*"

She stared at the floor in front of them. At least now, though, her attention seemed closer to hand.

Davide reached up and brushed her hair back behind one ear, moving closer to speak softly so only she could hear.

"*Amore, ti prego.* Please don't do this. Stay here, stay at the hotel if you wish and I'll give you all the time and space you need to be sure you want to go."

When he touched her arm, she didn't pull away, nor did she look at him. Her silence was enough to frighten him even more. Such distance when he was right beside her was unnerving.

"*Ti amerò per sempre*, Emilia. You know that."

"That's what you've told me. But since you can't give me what I've asked for, this is my only choice."

"Emilia, you *have* to stay. If you go, my asking you to marry me will sound like it's just a ploy to keep you here."

Emily breathed an exasperated sigh and shook her head and Davide's heart sank to his feet. She didn't believe him; she really thought it *was* a ploy.

"I promise, Davide," she said, "I *will* call you in a few days. One way or another, I'll let you know what I've decided."

All too soon, they were at the head of the line. She loaded her carry-on bag onto the conveyor belt and turned to face him for what he was becoming certain would be the last time.

Porca vacca...I may never see her again.

No matter how hard he sought them, no words came to mind. They seemed to dance just out of his grasp, evading his flailing attempts with maddening ease. When his eyes met hers, he willed her to stay with every ounce of energy he still had, until her stubborn resistance pulled her away from him at last.

Without speaking, he moved forward and framed her face in his hands, heedless of the protests of other passengers waiting to pass through security. He brought his mouth to hers, desperate to persuade her and hoping to convey his need for her with this final gesture.

As they parted she lingered, her lips brushing his, her eyes half-closed in a dreamlike expression. She drew away, nodded to the security guard who waved her forward and stepped through the metal detector, her passport and boarding pass held before her in one hand.

The security guard smiled at her and looked back at Davide, grinning. "*Questo è amore*," the man said, just loud enough for him to hear as Emily disappeared from his sight.

She was gone.

An hour later, it had only begun to sink in. Emily had boarded her flight and had departed for London.

First London, then Detroit, then home.

Behind where he sat in front of the check-in counters, a small child was crying. The initial sounds of unhappiness quickly escalated to plaintive declarations of dismay. Davide's heart crumpled in sympathy.

I know just how you feel.

He sat there while time stretched away before and behind him. Emily had once said the night Jacopo left her had lasted an eternity. Surely this was what she'd felt back then.

His eyelids suddenly felt weighted down, too heavy to keep open in her absence. He allowed his eyes to close while he half-listened to the sounds of passengers and their families talking around him. He could hear the tender farewells of other couples, their soft anticipation of meeting again, seeing one another soon.

It was hard to breathe now. His chest seemed gripped by an immense, unkind hand which squeezed his breath out of him with a slow, steady determination. The unfairness of it all seized him with equal unkindness and he realized he was shaking all over, his fingers cold and numb.

I want to sleep for a while. Not long—just a few years or so. That's possible, right? How could I have let this go so wrong? How could I let her leave?

His eyes began to mist up and he swiped at them with the heel of his palm. A faint beeping caught his attention and he plunged his hand into his coat pocket for his phone. For a brief moment he allowed himself to hope. *Emilia?*

His spirits fell. The number on the display wasn't hers.

"*Pronto?*"

"Davide? Where the devil are you?"

"Miki...." He exhaled a dispirited sigh. "I'm at the airport."

"The airport? What the hell are you doing *there?* You have a class sitting here waiting for you to walk in and start your lecture now!"

"I forgot."

"You *what?*"

Davide sank lower into his chair, despondent. "I forgot," he repeated, numb. "I'll be there for my next class."

"What's going on? Are you all right?"

"She's gone. She went home. I fucked things up again."

An interminable silence followed before Miki spoke.

"Fuck."

Amen, brother.

"Don't worry about the class. Go home. I'll tell the head that you have the flu or something; don't worry." Miki paused. "Do you want me to come over?"

Davide considered for a moment. "No. I think I'd like to be alone for a while," he said, further sickened by a dull realization emerging though the haze in his mind. "I'll see you tomorrow, maybe."

"All right, then. Davide?"

"*Sì?*"

"I'm really sorry."

"*Grazie. A presto.*" He closed the call, trying to ignore the lump in his throat at Miki's almost tender tone.

Never mind that. He got to his feet and walked toward the exit and the gray day awaiting him outside. *Maybe she'll change her mind even yet. I've just got to wait this out.*

43

"Ladies and gentlemen, the captain has turned off the seat belt sign. We ask that you remain seated with your seat belt fastened..."

Gazing out the window, Emily sighed. The Italian countryside below, a patchwork of browns and yellows with the occasional square of green, was already growing indistinct, soon the cloud cover eclipsed it all.

The seat next to her was blessedly empty and when her eyes burned with as-yet unshed tears, she blinked furiously to clear them without any self-consciousness. Her hand rose to her throat to stroke the aching, swollen sensation away and then dropped to her lap.

She drew her purse out from under the seat in front of her and prepared to sort through it, until Davide's face came to mind and stilled her hands. Desperate to force the image away, she turned her head to stare out of the window again at the glare of sunlight on the sea of white surrounding the plane. However, nothing could burn the vision away—the image remained no matter what she did.

Ears popping, she fumbled in her bag for a piece of gum or hard candy to relieve the pressure. Her hand closed around the edge of an envelope, tucked underneath her planner.

Jacopo's letter.

A dull throb replaced her heartbeat, seeming to echo in her chest from a long way away. Her hands trembled as she held up the envelope to examine it. She'd only given it a cursory look in Trevisan's office. Afterward, she'd been too distracted by Letizia and by Davide's tale to give it another thought.

Every step of the way, you insist on being there, don't you? You really do *manage to screw up any plans I make.*

Her fingers trailed over the envelope, her name written with an elaborate flourish. Once more, a flash of homesickness overcame her, accompanied by first Jacopo's face, then Davide's.

I'm going out of my mind.

She slid one finger carefully beneath the edge of the flap, noting the wax seal with Jacopo's initials pressed into it. She'd bought him the heavy brass stamp for his birthday seven years ago, knowing he'd appreciate a gift so traditional and extravagant.

A single folded sheet of cream-colored paper was inside. When she took it out of the envelope and read it, each and every swirl and loop on the page somehow brought his voice to mind.

> *"Emily,*
> *Don't let me hurt you anymore.*
>   *Jacopo"*

The sensation of his voice in her ear grew stronger, the words repeating until she fancied she felt his breath warming her ear, the weight of his hand over hers on the armrest. Her skin goosefleshed under the sleeves of her sweater and she shivered, trying to decide whether the sense of him so close was comforting or chilling. With effort, she forced her shaking hands to refold the sheet of paper and slip it back into the envelope.

"Goodbye, Jacopo," she whispered to the phantom alongside her. "Once and for all."

She moved to put the envelope away and her hand drifted restlessly through the detritus at the bottom of her bag. Her fingertips brushed against something unfamiliar.

Something small.

Something velvet.

She closed her fingers around it and instinctively understood just what it must be.

"No…" she murmured, taking it out. The box fit in the palm of her hand but seemed to weigh a ton. "He really meant it. I can't believe it." She took a deep breath and examined the box closely, glancing around at the other passengers before she attempted to open it.

The soft *creak* of the hinge opening sounded loud and she blinked in surprise at the contents. The rush of anticipation faded swiftly, winding down to simple puzzlement. With trembling fingers, she took out a slim metal object, wrapped in a sliver of notepaper.

Taking care not to fumble and drop them, she unfolded the paper and took out a house key. Davide's familiar chicken-scratch scrawl in blue ink made her smile in spite of herself.

"Whenever you're ready," it said.

Emily just missed the shuttle bus to Heathrow from Gatwick. After collecting her bags for the transfer, she went to the Arrivals area and sat, heedless of the time slipping away while she opened and closed the little velvet box more times than she could count.

"'Whenever you're ready', he says," she murmured to herself, confident her words would be lost in the noise of the hall. "I wish I knew when *that* might be."

Falling silent, she watched arriving passengers sweep into the waiting arms of their friends or families. Solo travelers, their faces for the most part empty of expression or perhaps showing relief at their arrival, trailed their luggage behind them as they skirted the larger, more exuberant groups gathering near the doors.

A few people hurried to the buses to make their connections to Heathrow, as Emily had meant to do. Instead, she continued to sit with her bags around her chair and the velvet box in her hands, listening to it *creak* open and closed, again and again.

At last she took out the key and the note and put the box in her purse again. She read and re-read the simple message in his familiar scrawl, recalling how she'd done the same with his note in Ypsilanti last year. Feeling the tell-tale tickle behind her eyes, she willed herself to hold her tears at bay.

She turned the key end over end, noting the way the light shone along the length of it, flashing and curving along the lines etched into the metal.

He's certainly determined. I guess I have to give him points for that.

Turning her attention to the arrivals once more, another lone passenger caught her eye. This woman walked with her shoulders slumped, an expression of weary resignation written on her face as she dragged her bags behind her toward the exit. There wasn't even a hint of happiness or hopeful expectation in her.

This time there was no faint tickle to warn her; tears spilled over to fall down Emily's cheeks, an overwhelming empathy washing through her.

For the first time since booking the flight home, Emily considered her arrival in Ypsilanti. She hadn't even called her mother to come pick her up in Detroit, or told Jenn she was coming home.

Why is that? I need to let them know I'm on my way, don't I?

She swiped at the trails from her tears. Perhaps she'd never really meant to go home. Had she been hoping Davide would say or do something to change her mind and convince her to stay?

Was that even an option now?

He'd never really apologized. Then again, what would he be apologizing for? His decision to try and spare her feelings, or for keeping the truth from her? As far as *he* was concerned, they were one and the same. That was his argument all along.

The farther she got from him, it seemed the more she understood.

Except for her father, there had never been a man in her life she could trust. Not Jason, with his fickle affections and sorry excuses, nor Jacopo, who had lied to her from the very beginning of their relationship. As for Davide...? Well...

Unlike Jason, Davide wanted her as she was—flaws and all. Unlike Jacopo, he had no ulterior motive, so far as she could tell.

She looked at the note again.

"Whenever you're ready."

After all the stress and fuss and argument, he'd still wanted her to stay. But when had he put this in her bag? The trip to Venice? At his apartment last night? In the cab?

Clutching the key tightly in her palm, she brought her closed hand to her mouth, her heart pounding.

He lied to me.

He lied to protect me.

He thought he was doing the right thing, even though he knew he could lose me if I found out.

He thought he was to blame. He always *thinks he's to blame.*

She remembered his letter to her in Ypsilanti, how he had felt responsible for adding to her pain in Milan when he'd misinterpreted her reactions to him. He'd done it then, too, hadn't he? Accepted blame and apologized for something which he'd had no part in?

Why would he do that? Why would *anyone* do that?

Digging in her purse for the box, her fingers strayed across the envelope from Jacopo and she paused, now considering his message.

"Don't let me hurt you anymore."

With shaking fingers, she drew out the velvet box and slipped Davide's note and key inside. She closed it slowly, her heart pounding, and put it away.

There's something else in Jacopo's note, isn't there?

Numb, she took out the envelope and opened it. She slid out the page inside and unfolded it, not reading it. Instead, she angled it slightly to catch the light, just so.

A watermark shone faintly, barely visible beneath his writing. The crown design was familiar, one she had seen from time to time when she'd lived in Rovigo and when she'd stayed at the hotel a short while ago.

Did he write the letter that night? After she'd spurned his advances and told him to go back to his wife?

Had he only understood then how much he had hurt her and still did?

But that wasn't altogether true—not now. She'd cut every tie to Jacopo she'd been able to and if not for Davide's belated revelation regarding her ex-husband, she'd have been well rid of him.

The reminders would always be there, no matter what she did, but she couldn't allow her past to shape her future any more. Not even Jacopo had wanted that.

More than the money, more than his well-intentioned bequests, Emily realized *this* was perhaps the kindest thing he had ever done for her.

The tears came again as she folded the page and put it back into the envelope, then tucked them away in her purse, alongside the velvet box. It wasn't quite sadness which made her cry, though.

The depth of Jacopo's lies had been far more profound than she'd thought. Hadn't he admitted he'd come to love her at the end? Wasn't that why he'd hurt her, to try and convince her to go? How long did he have to lie to himself, to make it feel like the right thing to do?

With a heady rush came new awareness: None of it mattered, not anymore. For one desperate moment, she longed to have Jacopo there, standing beside her.

She wanted to say goodbye and she wanted to say thank you.

"Apology accepted," she whispered and a feeling of lightness came over her so strong she felt as though she had been lifted from where she sat.

Emily stood on shaky legs, waiting until she was certain they'd support her before she gathered her suitcases and trundled them toward the lift.

She had a plane to catch and not a moment more to lose. She'd lost enough time as it was.

Davide lay on the bed in the near-darkness and stared up at the ceiling. His gaze traced around the design of the scalloped bas-relief surrounding the light fixture in the center, illuminated by light from the street below. He threaded his fingers together over his belly and his right index finger throbbed beneath the fresh bandage he'd had to apply after cleaning up the broken glass in the living room.

The broken frame was now in the garbage can in the kitchen, along with the photo of Letizia, scratched by the shattered glass. Strangely, he couldn't recall her face clearly now. Whenever he closed his eyes, he saw Emily.

Emily laughing.

Emily crying.

Emily leaving—always leaving.

Now that she was gone, he saw everything about her more clearly. Wasn't that always the way? As soon as they were gone, you truly appreciated them, or you appreciated just why they needed to go. Not that it made anything easier to accept, of course. It just meant her argument was fairer than he'd wanted to give it credit for being.

He'd never really trusted her, had he? Always in the back of his mind, there'd been doubt—a belief she'd leave at the first provocation. She'd taken so long to contact him after she'd gone back to the States, he'd thought she'd moved on. Then he'd held back from her for fear of pushing too soon and scaring her away.

And when she'd finally come to him and he'd found the courage to follow through?

He'd continued keeping a secret from her for fear she'd leave him for good. He hadn't trusted her to stay.

Had it been worth going through all this? Did having her here for a few short weeks justify all the anxiety and guilt, or the pain he'd caused her by waiting?

Of course not. Not at all. But the mistake had been made and that was it.

Done.

Worst of all, this time was vastly different from Letizia's departure. Letizia had committed her deceptions and acted on her desire to leave before he'd really understood what was happening. He'd never had a choice, had never had a say in the matter at all.

Emily was different. She'd only asked for some space, a little time to herself to consider her options and make her decisions. She'd only ever wanted a chance to think things through and clear her head.

He'd denied her that, even though he'd taken exactly the same for himself tonight.

He'd stayed in the airport for a few hours before hailing a cab home and then wandered around his neighborhood for a while, not wanting to see his empty flat, not wanting to feel it emptier than before.

Miki called again to offer a shoulder to cry on, to bring a few drinks over to drown any sorrows Davide might care to. "Or, if you prefer, we could just sit and watch the television or something. There's a match on later, I think," he'd said.

And Davide had turned him down, as gently as he could.

Then he'd gone to clean up the broken glass and had cut himself in the process. He didn't really feel the cut even though he'd seen the blood streaking the glass and the tile floor it had fallen onto. The sharp sting while he cleaned the wound was the first real sensation he'd had after coming home.

After bandaging the wound, he'd come into the bedroom, cleaned and straightened everything and lay down in the semi-darkness, atop the neatly-made bed. His eye still ached from time to time, though the swelling had gone down. His finger throbbed in time with his heart when he thought of her too deeply.

However, no tears came. There was only the aching, empty void in his center which he feared to contemplate. If he fell in this time, he'd never surface again. It wouldn't be worth the trouble.

He closed his eyes at last, a vague afterimage of the ceiling light's silhouette floating faintly behind his eyelids. He drifted in his head, consciously steering himself away from thoughts of her. It happened so often he realized he was thinking of her more than not, regardless.

If I had another chance, I'd take it. I'd never lie to her again—not for anything.

He became aware of a faint buzzing sound and his thoughts drifted toward it. It sounded like an insect was trapped in the nightstand drawer.

At this time of year? That doesn't make sense.

Then he recognized it for what it was—a text message on his mobile phone. He rolled over awkwardly to open the drawer and snatch the phone out of it, almost dropping it to the floor in his hurry.

Shaking, he pushed the button to open the message, the keypad suddenly seeming too small under his clumsy fingers. He held the phone up to read it, the back-lit yellow glow too bright in the gloom.

"I'm ready," it said.

At once he was shaking all over. He closed his eyes again, willing back the panicked feeling of *Too-good-to-be-true* which surfaced on the tide of his racing heart. He wanted to believe the message in his hand. He wanted to believe the sound of the doorbell was really there, beyond the rush of blood in his ears.

On unsteady legs he made his way down the hall toward the front door. The floor seemed to rock beneath him and he paused to steady himself with one hand against the wall.

A single *ding* of the doorbell came as he drew a deep breath and moved toward the door. The faint shuffle of feet outside gave him pause as he steeled himself for his visitor.

I probably dreamed the message. It's just Miki, I'm sure. He never could take a hint.

Davide raised his hand to look at the phone again, only to find he'd left it in the bedroom.

Never mind. I'm dreaming this part instead.

"Davide?" said a soft voice at the door.

He couldn't reach the door fast enough. He felt as though he was moving through heavy mud up to his thighs, the door handle under his hand strangely distant.

He nearly lost his grip on the door at the sight of her and Emily looked at him with wide eyes, her face flushed pink. Her suitcases were on either side of her and Davide felt a flash of regret that she'd had to carry them up the four flights of stairs on her own.

"Emilia."

It was all he could say, still afraid that he was dreaming her presence in front of him.

And then she was in his arms, the door closed behind her, her bags forgotten.

At first light, Emily opened her eyes to find Davide watching her.

"*Buongiorno*," he said, his eyes crinkling in an echo of his smile.

A small flurry of excitement shivered down into her belly at the sight and she curled up tighter into herself. "*Buongiorno*."

Silence, comfortable and natural, settled between them. Davide's eyes held hers across the pillowcase the two of them shared, his eyes impossibly dark in contrast to the white bed linens.

My God, but he's beautiful.

She slid a little closer to him and felt a hard lump beneath the pillow. Puzzled, she slipped one hand beneath it and closed her fingers around a small velvet box. With a small half-laugh she took it out and gave it a quick once-over.

This time, it was too small to hold a key.

Emily met Davide's eyes again, her heart racing. With exaggerated care, she opened the box and peered inside to find a white-gold ring. Two hands joined to hold delicately detailed flowers, a bright ruby centered in the middle of them. In the early morning light, tiny diamond chips sparkled brilliantly from within the velvet folds of the box.

"Emilia?"

With difficulty she tore her gaze away from the ring and looked at him again.

"*Sì?*"

"*Sposami.*"

"What?"

"Marry me, Emilia," he repeated, and then grinned slyly. "I need some sort of guarantee you won't try to run away again."

"Do you realize what this will get you into?" she asked, moving closer to him. "My mother will be your mother-in-law."

"And mine will be *yours*. I'm not sure who's getting the worst of this."

"Let's not think about that, then…"

Davide took the box from her and took out the ring, then slid it onto her finger. "You're not stopping me?"

"Well, that would be silly, wouldn't it? Why answer 'yes' if I don't want you to?"

"So this is your answer? 'Yes'?"

"*Sì, questa è la mia risposta*, Davide. Yes."

"Emilia?"

"Yes?"

"*Bentornata a casa, amore mio.*"

"Davide?"

"*Sì?*"

"*Chiedimi se sono felice.*"

Thanks and Acknowledgments

Although writing is a solitary task, it is rare that a writer completes a novel without some sort of help from others. This novel was no exception. I would like to thank everyone who helped me in one form or another while I wrote this story, but I am certain that—in spite of my best efforts—I will surely forget someone. I hope to make it clear that any omissions are purely unintentional, and any mistakes found within this story are mine and mine alone.

Thanks to my critique partners Nell Dixon and Jason Horger—knowing they were expecting more was great motivation to write, and the help they gave me in refining this story is immeasurable. I really couldn't have done it without their assistance. Thanks also to Bonnie A. Rubins for helping me with the first drafts, the final draft, and for helping steer the story in the right direction.

In fact, I'd like to give my thanks to *everyone* who read and commented on this story throughout its development. Without their input, this story could not have grown in the way it did. Thanks so much to all of them—their kind and instructive words gave me much encouragement to keep going and see this through.

Thank you to my family and my friends, for their support and belief that I could get this done. I hope you're all pleased with the results.

I seldom write in silence, much to the chagrin of my neighbors, and so I would like to thank the musicians whose songs inspired me in writing this story. While the list is far too long to detail every artist, a select few—especially the Italians—provided an incredible amount of inspiration. My desire was to put on the page the emotions those songs stirred in me. I hope I've achieved that here.

In a similar vein, I thank Italy itself for the inspiration it provides—particularly *La Grassa*, the city of Bologna. Home to artists, academics and some of the finest food in the world, if it's possible to have a crush on a city, I have one on her. *Non c'è una città più bella al mondo.*

Thanks most of all, of course, to my husband Alessandro. He endures so much, from my crazy crushes to my twisted comments while watching cycling and rugby, on down to the fact that I can disappear into my own little world for hours on end for the sake of telling stories. He provides vast amounts of inspiration for me every day. Not to mention that he went the extra mile and vetted almost all of the Italian contained throughout the story. His input has been incredibly valuable, in every possible aspect of this work, and without him, I never would have been able to see this through.

Alle, this story rings true because of you.

Grazie mille, amore mio. Ti amo tantissimo.

ABOUT THE AUTHOR

An aspiring writer from the age of eight, Kimberly Menozzi began writing her first stories instead of paying attention in school. While her grades might have suffered, her imagination seldom did. She managed to keep most of her stories together for years, then lost them after a move when she left a trunk full of papers behind. (She meant to go back and get them, but circumstances prevented her from doing so.)

So, she started over again. And lost those, too.

After a trip to England in 2002, she began work on *A Marginal Life (Well-Lived)*, inspired by the music of Jarvis Cocker and Pulp. The novel was completed in 2003, and is undergoing rewrites with hopes of publication in the near future.

Also in 2003, she met and fell in love with an Italian accountant named Alessandro. She married him in 2004. This necessitated her arrival in Italy and she has lived there ever since. After several months of working for language schools and writing blog entries for her family in the US to read, new story ideas began to develop.

Finally, in 2007, she began work on a new project, inspired by her love/hate relationship with her new home. The novel *Ask Me if I'm Happy* was completed in August of 2009 and was released on November 15th, 2010.

On April 28th, 2011, Kimberly published a prequel to *Ask Me if I'm Happy*, a novella, titled "Alternate Rialto".

Kimberly is presently at work on her next project, *27 Stages*, a novel set in the world of professional road cycling.